SUSAN KRINARD

CODE OF THE WOLF

First published in Great Britain 2012
by Mills & Boon, an imprint of Harlequin (UK) Limited,
Eton House, 18-24 Paradise Road, Richmond, Surrey TW9 1SR

ISBN: 978 0 263 89603 9
ebook ISBN: 978 1 408 97486 5

089-0612

Harlequin (UK) policy is to use papers that are natural, renewable and recyclable products and made from wood grown in sustainable forests. The logging and manufacturing processes conform to the legal environmental regulations of the country of origin.

Printed and bound
by CPI Group (UK) Ltd, Croydon, CR0 4YY

Praise for the work of
Susan Krinard

"A poignant tale of redemption."
—*Booklist* on *To Tame a Wolf*

"A master of atmosphere and description."
—*Library Journal*

"With riveting dialogue and passionate characters, Ms Krinard exemplifies her exceptional knack for creating an extraordinary story of love, strength, courage and compassion."
—*RT Book Reviews* on *Secrets of the Wolf*

"Susan Krinard was born to write romance."
—*New York Times* bestselling author Amanda Quick

"Magical, mystical and moving…fans will be delighted."
—*Booklist* on *The Forest Lord*

"Darkly intense, intricately plotted and chilling."
—*Library Journal* on *Lord of Sin*

For Lavon

CODE OF THE WOLF

PROLOGUE

Crockett County, Texas, 1877

"HELP ME."

The wind was cold and cutting, snatching the plea from Serenity's lips and carrying it away in a swirl of choking dust. Her eyes were caked with that same relentless dust, but she could see the shapes of the buildings, as gray as the late-winter landscape, huddled along the rutted road that passed for the town's main street.

She didn't know the town's name. She didn't know where she was, except that it was far away from the cave. She knew that her strength was failing her; the scratches and blisters on her feet had bled and scabbed over more times than she could count and she had almost forgotten the taste of water. If she had not been so weak, she would never have asked for help.

But now she had no choice. She took another step toward the nearest building, stumbled and fell to one knee. Gritting her teeth, she pulled herself up. A few more steps. Surely God would not be so cruel as to deny her succor now. Surely she had suffered enough.

She blinked, desperately trying to summon up just enough tears to clear her eyes. The building swam into focus. There was a crude, hand-lettered sign hanging askew over the door.

The tears came at last. The store was tiny, but it was better than the saloon a few doors up the main street, or one of the decrepit houses that seemed too isolated to be safe.

Serenity crept like a mouse left barely alive by a vicious cat, clutching what remained of her clothing close to her body. Somewhere a voice rose in argument. A man's voice. She didn't want anything to do with men. Not ever again. She crouched, shivering, and waited until the voice fell silent.

The store seemed very far away, but she went on, even when her legs gave out and she was reduced to crawling. She was nearly at the threshold when she heard a heavy tread behind her.

She thought she would collapse, pulling her body into a protective ball as she waited for the grabbing hands and rough laughter. But she turned instead, fingers curled into claws, pulling her lips back into a snarl like a cornered animal.

The big man stared down at her, his colorless eyes mere slits in a nest of sun-carved wrinkles.

"My God," he said. He reached down, his hands as rough as his bearded face.

Serenity cried out and tried to beat them away.

The man withdrew a step, palms outward.

"I ain't gonna hurt you, miss," he said. "You're hurt. I'm only gonna..."

She scuttled away on hands and knees. Better to die in the desert than let him touch her. There was no hope. Not here. Not anywhere.

"Wait!"

Sharp pebbles bit into her knees and lacerated her hands as she tried to escape. She had gone no more than a few yards when she heard footsteps again. Two sets this time, one lighter than the first. Nowhere to hide. They would take her again. They would—

"Here, now." The voice was soft and gentle and unmistakably feminine. "No need to be afraid. We only want to help."

The hands that touched her were small and strong, stroking her shoulders, her matted hair. Serenity felt the last of her strength give way. She fell facedown in the dirt. Those small hands lifted her, and all but carried her out of the battering wind. The sudden stillness as they passed through a door and inside was far more than a blessing. It was a miracle.

"Let's get her to bed," the woman said.

The hulking shadow beside her reached for her again.

"Don't!" Serenity said, though hardly any sound passed the constriction in her throat. "Don't let him… touch me."

Warm arms closed around her. "I won't," the woman said. "Don't be afraid."

Trust was a feeling Serenity had almost forgotten, but she found that it had not yet deserted her completely. She concentrated on forcing her legs to carry her through another door and into a neat little room with a bed just wide enough for two, covered with a simple, hand-sewn quilt.

Once Serenity had helped the other women at home make quilts just like it. In the old, happy days. Before…

"Lie down now," the woman said, flipping back the covers. "You're safe."

Serenity obeyed, letting her body sink into the mattress. The woman lifted her shoulders and tucked pillows under her head. A glass was pressed to her lips. The water tasted like dust. It could have tasted like cow dung and Serenity would have been grateful.

"Slowly," the woman said, and took the glass away. Serenity closed her eyes. Part of her—the lost, innocent part—was sorry that she was dirtying the kind woman's bed with all her dust and grime and sweat. The rest of her was too exhausted to care. The sheets and blankets settled over her, and cool wetness bathed her forehead, her cheeks, her lips.

After a while the ministrations stopped, and Serenity heard the woman draw away from the bed.

"Is she asleep?" the man asked.

"I think so." The woman clucked softly. "She's in a bad way."

"Why is she out here alone? What could have happened to her?"

"I have an idea, but we won't talk about it now."

The voices felt silent. The door closed. Serenity opened her eyes and stared at the ceiling as her earlier relief and gratitude burned away in the bitter cauldron of her heart.

The woman knew. It must be written in Serenity's very flesh, like the brand on a heifer.

Once Serenity would have been ashamed. Once, long ago, she had been. But shame, like love and faith and hope, had died along with her virtue, leaving space for only two emotions: fear…and hate.

A laugh like a raven's croak burst from her throat. Apparently she could still feel shame, after all. It was the fear that shamed her now, fear that turned her into a quivering animal. It was the enemy that refused to let her go.

But she wouldn't let it win. She would fight it as she'd never learned to fight *them*. Serenity closed her eyes again. Fear and hate. One to be defeated. The other to be cherished, for it would give her strength.

She would never, *never,* be helpless again.

CHAPTER ONE

Doña Ana County, New Mexico Territory, 1883

"I'M GOING TO enjoy this."

Jacob squinted up into the blinding New Mexico sun. Leroy Blake was only a black shape against the glare, but his gun was inches from Jacob's face, all too solid and seconds away from sending a bullet into Jacob's brain.

It wasn't easy to kill a werewolf, but a bullet to the brain would do it. Jacob knew his odds of survival were almost nonexistent.

"Too bad it'll be over so quickly," he said, wincing as a broken bone grated in his shoulder. "I would have been happy to watch you hang, but I'd have taken the most pleasure out of seeing you squirm as they built the gallows."

Leroy's gun slammed into Jacob's temple, knocking him to the ground. The outlaw's spittle flecked Jacob's cheek.

"You think you can trick me?" Leroy snarled. "You want me to give you a chance to escape? I ain't that stupid."

Jacob lay still. It wasn't just a matter of making Leroy think he was helpless, which he very nearly was. Broken ribs made it hard to breathe, and blood loss was rapidly draining what was left of his strength. He wasn't even strong enough to Change.

"You're…not stupid," he croaked, "but you're still a coward, Leroy. Still afraid…I can get away. I'm surprised you don't run right now and leave one of your men to do your dirty work."

The outlaw dug the toe of his boot into the ground and kicked dirt into Jacob's face. "You ain't *nothin',*" he said. "Nothin' but a dirty bounty hunter." He leaned down, bathing Jacob in his foul breath. "You want to die slow? That can be arranged." He stepped back. "Silas! Bring that rope over here!"

Silas, one of the four men left in Leroy's gang, brought the rope, stepping gingerly around Jacob's body. Unlike his boss, he had sense enough to recognize that there was more to Jacob than met the eye. He knew it wouldn't take much to spook him.

"Git over here, Stroud," Leroy snapped. "You, too, Ben, Hunsaker. We're gonna give this son of a bitch his final wish."

Jacob remained limp as the men heaved him up and dragged him away from the scant shelter of the rocky outcrop. It was full noon now, and though it was only early May, the desert heat was relentless. A man left without water or shelter would soon be dead. Even a werewolf, unable to Change, badly injured and already deprived of food and water, couldn't expect to live out the week.

But it was a chance. Jacob let them carry him out into the desert, far from any shade, and drop him to the parched earth. Stroud and Hunsaker bound his hands and feet, while Ben hovered nearby and Silas kept a wary distance.

"Don't think we're leavin' you out here alone, Constantine," Leroy said, holstering his gun. "We'll make sure you get nice and warm. See how you feel about things in the mornin'. Maybe you'll beg me to kill you quick…if you last that long."

Jacob didn't answer. He closed his eyes, concentrating on slowing his heartbeat and the blood still trickling from his wounds. That, at least, he could manage. Leroy and his men retreated to find a comparatively comfortable place to watch.

The night was slow in coming. The buzzards, who'd come looking for an easy meal some hours ago, resumed their stately aerial dance. By the time the sun set, Jacob's tongue was swollen, and the bare skin of his face and arms was seared like overcooked beef. His body was too weak to heal itself quickly enough.

The darkness that seemed so absolute to ordinary humans was bright to Jacob's wolfish eyes. Leroy and his men were huddled over a tiny fire built of dead mesquite and rabbit brush branches, their faces etched in eerie light and shadow.

"I say kill him now and be done with it," Silas said.

Leroy snickered loudly. "Why? You still scared of him?"

Silas shook his head. "He ain't no ordinary bounty hunter. You seen how quick he killed Davey. If Stroud hadn't shot his horse…"

"He's good," Stroud said, "but he ain't nothin' special. He'll die like any other man."

"Maybe not as quick as you think," Silas muttered.

"I ain't never seen a man take as much as he has and stay alive."

The men fell silent. Using what remained of his strength, Jacob worked at the ropes. They should have been easy to break, but his werewolf's natural stamina had been depleted by lack of sustenance, and the mere effort of staying alive had sapped his endurance almost beyond recovery. After six hours he had barely managed to loosen the ropes around his wrists. But not enough.

When dawn came, Stroud and Hunsaker rode out in search of game, while Silas came to look Jacob over. Jacob kept his eyes closed and his body still, but Silas wasn't convinced. He crouched beside Jacob's head and poked him in the shoulder.

"I know you ain't dead," he whispered. "I know… 'cuz I know you ain't normal."

Jacob knew better than to respond, and after a while Silas went away. The sun rose, hotter than it had been the day before. Jacob crawled into the dark, cool shelter inside his mind the way an injured animal finds some untroubled place to lick its wounds and wait out the crucial hours that will determine its fate.

Stroud and Hunsaker returned sometime later, and the smell of cooking rabbit drew Jacob from his private mental sanctuary. Though his wounds had healed over, they were still raw inside. His skin was badly burned from the sun's constant assault, and his mouth was far too dry to water in vain anticipation of food.

He began to realize that he had less time than he'd estimated. Presuming Leroy didn't decide to shoot him first, he would have to get out of the ropes before another night had passed.

It wasn't long before he realized he most likely wouldn't even make it to sunset. Silas came twice to stand over him and mutter about things that weren't quite human. Even Stroud came to look him over, and despite Jacob's efforts, he knew they weren't deceived.

"He ain't dyin'," Silas whined as the sun began its steady descent into the west. "We could be here for days, waitin' him out."

"I hate to say it, but I think he's right," Stroud said. "Constantine looks bad, but he's not near dead. We didn't come after him just to see him walk away."

Ben and Hunsaker muttered agreement.

Leroy, who had been sulking in the only patch of shade for half a mile, hawked and spat loudly. He didn't like to admit to anyone that he'd been wrong, let alone that his own captive might have played him for a fool.

He got up, and Jacob heard the sound of a gun sliding from its holster. "We ain't gonna stick around," he said. "A belly shot will see to him, and he'll still suffer enough to wish I'd shot him in the head."

"But what if he—" Silas began.

"Shut up." Leroy's boots stomped in the dirt as he marched across the dozen yards of parched ground to where Jacob lay. Jacob tested the ropes around his wrists. With a final burst of effort he might get his hands free, but his feet would still be bound. Even so, a carefully aimed kick would relieve Leroy of his weapon—if Jacob could find some last reserve of strength.

Leroy stopped inches from Jacob's body. He lashed

out with his foot, kicking Jacob and sending a fresh wave of agony through Jacob's ribs.

"So long, Constantine," Leroy said with a twisted grin. "Hope the buzzards don't start into you before you're dead."

He aimed his pistol. Jacob gathered his muscles for a single, straight kick.

The gun went off, but Jacob felt no shock of impact, no pain. Leroy howled, dancing like a man who'd just stepped on a red ants' nest.

Jacob didn't give himself time to wonder what had happened. He ripped his hands free of the ropes and threw himself on top of the gun Leroy had dropped. Someone shouted a warning. Stroud came running, and another shot from nowhere took his hat right off his head. He grabbed Leroy and fell flat on his belly.

Clutching Leroy's pistol, Jacob felt his muscles turn to water. He couldn't so much as raise the weapon above his head, let alone get to his knees. He rolled onto his back and concentrated on keeping his hand on the gun. Whoever came for him next would get a bullet between the eyes.

"Stay where you are!"

Jacob laughed. He couldn't have moved even if he'd wanted to. But after a dazed moment he realized the voice he'd heard didn't belong to Leroy or any of his men. It was higher-pitched, though it carried strongly enough.

A woman?

Blackness rolled like thunderclouds behind Jacob's eyes. He fought it, fought the helplessness that was coming. If there was a woman here, she didn't stand a chance against Leroy's gang. God knew what they would do to her once they…

The pistol fell from his hands. His senses dimmed. He heard hoofbeats.… One horse, three, six. The gang's mounts, plus his own. More gunshots, and a cry of surprise and pain. Seconds or minutes or hours passed before he heard a different set of horses—three of them—approaching from the west.

Jacob struggled to keep his eyes open as the riders drew up a few yards away. They dismounted, feet striking the ground more lightly than any man's would have done.

A silhouetted figure appeared, slighter and shorter than any of the outlaws, smelling faintly of perspiration, soap and chamisa. He could see nothing of her face. She stood over him, rifle in hand and at the ready. She prodded his hip with her booted toe.

"Is he alive?" she asked in the same voice that had rung with command so short a time before.

Another woman knelt beside him, and slender fingers touched his throat. It was the first soft, cool thing he'd felt in days.

"He is alive," the second woman said, speaking with a slight Chinese accent. "But he may not remain so for long." The fingers withdrew. "We must take him back with us."

"No man comes to Avalon," she said.

"But, Serenity," a third, younger, voice said, "he'll never survive out here! We have to bring him in."

Serenity. Jacob tried to remember what serenity felt like. He tried to imagine what kind of woman would have such a name. It didn't go with her hard, merciless voice.

"Very well," she said. "But only if we can tie him to one of the horses. I won't have him loose for a moment."

"He may not survive the ride," the woman with the cool fingers said.

"It's the only way," Serenity said. "If he makes one hostile move, we drop him."

Smart, Jacob thought dreamily. Smart—and tough. Tough enough to beat Leroy at his own game. But were the men dead? He'd heard those six horses running away, sure enough, but he doubted the outlaws would have fled if they hadn't been caught by surprise. If Leroy and his men were alive, they might come back at any time.

He had to warn these women somehow. He opened his mouth. His lips cracked. His tongue was like a chunk of stiff rawhide, but somehow he managed to move it.

"G…go," he rasped. "Get a—"

Lightning flashed inside his skull, and the blackness engulfed him.

SHE HATED HIM.

Serenity didn't have to know a single thing about the man slung over the back of Changying's horse. One good look at him was enough. It wasn't just the way he was dressed, not much different from his tormentors, or the fact that he had been so quick and graceful and handled the gun like an expert in spite of the severity of his injuries. She wasn't deceived the way Frances had been, assuming this was a helpless victim in need of succor.

No. Helpless he might be—for now—but he wasn't some innocent passerby set on by outlaws. Killers like those other men didn't bother to torture a captive for no reason, and this man had been shot and beaten and put out in the sun to fry like bacon on a griddle.

More than likely he was one of them, or someone just like them. His face told the tale. It was young enough. It might even be handsome under the grime and sunburn.

But it was also hard. Hard in the way only a killer's would be, narrow-eyed, thin-lipped, sharp as the edge of an ax blade. The kind of face people didn't stare into for long, because they knew one look too many might leave them wishing they'd never seen his face at all.

Serenity touched the butt of her rifle in its scabbard. For a red cent she would untie those ropes and leave him in the dust. He was like a sickness, a rot that would invade Avalon and steal its peace even if he never recovered at all.

Her hand closed around the rifle stock. One move…

Changying shifted behind her, reminding Serenity that she had more than her own wishes to consider. "It was right to take him," the Chinese woman said quietly. "I know you would never have left him to die."

Changying was right. She wouldn't have left him. No more than she would have left a beaten dog.

When they stopped briefly to rest the horses at the well, Changying reported that he was still alive. Serenity permitted the healer to set him upright just long enough to give him water, but the liquid only dribbled over his flaking lips. Serenity pushed on even after the sun had set, torn between wanting the security of home and hoping the man died before they reached it. There was still some danger that the other men might follow, though she knew she had wounded two of them, one badly.

A mile west of Avalon, Frances spurred ahead to warn the others. By the time Serenity, Changying and their cargo reached the ranch house, several of the other women were there: Victoria, Avalon's blacksmith, her bare arms still coated with ash from her shop; Helene, her belly bulging under her apron; Bonnie, her cascade of red hair falling into her face after a hard day of washing; Michaela and Nettie, both weary from their day's work. Zora, Caridad and Judith were still out on the southern range but should be returning at any moment. They would be of the most use if the man caused any trouble.

Not that she would let him get the chance.

Bonnie approached Changying's horse, her green eyes curious. She bent to peer into the stranger's face. "Frances said you were bringing a man back here, but I didn't believe it," she said. "Who is he?"

"He hasn't been able to speak," Serenity said as she and Changying dismounted. "He may not last the night."

"Yes, he will!" Frances said. "Changying will take care of him."

The other women turned to stare at the girl. "You seem very happy to have him here," Victoria said softly. "Haven't you listened to anything we've said?"

Frances thrust out her chin. "*I'm* not afraid of him just because he's a man! He can't hurt any of us."

Helene sighed, and Victoria shook her head. Victoria was right to be concerned, Serenity thought. Frances was their newest arrival, and though she'd defied a domineering father and escaped a forced engagement, she was anything but wise where the male sex was concerned.

We should never have taken her in, Serenity thought. But the alternative would have been to send her home, and in any case, it was too late now. There were more important things to worry about.

"Nettie, Michaela, will you help Changying get him to the barn?" she asked.

The two women fell in beside Changying as she led her horse toward the barn, and Serenity felt vast relief when they'd carried the man out of her sight. Victoria gave Serenity a long, troubled look and took the horses to the stable. Frances ran after her.

Bonnie fell into step beside Serenity as they walked to the house. "I never thought I'd see you bring a man to Avalon," she said, pushing stray hair out of her face.

"Neither did I," Serenity muttered.

Helene caught up to them just in time to ask Serenity to take off her boots before she went inside.

"I just swept the floor," she said apologetically. "If you wouldn't mind..."

Her meekness was like a constant reproach, though Helene would have been horrified to realize that Serenity regarded it as such. Serenity hated the idea that Helene had to apologize for anything, especially to *her.* They were supposed to be beyond that here.

They were supposed to be free.

Serenity sat on the bench on the porch and pulled off her boots, leaving them standing against the wall. She, Helene and Bonnie went inside, where Helene had already prepared a pot of coffee. They sat at the kitchen table and talked for a while, speaking of inconsequential things: the baby's increasingly frequent kicks, Bonnie's newly completed quilt and the beginning of calving season. There would be hard work aplenty soon, and most of the women, including Bonnie and Frances, would be riding out with the rest instead of helping Helene and Nettie with the domestic chores.

"I never saw myself making a quilt," Bonnie said wryly, "but I definitely never imagined I'd be working cattle."

"I wish I could help," Helene said, looking down at her chapped hands.

Serenity leaned over the table. "You *are* helping, Helene, much more than you should be in your condition. You're invaluable to us."

"Would you like more coffee?" Helene asked with a sudden grateful smile.

"You stay right where you are," Bonnie said. "I'll get it." She exchanged a quick glance of understanding with Serenity. In spite of their vastly different backgrounds, Bonnie and Helene were fast friends, and Bonnie shared Serenity's frustration with Helene's humility and shame over her condition.

I could have been like her, Serenity thought. If things had been different. If she'd gone home with an illegitimate child in her belly, if her family had turned her out as a fallen woman.

Of course, they never would have done that. None of it had been her fault. It wasn't as if she'd chosen to…

Stop. Sometimes the simple command was enough to keep her from thinking about it. But the stranger in the barn had brought it all back in a way the other men she'd dealt with—her fellow ranchers in the valley, the suppliers and storekeepers, the idlers and drunkards and ne'er-do-wells—never had.

She tried to focus her thoughts on other pressing problems, chief of which was what the men she'd shot at might do. Chances were they wouldn't be in any condition to look for their attackers, and she'd seen no sign that they'd been following. But there was always a danger that they would decide to salve their masculine pride by tracking the women who'd humiliated them.

They wouldn't like what they found at Avalon, but that didn't mean Serenity could afford to pretend the threat didn't exist.

"You're worried, aren't you?" Helene asked. "About that man. What happened?"

Serenity was considering her answer when Bonnie set a plate of beans and freshly baked bread on the table in front of her.

"Eat, Rennie," she said. "I'm going out to get Frances and Changying. They need to eat, too." She touched Helene's shoulder. "You just sit quiet and drink your coffee. The baby needs her rest."

Her. Serenity wondered what would happen if Helene gave birth to a boy. An infant was born into innocence, but could a boy be properly raised in a world of women?

She picked up her fork and tried to eat. Her stomach rebelled, but she kept at it, aware that Helene was watching her with hesitant but very maternal concern. She took her unfinished dinner over to the sink before Helene could move to take her plate, and went to her room.

Her gun belt was in the bottom drawer of her chest, along with her revolver. She buckled on the belt, readjusting to the weight of the pistol at her hip. Rifles were one thing; they had many uses on a ranch. But handguns were different. She hadn't felt the need to wear hers on this last visit to town, but she realized now that it would not be wise to leave it behind again.

She returned to the kitchen, admonished Helene to rest, then went out. She passed Frances when she was halfway to the barn. The girl was running toward the house and hardly spared a glance in Serenity's direction.

"Frances!"

The pelting footsteps slowed and stopped. "I'm in a hurry, Rennie!" Frances protested.

"Why?" Serenity asked, her stomach beginning to churn. "Has something happened?"

"No, but Bonnie said I had to eat. I want to go back and help Changying."

Serenity didn't believe that the healer needed any help. Frances's fascination with the man was becoming worrisome. Under the circumstances, Serenity might have to forbid Frances to go anywhere near the barn.

She waved the younger woman away and went on,

measuring each step. She would deal with this man. She would allow him to stay until he was fit enough to be taken into town and not a moment longer. She would keep him tied up at night, and at least one woman would guard him at all times.

It was a damned waste of precious resources, and Serenity hated him all the more for that.

A shout brought her out of her grim thoughts. Caridad rode with her usual flourish into the yard, Zora and Judith right behind. Caridad leaped from the saddle, removed her hat and unbound her straight black hair with a flick of her fingers. She studied Serenity's face, her grin giving way to a frown.

"What is it, *mi amiga?*" she asked. Zora came up behind her on silent feet. Her sun-bronzed face showed little expression, but Serenity could see the concern in her eyes.

Serenity told them in as few words as possible. Caridad's face went slack with astonishment. Judith shot a wary look toward the barn. She was the oldest woman at Avalon and didn't say much, but her disapproval was manifest.

"I need to talk to Victoria," Judith said. "I'll take the horses."

Once she was gone, Caridad burst into an eloquent string of curses. "*Madre de Dio*s*!* How can this be, *mi amiga,* that you should bring such a man here?"

"I am sure Serenity had her reasons," Zora said. She met Serenity's gaze. "Do you think he is dangerous?"

"Dangerous enough to warrant careful watching," Serenity said, glad to dodge Caridad's incredulous question. But the former *bandida* wasn't finished.

"If only I had been with you," Caridad exclaimed. "I would have stopped you from making such a mistake."

And Serenity would have been forced to defend the man, which would have been unbearable.

"I'm glad you weren't there, Cari," Serenity said, touching the woman's arm. "You would have gotten yourself killed."

"Ay! To miss such a good fight…"

"There may be another, if those outlaws decide to come after us."

"We will be ready." Caridad glanced at Zora. "We can ride out again and watch."

"I don't think they'll come at night, but we'd better be prepared in the morning. If they haven't shown up in a few days, we should have no reason to worry."

"And by then we will know who this man is," Caridad said. "And whether or not we must be rid of him."

For a woman who had once ridden on the wrong side of the law in her native land, Caridad was far from merciful to one who might be in the same profession. But then, she had no reason to be, no more than did Serenity herself.

"I may need you in the morning," Serenity said. "You should sleep, Cari."

"Not yet. I must see this man."

Serenity knew better than to argue. Caridad charged ahead, and Serenity might have been worried if she'd thought for a single moment that the Mexican woman would act against her wishes.

But she wouldn't. For all her wild talk, Caridad accepted Serenity's leadership, just like the others. Sometimes, in her darkest hours, Serenity wondered why.

"Do you want me to come?" Zora asked behind her.

Serenity shook off the desire to lean on Zora's quiet, seemingly unshakable strength. "At least *you* should get some food and rest. Helene has a pot of beans on the stove."

Zora obeyed without protest. Serenity went on alone, her feet as heavy as Victoria's anvil. The barn door was open, spilling light from the lantern hung just inside, and she smelled the comforting scent of fresh straw, the warm bovine bodies of their two milk cows, and the newly sawn planks where Victoria and Judith had made repairs to the back wall. A horse nickered from the stable on the other side of the far door.

Ordinarily it was a place of peace, but not tonight. Changying, Nettie and Michaela had settled the stranger in one of the unoccupied stalls where they kept ailing cattle, or calves needing special care. From the look of him, he hadn't improved. Caridad stood with hands on hips, staring down at him with a ferocious scowl.

"Don't waste your time, Changying," she was saying as Serenity approached.

The Chinese woman looked up. "He has taken a bit of water," she said. "I believe he will be well."

Serenity closed her eyes. Changying was too good at her craft to speak up if she didn't believe it.

"Has he been awake?" she asked, joining Caridad.

"Only for a moment," Changying said. "But he is already better than he was."

"He is an evil-looking man," Caridad said. "*Un hombre malo.*"

It was exactly what Serenity had been thinking, yet the words seemed far more harsh than her private thoughts. Now that the man was out of the glare of sunlight and in such quiet surroundings, he didn't seem nearly so terrible. Still potentially dangerous, to be sure, and never to be trusted. Hard as the New Mexico desert. Yet his face wasn't quite so much like a villainous mask, and there was an easing around his mouth as if he knew, even in his sleep, that he was safe.

The inexplicable impulse to defend him against Caridad's harsh judgment frightened her. She couldn't afford to let down her guard. Not ever.

"If he is all right for now," she said to Changying, "you should go and get your supper. I'll watch him."

"And I," Caridad said.

"You just rode in," Michaela said. "Let us do it."

Serenity shook her head. "He's my responsibility. Cari, get a little sleep. I'll need you and Zora to do some scouting in the morning."

Caridad heaved a great sigh. "If you insist, *jefa*." Adjusting the twin bandoliers crossing her chest, she strode out of the barn. Nettie and Michaela followed reluctantly.

"If he wakes, try to give him a little water," Changying said as she got to her feet. "I have treated his wounds as best I can, but he must take proper nourishment if he is to heal."

"I'll see to it," Serenity said. She couldn't do less than Changying, even though she loathed the idea of touching him again.

Moving almost as quietly as Zora, Changying left. Serenity leaned against the partition between the stalls, refusing to look at the man's face again, unwilling to see anything in it she hadn't already judged to be there.

But when she looked down and away, she saw other parts of him that disturbed her just as much. Changying had stripped him of his clothes—a fact Serenity had been trying to ignore—and covered his lower body with a blanket. And though Serenity was able to avoid thinking about what the blanket covered, she couldn't fail to notice the strength of his arms, the muscular breadth of his chest, the slim, lean contours of his waist.

She didn't want to notice them. The last time she'd seen a man undressed…

Covering her face with her hands, Serenity turned her back on Changying's patient. She should have felt utter loathing. She'd deliberately cut off even the remotest physical reaction to any man since her escape six years ago. She had believed herself incapable of experiencing such attraction again.

And she wasn't experiencing it now. It was only the poison this man had brought with him that had infected her brain like a fever. That made her view his body with admiration instead of disgust.

Slowly she turned around again and deliberately examined him with the cool detachment Changying had displayed. It was only a body. A magnificent example, but only a body nonetheless. It had no power to frighten or attract her.

Slumping back against the partition, she closed her eyes. She didn't realize how exhausted she was until she woke suddenly from a standing doze. Instantly she looked down. The man was staring back at her with cool gray eyes.

"Ma'am," he croaked. "Would you mind telling me… where am I?"

CHAPTER TWO

THE WOMAN DIDN'T answer at first, and that was just as well. Jacob was far from ready to get up, and talking at all was difficult. He was naked under the blanket someone had thrown over him, his gun and knives were gone, and he had no idea where he was.

But his wounds hurt less, his mouth had a little moisture in it, and he was finally able to get a good look at his savior. What he saw surprised him.

At first glance she didn't look like the kind of woman who could face down a band of outlaws and outshoot them with exquisite precision. She was petite and fine-boned, with almost delicate features and dark blond hair pulled severely away from her face.

And she was pretty. By no means a great beauty, but then, a woman who carried a gun on her hip wasn't likely to be overly concerned with her appearance. Her face was tanned and unpainted, her figure completely concealed by baggy boy's trousers and a shirt, with only a telltale dip at the waist where her belt held her clothing closer to her body. He was willing to bet she wasn't wearing a corset, either. Most men would have judged her appearance beyond the pale of anything proper for a female.

Once Jacob might have done the same. He wondered

about her male kinfolk; few men worth their salt would let a wife or daughter or sister dress that way, or ride into the desert with only a couple of other females as an escort. It was a man's place to protect his women, and there was no excuse for such a lapse. No excuse at all.

Yet for all her small size, nothing in the lady's appearance or in her steady glare suggested weakness or dependence on anyone.

He remembered her name. Serenity. The woman who was anything but serene.

Without a word, she retrieved a pitcher standing on a stool against the wall to his left and sloshed water into a glass. Jacob remembered someone giving him water before, but he didn't think it had been this woman. The hands had been gentle, the face—what he had been able to see of it in his delirium—entirely different.

Stiffly the woman bent over him, as if she hoped to put the glass to his lips without coming anywhere near him. After a moment she knelt, still keeping her distance, and put the glass down just long enough to push the sack of grain that served as his pillow higher under his shoulders.

"Drink," she said, and set the rim of the glass to his lips. The water tasted like ambrosia as it coated his mouth and trickled down his throat. The moment he had had enough, the woman put the glass down, stood and resumed her place against the wall.

Jacob half closed his eyes. It was difficult to keep them open, but he had to know more about this woman and why she, though so obviously hostile, had helped him.

"Ma'am," he tried again, "I'd be obliged if you would tell me where I am."

She crossed her arms over her chest and stared at some point behind his head as if she could burn a hole in the wall with her stare. "You're at Avalon," she said.

Avalon. He'd heard her speak the word before, but it also echoed in other memories. Somewhere, sometime long past, when he'd been only a boy, he'd heard the name. It meant nothing to him now.

"A ranch?" he asked.

"Yes."

Her voice was no longer distorted by distance or his delirium, but it still didn't match the delicacy of her face. It should have been soft and soothing, not harsh, as it was when she spoke to him. It should have been like Ruth's.

But Ruth would never have put on a man's clothes or carried a gun. The thought would never have entered her mind.

Whatever was in *this* woman's mind, she wasn't going to offer him any more information without real encouragement. He braced himself on his elbows and tried to sit up. She flinched, controlling the involuntary movement so quickly that he doubted an ordinary man would have noticed.

"I'm…obliged, ma'am," he said. "For what you did out there."

Her jaw tightened, and she finally met his gaze. "It's

strange," she said, "how quickly you've come from nearly dying to acting as if you weren't hurt at all."

No pleasantries with this lady. Not that he was inclined to them himself. But there was considerable suspicion in her words, as if she believed he'd feigned his condition.

But why would such a thought even occur to her? That she didn't trust him was clear, and she was smart not to, but she had no call to think he'd had any reason to pretend.

Unless she'd sensed something different about him. Some regular folk did. Jacob had made a mistake in letting her see just how fast a werewolf could recover from serious injuries once he had the resources to do it.

Still, he figured it wouldn't do much good to assure her that he wasn't a threat, sick or not. He sure as hell wasn't ready to get up and dance a jig anytime soon.

"The water and shelter helped, ma'am," he said honestly. "But if it's all the same to you..." He glanced at the pitcher on the stool. There was no chance that he would beg for another glass of water, but at least the words were coming easier now. "I'd like to stay here a little while longer."

Her hand hovered near the grip of her gun. "Who were those men?" she asked.

Her question told him that she'd had precious little idea of what had been going on when she and the other women had rescued him. "They were...part of Leroy Blake's gang. I was taking Leroy to Las Cruces when his partners—"

He stopped, wondering why he should admit how stupid and careless he'd been to let the likes of Leroy's men get the drop on him.

His throat was too raw for laughter. It caught in his chest like a cough. Hell, she'd already seen him at his weakest. Maybe it was contempt he saw in her face. It would be more than justified.

The idea stung in a way that bothered him considerably. He couldn't remember the last time he'd given a damn about another man's opinion. Or any woman's since Ruth had died.

"They set up an ambush," he said.

There was as little feeling in her face as there was in his words. "You weren't with them?"

So that explained it. She thought he might be one of them. It wasn't as if outlaws didn't turn on their own kind plenty often.

"No, ma'am," he said. "Like I said, I was taking Leroy to Las Cruces. Five of his men were waiting for us two miles south of San Augustin Pass."

"There were only five men with you. There was another one?"

"Yes, ma'am, but he won't be bothering anyone again."

He could see the questions in her eyes, but he had concerns of his own that had to come first. "How many did you get?" he asked before she could speak again.

She touched the grip of her gun. It was a good one—a Colt single-action Peacemaker, well used but obviously well cared for, as well. "They got away," she said, every word grudging. "I hit at least two of them, though, including the man who was trying to kill you."

"Did *you* intend to kill *him?*"

"No," she said shortly.

Jacob believed her. He could see the idea bothered her, which was something of a relief. She wasn't quite as hardened as she obviously wanted him to think.

He lay back down again, suddenly winded. "You're a good shot, ma'am."

If she appreciated the compliment—the kind he very seldom gave to anyone—she didn't show any sign of it. "Will they come looking for you?" she asked.

Smart of her to consider that possibility. It was the same one that had been on his mind since he'd woken up.

"I don't think they have the stomach for it," he said. "Especially since Leroy's wounded, and you said you got one of the others. But—" He sucked in a breath as a wave of nausea reminded him that he wasn't as strong as either he or the lady had believed. "I don't plan to be here long, but I'll be happy to tell your menfolk whatever they need to know."

She gave him a look of bitter amusement. "It would be best if you told *me,*" she said.

Even the dim light from the lantern was beginning to hurt his eyes. He closed them and sighed.

"You're a fine hand with a rifle, ma'am, and maybe with that gun, too. You're braver than most men I've met. But your menfolk won't want you risking your life again, and as long as there's a chance—"

"So you would like to speak to the ranch boss?"

"Yes, ma'am. That would do fine."

"In that case, you *are* speaking to her."

It took about five seconds for him to realize what she'd said. He opened his eyes and stared at her. She was as dead serious as anyone he'd ever seen.

"Are you saying…you run this outfit, ma'am?"

"Yes."

Now he understood that bitterness. She must think this was quite a joke on him. But it didn't make one lick of sense.

The only possibility he could see was that she was a widow and had no other close male kin to take over the ranch when her husband died. Or maybe she was the only child of a father who'd died and left her with no choice but to manage on her own.

Either way, she couldn't have been at it for long. The odds would be too stacked against her in this country, where any female boss, even if she proved strong enough to keep her hands and manage the finances and other business, would have to contend with constant challenges from men and nature no woman should have to face.

But she'd done a pretty damned good job of driving off Leroy's gang, and what he could see of the barn didn't suggest she was struggling to survive. It was well built and clean, the horses he'd seen were of good quality, and the woman herself hardly looked like someone living on the edge of ruin.

The fact was that he didn't know a damned thing about this place or this woman who claimed to run it, let alone if she was telling the truth.

"I've been remiss in introducing myself, ma'am," he said, instinctively reaching up to touch the brim of his missing hat. "My name is Jacob Constantine."

He wasn't particularly surprised when she failed to provide her name in return. "And why were you taking this man Leroy to Las Cruces, Mr. Constantine?" she asked.

Not everyone who heard his profession admired him for it. In fact, he would have to say most didn't have a very high opinion of bounty hunters. But his only alternative was to lie, and he made it a habit to tell the truth. That was part of the Code he lived by. The Code that kept him sane.

"Leroy Blake is wanted in one state and three territories for murder, robbery and other crimes," he said. "I was taking him in for the bounty."

Her expression didn't change. "He sounds like a very bad man," she said. "Why didn't you get the rest of his gang when you captured him?"

"They weren't with him, ma'am."

"Even if they had been, you couldn't have taken all of them, could you?"

He might have been able to, given the right circumstances, but he couldn't tell her why. "The chance didn't present itself," he said.

"And it never occurred to you that they might realize you had their boss and come after you?"

Her scorn was obvious, and Jacob felt his temper begin to rise. That was the worst stupidity of all. He had no call to be mad at her, and he'd learned a long time ago to control his passions. Especially where women were concerned. That was part of the Code, too. Rare were the times he'd ever been discourteous to a female, no matter what her stripe.

Even more rarely would he let himself get into a position where he had to apologize, explain himself, or become beholden to any man, woman or child.

"Ma'am," he said, "I regret that you had to get tangled up in this. By tomorrow—"

His words were lost in a ruckus as the barn door burst open and a brown-haired girl ran in, closely followed by an older female with thick red hair and the Chinese woman who had tended him before. The girl dashed right up to Serenity and stopped, her skirt slapping around her legs.

"Oh!" she said, staring down at Jacob with wide brown eyes. "You're awake!"

The redhead came to stand behind the girl while the Chinese woman set down the still-steaming teakettle she had been carrying, retrieved the pitcher and filled the glass with fresh water. He noticed for the first time that she was wearing soft trousers and a long tunic, the typical dress he'd seen in places where the Chinese were more common.

Jacob quickly examined the other two. The girl was probably no more than seventeen—pretty, coltish and clearly high-spirited. The redhead had a look about her Jacob had seen plenty of times before, in dance halls and saloons and less savory places where women sold their bodies for money and board.

But she didn't seem beaten down by the work like most of them. There was a sparkle in her green eyes and a gentleness in the hand she laid on the girl's shoulder, and she hadn't yet lost the beauty that would have drawn men to her bed.

"Drink this," the Chinese woman urged, offering him the glass.

He drank slowly, nodded his thanks and tried to sit up again.

The woman shook her head.

"You must lie still," she said in her accented English.

"He looks so much better, Changying!" the young girl said. Her gaze sought Jacob's. "Who are you? What were you doing out there with those men? Did you see—"

"Frances," Serenity said in a firm, quiet voice that silenced the girl instantly. The way she spoke now had nothing in common with the way she'd talked to Jacob. It was all the difference between dealing with a friend and an enemy.

"I'm Jacob Constantine," he repeated. "As I said to Miss..." He glanced up at Serenity. "I never caught your name, ma'am."

"Serenity Campbell," the redhead said, stepping around the girl. She wore a simple modest skirt and bodice more suitable for a hardworking farm wife than a dance-hall girl, and there was an open friendliness in her manner that gave the lie to the weary lines around her eyes and mouth.

"My name is Bonnie Maguire," she said. "This is Frances Saunders." Then she gestured toward the Chinese woman, who was measuring out a fine dark powder into a tiny spoon. "Liu Changying, our healer."

Serenity Campbell seemed unperturbed by the older woman's assumption of introductions, but her attitude toward Jacob didn't thaw one bit. If anything, her glare seemed even more hostile.

"Changying?" she said.

"He appears much better," the Chinese woman said, carefully pouring hot water from the teakettle into a plain brown mug. She emptied the contents of the tiny spoon into the water. "How is your pain, Mr. Constantine?" she asked, resting her cool hand on his forehead.

"Almost gone, ma'am," he said, which wasn't the whole truth but would be soon enough.

Changying eyed his bandages but didn't look underneath them, which was a very good thing. "Your fever is slight, Mr. Constantine," she said in her soft lilt. "Your skin is no longer burned. You have healed very quickly."

"If I have, ma'am," Jacob said, "it was your care that did it."

She frowned a little, her dark eyes probing his. He could feel her curiosity and doubt, but she set them aside and reached for the mug.

"Please drink this," she said.

Jacob took in a deep whiff of the stuff. It smelled like some kind of tea made with herbs, but he didn't recognize the plant from which the powder had been ground.

He would have been a fool to drink it anywhere else. But he read people pretty well, and there was nothing about the Chinese woman—about any of them but Serenity—to suggest they wanted to do him any harm. His body would tell him soon enough if the tea was bad.

So he drank it, and a deep, penetrating warmth spread throughout his body. The slightly bitter taste lingered on his tongue.

"It will help you sleep and cool your blood," Changying said.

"But he just woke up!" Frances protested. She leaned toward Jacob as if she were standing on the edge of a mesa ready to throw herself off. "Where do you come from, Mr. Constantine? Why were those men trying to kill you?"

"He can answer those questions later," Serenity said. "I think Changying would prefer we leave him to his rest."

The Chinese woman rose and bowed toward Serenity. "It would be best, yes."

With a little pout, Frances allowed Bonnie to lead her away.

Changying touched Serenity's arm.

"Will you sleep?" she asked.

"Soon." Serenity smiled—a full, warm, affectionate smile—and gave a little bow to Changying in return. "Thank you, Mei Mei."

Changying returned a small smile and retreated. Serenity stared after her, the smile fading.

An odd sensation, as if he were floating on cotton and clouds, seeped through Jacob's body. It made him feel almost peaceful.

"Those women…live here with you?" he asked Serenity.

"Those women," she said, looking down at him, "are my friends and fellow workers here at Avalon."

Well, he'd known Changying and Frances had been with her during the gunfight, even if he'd been only half-aware of their presence most of the time. But he still wondered why none of her male hands had looked in on him, if only out of curiosity. If she was so suspicious of him, why hadn't she sent one of them to stand watch over him?

"I told you I didn't think Leroy's men would follow me," he said, his words beginning to slur, "but it would be a good idea for you to send some of your men to keep a lookout. Is your foreman—"

"We have no foreman," she said, a flame of defiance dancing in her eyes. "There are no men here."

No men. For the second time he had to think before he was sure he'd heard her right. No men? None at all?

No wonder she kept a hand on her Peacemaker, and looked at him as if he might jump up and throw himself on her like a savage. Jacob couldn't think how a ranch run only by women could exist in the first place.

He wanted to ask her how such a thing was possible, how far they were from where they'd found him, what defenses they had against marauders...all the things he would consider if he had to arrange protection for people incapable of taking care of themselves. Not that he'd had to do anything like that for years, much less wanted to now.

But he'd lived by the Code almost from the day Ruth had died, when he'd realized that it was either that or become exactly what he hated. He had devoted himself to the cause of bringing criminals like Ruth's killers to justice, but having a cause wasn't enough. It was the Code that kept him within the bounds of civilization and decency—a code that prevented him from prolonging the bloody feud that had led to Ruth's death, a code he'd never abandoned in all his years as a Texas Ranger and bounty hunter.

The Code said he couldn't let a debt go unpaid. Not when he'd brought trouble on innocent folk who could suffer for his mistakes. Especially not when he owed his life to three females who had risked their own lives for a stranger, a stranger their leader had so clearly despised from the very beginning.

But there was an obvious way to pay the debt and finish his job at the same time. He could make sure that Leroy's gang wouldn't be making any more trouble for these women if he went after them while the trail was still hot.

If Serenity Campbell would let him leave.

At that point his thoughts lost their shape and puddled inside his skull like melted butter. His eyes wouldn't stay open. It took a powerful concoction to affect a werewolf, but whatever Changying had given him was doing it. And there wasn't a damned thing he could do to stop it.

He was at Serenity's mercy. And he had an idea that if it hadn't been for the other women, she might shoot him right through the heart.

IT WAS MIDNIGHT when Jacob woke.

He opened his eyes, instinctively flexing his muscles and stretching his body to its full length, testing every bone and muscle and sinew.

The worst pain was gone. His wounds weren't completely healed, but that wasn't a concern if he was strong enough to Change.

At least there wouldn't be much risk in trying. He could already smell that no one was in the barn with him. He pricked his ears, listening for movement outside.

Someone was there, sure enough. The woman called Caridad, so eager with her guns. There was some chance that she might come in on him while he was still in wolf shape, but he was willing to take that chance.

He sat up, wincing at the pull of his scabs and the knitting flesh beneath. It took some effort even to cast off the blanket. He was grateful the healer had stripped him, if only because he didn't have to remove his clothes. Modesty wasn't much of a consideration at a time like this.

It was certainly possible to Change while sitting or even lying down, but Jacob had always preferred to stand. Pulling himself up with his hands braced against the side of the stall, he got to his feet. Nausea made it difficult to hold up his head, but somehow he managed it. He closed his eyes and concentrated.

The Change came stuttering like an ancient steam engine. For a moment he wavered between human and wolf, not quite able to make the transition. He clenched his fists and sucked in a deep, shaking breath.

At last his resisting body gave way, and he dropped to the straw on four broad paws. Every scent and sound became almost painfully sharp and distinct. The milk cows snorted and stirred in their stalls, spooked by the presence of a predator. Soon they would start lowing, sending an alarm that the woman outside couldn't possibly miss.

But Jacob didn't need much time. The Change had made him whole again, though he knew there might be some lingering weakness. The transformation itself took no small amount of strength.

It felt good to be in wolf shape again, but he couldn't risk staying in it. There was too much of a chance that someone might walk in on him. One of the milk cows began to bawl, making his situation even more precarious. He braced himself and Changed again, finishing just in time. Caridad rushed into the barn, a gun in each hand.

She stopped abruptly when she saw Jacob leaning against the partition. "What are you doing?" she demanded.

Jacob raised his hands. "Nothing, *señorita,*" he said. "Only seeing if my legs will hold me up."

"Sit down," she said, jerking her guns in emphasis.

There was no point in deliberately antagonizing a trigger-happy female, and Jacob had done what he'd set out to do. He eased himself to the ground and pulled the blanket up to his waist, shivering for effect.

"You know where the rest of my clothes are, ma'am?" he asked.

"Do you think you are going somewhere, *señor?*"

"Not just yet."

Eyeing him suspiciously, Caridad stalked past him to look in on the cows. She seemed satisfied, for she quickly returned, stopped to regale Jacob with another threatening stare, then left the barn.

With a sigh, he settled back on the straw. He would need a good sleep to let his body recover from the forced Change. By dawn he would be almost as good as new.

And then he would be fit for whatever his conscience decided he should do.

THERE WAS NOT the remotest chance of intimacy with the man in the barn.

Constantine, Serenity reminded herself. A strong name. The name of the first Christian Roman emperor.

Christian this man might be, but her opinion of him had not changed, at least not in its fundamentals.

She released the calf she'd been examining back to its anxious mother and crouched back on her heels. Her finger stung where she had pricked it through her glove on a cactus spine, all because of her carelessness. And *that* was because she'd been thinking about Constantine.

About the way he talked: soft, low and courteous, as if he actually had respect for her and the other women. He had expressed gratitude, and at no time had he offered any threat. He'd warned her about the outlaws, and he'd admitted that he'd permitted the outlaws to ambush him.

He had even complimented her.

That had surprised her, caught her off guard for a moment or two. But of course it wasn't really a compliment to say she was a "good shot." He was just surprised that a woman could be handy with a gun. Just as he'd been more than surprised to learn that a woman could be a ranch boss.

Of course, she hadn't meant to admit that there were no men at Avalon; she still had no idea why she'd done it, except that his assumption that he would need to speak to her "menfolk" about the possible dangers posed by the Blake gang had made her reckless.

Foolish. The stupid mistake of a child.

Serenity got to her feet and looked across the range in the direction of the house, a quarter mile to the west at the foot of the rocky, yucca-clad hills that rose steeply to the base of the Organ Mountains. It was still early in the morning, but her feet already itched to get back to the barn.

Constantine had been sleeping—or at least pretending to be asleep—when she'd checked on him just after dawn. Caridad had been standing watch since midnight, at her own insistence, while Serenity snatched a few hours of sleep. Since sunrise, Zora, Nettie and Victoria had been out looking for any sign of intruders. Serenity was nagged by the constant worry that they might find what they were looking for.

She had her own chores to do, but she found she couldn't concentrate. She trusted Caridad completely, but Constantine wasn't Cari's responsibility.

He was *hers.* And even after his warnings and compliments and admissions of mistakes, all his sincere looks and honorable words, she never doubted that he was still dangerous—and would become even more so when he recovered.

Whistling softly to Cleo, she mounted and started back for the house.

Bonnie came to meet her as she rode in.

"I'm glad you're here," she said, wiping her hands on her apron. "Changying asked me to tell you that Judith and Frances are ill. She has confined them both to bed with…" She paused and then continued as if reciting lines she had been given to repeat. "'Disturbance of the upper *jiao,* congestion of the lungs and nostrils, lethargy, shaking chills and a general imbalance of *qi.*'"

Changying was not prone to exaggeration, and Serenity had heard enough of the Chinese woman's odd medical terms to know the illness was not a mild one. She slid down from Cleo's back, led the mare to the inner corral and quickly unsaddled her. The moment she was finished, she strode into the bunkhouse, where Changying was spooning one of her herbal teas into Frances's mouth.

"How are they?" Serenity asked.

Frances turned bleary, bloodshot eyes in Serenity's direction. "I'm all right," she whispered. "Changying won't let me get up, but I—"

"Do not attempt to speak," Changying said, feeling Frances's forehead.

Serenity glanced toward the other occupied bunk where Judith was shivering under several blankets.

"What is it?" she asked, worry clogging her throat. "How could this have happened so quickly?"

"It is one of the sweating sicknesses," Changying

said, rising. "I have seen it come on very quickly when many people are together in one place."

And that would have been when Serenity, Frances and Judith had gone into Las Cruces a few days ago. Suddenly Serenity remembered Frances's sniffles and complaints of a stuffy nose the day before, which Serenity had put down to the blowing dust and the excitement of the rescue.

"They will be all right?" she asked.

"With a week's rest, yes. Perhaps two."

Two weeks. Serenity was beyond grateful that the illness wasn't as serious as it had sounded when Bonnie had spoken of it, but it could not have come at a worse time. Not with Constantine here, and the start of branding season only a few days away. Every woman at Avalon would need to be working from before dawn to after dusk for the next month, and there were hardly enough of them to do the job even then.

"Let me know if anything changes," Serenity said, and left the bunkhouse with Bonnie right behind her.

"What are we going to do?" Bonnie asked. "Helene can't ride in her condition, let alone work cattle. With only seven of us…"

"We will do whatever we have to," Serenity said. "We have no choice."

"We might hire a couple of boys from town, just for the branding."

Serenity came to a sudden stop. "You know that isn't possible," she said.

"We could lose dozens of calves to the Coles. You

know they'll steal any unbranded beef they can get their hands on."

That was true, but it couldn't be helped. "We will do what we have to," she repeated.

And the first thing to do was get rid of Constantine. She had a feeling he would be glad enough to leave as soon as he was capable of it. Of course, he didn't have his own mount, but Serenity would be more than happy to give him one just to get him away from Avalon.

And she prayed he was telling the truth about being a bounty hunter, which put him at least marginally on the right side of the law.

She and Bonnie parted ways, and she started toward the barn. The door swung open, creaking on its hinges, and Jacob Constantine walked out, wearing his filthy, torn trousers, his bandages and little else. He was scanning the yard with intense curiosity, and when his gaze settled on her, his gray eyes seemed to stare right into her soul.

CHAPTER THREE

CARIDAD CAME RUNNING from the barn, guns in hand and a furious scowl on her face.

"Stop!" Cari shouted, pausing to aim at Constantine's naked back. "Stop, or I will kill you!"

Slowly the man raised his hands. Serenity was stunned at his condition. He was moving gingerly and with a slight limp, it was true, but he was on his feet when only yesterday he had barely been able to sit up.

"Cari," she said calmly, "it's all right. Isn't it, Mr. Constantine?"

He lowered his hands with a slight wince of pain. "Yes, ma'am," he said, never looking away from Serenity's face. "As you can see, I'm unarmed."

Unarmed, except for a remarkable strength that had allowed him to recover from serious injuries in less than twenty-four hours, not to mention a body made for fighting. A body he seemed perfectly comfortable displaying in public.

Bonnie came up behind Serenity. "Well, I'll be damned," she said.

Victoria came running out of her workshop and stopped suddenly when she saw Constantine.

Caridad holstered her pistols and stalked around him, scowling.

"I'm sorry," she said to Serenity, practically seething with anger and embarrassment. "He…deceived me, the *cabrón.*"

"Did you, Mr. Constantine?" Serenity asked, forcing herself to take a few steps closer to him. "That is hardly a sign of good faith. Or do you want to get yourself shot?"

"Not so soon after the last time," he said with a wry curl of his lips. The expression would have been disarming to most people. To most *women,* Serenity thought. It had the effect of transforming his face just as his earlier vulnerability had done, making it appear a little softer, good-natured, almost friendly.

"You seem well enough now," she said.

"I'm getting better," he said mildly. He glanced around the yard a second time, then up at the granite and limestone pinnacles of the Organ Mountains towering above the house to the west. "Mighty fine place you have here, Miss Campbell." The gray eyes fixed on hers again. "It *is* 'Miss,' isn't it?"

"What business is that of yours?"

"Easy, now. I just wanted to know how I should speak to you."

I'd rather you didn't speak to me at all, Serenity thought. His condescension scraped at her already raw nerves. "'Ma'am' is perfectly suitable," she said.

He touched his forehead in a salute that might have been mocking if he hadn't looked so grave. "I don't believe I've met this lady," he said, indicating Victoria with a slight nod.

"Our blacksmith, Miss Curtis," Serenity said. "How soon do you think you'll be fit to ride, Mr. Constantine?"

He hesitated. He cocked his head as if listening to some internal voice.

"Tomorrow," he said. "If you'll lend me a horse." Caridad snorted, but he went on, unperturbed. "I'll be riding directly after Leroy and his men. They took my horse and stole my money, but I'll get them back. I'll repay you as soon as I can."

His confidence had a strange effect on Serenity, filling her with envy, anger and admiration all at the same time. He was so sure of himself, when she so seldom was.

"You are assuming they aren't waiting to ambush you again," she said.

"You haven't seen any sign that they're on your range, have you?"

"My riders haven't reported anything."

"Then it's a safe bet they didn't come after me."

"You are a stubborn man, Mr. Constantine."

"I have to be, in my line of work," he said.

A hunter, probably little better than those he hunted. *Let him go after them,* she thought. *It's no business of mine if he gets himself killed.*

"Do you mind if I sit down, ma'am?" he asked with that same incongruous courtesy.

"You are free to return to the barn," she said coldly.

"I'd like a little fresh air, if it's all the same to you."

It wasn't the same. But Serenity could see that his face had gone a little pale, and there was a sheen of perspiration on his forehead.

She jerked her head in the direction of the house. "You must be hungry," she said. "Changying would want you fed."

"You are going to let him into the house?" Caridad demanded.

That wry, amused expression crossed Constantine's face again. "I would appreciate it, Miss Campbell," he said.

"There's fresh bread and soup in the kitchen," Bonnie offered.

"Obliged, Miss Maguire," he said, inclining his head. Serenity could have sworn that Bonnie blushed—and there wasn't much in the world that could make her blush.

Could it be that she admired Constantine? Perhaps even found him attractive?

"I hope Miss Liu and Miss Saunders are well?" he asked.

Serenity had no intention of telling the man just how unwell Frances was.

"They're busy," she said, and looked Constantine up and down with the deliberate detachment of a buyer assessing the merits of a beef bound for the stockyards. "Your clothes are ruined, and we have nothing here that will fit you."

"I'm sure Helene can sew something up for him," Bonnie said.

"Mr. Constantine is leaving tomorrow," Serenity reminded her.

"But we can't send him out like this!"

She was right, as much as it pained Serenity to admit it. "Mrs. Tompkins will take your measurements when you go inside," she said to Constantine. She thought of asking him to put on his boots, but there wasn't much point, when Helene would only want them off again.

Helene hadn't been to the barn to see Constantine. What would she make of him, considering how badly her fiance and family had treated her?

"You're very kind, ma'am," Constantine said, holding her gaze.

"Imprudente," Caridad muttered. "Kindness will get you killed."

Serenity pretended she hadn't heard. Not waiting to see if he would follow, she returned to the house.

Constantine caught up with her.

"Most of your hands are out on the range?" he asked, falling into step beside her.

She kept her pace steady in spite of his uncomfortable nearness, and her uneasy awareness of his physique and masculine scent. Was he trying to find out how many women lived at Avalon?

"Everyone is occupied with chores," she said. "Including watching for those outlaws of yours."

He didn't take any visible offense at her tart reply. He glanced up at the sun rising over the vast Tularosa Valley. "You must be about ready to start branding," he said.

"Yes," she said shortly, as they stepped up onto the porch.

Nothing more passed between them until they had gone into the kitchen, where Helene was sitting at the table mending the hem of a well-worn skirt. She bolted from her seat when she saw Constantine. He stopped where he was, tucking his hands behind his back. Serenity moved closer to the other woman.

"Mrs. Tompkins," she said, "this is Jacob Constantine. Mr. Constantine, Mrs. Tompkins."

"Ma'am," Constantine said. His eyes barely flickered down to Helene's distended belly. "Pleased to meet you."

Helene sank back down into her chair. "Good morning, Mr. Constantine," she murmured, regaining her composure.

"Bonnie tells me there's soup and bread," Serenity said, as if everything were perfectly normal.

"I'll get it."

Before Serenity could stop her, Helene began to rise, lost her balance and tilted sideways. Constantine was there in an instant, supporting her arm.

"You should rest, ma'am," he said. "You've got someone else to think of now."

Helene stared up into his face with something like wonder. For a moment Serenity saw what the other woman did: simple kindness and concern.

"Th-thank you," Helene whispered. "I think I will lie down for a while."

With an unreadable glance at Serenity, she waddled out of the dining room.

"I will thank you not to offer advice to my friends," Serenity said stiffly.

He leaned against the wall, muscles bunching and relaxing as he folded his arms across his chest. "Seems the Missus hasn't been getting very good advice so far."

Heat washed into Serenity's face. "You know nothing about us and our ways," she said. "You think of women as weak vessels suitable only for…for—" She broke off and began again. "Helene…Mrs. Tompkins is far stronger than she looks. Too much bed rest will do her no good at all."

His eyes were so clear, so knowing, but they did not mock. “You’re right,” he said. “I know nothing about you and your ways. Why don’t you tell me how a place like this came to be and how it manages to keep going?”

He seemed to know every single thing to say that would make her angry. “Because it’s run by women? You wonder how we can do work usually done by men?”

A lock of dark hair fell across his eyes, and he pushed it aside. “It had occurred to me,” he said.

Oh, the arrogance. So completely typical. “This ranch has been operating for three years,” she said. “We have fifteen hundred head of cattle. And we own this land outright.”

“We?”

“All of us together.”

“That is impressive, ma’am,” he said softly. “Especially in this rugged country. How did you come to be here without any men?”

“We have our reasons.”

“They must be pretty strong ones.”

She had had enough. “Do you know who keeps the farms and ranches of the West from sinking into barbarity and filth? Who brings learning and civilization to the cattle towns? Who does the washing and cooking and raising of children, and all the other things most men would never—”

Constantine raised a hand. “You’ve made your point, ma’am. But everything you’ve said is about women working in the home, where they are protected.”

Protected? As *she* had been? “And you, a complete

stranger, are so deeply concerned for our welfare," she said.

"Any decent man would be."

"Are you offering to be our 'protector,' Mr. Constantine?"

His lids dropped over his eyes, and a muscle jumped in his cheek. Serenity turned her back on him, took a bowl from the cupboard, ladled soup from the cast-iron pot on the stove, and set the bowl down hard on the table. She returned to the worktable, uncovered the bread, sawed off a chunk and tossed it on a plate. She plunked it down beside the soup, along with a spoon.

Constantine continued to stand. After a moment she realized that he was expecting her to sit first. She wanted to storm out, but that would be giving in. And she would *not* give in.

She took the chair farthest from him and sat very still, staring at the table while he ate.

"My compliments to the cook, ma'am," he said. His voice sounded almost hollow. Had she actually said something that had shaken his seemingly unflappable calm?

What kind of man was he, really? It had been a very long time since she'd bothered to consider what "type" any man was. They had all become the same to her, and she never attempted to look beyond her assumptions. She didn't even want to try.

Why, then, did she look at *this* man and feel that somehow she had been wrong in her first judgment of him?

"I would like to ask *you* a question, Mr. Constantine," she said. "How does a man come to be a bounty hunter?"

His face became a perfect blank. "Most do it for the money," he said.

"But not you?"

"I reckon my reasons are my own, just like yours."

"And do you consider yourself to work on the right side of the law?"

Every one of his muscles seemed to contract at once, and he set the spoon down with exaggerated care. "Yes, Miss Campbell," he said, matching her ice for ice. "I do. If you'll pardon me, I'll be going back to the barn."

She had offended him. Truly offended him. And she felt no satisfaction at all.

"Wait," she said. "Helene didn't take your measurements."

"It isn't necessary," he said brusquely, heading for the door.

"Bonnie won't be happy if I let you leave tomorrow half-dressed."

He hesitated, looking back at her, searching her face. Her heart turned over. She knew where the sewing things were; she'd done plenty of mending herself. It would only take a moment to get the measuring tape.

But to touch him, to lay the tape over the firm breadth of his back and shoulders, to feel his warm skin under her fingertips…

"I'll ask Bonnie to do it," she said, darting past him and out the door.

Bonnie was carrying a pail of fresh milk toward the house when Serenity met her.

"What's wrong?" Bonnie asked, setting the pail on the ground. "What did he do?"

"Nothing," Serenity said, releasing her breath. "Helene is resting. Can you take Constantine's measurements?"

The redhead grinned. "It will be my pleasure."

"You find him…attractive, don't you?"

"What woman wouldn't?"

It was not as appalling a question as it sounded. Bonnie knew very little about Serenity's past except that she had had some trouble with men. Everyone at Avalon had, at one time or another. But Bonnie's own troubles and former profession hadn't crushed her spirit or her ability to be drawn to the opposite sex. Even to a complete stranger.

Serenity couldn't imagine what it would be like to be as strong as Bonnie.

The older woman lost her smile. "I'm sorry," she said. "That was a stupid thing for me to say." She looked at Serenity more carefully. "He said something to upset you, didn't he?"

"Don't be silly."

But Bonnie continued to peer into her face, searching for the answers Serenity had never been able to give her. "You're upset about the branding. I suggested we hire a few boys from town—" She held up her hands before Serenity could protest. "I know. But in fact we have someone right here who could help."

For a moment Serenity didn't understand. When she did, her answer was immediate.

"Never," she said. "I want him gone."

"Even if he could make all the difference between a good season and a bad one?"

"Even if he were willing, and I don't see why he should be, he is only one man. How can he make a difference?"

"If it's that you don't want to ask him, I can—"

"No. He'll ruin everything. He—" Serenity swallowed and took a deep breath. "We all agreed on terms when we came together here. We would never ask for the help of any man. Do you want to go back on that promise, Bonnie?"

"She won't have to."

Constantine came sauntering down the stairs from the porch, a blanket draped over his shoulders, quiet as a panther. Serenity hadn't even been aware he'd come outside, let alone that he'd been listening.

"I didn't mean to eavesdrop, Miss Campbell, Miss Maguire," he said, nodding to each of them in turn, "but Miss Maguire is right. And, I owe you a debt, and I'd be glad to help out for a week or two."

IT WAS A MISTAKE, and Jacob knew it.

He thought he'd made his decision. He'd intended to leave tomorrow, just as he'd promised Miss Campbell...borrow a horse and get right on Leroy's trail. It wouldn't have gone too cold for a werewolf. Not yet.

But it might be in a week or two. He was about to sacrifice not only the bounty, which he needed, but the chance to bring another bad man to justice. And Serenity Campbell had been right to mock him when she'd asked him about becoming "protector" to these women. He'd pried into their business when he had no right or reason to, and every reason *not* to. God knew he wasn't fit to offer protection to anyone, let alone…

He tried without success to shake off the bitter memories. He hadn't taught Ruth to protect herself. She'd been a gentle soul, and he hadn't thought it was necessary. He'd sworn never to make himself responsible for any woman again.

If it weren't for the Code—the same code that wouldn't let him forget a debt—he wouldn't be here now, able to make a choice like this. He would have been dead—if not physically, then in every other way that mattered. He would have thrown himself into a fight he couldn't win, walked right into the Renier stronghold to take his revenge for Ruth's murder and started shooting without caring who he killed.

But he was alive because of these women. They had saved him at considerable risk to themselves. He hadn't intended to overhear their discussion in the yard, but his keen wolf's hearing had made it impossible for him to avoid it. Now he knew how much they needed him.

He couldn't do anything about their tricky situation here, surrounded by men who would no doubt be glad to take advantage of them and steal their cattle, if not their land. All he could do was discharge his debt, and maybe buy them a little more time.

"That is very generous of you, Mr. Constantine," Bonnie said. "If you're sure you're able to—"

"No," Serenity said, looking away. "Mr. Constantine has his own work to do. We would be selfish to keep him here."

"Not at all, ma'am," Jacob said. It was so easy to see through that tough facade to the scared woman beneath it. Scared of *him.* And he was sure that fear had something important to do with why there were no men here, why these women had made some kind of pact to keep the male sex from intruding on their domain.

He didn't like to scare women. He'd known right off that Serenity had been bothered by seeing him without his shirt. It wasn't just some kind of prudish disapproval. No, it went a lot deeper than that. If he'd known how hard she would take seeing him that way, he would have found something to throw over himself earlier.

She didn't seem to appreciate that he'd done it now. "You don't owe us anything," Serenity said. "You can be on your way with our blessing."

Bonnie Maguire met his gaze, begging him not to accept Serenity's dismissal. She, along with the girl, Frances, and Changying, had no difficulty in accepting his presence here, while Caridad shared Serenity's intense dislike. They weren't all of the same mind.

"I pay my debts," he said. "I know how to work cattle. I may be one man, but I'm good at what I do."

"I said we don't need you."

"I think you do, and if you cared about this outfit and these friends of yours, you'd realize that."

Angry blue eyes fixed on his. He had to admire Serenity Campbell in spite of himself. Scared she might be, but she would do everything in her power not to let him see it, not to show by a single word or deed that she was weak in any way. Just like she would do her best to hide her womanliness under ill-fitting boy's clothes.

"Let him help us," Bonnie said, resting her hand on Serenity's arm. "Most of the branding will be over in a few weeks, and then he'll be on his way. Won't you, Mr. Constantine?"

Nothing in the world could keep me here, he thought. "That's right, ma'am," he said aloud. "Miss Campbell, you don't have to worry. I'll do my work and never trouble you again."

Serenity weighed his words as if she were Blind Justice herself. "Let me make one thing clear, Mr. Constantine," she said. "You will be here on sufferance. You will treat every woman here with courtesy and respect. You will give no orders. And you will make no advances. None of any kind."

As if he would ever touch any woman who didn't invite him to do so. That generally meant whores who made their living entertaining men. They didn't expect anything from him but his money. Unlike Ruth, they could take care of themselves.

The woman standing before him would never invite any man to touch her.

"Do those rules suit you, Mr. Constantine?" she asked. "Because if they don't—if you break a single one of them—we will drive you out. And if you fail to do your share of the work, or prove less competent than you claim, we will dispense with your services."

Jacob hitched his thumbs in the waistband of his trousers. "I reckon you've made yourself clear, ma'am."

It wasn't the answer she'd expected. She'd wanted him to take offense, walk away and save her the trouble of dealing with him one moment longer.

"Bonnie," she said, turning her back on him, "he still needs to be measured."

"I'll see to it."

But the other woman didn't move, and Serenity was the first to leave. She set off at a pace that must have challenged her small body and went into the bunkhouse.

"I'm sorry," Bonnie said. "Serenity didn't mean what she said."

Jacob studied the redhead with interest. "I think she did," he said.

Bonnie glanced down at the milk pail by her feet. "I'd better take this inside before something gets in it," she said. "Come on in."

He moved to pick up the pail, but she beat him to it. He followed her into the house, and watched as she carefully poured the contents of the pail into several bottles and capped them. "Where did you work cattle?" she asked.

"Lots of places," he said, leaning a hip against the table.

"But you're a bounty hunter now."

"That's right, ma'am."

"Call me Bonnie."

He wondered if calling her by her Christian name would break one of Serenity's rules of conduct. "Have you been here long, Bonnie?" he asked.

"About a year." She looked over her shoulder. "It's a good place, with good people."

"Miss Campbell didn't want to tell me much about it," he said. "Or about herself."

"She never talks about herself, not even to us," Bonnie admitted. "Don't expect her to confide in you, of all people." She turned to face him, bracing her hands behind her on the worktable. "Serenity bought this land three and a half years ago," she said. "The owner of the land had died, and his kinfolk wanted nothing to do with this country. There was nothing on it but a few corrals, and an old adobe *casa* that had already been done in by wind and rain. She, Zora and Caridad started with only a few cattle. Within two years there were ten women working here, and a lot more cattle."

"Only ten women?" he asked.

She shrugged. "Usually it's enough. Helene can't ride, of course, but…"

Jacob paced away from the table, crossed the room and swung around again. "Do you all feel the same way about men as Miss Campbell does?"

She laughed. "I guess it's pretty obvious, isn't it?" She sobered. "I can't talk for the others, but just about everyone here has some reason for wanting to get away from men. Some just wanted their freedom. Others wanted peace. I wanted…" She hesitated. "I think you know what I used to be, Mr. Constantine. I see it in your eyes. Well, I'd had enough of that life, and it seemed to me that the best way to start fresh was to go somewhere and do something that had nothing to do with whoring."

"Why do you trust me, Bonnie?"

"I'm a pretty good judge of men. I think you're honest." She hesitated. "I see something else in your eyes, too. You want to know about Serenity. But I can't tell you. If she decides to trust you, maybe she'll tell you herself."

Jacob wasn't used to being so easy to read, or to being so firmly put in his place.

By unspoken agreement, he and Bonnie let the conversation lapse, and she went in search of the sewing things. She returned with a tape measure and set about recording the length and breadth of his chest, shoulders and arms.

Jacob felt nothing when she touched him. Bonnie's movements were as efficient and impersonal as they could be. For some reason he couldn't fathom, his thoughts turned back to Serenity.

She'd touched him less than a half-dozen times, usually as if he were a side of beef or a sack of flour, but even those brief contacts had stirred him in a way he didn't like. It was wrong, and he knew it. Just as it was wrong to wonder what had made her what she was.

There was no reason to give it any thought at all. In a few weeks he would be gone.

CHAPTER FOUR

IT WAS A MATCH made in hell.

If there had been any other way, Serenity wouldn't be riding beside Jacob Constantine, constantly aware of his presence, of the smell of him, of the easy way he sat on his horse. If she hadn't been so bent on protecting the other women from him—even Bonnie, who was far too trusting, and Caridad, who might shoot him and have to live with the remorse—she would gladly have sent him out with someone else.

But he was *her* responsibility. So she rode out with him in silence to the southwest quarter of the range, beginning the search for calves in need of branding. No words passed between them; she didn't offer conversation, and he seemed content to concentrate on the work.

He doesn't want to know me any more than I want to know him, she thought. And yet, in spite of herself, she began to notice little intriguing things about him that broke her concentration and awakened a far from easy curiosity.

First, there was the way he worked the cattle. She had to admit that Constantine was worth several men in terms of skill and efficiency. He was just as good as he'd implied, guiding his horse with his knees and hardly a touch on the reins, handling the beeves as if they were harmless little lambs.

Ordinarily, branding required a minimum of three riders for each quarter of the range, and weeks of grueling work. But Jacob didn't need any help at all getting the calves down, holding and tying them while she wielded the branding iron. In fact, he seemed to put very little effort into the work at all, and yet he achieved results that almost aroused her admiration.

Then there was the way he treated her. Though they seldom spoke, he was invariably courteous when he addressed her, never attempting the slightest intimacy or asking a single personal question. If he saw her as anything but a working partner, he showed no evidence of it.

She, however, could never be less than keenly aware of his lean, broad-shouldered frame, or the face she had been forced to concede was handsome in its own rough way. Nor could she pretend she wasn't aware of her own body, even though she had long ago made it a habit to forget it was anything but a living machine to be fed and cared for as one would any valuable animal.

The first night they made camp beside the well at the far west border of the property—one of several that, along with a natural spring, made Avalon so valuable. There was enough of the branding fire left to cook the brace of cottontails Constantine had provided, a welcome addition to the coffee, beans and biscuit makings Serenity had brought.

When he'd left camp to go hunting, Serenity had been half-convinced that he'd gone for good. Maybe he thought his debt had been paid with a day's hard work.

The fact that he hadn't taken his horse didn't convince her otherwise; it just meant he wasn't a horse thief.

But when he'd come back he'd had the rabbits in hand and had laid them on one of the nearby rocks without comment. She had thanked him briefly, brushed aside his offer to cook the rabbits and set up the spit herself. While the first one cooked, the two of them shared not so much as a single word. Jacob sat very still, listening to the night sounds, alert but relaxed. Serenity only wished she could feel the same.

When the first rabbit was ready, Serenity found herself offering it to him just to break the silence.

"No, ma'am," he said, meeting her gaze. "I reckon you're entitled to it."

His easy refusal angered her out of all proportion to his words. "Because I'm a woman?" she snapped.

"You've worked as hard as any two men combined. You need to keep up your strength."

And why should he care about her strength? Why bother with such compliments when she had never shown the slightest indication that she had any use for them?

"You're the one who's been hurt," she said.

"I can wait."

He wasn't going to back down, and she was too exhausted to argue. She hung the other rabbit on the spit and began to eat. She was far too hungry to be dainty about it, but Constantine didn't pay the least attention.

He accepted the second rabbit and ate with remarkable tidiness. When he'd finished, he picked up the battered tin plates.

"We don't want any coyotes bothering us," he said

with a slight, wry smile and walked out into the dark to wipe them clean in the sand. His words and that smile made it seem almost as if he was keeping some secret joke she wasn't meant to understand.

Her temper flared again, and she was forced to acknowledge that her emotions were out of control. All the feelings she had tried to master over the past six years were bubbling to the surface, and Jacob Constantine was the one who'd set them to boiling.

But blaming him for her upset wouldn't help her. She knew that her anger was a sign of her own weakness, a dangerous vulnerability, a painful reminder that she had yet to erase the brand Lafe Renier and his gang had left on her soul. As long as she carried that brand, she would be a prisoner to her past. And her pain.

She had always known there was only one way to conquer that pain squarely: stare it in the face and spit in its eye. Unfortunately, she hadn't yet found the means to put that plan into action.

But there was something else she *could* do, here and now: refuse to give Jacob Constantine the satisfaction of knowing just how thoroughly he disturbed her. And she could learn as much about him as possible. If she understood him even a little bit, she would know how to deal with him, how to react, how to ignore him when it suited her. She would be able to defend herself.

From what? she thought. But she shoved the thought aside and considered what question to ask first.

"How did you become a bounty hunter?" she asked abruptly when he returned.

She'd asked him a similar question before, and he'd

rebuffed her. She was prepared for the same reaction this time, but he surprised her.

"You've heard of the Texas Rangers?" he asked.

"I lived in Texas as a—" She broke off, took a deep breath and started again. "I have heard of them."

Constantine pulled his hat over his eyes and stretched out on his back, supporting himself on his elbows. "I was a Ranger for ten years," he said.

Most people would have considered that something to admire, but there hadn't been Rangers around when the Reniers had attacked Serenity's home, killed Levi and her parents, burned the house and taken her away.

She picked up a small stick and idly poked at the ashes. "What made you stop?" she asked.

"It was good work, but the time came when it just didn't suit me anymore."

"Why not?"

He turned his head to look at her, his eyes glittering red in the firelight like a coyote's. "Everyone changes," he said.

He returned his attention to the darkness beyond the fire, but Serenity had the feeling that he was listening intently to every breath she took. Gooseflesh crept up her arms.

"Are you good at what you do, Mr. Constantine?" she asked. "When you're not being ambushed, I mean?"

"Jacob."

The suddenness of his reply startled her. She'd deliberately provoked him, but instead of reacting with annoyance or anger, he'd offered her his Christian name.

Once she would have found such informality natural, as it had been among her kinfolk. But she knew she and Constantine could never be friends, let alone intimates. He must know that as well as she did.

And yet to refuse his request would be surrendering to the very fear she rejected. She had no obligation to reciprocate with a similar invitation.

"Jacob," she said.

He nodded briefly without looking at her. "Yes, Miss Campbell," he said. "I am good."

It wasn't just arrogance on his part. He was confident with good reason. She had seen how supremely competent he was, how at home in his own body, graceful and powerful at the same time. Never a wasted motion, like a wolf in pursuit of its prey.

"How many criminals have you caught?" she asked.

"As a Ranger, or a bounty hunter?"

"Both."

"Maybe fifty or so."

It seemed an incredible number, but she didn't doubt him. "How many did you kill?"

His jaw set. "I don't kill unless I have no choice."

"Even when someone tries to kill *you?*"

"I defend myself like any man."

"You would have killed Leroy, wouldn't you?"

He gave her another of those long, flat stares. "If I had to. My aim is to take them in alive."

"What happens when you deliver a wanted man to the authorities?"

"He's tried by a judge and jury."

"Have you ever arrested an innocent man?"

He looked away again. "Not that I know of, ma'am."

Ma'am. It was a safe word, a respectful word, but suddenly she hated it.

"Serenity," she said.

Constantine—Jacob—was silent for a time. "It don't seem right, Miss Campbell."

"You asked me to call you Jacob."

"It's not the same."

"Because I'm a woman?"

"That's what you are, Miss Campbell, even if you don't want to admit it."

She scrambled to her feet. "Not as far as you're concerned, Mr. Constantine."

His mouth twisted in that familiar smile. "Don't worry. I'll stick to my side of the bargain." His smile faded. "Maybe you have good reason to distrust all men and refuse to have any on your place. I just can't help wondering what that reason is."

JACOB HADN'T MEANT TO ask such a direct and personal question. He should have discouraged Serenity's curiosity about him as soon as she started to talk. He'd told himself he didn't want to know anything more about her, but the longer they were together, the less true that seemed.

He hadn't lied when he'd said she worked as hard as any two men, and just as well. Her skill wasn't in question; wherever she'd learned to handle cattle, she'd taken to the lessons like a dog to a bone. And she'd never asked a single favor of him, never expected him to take on dirty work she wouldn't do herself.

The fact was that she'd been easy to work with, and he'd had more than one assumption about female ranchers proved wrong—which only made his need to understand Serenity that much stronger.

Now she stared at him, her full lower lip caught between her teeth, and he noticed again just how pretty she was. Fresh and clean, like a desert night.

"We have discussed this before," she said. "Does it really seem so strange to you that women might strike out on their own simply because they have the means and courage to do so?"

Her response was much less defensive than he'd expected, which pleased him for no reason at all. He phrased his answer carefully.

"There are easier ways to strike out on your own than to try running an outfit like this."

Serenity uncorked her canteen and took a long drink. "We don't just try, Mr. Constantine. We succeed."

No easy answers, just as he'd expected. "You were lucky to get a place like this," he said. "You have a spring here?"

"Coming out of the Organs," she said. "We also have two good wells."

"There are some pretty big outfits in the county," he said. "The owners must envy what you have here."

"Their envy is no concern of mine," she said, the ice returning to her voice.

"They never give you trouble?"

"What trouble could they give us?"

"You've never been pressured to sell?"

"We are capable of defending ourselves, Jacob. There are plenty of good shots at Avalon. Anyone who comes here looking for trouble will get it."

"You've had no problems with rustlers?"

"None to speak of," she said.

Only because they'd been lucky, which didn't make

Jacob feel any easier in his mind. Even if the more powerful ranchers in the area didn't find a way to move them off the land, some gang like Leroy's was bound to see Avalon as a plump chicken waiting to be plucked, come in force, and then—

He cut off the thought and took another tack. "If you're having trouble with branding," he said, "what do you do when you set up a drive?"

"We supply cattle to Fort Selden and Fort Cummings. We manage very well on our own."

And they must leave the ranch pretty much undefended at such times, which seemed like sure suicide.

Unreasonable anger gathered in Jacob's chest. "You think you've found some kind of freedom here," he said harshly, "but this peace won't last forever."

She sprang to her feet. "You have no stake in our success or failure," she said, her voice husky with emotion. "You won't see any of us ever again once you leave."

Why did that simple fact make him want to argue with her? She was right. But he still hadn't learned a damned thing about what drove her. He knew generally why these women had come here, but not what made *her* so wary of men, or why she would risk so much to prove she didn't need them. She must have had a father, a brother, maybe even a husband. The thought of her having been bound to any man had a strange effect on his heart. It made him forget to be careful.

"You saved my life," he said. "That gives me some reason to care what happens to you."

She froze in the act of turning away, her face caught in a rare moment of vulnerability. "You don't have to worry," she said. "We know the risks. We live our own way and make our own rules. No one here has to be afraid…"

She didn't finish the sentence, but Jacob recognized how close she'd come to revealing something important about herself. She must have realized it as well, for she suddenly broke into a brisk walk and strode out into the darkness.

Jacob could still see her. He knew she wasn't in any danger, and she wasn't angry or reckless enough to stray far from the fire.

Still more than a little angry himself, he adjusted his saddle under his head, folded his arms and closed his eyes. *Four weeks, at most,* he reminded himself. *Only four...*

He dozed for a while, half-awake as he listened for Serenity's return. Only when he heard her soft footsteps approaching her bedroll did he allow himself to sink into a deeper sleep, though some part of his wolf senses remained alert.

It was those senses that woke him first when the gun went off. He sprang up, shaking the sleep from his mind and body, and listened for the echo of the distant report.

"What is it?" Serenity asked, her voice muffled as she sat up and pushed her blanket aside.

Of course her human ears hadn't heard it. "A gunshot," he said.

In a moment she was on her feet beside him, fully alert. "Where?"

"Two, maybe three, miles to the east," he said.

Which would be somewhere in the cluster of what

passed for foothills not far from the house. Serenity didn't even ask how he'd heard a shot so far away. Her face went pale in the breaking dawn light.

"Bonnie and Zora," she said. Without another word, she buckled on her gun belt, ran for the horses and swung up onto her gelding's bare back. She kicked the horse into a hard run, not waiting to see if Jacob would follow.

He cursed under his breath, mounted his own horse and urged it after her. Serenity obviously knew she couldn't push the gelding at a full gallop for three miles across the desert, but she never let him fall below a trot, and the horse was willing enough.

Jacob's own mount proved equally willing. Little by little, he pulled into the lead, knowing that Serenity could only guess where the shot had come from.

He *knew.* Just as his nose and ears told him that Leroy and three of his men were waiting in ambush in one of the deep arroyos cutting east away from the Organ Mountains.

There was no time to warn Serenity. He cut across her path, forcing her horse to turn with his. He aimed for a jumble of high rocks a dozen yards from the arroyo. Once the horses were behind the rocks he jumped down, grabbed Serenity around the waist and pulled her after him.

Her fists pounded his chest in a drumbeat of panic. Her eyes were wild, though she didn't make a sound. He wrapped his arms around her.

"Be quiet," he whispered. "There are men in that arroyo just waiting for us to stumble over them."

Her rigid body went still. "Leroy's men?"

She read the answer in his eyes. Her shoulders slumped, and she went limp as the tail of a newborn calf. Just as he was about to release her, she jerked free and put a good dozen feet between them.

"Don't ever do that again," she said, very softly.

He ignored her warning. "Bonnie was working out here?" he asked.

"With Zora."

He didn't know who Zora was, but this wasn't the time to ask. He was too busy keeping an eye on Serenity, who had pulled her rifle from its scabbard and moved to a point where she could see around the rocks to the lip of the arroyo. "How do you know Leroy is there?" she asked.

He couldn't very well tell her the truth. "I saw one of them stick his head up," he said. He didn't tell her that he smelled blood. He hoped it belonged to one of the gang.

"I have to find Bonnie," she said. "Zora can take care of herself. But Bonnie—"

Her voice broke. She was sick with worry, and there was little Jacob could do to reassure her. "Miss Maguire struck me as a lady who can take care of herself, too," he said. "They may have the men pinned in the arroyo." He adjusted his gun belt. "Let's just hope your friends don't shoot at me when I—"

"You don't have to worry," she said. Her face was as hard as one of the granite peaks rising above them. "I'm going out there myself."

"Don't be stupid," he said. "They'll shoot you down as soon as you stick your head out. I know how to get around them. You cover me."

Before she could protest, he was running around the rocks, crouched low and ready to shoot. He heard Serenity's feet crunch on the gritty earth behind him. He prayed she was only getting into position to shoot if one of Leroy's gang spotted him.

They didn't see him until he was within a few feet of the arroyo, and then only because someone out of his sight nearly got him in the leg. He half fell into the arroyo, twisting like a cat so that he landed on his feet and was firing before his boots touched ground.

There were four horses and three men crowded between the steep walls of the arroyo—Leroy, Hunsaker and Silas—and two bodies sprawled behind them, one male and one female. The man was Stroud, clearly dead, and the woman was Bonnie Maguire. She was lying on her stomach, very still, but breathing.

Leroy was heavily bandaged, but he wasn't as badly hurt as Jacob had hoped when he'd seen the outlaw shot. Leroy's eyes blazed with a very personal hatred.

Three guns aimed at Jacob. He got Leroy in the bad shoulder again and watched the man go down before the first bullet grazed his own arm. He twisted out of the path of two more bullets and fired again.

His shot missed, but someone else's didn't. Hunsaker fell with a cry. The horses shied and squealed. Hoofbeats pounded at the edge of the arroyo.

Serenity had ignored his warning.

"Go back!" he ordered.

"You'd better give up!" Serenity shouted from her position somewhere above them. "You're outnumbered!"

Silas looked wildly toward Jacob and aimed his revolver at the female body at his feet. "Tell her if anyone shoots again, I'll kill this bitch!"

Jacob lowered his gun. "Serenity!" he called. "Can you hear me?"

"I hear you. Are you all right?"

"Yes." The slight wound on his arm was already healing, and he was too worried to feel much pain. "Don't shoot, and tell your friend to hold her fire. They've got Bonnie."

Neither Silas nor Leroy heard Serenity's soft wail, but it tore at Jacob's heart. He swallowed a growl and faced the two men who remained.

"I warn you," he said, "if you hurt the woman, you'll never get out of here alive."

CHAPTER FIVE

SILAS LAUGHED NERVOUSLY. "You're going to let us go, Constantine, and we'll be taking the woman. We'll release her when we're good and ready. If you try to follow us—"

He continued with his threats, but Jacob was concentrating on the sounds of movement above the arroyo. Serenity had dismounted and was walking away. Not abandoning him or Bonnie, he knew, but planning some new and foolhardy tactic. He had no way to stop her, but at least the men hadn't heard her. He could keep them occupied until something—or someone—broke the stalemate.

"How do I know the woman is still alive?" he asked.

"She's alive," Leroy said, clutching his bloody shoulder and rolling to his knees, his face pale as milk. "But she won't be much longer if you don't do what we say. Drop the gun."

Jacob let his pistol fall and raised his hands. "Why did you come back?" he asked.

"You think I'd let a bunch of ugly bitches drive us away?"

"So you thought you'd make them pay."

"They *will* pay."

"Didn't you plan to take the woman and leave?"

"I'll be back."

"And I'll find you. You think I believe you'll let the woman go once you're out of here? You'll kill her, and there won't be anything to stop me from getting you."

Leroy glowered. It was obvious he knew Jacob wasn't bluffing. The fight seemed to go out of him all at once, but Jacob wasn't fooled.

"I've got a deal for you, Leroy," he said. "Me for the woman."

Silas giggled, but Leroy was listening. "What's your relation with these females, Constantine?"

"They saved my life."

"You want me to believe you'd give yourself up for some bitch you hardly know?"

"That's right. I'll ride with you, unarmed. Once we're at the pass, you let the woman ride back, and you can do whatever you want with me."

Leroy's eyes narrowed in calculation. He was smart enough to realize that Jacob would never expect him to keep his part of the bargain, and he had a hard time believing Jacob would keep his.

But he couldn't resist the temptation. "Okay," he said. "I want to see you strip buck naked so I can make sure you don't have any weapons on you. And you tell them bitches to keep away."

"I need proof the woman's alive and well enough to ride."

Leroy jerked his head at Silas, who knelt beside Bonnie and turned her over. Her jaw was already black-and-blue from a nasty blow, but there was no visible blood on her clothes.

She groaned and tried to push Silas away. He helped her sit up, and she opened her eyes.

"Jacob?" she whispered.

"I'm here. You save your strength."

"All right, Constantine," Leroy said. "Throw your duds and gear down there, then climb up top and tell them females not to fire afore you come back."

Without hesitation, Jacob began to remove his clothes. He unbuckled his gun belt, set his belt knives in their sheaths on the ground, took off his bandanna and vest and shirt, pulled off his boots, and removed the tiny knife in its boot sheath. When he'd taken off the rest, Leroy gestured sharply with his gun.

Jacob knew he could Change in an instant and be on the men before they recovered from the shock. The Code was plain about bargains and promises: you didn't break your word, even if you were dying. But he'd been careful in his agreement with Leroy; he'd agreed to ride out with them, but hadn't made any promises about what he would do before.

Still, something held him back. He didn't want to risk Serenity seeing him Change. She had enough to worry about without facing that kind of terror.

But he still had his superior speed and strength. He began to climb up the side of the arroyo, letting his feet slip as if he found the effort difficult. As soon as his eyes reached ground level, he saw Serenity flat on the ground a few yards away, rifle in hand, waiting for the chance to get near the ravine. She met his gaze, her eyes dark with emotion and fear.

But not for herself. He knew that as clearly as if she had told him.

He turned his head to search out the other woman he could smell nearby. She was crouched a few yards away on the other side of the arroyo, ready to fire her own Winchester.

"Tell them!" Leroy snapped behind him.

The muzzle of a gun poked into the small of Jacob's back. He dug his fingers into the dry, crumbling dirt at the lip of the arroyo. It began to disintegrate under his grasp.

"Serenity!" he shouted. "Don't—"

The soil under his hand gave way, and he fell backward. Leroy cursed as he buckled under Jacob's weight, firing blindly. The bullet just missed Jacob's hip. A second bullet flew over his head as he spun around and knocked Leroy's gun from his hands.

Silas's hands were shaking, but he had moved within point-blank range and was about to shoot Jacob through the heart. His finger twitched on the trigger.

The gun never went off. The muzzle of a rifle poked over the edge of the arroyo, and a bright red blossom opened on Silas's shirt. He opened his mouth, staggered and fell.

"Jacob!" Serenity cried. "Are you all right? Is Bonnie—"

He was distracted for one fatal instant. Leroy scrambled up, dodged Jacob's reaching hands and fell on top of Silas's body, snatching at the fallen man's revolver. His bullet caught Bonnie full in the chest. Serenity screamed, dropped her rifle and threw herself into the arroyo just as Jacob lifted Leroy and tossed him against the rock wall.

Then there was silence, broken only by Serenity's quiet sobs.

Jacob turned slowly, barbwire coiling in his gut.

Serenity was holding Bonnie in her arms, rocking her gently and singing some kind of lullaby as she wept. She was no longer aware of Jacob at all.

Jacob crouched where he was, remembering. Remembering Ruth and how he'd found her body, shattered and abused and shot. He had promised to protect her when he'd made his marriage vows, and he'd failed her. He had made himself responsible for Serenity and Bonnie when he'd gone after Leroy and his gang in the arroyo. He'd failed *them,* too.

The almost inaudible crunch of soft footsteps above alerted him to the other woman's approach. She knelt and looked into the arroyo, black hair falling across her face. Her dark-eyed gaze brushed over Jacob and his naked body, dismissed him, and settled on the women below. She jumped lightly to the ground and knelt beside Serenity.

Jacob felt the shock of recognition through the dull haze of his despair. Zora had to be half Indian, probably Apache by the looks of her, but she was at least half werewolf, as well. And she recognized the wolf in him, too.

Right now, though, she wasn't interested in anything she and Jacob might have in common. She put her arm around Serenity and spoke low in Apache, a murmur of farewell and sorrow.

The last thing either of them wanted, he knew, was his commiseration. He made sure that Hunsaker and Silas were dead, then crouched beside Leroy to keep an eye on him, averting his face from the women's suffering.

After a while the weeping stopped, and Serenity lowered Bonnie's body gently to the ground. She smoothed the woman's flyaway red hair from her face, removed her own coat and laid it over Bonnie's chest to cover the ugly wound.

"We'll take her home," she said. She rose and glanced around the arroyo at Leroy and the dead men, her face expressionless, eyes red-rimmed and empty. She turned to Jacob.

"Is Leroy dead?" she asked

"Miss Campbell," he said, "I'm sorry."

She looked right through him. "Is he dead?"

"No. But I swear to you—"

"Why didn't you kill him?"

"I'm taking him in," Jacob said. "He'll suffer a lot more waiting to be hanged than he would if I killed him now."

Even to his own ears, the words sounded cold and indifferent.

Serenity began to shake. "He is not going anywhere," she whispered.

"I will do it," Zora said. Her voice was as soft as her tread, but her eyes were hard. She pulled a knife from its sheath at her belt.

Jacob rose to stand between Leroy and the Apache woman. "I can't let you do that."

"He killed Bonnie," she said.

No fire, no hatred. Just simple fact. That was enough for Zora. But Serenity might still be reasoned with.

"He has to be brought to trial," he said. "You talked once about women making the West civilized. I aim to keep it that way."

Serenity stared at him as if he'd gone loco. "Civilized?" she repeated blankly. "What is civilized about any of this?"

Nothing. And that made the law even more important. No matter how much he might wish he could kill Leroy here and now, the Code wouldn't let him. Killing in self-defense and to protect innocents was sometimes necessary, but he'd sworn years ago never to murder a man in cold blood, no matter what the reason. To do any different would make him just like those he hunted.

One slip would send him plummeting into the pit.

"I'm sorry," he said again, meaning it with all his heart. "But the law is the law. I promise he'll pay the price for what he's done."

Serenity's shaking had stopped, but he knew she wasn't half ready to concede. "You want him to go to trial?" she asked. "We can arrange that right here at Avalon."

The idea took him aback. "Miss Campbell," he said, "this is no place—"

"He would have a chance to tell his side of the story," she said.

As if that would matter. Serenity had held Bonnie in her arms as the life had drained out of her friend. Her devotion had gone deeper than Jacob had guessed. There wouldn't be even a semblance of justice in what she was proposing.

He looked at Bonnie's body. She'd been a good woman. She might not be suffering, but Serenity and the others would go on grieving. Revenge wouldn't ease those feelings, no matter what they thought. Revenge was a disease that ate you up inside and left nothing but a rotted soul.

"I can't let you do it, Miss Campbell," he said.

He'd underestimated Serenity and her women when he'd first come to Avalon. He should have known better than to do it again.

Serenity pointed her rifle at his chest.

"I'm sorry, Mr. Constantine," she said. "Zora?"

The other woman advanced on Jacob, knife in hand.

Jacob held his ground.

"You won't hurt me," he said.

Serenity's eyes were clouded with the blindness of grief, but he could see the battle roaring inside her. She had no desire to threaten him, but she saw no other choice.

She didn't trust the law to take care of Leroy. She didn't trust Jacob to finish what he'd started. And maybe she blamed herself for Bonnie's death, for not taking better care of her people.

That was something Jacob understood. When he'd first set out to track Ruth's murderers—killers who had taken pains to leave obvious evidence of their identities—the trail had already gone cold and he hadn't known where they'd taken refuge. He'd thought his need to kill them outright would never fade, no matter how long he searched.

But it had. He'd seen the pit opening up in front of him and had stepped back just in time. He'd found the Code. It had restored his sanity and given him new purpose. Serenity didn't have the Code, or anything like it, to make her path clear.

And he knew there was something darker behind her need for violent retribution.

Zora moved closer to Jacob, her gaze never leaving

his. She knew just how dangerous he could be. He knew he could overpower her, but she or Serenity might get hurt in the struggle.

That was a risk he didn't want to take. He would go along for now, but he wouldn't make any promises he couldn't keep.

"All right," he said. "You mind if I get dressed?"

Serenity blinked, as if she hadn't noticed his state of undress until that moment. She flushed and gestured with the rifle. With Zora right behind him, Jacob returned to his pile of clothes and, ignoring his long johns, pulled on his trousers, careful to avoid the knives he'd dropped a few feet away. Zora gathered them up and pushed the sheaths into her belt.

"You'll carry Leroy out of the arroyo," Serenity said to him. "I'll stay with you while Zora gathers the horses."

"Leroy's hurt pretty bad," Jacob said. "We'd better bind him up, or he's likely to bleed to death before we get him to the house."

"Can you do it?" she asked.

Jacob nodded and knelt to tear strips of cloth from the cleanest parts of the dead men's shirts. Serenity watched intently while he pulled Leroy into a sitting position and bound his shoulder. The outlaw groaned but remained only half-conscious. When he was finished, Jacob hauled Leroy to his feet.

"That way," Serenity said, gesturing east. She followed Jacob as he carried Leroy past the huddled, frightened horses along and out of the arroyo. Jacob rolled Leroy off his shoulders and waited until Zora drove the gang's horses up behind them. She led one of them to Jacob.

"Put him up," Serenity said.

Leroy groaned as Jacob heaved him into the saddle. Serenity threw Jacob a length of rope. He tied Leroy's hands to the saddle horn and his feet into the stirrups. Zora set off for the rocks where Jacob had left his own horse and brought the gelding back, along with Serenity's mount and two other horses he assumed were hers and Bonnie's. Then she went back into the arroyo. She returned with Bonnie cradled in her arms. Serenity slumped, her head bowed in inconsolable misery.

Jacob knew that if he planned to make an escape and take Leroy with him, this was the time. Zora couldn't come after him now, and Serenity was too lost in her grief to stop him. She probably couldn't hit him with a bullet even if she were standing right next to him.

But Jacob couldn't seem to move. Zora gently laid Bonnie on the ground, rising swiftly to face Jacob again as she cut a length of rope from the coil tied to her saddle. Her intention was obvious. Jacob held his hands out before him, and Zora began to bind his wrists. She knew he could snap the ropes if he set his mind to it, but she wasn't going to make it easy.

Averting her eyes, Serenity moved to unbuckle the cinches from two of the outlaws' horses, then swung the saddles over the bare backs of her mount and Jacob's. When she was finished securing the tack, she stepped back and looked from Bonnie to Jacob. He knew she was wondering how to get Bonnie back to the house when she and Zora needed their hands free to keep him and Leroy under guard.

The words came out of his mouth before he had time to think.

"I'll take her," he said.

Zora's eyes narrowed.

Serenity released a ragged breath.

"Why should I trust you?" she asked. "Maybe you only want us to untie your hands. You could…you could use Bonnie to make us let you go."

Her accusation was more painful to Jacob than any wound he'd suffered since Leroy's gang had ambushed him. "I wouldn't do that, Miss Campbell," he said stiffly. "I would never desecrate the dead that way, least of all Miss Maguire."

Serenity stared at the ground. "I'll still shoot you if you try to take Leroy."

Better to make her think he believed her. "I know," he said.

Serenity looked up again. "Zora, untie him."

Zora clearly didn't want to do anything of the kind, but she slashed the ropes and stepped quickly away. Jacob set his foot in the stirrup and mounted, sliding as far back in the saddle as he could. His horse snorted and tossed its head at the smell of death so near.

With visible reluctance, Zora lifted Bonnie into the saddle. Miss Maguire had been a slight woman; she fit easily into the space between Jacob and the pommel. He put his arms around her and found that his throat had closed up on him. Her body was still warm. A thick tide of grief and memory painted a wash of moisture over his eyes.

I'm a pretty good judge of men, she'd said to him only a couple of days ago. *I think you're honest.*

But his honesty hadn't been enough to save her.

Zora went for another piece of rope and reached up to tie Jacob's hands in front of Bonnie's waist.

"Leave him be," Serenity said.

Zora didn't question Serenity's order. She strode back into the arroyo a third time and emerged with the outlaws' guns, and Jacob's six-shooter and knives. She kept one of the guns, tucked the rest in her saddlebags, and mounted her own pony. She kept the gun aimed at Jacob while Serenity slid her rifle into the scabbard attached to her saddle, then tied lead ropes to the five spare horses' bridles. She tied three horses to Zora's saddle and two to Jacob's, fixed the lead of Leroy's horse to her own saddle, and swung up onto her gelding's back.

"You ride ahead," Serenity said to Jacob.

He gave his horse a gentle kick and turned it in the direction of the house. Serenity and Zora took up positions behind him. He could feel the iron eye of Zora's rifle aimed at his back.

It took them about two hours to reach the house. Sometimes Serenity rode beside Jacob, just out of reach, and looked at him with a battle raging behind her eyes. Leroy began to groan loudly not long after they left the arroyo, and within an hour he was cursing and hurling threats.

By the time they reached the outer corral, Leroy was too hoarse and thirsty to do any more complaining. The yard was empty when they rode in, but Helene soon hurried out of the house with a little exclamation of surprise and alarm.

"Serenity?" She looked from Leroy to Jacob and Bonnie. Her knees buckled.

Serenity jumped out of her saddle. She caught Helene and supported her until she could get to her feet. Changying ran from the bunkhouse a moment later. She came to a sudden stop when she saw Bonnie.

Zora sheathed her rifle, dismounted and stood beside Jacob's saddle. Jacob eased Bonnie into Zora's arms and swung down. Changying rushed up and pressed her fingers to Bonnie's throat, though she must have realized that the other woman had been gone for hours. No one could have survived the wound she had taken.

Slowly Changying lowered her hand and met Jacob's gaze. Her expression remained quiet, but there was as much turmoil behind her eyes as Jacob had seen in Serenity's.

Zora firmed her hold on Bonnie and started for the house. Helene was sobbing, and Serenity remained behind to comfort her. Jacob waited awkwardly, unable to help, unable to do anything to restore any part of what had been taken. Changying shot him a troubled glance and followed Zora. Leroy had slumped over the saddle horn, begging for water in a ragged whisper.

Last chance, Jacob thought. With Zora and Changying out of sight and Serenity occupied with Helene, he wouldn't find it difficult to take Leroy away. The fact was that Serenity was making it easy for him.

Did she trust him after all? Or did she *want* him to take Leroy, so she wouldn't have to act on her darkest impulses? He was pretty sure she'd killed Hunsaker, but that had been in the heat of battle. There was too much goodness in her, too much basic decency, to go through with what she'd planned for Leroy. She had to know that everything she and the others had worked for could be destroyed with a single mistake.

He could spare her that. All he had to do was jump back into the saddle, cut the lead of Leroy's horse and ride away.

"Jacob."

Serenity's arm was still tight around Helene, but her gaze was all for him, and this time she didn't look away.

"Thank you," she said. "Thank you for bringing her back."

Jacob struggled for the right words. "She was a good woman," he said.

"Yes," she said. "One of the best." Helene nodded, dabbed at her eyes and walked to the house.

"She told me she'd only been here about a year," Jacob said once he and Serenity were alone again.

"You spoke to her?"

He was surprised to hear more yearning than anger in Serenity's voice. No hostility, only a sad curiosity. Maybe she wanted to know what Bonnie had talked about in the hours before her death.

"She told me a little about the ranch," he said, "and why she came here."

Fresh grief welled in Serenity's eyes. "She had a hard life before. She didn't have enough time to be happy."

Jacob almost couldn't bear her pain. He raised his hand halfway, clenched his fist and dropped it back to his side.

"I wish I'd been there sooner," he said.

"So do I."

Her voice was rough with more than sorrow. Jacob knew she blamed herself. She believed she was personally responsible for every woman at Avalon. She would be ready to comfort anyone who needed it, but who would comfort her?

"It wasn't your fault," he said.

"I sent Bonnie out when I knew she wasn't any good with a gun. I thought if she was with Zora…" She covered her face with her hands. "I should have known it wasn't safe. I should have known."

Just as he should have known that he and Ruth had no chance of escaping the feud that had haunted the Constantines and Reniers for a hundred years.

Without considering the consequences, Jacob walked up to Serenity and took her in his arms. For a few fragile seconds it seemed that some profound understanding passed between them. It didn't matter that Serenity didn't know about Ruth or his own guilt. Somehow, instinctively, she sensed they shared something that words couldn't define.

Then she remembered who she was. She pulled away, stumbling back in confusion. Her face was deeply flushed, but there was no anger in her eyes. She moved close to Jacob's gelding and stood beside the horse's head as if the animal's sheer bulk could protect her.

Jacob realized he was just as shaken as she was. He swallowed a mouthful of curses.

Serenity leaned her cheek against the gelding's broad forehead. "Why didn't you take Leroy when you had the chance?" she asked suddenly.

Her voice was almost unnaturally quiet, and there

was no accusation in it. But Jacob knew he'd failed her. He'd intended to spare her the ugliness of revenge, but he'd been too slow to act. He could no longer make any sense of the thoughts in his own head. Or the turmoil in his heart.

Unaware of his impending fate, Leroy croaked another desperate plea for water. Serenity flinched. That alone made Jacob wish he could put a bullet through Leroy's brain.

"We'll have to give him something to drink," Jacob said. "I'll take care of it. You go on inside and see to Miss Maguire."

They gazed at each other, neither quite ready to sever those last remaining threads of understanding that had so briefly bound them together.

"Jacob," she said softly. "Promise me you won't try to take Leroy away."

The spell was broken. Jacob felt his body become heavy, weighted with the soul-deep knowledge that the answer he gave her would have greater consequences than he was prepared to face. If he refused, he knew he would lose something precious, something he hadn't even known he'd found. Something as deadly as it was sweet.

He laughed at himself. The desert sun had addled his brain, and he had to get it straight again before he made a mistake he couldn't undo. There was only one answer he could give.

But when he gave it, it wasn't the one he'd planned on.

"You have my word," he said. "On one condition."

CHAPTER SIX

SHE WENT VERY still, and it felt as if she'd put the whole of New Mexico Territory between them.

"What is it?" she asked.

"You said when you gave Leroy his trial you'd let him speak on his own behalf. I want to do it for him."

"You want to *defend* him?"

"I'll just tell the other women what I told you. About seeing that justice is done the right way, even when it seems hard to trust to the law." He paused. "Of course, they might decide to go against what you want if I convince them."

It was a test, and she knew it. However much she hated Leroy, she couldn't pretend it would be any kind of trial if no one was allowed to speak except those who wanted the outlaw dead.

"Very well," she said coldly. "You do what you must, and I will do the same."

She turned sharply and began to walk away.

"Wait," Jacob called after her.

She didn't turn around. "What is it?"

"Where do you want me to put him?"

"In the shed, if you think you can tie him up well enough to make sure he doesn't escape."

Serenity went on to the house without another word.

Jacob removed his hat and ran a hand through his

sweat-soaked hair. He'd broken the brief truce between them for the sake of a man he hated, but there hadn't been any choice. If he was going to compromise the Code in one way, he had to make up for it in another or let it die. And if it died, the man Jacob had pieced together from the shards of his old life would die with it.

Feeling more tired than he had since he'd woken up in Avalon's barn, Jacob untied Leroy's feet and hands, and pulled him down from the saddle. While the outlaw sprawled on the ground, too weak to move, Jacob went to the yard pump and unhooked the tin cup that hung from the adjoining post. He filled the cup and carried it back to Leroy.

"You…you sorry son of a bitch," Leroy rasped. "Takin' orders from them—"

Jacob grabbed a fistful of Leroy's greasy hair, lifted the outlaw's head and pushed the rim of the cup against his cracked lips. Leroy sucked greedily until the water was gone. Jacob jerked the cup away.

"These women would like to see you hang," he said. "And they don't plan to wait for any judge and jury. I don't think they'll much care if I haul your dead carcass to Las Cruces and collect the bounty."

Leroy grinned raggedly. "You won't let them hang me, Constantine. You're too—" he hawked and spat "—honorable."

Jacob shook his head. "I don't think there's much I can do to help you now, Leroy," he said. "Still, you got a better chance with me than you do with these women you despise so much. If you cause one speck of trouble, you won't get any chance at all."

The outlaw tried to laugh, but he ended up choking instead. Jacob set the cup down, seized Leroy by the front of his torn shirt and dragged him to his feet. Leroy cried out in pain and went limp. Jacob half pushed, half carried the outlaw toward the shed.

Once he had Leroy well tied up and had given him another drink of water, Jacob returned to see to the horses and found Zora leading the four from Avalon toward the stable adjoining the barn. He collected the outlaws' horses, tied them to the fence of the corral just outside the stable, and went inside.

Zora didn't acknowledge him until she had the horses secured and had begun to remove their saddles. Even then, she only glanced at him, her dark eyes unreadable, and went on with her work without speaking.

Jacob didn't see any reason for delicacy. "You know what I am," he said, picking up a brush and setting to work on Serenity's mare.

Zora gave a short nod. "I know," she said.

Her English was perfect, if formal, and that told him she'd had a decent education somewhere, maybe in an Indian school. Still, most Indians Jacob had known didn't talk unless they had something to say, and Zora was obviously no exception, half-breed or not. If she felt any curiosity about him, she wasn't going to let on. It was up to him to keep the conversation going.

"Do they know what *you* are?" he asked.

Her hands stilled on her horse's bridle. "No," she said. "And they will not."

He didn't have to ask her why she spoke so firmly. There were a fair number of werewolves in the West, but most of them took pretty great pains not to let ordinary folk know they existed. A few were less cautious, but they were the ones with the least to fear…the ones who had the kind of power that made people reluctant to look too closely.

A woman who was half Apache, half white, would have double the reason to be careful.

"What brought you here?" he asked as he bent to examine the gelding's forefoot.

"Why do you ask so many questions?"

No anger, not like she'd shown when she'd threatened to stab Leroy, but Jacob wasn't deceived. "Wouldn't you, in my situation?" he asked.

She hung the bridle over a hook on the wall and faced him. "You do not have to stay here," she said. "It would be better if you left today."

Without Leroy, she meant. "I've given my word to Miss Campbell that I won't try to take Leroy," he said. "But I'm making my case that he should have a real trial."

Her impassive face flared with emotion. "You have brought nothing but pain to this place," she said. "No one wants you here."

"Miss Campbell seems to think I did some good today."

Zora made a cutting motion with the side of her hand. "Those men would not have been here if you hadn't come."

"You're right. But I said I'd work off the debt in trade for saving my life, and that's what I aim to do."

She stared at him so long that he began to see the little flecks of yellow suspended in the black of her eyes. "It was men like you who hurt Serenity," she said. "If you ever give her even one moment of pain, I will kill you."

"You'll have to stand in line," he muttered. But his thoughts were snagged on the other thing Zora had said.

"Men like you." Was she comparing him to Leroy? He would have thought he'd proven to these women that he wasn't that kind. And he didn't think Zora meant bounty hunters.

"Are you saying it was werewolves who hurt her?" he asked in amazement.

Zora's expression became stolid again. "Yes."

His heart began to race. "How?"

"Why should I tell you?"

"How can I make sure *I* never hurt her if I don't know what makes her the way she is?"

"There is nothing wrong with her."

But Zora's voice told Jacob that she didn't believe it. She frowned, letting the silence drag on so long that Jacob thought she'd decided not to answer.

"Her parents were killed," she said abruptly.

It wasn't what he'd expected. Hell, he hadn't known what to expect, though he'd decided that she must have suffered some abuse at the hands of a man to hate them so much. But this was worse. He felt it all the way to his bones. The hair on the back of his neck bristled, and a growl rumbled in his chest.

Werewolves had hurt Serenity, just as they had killed Ruth.

That was why Zora didn't want Serenity to know what she was. Why Jacob could never let her catch even a glimpse of his true nature. Because she would hate him even more than she had in the beginning.

"How much does Serenity know about our kind?" he asked.

Zora gave him a long, assessing look. "I think she knows there are others. But she has no reason to believe they are not all killers."

She would have no reason to think otherwise even if she'd never met any werewolves. It was natural for regular folk to feel horror and fear when they found out such creatures existed, even though most werewolves lived peacefully among them, never causing a lick of trouble or hurting anyone. Jacob's family had been like that, except when it came to the feud, and that had nothing to do with humans.

"Do you think I'm like the ones who killed her parents?" he asked.

"Are you?"

"No more than you are," he said, holding her gaze with his most aggressive wolfish stare.

Zora was the first to look away. "Then maybe you would help her," she said.

Her sudden change in attitude caught Jacob off guard. "I thought you wanted me gone."

"Maybe I was wrong."

His fingers curled around the brush so hard that he crushed the sturdy bristles. "How can I help her?"

"She will never be free until someone finds the ones who hurt her."

"Were there many of them?"

"A gang, like Leroy's."

Icy claws raked down Jacob's spine. "What were their names?"

"If she knew, she never told me."

Jacob closed his eyes. There was more than one outlaw werewolf gang in the West. The odds of any connection…

"Where did this happen?" he asked.

"In Texas."

Where Ruth had died. A breath of hot wind gusted into the stable, licking at the cold sweat dripping down the nape of his neck.

"Are you suggesting that I should go after these men?" he asked, struggling to keep his voice as level as Zora's.

"You are a hunter of evil men," she said. "You can track them as a human could not. I and others here have saved money. We will give it to you if you—"

"Is this what Serenity wants?" he asked.

"She would have done it herself long ago, if she could. But she does not know how to find them, and—"

"And you won't help her."

Zora hesitated. "I cannot."

"Because you don't want to lose her friendship by admitting you could do it."

"She would try to follow me. With you, it is different. You will leave anyway. She does not have to know." She searched his eyes. "If she found them, she would try to kill them herself."

"Has she killed many men?" he asked, hoping to hear the right answer.

"No. The man in the arroyo was the first. It would not matter. She would still try. Her courage cannot be doubted, but courage is not enough."

Jacob's imagination conjured up the picture Zora

evoked far too clearly. Ruth had been brave, too. But she hadn't been strong.

What if they are the same men?

"No." He dropped the ruined brush and backed away, stopping only when he reached the wall behind him. "I'm not in the business of revenge for hire."

Zora's gaze followed him, dark and implacable. "You do not care for Serenity."

"I don't know her."

"You know enough. You are one of the few of our kind who fight for the laws that protect men from those who would harm the weak. The evil ones are bound by no law. Who will prevent them from killing again?"

Who would stop the werewolves who had killed Ruth? Jacob had chosen to let them go rather than shed more blood that would stain Ruth's memory and feed the feud that would continue to take more lives.

But these men weren't likely to be Reniers, no matter how much his overwrought suspicions tried to conflate them. He might be able to stop them…not for his own sake or Ruth's, but for the greater good.

He caught Serenity's scent before he heard the rustle of hay and the scrape of a foot in the doorway. He and Zora exchanged glances.

Had she been listening to their conversation? Ordinarily, no human could approach so close to Jacob, or any werewolf, without giving herself away. But both he and Zora had been distracted and focused on each other. There was no telling what Serenity might have overheard.

Zora moved quickly to the door. Jacob joined her. Serenity had already disappeared.

"Maybe she didn't hear anything," he said without much hope.

Zora's strong hand gripped the doorjamb, setting the wood to creaking in protest. "If she knows what I told you," she said, "it will hurt her. But if she realizes what we are…"

She turned and walked back into the stable. Jacob was torn between staying to ask more questions about the gang that had killed Serenity's family or going after Serenity…to what purpose he didn't know. If she'd heard everything, she wasn't likely to want him anywhere near her.

And right now he had to spend a little time alone, figure out just what he was going to do—not only in trying to defend a man he despised, but after the trial was over.

He walked away from the barn, past the outbuildings and well out of sight of the house, before he Changed. The vastness of the desert lay open before him, and he let the wolf take him.

SERENITY'S HEART was beating with such force that she was afraid Jacob would hear it from across the yard.

He could do it. He could exact the retribution she herself could not. She knew from painful experience just how keen those animals' senses were, and how difficult it was to deceive them. She was still amazed that he hadn't heard her enter.

And Zora… Serenity darted inside the bunkhouse and struggled to catch her breath. Zora was one of *them.* Serenity had never suspected, never questioned

Zora's extraordinary tracking skills, her keen senses or her ability to heal so quickly.

Was it because she was a woman? Serenity had known only male werewolves. She hadn't even been able to imagine how any woman could…

Voices—Changying's and Frances's—sounded from the sickroom, and Serenity pressed herself to the wall. None of the others knew. Not about what had happened to her, let alone that creatures such as Zora and Jacob existed. Zora, who never seemed afraid of anything, had obviously never wanted anyone to know what she was, least of all Serenity.

She had every reason to hide it. Zora had been rejected by both Indians and whites, belonging to neither world. It was bad enough for any person to live as she had, with no place and no people. But if anyone had ever seen her Change, it would have been far worse.

Had Zora's parents been like her? How many others had she herself known without realizing it? And Jacob…

A chill of horror gripped Serenity. She had ridden beside Jacob Constantine, spoken intimately with him, fought beside him, and he had never once looked at her with cruel lust in his eyes. He had never become an animal in her presence. He had kept his word about Leroy.

And he had held her in his arms and told her Bonnie's death wasn't her fault. She could still feel the strength of his body, the solid beat of his heart, the warmth of his breath in her hair. She had wanted him to hold her forever.

Until she had remembered.

Serenity's legs crumpled. She crouched, half leaning against the wall, pressing her hand to her chest as if she could soothe the wild thing leaping madly inside her ribs. Her emotions were so raw that she knew the only way she could master them was by keeping them locked within. Above all else, she had to make sure Jacob never knew what she had learned. After the trial, she would see that he left Avalon immediately. She would find some excuse to send him on his way.

Yet once she was calm again, she was able to recall the other things Zora and Jacob had discussed. Zora was the only woman at Avalon who knew the whole truth of Serenity's past, but she had told Jacob only part of it. Had she confided in him because they were the same kind? Because she really thought Jacob would be willing to find the Renier gang?

"You are a hunter of evil men," Zora had said. He'd been shocked when she had told him that the killers of Serenity's family were werewolves, but then he had asked for their names. He had spent many years tracking outlaws. Could he know something about the Reniers?

Serenity sucked in a deep breath, got to her feet and walked into the sickroom where Changying was hovering over her patients. Frances was sitting up, while Judith lay on her bunk, breathing through her mouth.

"How are they?" Serenity asked.

"I'm fine!" Frances said before Changying could answer. "When can I ride again?"

"In a few days, if you continue to rest," Changying said.

Frances cast her a rebellious glance. "I should have

been with Bonnie and Zora." Her eyes filled with tears. "If I had, maybe—"

"You couldn't have done anything," Serenity said, as gently as she could manage.

"I know what I'll vote for when we have the trial!"

"You're too young to be involved in something like this," Serenity said. She turned to Changying. "We'll bury Bonnie tonight, as soon as Caridad and the others have returned. Then we'll hold the trial. Is Judith well enough to attend?"

"I'll come," Judith said, poking her head up from underneath her blankets. "I want to…help put Bonnie to rest. And make sure that man…" She shivered and sank back down.

Changying hurried to her side, laid her palm on Judith's forehead and tucked the blanket higher around Judith's neck. Then she turned back to Serenity.

"Would you condemn this man so soon after Bonnie is laid in the earth?" she asked.

Changying's distaste was evident in her soft voice, but she had seen Bonnie's body. Serenity couldn't believe she wasn't just as eager to see Leroy punished as the rest of them were.

"We can't afford to hold him prisoner," Serenity said sharply. "There is too much work to be done, and Bonnie would want—"

"She would not wish this," Changying said. "Constantine could take him away."

"That's not good enough."

"You have already decided this man's fate."

"He'll have a chance to speak for himself."

Except Jacob would be speaking for him. And she would have to listen.

She walked away before her discussion with Chang-ying could turn into a quarrel. Nothing the Chinese woman could say would make a difference, not to her or anyone else who had loved Bonnie.

Unable to eat and afraid to think, Serenity went to the bedroom where Bonnie lay and sat beside the bed, letting anger and hate fill up all the empty spaces in her heart. The hours passed, and sometime late that afternoon she heard Caridad, Nettie and Michaela ride in. She went to meet them, and soon most of the other women were gathered in the yard. Zora hung back, but Serenity felt her glances and was certain that the Indian woman knew that her true nature was no longer a secret.

But now there were other, more urgent concerns. Telling Caridad and her partners about Bonnie was horribly difficult, and by the end everyone but Caridad and Zora was weeping. Caridad gripped her guns and stared at the shed.

"Cari," Serenity said, "shooting is too good for him."

With a brief nod, Caridad took her horse toward the barn. Nettie and Michaela followed, heads bowed and steps heavy.

Serenity knew she had to be strong for all of them. Strong enough to face her greatest fear without flinching. She went to join Zora.

"It's all right," she said.

Zora needed no other reassurance. The tension in her face relaxed. For a moment Serenity thought she would speak of Jacob, but she only touched Serenity's arm lightly and slipped away.

ALL THE WOMEN assembled by the house an hour later. Victoria had spent the time making a proper coffin out of spare wood. Now she, Helene and Serenity dressed Bonnie in her best dress, laid her gently in the coffin, and then covered her sleeping face with a beautiful lace shawl that Helene had brought with her when she'd come to Avalon.

The place they had chosen to bury Bonnie was just at the base of the foothills that rose steeply out of the valley, climbing around narrow arroyos and rocky outcrops toward the abrupt wall of the mountains. All of the women took turns digging, and well before dark they had made a space big and deep enough for the coffin. Nettie offered a quiet prayer, and then they slowly covered the coffin with earth. Michaela planted a cross she had made at the foot of the grave. There was no sound but quiet weeping; even the coyotes were silent.

When Serenity finally turned away, she found Jacob watching from a low rise above the grave. He had come so silently that not one of them had noticed him. His head was bowed, but as she walked toward him, he lifted his head and met her gaze. He didn't look any different than he had when they'd ridden back with Bonnie that morning. There was nothing to show him for what he was, but she saw in his eyes, as she had in Zora's, that he knew what she had overheard.

Yet she couldn't speak to him, though she knew herself for the very coward she had sworn not to be. She walked past him without a word.

It was full dark when the women gathered again in the dining hall. Changying, Judith and Frances sat in the back of the room, Judith still wrapped in her blankets.

Jacob was nowhere to be found, and Serenity hoped with all her heart that he had decided to leave Avalon. She was about to send Caridad and Zora to fetch Leroy from the shed when Jacob walked into the room, pushing the outlaw ahead of him by the collar of his shirt. Serenity felt an almost painful surge of relief, followed quickly by amazement that she hadn't noticed how like a predator he moved, how casually, powerfully inhuman he was in every act and motion.

"We've been waiting for you," she said.

He looked at her silently for a long moment, the gold flecks in his eyes burning like flames suspended in a stormy sea.

"Where do you want him?" he asked.

Serenity gestured toward the chair facing the benches and tables on the other side of the room. Jacob forced Leroy onto the seat and knelt to bind his hands behind the chair's back.

Leroy stared at the cold faces of the women who were to sit in judgment. His lower lip trembled. Jacob spoke to him in an undertone, and the outlaw shook his head violently.

Serenity began to speak, relating the story in all its ugly detail. She never raised her voice or revealed her anger and grief. Leroy stuttered in protest several times, but Jacob quickly silenced him each time with a cold stare and a quiet word.

Then it was Jacob's turn. He didn't offer any real defense. He briefly mentioned that it had been Leroy who shot Bonnie, but it was merely a dry statement of fact. He admitted that Leroy was a bad man who deserved to hang. But he went on to repeat what he'd said before to Serenity: that every man deserved a fair trial with a judge and jury of his peers, no matter what he had done. He made plain that all the women involved would be able to testify against Leroy in a court of law, and that there was no possibility he could avoid the lethal punishment he had earned.

He was eloquent, though he, like Serenity, never raised his voice. Even Serenity was drawn in by his reserved but earnest passion for the law. Every word he spoke served to remind her that he was utterly unlike her tormentors.

But when he was done and a tense silence had fallen over the room, there was not a face that had softened. Even Helene, the gentlest of them all, wasn't moved.

"You've heard Mr. Constantine give his testimony," Serenity said. "I know he intends to take Leroy back and see him put in jail. But beyond that, he has no control over what happens. Even *he* cannot guarantee this man's punishment."

"He won't get away," Jacob said. "I won't leave until he's tried and hanged."

Serenity didn't look at him, knowing she couldn't bear what she would see in his eyes. "We will put it to a vote," she said. Victoria rose and handed out small scraps of paper and pencil stubs to the other women.

"Write 'go' if you think we should let Mr. Constantine take Leroy," Serenity said when everyone was ready. "Leave the paper blank if you disagree."

Not a pencil moved. Victoria collected the scraps of paper. She brought them to Serenity.

Every one was blank.

Hands shaking, Serenity turned to Jacob.

"It's decided," she said.

Leroy spat a stream of curses. "You ugly bitches ain't gonna hang me!" he shouted. "If you try and touch me, I'll kill every last damned—"

Jacob seized Leroy by the back of his neck, tore the ropes free with his other hand and lifted the outlaw out of the chair. "You should be grateful, Leroy," he said. "At least you won't have to rot in your own piss waiting to die."

"No!" Leroy shrieked, struggling in Jacob's grip. "I have a right to a fair trial!" But it was clear that the stuffing had gone out of him.

"You should have thought of that before you came back looking for blood and an innocent woman ended up murdered," Jacob said. He held Leroy firmly as Caridad produced a long rope with a neatly tied noose at one end. Changying rose, took Frances's arm, and led the protesting girl from the room.

"You don't have to take any part in this, Mr. Constantine," Serenity said, staring after them. "You can leave whenever you want."

"I'm already a part of this," he said.

"Then bring him outside," Caridad said, gently swinging the rope. "We have just the right place."

She strode out of the bunkhouse, and the other women filed out after her. Serenity hung back until she was certain that Jacob had followed with Leroy.

He wouldn't break his word. She believed that, even

though that belief went against everything she had accepted as truth about his kind.

She went on to the barn, where several lanterns had been lit and Caridad was tossing the rope over one of the sturdy roof beams. Zora had brought a stool, and as Leroy cursed and fought in Jacob's grip, she placed it under the dangling noose.

Jacob hoisted Leroy onto the stool as easily as he would an infant. The outlaw collapsed, his legs sprawling on either side of the stool, and started weeping uncontrollably.

Jacob looked at Serenity. "You sure you want to do this, Miss Campbell?" he asked.

A bubble of shame formed in Serenity's stomach and climbed into her throat. She swallowed it down.

"Please step back, Mr. Constantine. Zora?"

With Zora's help, Serenity lifted Leroy to his feet. He didn't even struggle as she dropped the noose over his neck. Caridad stepped forward, ready to kick the stool out from under Leroy's feet, but Serenity shook her head. It was her responsibility, and hers alone.

She closed her eyes and swung her leg back. She never completed the motion. The deafening blast of a gun went off beside her, making her stagger and setting her ears to ringing. Leroy's head sagged in the noose, and his body went limp.

Jacob holstered his gun. Serenity had never even seen him draw it. She felt an almost tangible wave of shock as the others realized what he had done.

"Through the heart," Caridad said with unwilling admiration. She glared at Jacob. "*Cabrón!* You have robbed us!"

Spinning on his boot heel, Jacob headed for the barn door.

Serenity caught up with him.

"Why?" she asked. "Did you think you were being merciful?"

He met her gaze. His eyes were cold.

"I couldn't let you do it," he said.

"You didn't have the right!"

"Did you want it that badly, Serenity?" he asked. "Is blood the only thing that will satisfy you?"

The growl in his voice left her bereft of an answer. Without another word, Jacob strode out of the barn and stalked across the yard toward the outer corral.

Victoria came up beside Serenity, laying her rough hand on Serenity's shoulder.

"He's dead," she said. "That's all that matters, isn't it?"

Her voice was as flat as the Texas prairie, but Serenity knew the blacksmith was troubled. She glanced at the other women. They were avoiding each others' eyes, and none of them would look at Leroy's body.

Was it guilt? Did they feel what Serenity felt now, forced by Jacob's blunt accusations to recognize something ugly in themselves?

No. The ugliness had all been in Leroy and the men who had killed Bonnie.

Serenity returned to the stool, pushed it out from under Leroy's feet and climbed up onto it. She drew her knife and slashed the rope. The body fell.

"He'll have to be buried," she said. "Who will help me?"

The others began to stir as if they'd just wakened

from a terrible dream. Victoria, Caridad and Michaela offered to assist her. Victoria led one of the horses to the barn door, while Michaela brought two shovels from the shed. Caridad took a lantern, and then they heaved Leroy's body over the horse's back and set out across the range, leading the horse in the opposite direction from Bonnie's resting place.

The work was hard and worse than unpleasant. Each of them took turns with the shovel, and they finished in an hour. No one suggested putting a cross at the head of the grave. When they were done and had returned to the house, Victoria went directly to her smithy, while Michaela headed for the bathhouse. Caridad muttered something unintelligible and walked toward the bunkhouse.

Serenity felt filthy in body and soul, but she had another task to complete before she could indulge her personal needs. She went looking for Jacob and found him in the dark tack room, sitting on the bench and briskly rubbing wax into his borrowed saddle. She braced herself and walked through the door, pausing just inside where there was enough moonlight to see by. Jacob didn't look up.

"Why did you shoot him?" she asked.

He set down the rag and ran his hand over the polished leather. "I told you," he said.

"You said you couldn't let *me* do it. Why?"

Jacob raised his head. "He was never yours to judge," he said.

"But *you* killed him. Was it all a lie, your talk about justice? Did you plan to shoot him all along?"

The muscles in his jaw bunched and flexed. "No," he said.

Serenity knew she could have told him to leave right then. She could pretend she didn't know what he was and make some other excuse to send him away.

And Avalon would suffer because of it.

The fact was that she needed him, and not only for the branding. In her heart, she knew why he had taken Leroy's life before she could. He had wanted to spare her the responsibility. He hadn't wanted her to become a killer. Like him.

"I know," she said. She pressed her hands flat against the wall at her back, praying her legs would hold her up. "I know you're one of *them*."

CHAPTER SEVEN

SERENITY DIDN'T HAVE to explain herself. She wasn't speaking only of his being a werewolf, though he was sure that was what she meant. She was also reliving her most terrible memories. The fact that she was so calm astonished Jacob.

He wasn't calm, not inside. He had known it wouldn't be easy when she was finally ready to talk to him. Hell, it hadn't been easy when she'd avoided his eyes and tried to ignore him.

But this was worse than he'd imagined, seeing the world of anguish in her beautiful eyes. It made him want to find those men and slit their throats, hang them up by the balls and watch the life drain out of them. Just as he'd once planned on doing to the men who'd murdered Ruth.

"I'm sorry," he said, hoping she believed him. "I figured something bad had happened to you the first time we met. If I'd known it was because of my kind—"

"Your kind," she said, clenching her fists. "Savages."

No, she wasn't calm at all. She was fighting for control with every breath she took.

Once he hadn't much cared if she hated him. Now he couldn't stand the thought of it. He couldn't stand the thought of her being afraid of him because he wasn't human.

"Is that what you think of Zora?" he asked.

She turned away from him, her arms locked across her chest. "I *know* Zora," she said. "She would never do the things that—"

"Because she's a woman?"

"Yes!" Serenity twisted around to face him again. "Maybe that's what makes her decent, instead of a monster."

Jacob knew then that he had to explain a lot of things to Serenity, things she wasn't going to want to hear. She would be glad to see the back of him, and he knew he had to go. But he couldn't leave knowing she would go on believing that all werewolves were ruthless killers. That *he* was a monster.

He got up, unhooked the lantern hanging by the door and lit it with a match from a box on the shelf next to it. He crushed the match head between his fingers and let it fall.

"Do you think all men are like Leroy?" he asked softly. "Even your pa?"

She stared at him as if he'd spoken some rare foreign language. "How dare you—"

"Do you?"

"No," she whispered.

"But you judge all men the same anyway."

Serenity released a long, shuddering breath. "Zora told you what happened," she said.

Jacob sat back down on the bench. "I guess you heard just about everything we said."

Serenity bit down hard on her lower lip. "I wish I hadn't," she said. "I wish I hadn't found out."

He ached to go to her, hold her in his arms the way

he had when they'd brought Bonnie home. "I'm no different now than I was before," he said.

"What I *thought* you were before," she said. "Now I know that you can become an animal. Maybe you've already done it, right here. You've turned into a beast that has no law, no conscience."

"Maybe you don't know animals as well as you think you do," he said. "Folks think wolves are killers that slaughter livestock for fun. But even regular wolves don't do half the things people like to think." He shifted on the bench, moving slowly so Serenity wouldn't think he was going to get up. "There *is* a wolf part of us, but the human part isn't lost when we Change. We're good and bad, just like normal folk."

She gave her head a sharp jerk of denial. "I saw my parents' murderers turn into vicious animals. I saw them dance naked around the house before they set it on fire."

It was happening for her all over again, and there was nothing Jacob could to do help her. She wouldn't let him.

"How did you get away?" he asked carefully.

"I had gone out with one of the horses. I came back in time to see…" She hunched her shoulders. "They never saw me."

"Did you know those men?"

Her whole body flinched away from his question. "I'd never seen any of them before."

"Do you have any idea why they did it?"

"Why should they need a reason?" She squeezed her eyes shut. "We never did anything to them. We didn't even know such creatures existed."

And her first knowledge of them had come with death and ruin.

"I wish I could tell you that the men who killed your family were the only werewolves who do evil things," he said. "But there are more of us who don't. My folks were good people. They lived quietly beside their human neighbors. No one ever had cause to be afraid of them."

Serenity looked at him again, blood beading on her lower lip where she'd unconsciously bitten it. "Your family?" she said.

Maybe if he told her about Ruth, Serenity would find it easier to believe. But he couldn't. Not now. Maybe not ever, even if he was still here in the morning.

What he wanted to do was stroke the blood from her mouth and soothe her lips with his own.

Loco. Here she was thinking he was the enemy, and he was thinking about kissing her. Nothing would make her hate him more.

As if she'd heard his thoughts, Serenity touched her lip and stared without comprehension at the red stain on her fingertip.

"Werewolves are just like anyone else," Jacob continued, trying to distract himself from his very inappropriate thoughts. "We have mothers and fathers and brothers and sisters and all the rest. Fact is, for most of us family is pretty important. Some clans stretch all the way across the country."

"How many of you are there?" she whispered.

Just like that, he was on solid ground again. "I never tried to find out," he said. "I reckon most of us in America live in the West, where it's open and there are less people to notice that we're different."

"The animals who killed my family didn't care if anyone knew what they were," she said.

"Because they knew…" *That they would leave no survivors.* But Jacob couldn't bring himself to say it aloud. "My people wouldn't survive if we didn't live by most human rules. A lot of folks hate what they don't understand."

Her expression cleared. "You mean…you think you're in danger from humans?"

"There are a lot more of you than there are of us. We heal fast, and we're strong, but we can be killed. I would have died if you hadn't saved me."

"Is Zora…afraid of *me?* Is that why she never told me?"

"She cares about you. She didn't want you to hate her."

Slowly Serenity sank to the ground. "She was the only one who knew what happened to my family. I told her about the beast-men, and how much I—" She pressed her hands to her face.

Jacob started to rise, then sat down again.

"Serenity?"

It was only the second time he'd called her by her first name. Somehow it didn't make her feel any better.

"I'm all right," she said. She drew her knees up to her chest. "I never thought…it could be the other way," she said.

Jacob braced his hands on the bench and dropped his head between his shoulders. "Killing doesn't know any boundaries of race or blood. Werewolves even kill each other, just like men do."

"Have you?"

If she knew about the feud between the Reniers and Constantines, would she understand? Or would she see it only as another justification for her suspicion and hatred?

"No," he said, raising his head. "I told you when I kill, and why. Leroy was…" He shook his head. "I'm not like those men, Serenity."

Her eyes glazed with tears. "How do I know you're telling the truth?" she asked. "How can I know what you did before you came to Avalon?"

Jacob found it very hard to keep his voice steady. "I've never killed a child, a woman or an innocent man," he said. "Human or werewolf."

"I want to believe you."

"I want you to believe me."

She finally met his gaze. "Zora said you were one of the few of your kind who fight for the laws that protect the weak. When we brought you here, you seemed concerned about the ranch. Do you usually try to help people like us?"

"I live by a code, Serenity. I don't leave women defenseless when there's trouble."

"But we were never defenseless." Her voice was calm again, and Jacob began to hope he was getting through to her. "We could have handled Leroy's gang if Bonnie hadn't gone out with Zora. We needed her to work, but she wasn't a fighter."

"I brought this down on you. I would have let Leroy

go if I'd thought someone else would suffer because I took him through this country."

"You couldn't have known."

The acceptance in her voice was real, as real as her anger and fear and doubt had been before. She lowered her chin to her knees, lost in thought, and Jacob left her alone. He'd given her more to consider in one hour than anybody should have to deal with in a year.

And she was dealing with it better than he could have hoped. She was one of the bravest women he'd ever known, but she would never believe him if he told her that.

When she spoke again, there was a new light in her eyes. "In all the time you've been a bounty hunter," she said, "have you ever hunted another werewolf?"

Jacob shook off the deceptive mantle of peace that had lulled him into believing the worst was over. Serenity had overheard Zora's offer to hire him to track her enemies. He'd just been too worried about easing Serenity's fears to think she would seriously consider what her friend had suggested.

Now he had to face the fact that he'd done too good a job giving her reasons to trust him again. She had an idea in her mind, and she wasn't going to let it go. Zora had said Serenity would have killed her parents' murderers if she could. She hated them enough to do it. She would have kicked the stool out from under Leroy if Jacob hadn't moved first.

He'd done that for one reason only. Serenity hadn't understood what she was about to do. She'd killed before to save her friends, to save *him*. But Leroy's hanging had been different, and Serenity was no murderer.

Sooner or later the guilt would have come, and it would have begun to destroy everything good inside her. He'd almost let that happen to him, and he wouldn't let it happen to her. Even if he had to make himself look like a coward in her eyes.

"No," he said curtly. "I told you, we're careful to hide what we are. No werewolf is going to be taken easily, and there's a good chance Changing would be involved in the taking. The last thing I need is that kind of fight. It would be too risky."

"So you wouldn't go after them even if you knew exactly who they were and what they'd done?"

It sickened him to lie again, even though the lie was partly true. "No," he said. "I wouldn't."

She unfolded her legs and got up, refusing to look at him. "My parents' murderers were never caught," she said. "But you don't care about that, do you?"

Jacob swallowed the bile in the back of his throat. "I'm sorry about what happened to your folks, Serenity. But if it's a choice between protecting my people from exposure and stopping a handful of outlaws..."

"I don't believe you." She was trembling as if her whole body might shake apart. "I want the beast-men who slaughtered my family, and you're the only one who can find them for me."

Rising from the bench, Jacob took a few uneven steps toward the door and stopped. "It's the same as with Leroy," he said. "You don't want justice. You want revenge."

"I want both."

He extended his hands toward her. "It won't bring you peace, Serenity. I know."

"How do you know?"

"Because I've seen what it does to people, whether they get what they want or not."

"You underestimated all of us at Avalon," she said, moving near enough to dizzy him with her scent. "Don't underestimate me now."

He couldn't help being affected by the passion in her face and the blaze in her eyes. Even as angry as she was, as wrongheaded, she was beautiful. And she was standing too close. Much too close.

"A few minutes ago you hated me," he said, hardening his voice. "Now I'm of some use to you, and everything has changed."

She flinched. "No," she said. "It isn't like that at all."

"As I told Zora, I'm not in the business of revenge. I can't help you."

"I'll pay you any amount. I have a large sum in the bank. All you have to do is locate these men for me. I won't expect you to fight them."

"But you *will?*" He laughed, deliberately mocking her. "Will you shoot them down as they come running at you, ready to rip your throat out?"

"I've been waiting six years for a chance to find those killers, and I'm not going to wait any longer. If you won't help me, I'll convince Zora to do it. And if she won't, I'll find them some other way."

There was no laughter in Jacob then. Zora had warned him. Serenity would try to do exactly what she'd said. Whatever had held her back for the past six years, his coming to Avalon and everything that had happened since had broken something loose inside her.

She was willing to give up everything she cared about to pursue a hopeless cause.

"You're talking about abandoning the ranch," he said. "Abandoning your friends, people who depend on you. You're their boss, and a boss doesn't just walk away from her responsibilities."

A shadow of doubt flickered across her face. "Caridad could run the ranch while I'm gone," she said. "Zora could do it, too, or Michaela. They don't need me."

"You sure as hell act as if they can't live without you," he said.

"Maybe I've only made things worse for everyone."

"Dammit, Bonnie's death wasn't your fault!"

She stared at him, dry-eyed and unbending. "I have even more reason now to find those murderers. I'm sure they've already killed someone like Bonnie. Maybe many like her."

Jacob remembered all the times he'd convinced himself that keeping the feud alive would result in far more deaths than leaving the Reniers free. But Ruth had died eight years ago. He hadn't heard about the feud since. Maybe it was over.

Maybe his only excuse now was his fear of turning into the very kind of monster Serenity had described.

"You know I'm sorry about Bonnie," he said. "I would have given my life for hers if I could. But you can't bring her back. You can't bring your folks back."

"Is there nothing I can do to convince you?" she asked.

He swallowed hard. "No. I'm sorry, Serenity."

She backed away slowly. "If I didn't know you,"

she said, "I'd think you only wanted to protect your own skin. But you're not a coward. It's just that you only care about your own kind. You don't give a damn about—"

"I *do* give a damn."

"Then show it!"

Only half-aware of what he was doing, Jacob grabbed her by the shoulders and kissed her. He wasn't rough, but it wasn't a peck on the cheek, either. He tasted her lips, gentling her when she resisted him, stroking her arms as she melted into his chest. The fight went out of her body. All the intensity of her anger transformed into a passion that fired his blood and made him forget she despised him.

But it didn't last. She broke free, breathing fast, her flushed face losing all its color in an instant.

"Is that what you want, Mr. Constantine?" she asked hoarsely. "Is that your price for helping me?"

Jacob recoiled. She couldn't have hit him harder if she'd struck him with a blacksmith's hammer.

"No, ma'am," he said, his own voice gone flat. "My behavior was inexcusable. I beg your pardon."

"You want me, don't you?" she asked with a terrible calm.

God help him. "Miss Campbell—" he began.

"Why the formality now, Jacob?" she asked with a twisted smile. "People who have kissed ought to be on a first-name basis, don't you think?"

If she was trying to be seductive, she wasn't succeeding. That kind of game wasn't in her. But she kept on gazing into his eyes, making it difficult for him to think with anything but his cock.

"I'm not blind or without feelings," she murmured. "You don't have to apologize to me. I wanted it, too."

He couldn't believe it. She was offering what she thought would buy his cooperation because he was a man and a "savage," and claiming to want it, too. Except when he'd embraced her that morning, nothing in her behavior toward him had ever suggested that she wanted anything of a physical nature to happen between them. Far from it. And now that she knew what he was, she should be doubly repulsed.

Yet her response to his kiss hadn't been feigned. He'd smelled her arousal, felt it in the heat of her skin. Her body *did* want him. It was the rest of her that didn't.

Hell, he'd been pretending almost ever since he first saw her that he wasn't interested in her that way, either. He'd been aware of her as a woman, but he'd seen nothing in her to attract him, even if he'd been so inclined.

Now he knew how badly he'd been deceiving himself.

"What I did was wrong," he said. "Let's leave it at that."

She reached for him. "Why?" she murmured. "We can both get what we want."

If she made herself into his whore.

"There can't be any more between us, Miss Campbell," he said.

She rested her palm on his chest, fingers spread, as if she could capture his pounding heart in her hand. "You didn't answer my question, Jacob," she said. She pressed her face into his shoulder. "You can have me whenever you want me. Every night. All you have to do is help me."

Jacob jerked away. Her desperation didn't make him think the less of her. It made him feel dirty that he'd driven her to this.

"I don't take advantage of innocent women," he said.

"Why do you think I'm innocent?" She dropped all pretense of seduction and met his gaze unflinchingly. "It's a bargain, like any other. You'll be risking your life. What I can give may not be worth that risk, but if you're willing—"

"Stop," he commanded, holding up his hands. "You were right when you said I cared more about my own kind than any human."

Her expression went flat. "If you don't care about anything else, then why have you been helping us? Why have you been acting as if I…*we* meant something to you?"

Her new strategy left him dangling like a wolf pup in its mother's jaws. There were a hundred meanings behind the word *care,* and he didn't know which one Serenity meant. Was she talking about friendship, and that as a friend he should be willing to do as she asked? Or was she implying something stronger?

He laughed inwardly at his own arrogance. Satan would sup at St. Michael's table before she admitted to anything more than friendship. An unbreachable barrier stood between him and Serenity, a barrier that Ruth had ignored when she'd married him. It hadn't made any difference to *her* that he wasn't human.

That was why he could never feel for any woman what he'd felt for Ruth. He could want Serenity and choose not to act on his lust. He could *care* about her, but the Code told him where that caring had to end. He could never be involved with a woman again.

Serenity's hatred of his kind would tell her the same thing, if she would ever let herself think of him as anything but a useful tool.

"I didn't lie," he said. "I care enough to stay until the branding is over. That's the only promise I can make."

Her hands fell loose at her sides. "I understand," she said. "I'm grateful you're willing to help us. You see, I do care about Avalon, Mr. Constantine, whatever you may believe." She seemed to look right through him. "Thank you for hearing me out."

Just as she turned to leave, he saw her expression change. He had seen that same look on an outlaw's face just before he rode straight over a cliff rather than be taken alive. It came from an emotion that went beyond desperation into the territory of blind determination, the kind that made people do hopeless things with no thought of survival.

Whatever drove Serenity, it was too powerful for anyone to stop, least of all herself. She hadn't given up because he'd turned her down. She would go on just as she'd threatened, and the price would mean nothing to her.

"Serenity."

She was already halfway out the door, and he didn't think she was going to stop. But she did, keeping her back to him and cocking her head as if she'd heard some noise she couldn't identify.

"There's something I want you to see," he said.

"I have work to do."

"Please come back, Serenity."

The tone of his request must have surprised her, for she turned and started back for the stable. Jacob retreated into the shadows away from the lantern light and began to unbutton his shirt. He tossed it over the nearest partition, pulled off his boots and went to work on his trousers.

Serenity moved farther into the room.

"Where are you?" she asked.

He emerged from the shadows. Serenity went still. Her gaze swept over him with the same detachment she'd shown when he'd climbed naked out of the arroyo. After a moment she went back to the open door, swung it closed and undid the top button of her shirt.

"No one will disturb us," she said.

"Serenity," he snapped, cursing himself for a fool. "Look at me."

She paused, fingers poised on the second button, and met his gaze. He Changed. The process was swift, and to most human eyes it would have seemed like no more than a vague movement behind a veil of dark mist.

To Serenity it must have been terrifying. But she held her ground, watching steadily, until he was fully in wolf shape. She looked over every part of him, from muzzle to tail-tip, with remarkable calm. Then she knelt in the straw, hands on her thighs, and met his gaze.

"Is that all?" she asked.

CHAPTER EIGHT

THE WORDS WERE brave. Serenity prayed that Jacob believed them.

She schooled her face to display only the most dispassionate curiosity, the same expression her father used to show when he was studying one of the native plants he had collected in the open fields and oak woodlands beyond the pasture.

She thought she was successful. She thought she kept herself from trembling too much, her heart from pounding so fast that he would hear it.

But it took all her self-discipline to confront the huge black beast, so much bigger than any common prairie wolf, bigger even than the biggest of the Reniers. His eyes glowed with intelligence, like and unlike Jacob's at the same time. He kept his teeth hidden and his ears low, deliberately unaggressive, but Serenity wasn't deceived. He could kill her in an instant, break her back and tear out her throat with hardly any effort at all.

And all the while he was watching her watching him, waiting for some sign of weakness. She'd already surrendered the last of her pride by offering herself to him, a proposal she wouldn't have believed possible until just before she made it. The idea of giving herself to any man, let alone one like *him,* would have nauseated her only a week ago.

But she hadn't felt sick. When Jacob had kissed her, a very different thing had happened. She'd looked into his eyes and felt something extraordinary. It was the same powerful emotion she'd briefly experienced when he'd held her that morning, but she hadn't let herself think too much about her feelings then.

Now she couldn't help herself. This time, for a few precious moments, she hadn't been afraid. She hadn't wanted to shoot him, or run away. She'd felt safe, protected, warm. And hungry. Not only her body, but a part of her the Reniers had never touched. The last time she'd felt anything like it had been when she and Levi had walked hand in hand along the Guadalupe, speaking of their coming marriage and the quiet, peaceful life they would make together.

Once she hadn't thought beyond saving herself for Levi. She had loved him, and she had thought that kind of love, so pure and innocent, would be enough for her whole life. She would never have known any different if the beasts hadn't taken her.

They had destroyed that love and every gentle feeling in her heart. But when Jacob had kissed her, a world she had never had a chance to explore opened up for her, neither innocent and pure nor bitter with pain and hate.

But then the old fear had returned. She had destroyed that miraculous world with a cruel proposition born of her fear and fed by desperation. She had made herself safe again. Safe from anything Jacob could do to her. Safe from anything he could make her feel.

Except what she was feeling now.

She caught herself and returned her attention to the

reality in front of her. This was what Jacob *was*. Knowing he was a werewolf and seeing it were two very different things. She would never be able to forget what she had just witnessed, no more than she could forget what had happened seven years ago. Every moment she was around Jacob, she would think of this awful transformation. He could Change in an instant, at whim, like the Reniers, and in her mind one would blur into the other, until…

Closing her eyes, Serenity deliberately relaxed every muscle in her body one by one. There was one thing she couldn't forget. The very animal nature that made her recoil was inextricably linked with the part of him she had wanted only minutes ago. She couldn't take one without the other. And she needed the wolf even more than the man.

I'm not afraid, she thought, then opened her eyes to meet the wolf's dreadful stare. "I'm not afraid," she said aloud.

Silently the wolf inclined his beautiful head. The dark mist materialized again, wreathing his body in a kind of smoke that had no odor or substance. Something shifted behind the smoke, a figure casting off its fur and standing upright as the mist dispersed.

Then he was human again, magnificently naked, his human body honed like the wolf's to live and hunt under the most difficult conditions.

He *was* beautiful.

Shaking, Serenity averted her gaze as he retrieved his clothes and put them on again.

"Miss Campbell?"

She raised her head. Jacob was offering his hand to

pull her up, his manner almost formal, his expression unreadable. She took his hand. It was strong; he could have crushed her fingers with no effort at all. But he applied only the slightest pressure as he raised her to her feet. He released her almost immediately, and she had to rub her palm on her trousers to get the tingle out of it.

"You all right?" he asked.

"I am perfectly fine," she said. "Did I pass your test?"

"Only you can decide that, Miss Campbell."

At least he didn't deny that was what he'd intended. "Why?" she asked.

"Because I've decided to help you. Under three conditions."

His sudden capitulation left her speechless. She'd thought she would have to continue to work on him, wear him down over days, maybe weeks, as the branding progressed. But he had just done something she'd never expected, and she was cast adrift.

"What…are these…conditions?" she stammered.

"Assuming these men can be found, I'd be the one to bring them in. You wouldn't have any part of it."

Familiar anger brought her safely to dry land again. "Out of the question," she said.

"I work alone," he said harshly. "You'll only get in the way, and I won't risk your life."

"I can shoot. I know how to travel in the desert. I won't get in your way."

"You'd try to kill them if you got anywhere near them. I won't let what happened to Leroy happen again."

And that was the crux of it. He didn't only want to prevent her from risking her life. He didn't want her killing the outlaws. He'd shot Leroy rather than let her hang him.

In spite of what he was, he hadn't lied when he'd said he believed in justice. *His* kind of justice.

"How will you do it alone?" she demanded. "How will you keep them from killing you if you don't kill them first?"

"You don't have to worry about that. I'll take them and see that they face the law."

"Human law? How will you stop them from using their werewolf abilities to escape?"

His upper lip lifted, showing a flash of white teeth. "I'll stick with them until they're hanged."

Serenity couldn't doubt his conviction, or the strength of his will. But he couldn't promise the outlaws would face the hangman's noose any more than he could have sworn the same for Leroy.

"So you agree to the first condition?" he asked.

The lie was even more difficult under the grim weight of his stare. "I'll heed what you tell me," she said. "What is the second condition?"

He cocked his head, brooding over her answer, and then seemed to accept it. "The second condition," he said, "is that you do everything I tell you without question. You're used to giving orders, but now you'll have to learn to take them."

That was easier to promise, though she knew she would break her word if she had to.

"I agree," she said. "The third?"

He looked away. "You have to accept me for what I

am. Completely, and without reservation. I'm not going to spend the trip to Texas hiding half of myself."

That was the biggest challenge of all, the one thing she couldn't conceal.

But she would have to. Every minute, every hour, every day. One slip and she would lose her chance. If she could keep remembering that he was still more human than wolf…

But was he?

"I passed your test, didn't I?" she asked.

He breathed out sharply and nodded. "All right." He walked back to the front of the stable, reached for the polishing rag, then let his hand fall. "You have any notion of where we can start looking for these rogue werewolves?"

All the blood in Serenity's body seemed to pool in her feet. "I can take you to the town where I…" She stopped herself. She'd been about to tell him how she'd escaped, but she wasn't going to so much as hint at what had really happened to her unless she had no other choice.

"The town?" Jacob prompted.

"Yes. The town where the outlaws were seen not long before they…attacked our farm."

"Where might that be?" he asked gently.

"A place called Bethel."

"I've heard of it. How did you happen to find out they'd been there, if you didn't know their names?"

She had to be much more careful. To even hint that she knew the identities of the killers would arouse too many other questions. "After…for a little while, I asked if anyone had ever seen men like them. I heard rumors that led me west. Months later, by the time I got to Bethel, they were long gone."

"Where was your farm?"

Something made her hesitate to tell him the real location. "In Gillespie County," she said. "A few miles from Fredericksburg."

"You can describe these men to me?"

For so long she had deliberately driven their faces from her mind. They had become a blur of viciousness and cruelty, more wolf than human.

"I think I can sketch them for you," she said thickly.

He turned and caught her gaze. "You did get close to them."

"Sometimes, when something bad happens, you see things you couldn't otherwise." She swallowed. "Terrible things…"

"Are burned into your mind," he finished.

For a few seconds his expression was full of vulnerability, as if he had been stricken with bad memories of his own. Memories of *his* family, perhaps. She still knew nothing at all of his past, except for his time in the Texas Rangers. Had he lost someone, as she had? Had he lived with grief for years, as she had?

He must have felt her stare, for abruptly his expression relaxed and he was all business again.

"How many were there?" he asked.

Somehow she kept her voice from shaking. "Five."

"Did they seem close, as if they were related, or—"

A bell rang outside. Serenity offered up a little prayer of thanks.

"Helene must have supper ready," she said. "You haven't eaten all day."

"I think I'll skip it," he said. "I'm not hungry."

Neither was she. All at once she was remembering Leroy's face just as she had been about to kick the stool out from under him.

"At least you should get something to drink," she said. "We have a little brandy."

He hesitated, but when she left, he went with her. All the women but Zora were gathered in the dining hall. Helene was serving a simple stew and freshly baked bread. Everyone looked up when Serenity and Jacob walked in, and every face was solemn. If the others had discussed Leroy's death and Jacob's part in it, they were unwilling to broach the subject now.

Jacob stood close to the door while the women ate, most of them picking at their food. Caridad was one of the few who devoured her supper with obvious relish. Serenity offered Jacob a flask of brandy, but he refused. Changying cast several surreptitious glances from Jacob to Serenity and back again. Frances stared at him with open admiration.

Jacob slipped out before the meal was finished. Serenity sat staring at her nearly full plate, wishing she dared drink some of the brandy.

But that would mean giving in to her fears again. The time of running away was past. Now she could only go forward.

Frances, still a little pale from her illness, slid onto the bench next to Serenity.

"What's wrong with Mr. Constantine?" she whispered. "Is it because he shot that evil man?"

Serenity was eager to avoid the subject. "I don't

know," she said. "I don't think he enjoys having to kill anyone."

"That man deserved what he got," Frances said passionately.

Serenity speared a piece of cold beef with her fork and chewed it slowly. It tasted like dried cow dung.

Frances continued to stare at her.

"You were with Mr. Constantine a long time in the stable," she said.

No doubt many of the women had noticed. "We had much to discuss," Serenity said.

"What, in particular?"

Sometimes, in spite of her young age, Frances seemed all too perceptive.

"I'm going away for a little while, as soon as the branding is finished."

Frances sat bolt upright. "Going away? But you can't leave! How can we get along without you?"

"I'm not indispensable, Frances. There are others perfectly capable of running things while I'm gone. It is—"

"But where are you going?" Frances glanced toward the empty doorway. "You're going with Jacob, aren't you?"

"Yes."

"I knew it," Frances said, scowling fiercely at the table. "You *want* to take him away from me—from *us*. You're in love with him."

Serenity dropped her fork. It clattered loudly, drawing the attention of the women lingering in the dining hall. Caridad frowned in her direction, and Victoria paused on her way to the door. Helene shot her a look of concern.

Serenity's face grew hot. "I am *not* in love with him," she said. "He is going to help me find someone."

Frances's obvious jealousy was not appeased. "Who?"

"I'm going to explain tonight," Serenity said. "You can help by letting everyone know that I'd like to speak to them in an hour."

"But—"

"I'll clarify everything then, Frances." Serenity winced inwardly at the lie. "Mr. Constantine will be there, as well. He and I have already come to an agreement. Promise you won't tell anyone else what I've said to you."

Frances looked away, sighed and began to climb off the bench.

"Oh!" she said, reaching inside her shirt. "I forgot!" She squirmed uncomfortably and pulled out an envelope. "When we went into Las Cruces last time, I went to the post office. They had something for you, but I forgot to give it to you, and then I got sick. I'm sorry." She passed the envelope to Serenity and beat a hasty retreat.

Serenity stared at the nearly illegible address on the battered envelope. It was muddied, smeared and dog-eared, but whoever had sent the letter had known her name and enough about her current whereabouts to send it to Las Cruces.

No one in New Mexico would have reason to contact her by mail. She had no friends outside Avalon, and only business acquaintances in the Mesilla Valley.

This was obviously a woman's writing, which made it all the more peculiar.

But she didn't want to think about it now. She tucked the envelope inside her vest and was about to get up when Caridad sat down beside her.

"Well?" the other woman said. "What has he done to upset you now?"

"Nothing."

"You cannot deceive me, my friend. Your face is as white as a *Federale's* bones."

Serenity knew better than to avoid Cari's eyes. "Mr. Constantine has been very helpful."

"You mean by shooting that *cabrón* Leroy? Such a quick death was too good for him."

Sudden shame burned Serenity's skin. "I was wrong about Mr. Constantine," she said. "I believe he can be trusted."

Caridad snorted. "Forgive me if *I* do not trust him."

When Cari made up her mind, it wasn't easy to change it. She would probably object more strongly than anyone to Serenity setting out with Jacob. But she, unlike Frances, knew a little of Serenity's past, though much less than Zora. She would be the first to understand *why* Serenity had to go.

Serenity told Caridad about the meeting, and the Mexican woman narrowed her dark eyes. "What goes on between you and Constantine? I saw you in the yard."

"He was…comforting me, that's all."

"Comforting." Caridad's frown deepened. "I warn you, *mi amiga*. Stay away from him." The former *bandida* left with a shake of her head.

A half hour later, after she and Nettie had helped Helene clean up, Serenity sat down at the kitchen table with a sheet of paper and began to draw.

Every line she set down was agony. If Aunt Martha hadn't worked so hard to teach her to sketch, she might have been spared this. But she was good, and the pictures formed quickly.

She finished just before the time she'd asked the women to meet. She went to the bunkhouse, more than a little worried now that she had so much to explain. She waited at the front of the room, while Jacob took a position by the door.

Perhaps Frances hadn't kept Serenity's secret, for there was an air of expectancy among the women, low murmurs and worried frowns.

Straightening her spine, Serenity began to speak.

First she told them what had happened to her parents. They became very still as she explained how long she had waited for the right time and circumstances to seek the outlaws, and why she was leaving with Jacob. Caridad and Changying were clearly not happy, and there were little cries of protest and dismay from the others. Zora, who stood far back in the room, showed no expression at all.

Victoria was first to speak up. "I understand why you want to go," she said, "but shouldn't you let Mr. Constantine go alone? If he is willing to look for them—"

"I would never send anyone else to bear the responsibility," Serenity answered, meeting the blacksmith's troubled gaze. "Mr. Constantine has agreed to help me find these men for a fair price, and I believe he will succeed."

Jacob stirred behind her. They hadn't discussed an actual price yet, but she had already planned to pay him generously for his assistance. To do less would always leave doubt as to how she planned to recompense him for his trouble, and after the incident in the stable, she never wanted to face that situation again.

"What about the ranch?" Michaela asked.

"I will not be gone more than a few months," Serenity said, praying that was true. "We will finish the branding, and everything will be in order before we leave. I know that all of you can manage the work to be done for the remainder of the summer. Caridad, if she agrees, will take my place as boss." She looked at the Mexican woman. "Is that acceptable, Cari?"

Caridad jumped to her feet. "And what if you do *not* return?"

Changying joined her. "If these men would kill your family," she said, "they will kill you just as quickly."

"Not while I'm with her." Jacob moved to stand beside Serenity. "I know what these men are like, and how to handle them. I promise you that Miss Campbell won't be exposed to any unnecessary danger."

Serenity knew that he really believed what he was saying. And she would let him keep on believing it until the last possible moment.

Caridad glared at Jacob and folded her arms across her chest. "I see no reason why we should let her go alone with you," she said. "I will come. Another can be boss."

"No," Serenity said. "You are our best shot, along

with Zora. You'll be needed here, if only to protect Avalon from the ranchers who would be pleased to take it from us."

"*They* won't bother us again after the last time. We got rid of them fast enough."

"What about outlaws like Leroy?"

"We will see that it becomes known how he and his men died when they came here," Caridad said.

"I would still be grateful if you would stay."

Even Caridad could recognize defeat. "Very well," she said. But there was no relenting in her dark eyes when she looked at Constantine.

"If you fail or betray her in any way," she said, "we will find you."

Jacob inclined his head. "I hear you, *señorita*."

When Cari sat down again, Serenity explained something of what she and Jacob had discussed. In spite of her reassurances, the other women continued to show concern, ranging from Caridad's outright rebellion to Changying's troubled glances. Several of the other women gathered around Serenity to ask questions, and express their doubts and worries.

When the last questions had been answered—as thoroughly as she was willing to answer them—Serenity wished Jacob a good night and wearily returned to the house. She knew she should have felt more relief because she was finally able to put her long-deferred plan into action, but she couldn't erase the thought of Jacob's transformation from her mind. She was keeping big secrets from him, and she couldn't predict how he would react when she admitted the truth about what had really happened to her at the hands of the men they hunted.

How could she ever tell him, given what he was? Would he be shocked? Would he pity her as a victim of circumstances beyond her control?

Because she was *not* a victim, and she wouldn't let any man, not even a werewolf, turn her into one again.

Passing through the short hall, Serenity walked by Helene's closed door and paused to look into Bonnie's room, staring at the bed where the other woman had so recently lain. She stayed there for a while, then went on to her own room.

She sat on the bed and pulled the letter from inside her vest. The paper felt brittle under her fingers as she broke the seal and opened the envelope. The letter was dated over three months ago, and the salutation…

Serena. She closed her eyes and let the letter fall into her lap. No one had called her that since before the attack. It had been her father's pet name for her, and not many people had ever used it. All but a handful were dead.

Slowly she picked up the letter and began to read.

For a long while afterward she sat with the paper crumpled in her fists, listening to the unspoken words rattling inside her head like brittle tumbleweeds.

...hope we have found you... We have returned to rebuild... Come home to us. Kind, gentle words from people she had loved until that horrible day. That day, and all the days after, when she had convinced herself that the outlaws would never have attacked if only Aunt Martha and Uncle Lester and the others hadn't left her

parents to return to the home settlement in San Antonio.

The sensible part of her mind knew it wouldn't have made any difference if they'd remained. Quakers were taught not to fight their enemies. The outlaws would probably have killed every last one of them.

But their decision to abandon the settlement near Kerrville had haunted Serenity for too long. She had no use for Quaker ways now, not for peace and humility and turning the other cheek. Undoubtedly the Friends would accept and welcome her if she went "home"—until she told them everything that had happened. They would lecture her with heartfelt sincerity about forgiveness and rebirth into a new and better life. They would try to shepherd her into a fold that could never again contain the black sheep she had become.

It was past midnight when she dropped the badly wrinkled letter into the bottom drawer of her chest and began to undress. But there was no hope of sleep. Two hours later she was dressed again and outside, her sketches in hand, wondering why she thought seeing Jacob at such an ungodly hour would make her feel any better.

In fact, it was downright dangerous. But talking to him about their hunt would take her mind off her aunt's sweet, unwanted sentiments and the life she'd forever left behind.

Only when she was standing outside the barn door did she recognize her own foolishness and start to turn back toward the house. But it was too late. Jacob had already appeared, barefoot and dressed only in his trousers, waiting.

"Something wrong, Miss Campbell?" he asked softly.

Serenity turned back quickly and showed him the handful of papers. "I've finished the sketches, but they can wait until morning. I'm sorry to have woken you."

"You didn't wake me." He rolled his shoulders and lifted his head as if to smell the air. "I was thinking of going for a run."

As a wolf, he meant. She shivered in spite of herself.

"Then you want to look at these sketches now, or in the morning?"

His eyes caught the moonlight as they met her gaze, reflecting red behind the gray and gold. "Might as well do it now," he said. He stood aside to let her precede him into the barn, where he lit the lantern and hung it up beside the door. Serenity handed him the first of the sketches. He spread it flat against the wall. His long fingers arched, curled, tore into the paper as if it were woven of air.

"Do you recognize him?" Serenity asked, her heart tripping wildly.

"I've seen him," he said. "He's a Renier."

So he knew them. Maybe they'd been acquaintances, or even friends. Maybe he'd ridden beside them, on the wrong side of the law.

But those thoughts were crazy. They had to be.

Very carefully, Jacob smoothed out the irreparably torn paper. "You have more?"

She took the first sketch away and gave him the second one, hardly daring to breathe. He glanced at it, returned it to her and nearly snatched the third one from her hand.

"All Reniers," he said, dropping the last sketch to the floor. "They're one of the biggest werewolf clans in the West."

Serenity closed her eyes. "How do you know them?" she asked.

He was so quiet she thought he'd left the barn. She opened her eyes again to find him bent nearly double, shrunken in on himself like an old man.

"I know *of* them," he said, straightening quickly. "Every werewolf in the West knows of them. They have ranches and property all through Texas and the Territories, and they're not friendly to outsiders."

"You mean they hate ordinary people?" she asked.

"And other werewolves."

"But they aren't all outlaws?"

He had hardly touched on the relationships between werewolves when he'd explained about them, but she knew that wolves were very protective of their territories. Violently so.

"They aren't all outlaws," he agreed, though his voice was clipped and strange. "But there are connections and alliances among all the Renier families, just as there are among humans. The men we're looking for might have found shelter among their own."

The biggest werewolf clan in the West. Hundreds, perhaps thousands, of beast-men.

He must have sensed her alarm, for he gave her a probing look. "The Reniers, like most werewolves, have to live among humans. They won't want to acknowledge killers among them, and they might not take much trouble to protect fugitives." He pressed his lips together. "Still, we won't draw attention to our search."

His speech had given Serenity time to recover again. "Do you know where we might find them?"

"They could be anywhere," he said. "We'll begin just as we planned, with the town where you said the outlaws were seen not long before the attack."

Which had been *her* lie. And now, when it was too late, she realized the difficulty returning to Bethel might place her in. Someone was bound to recognize her as the girl who had crawled through a dust storm to find sanctuary at the Morgans' home. What if the old couple were still there?

She would have to hope that she had changed enough so that no one would connect her with that pathetic, beaten girl.

The girl she would never let Jacob Constantine see.

Serenity bent to pick up the sketch Jacob had dropped. "We never finalized your payment," she said. "I meant it when I said I can afford to give you whatever you ask."

"I don't need your money," he said. "If they're killers, they're probably wanted by the law. There's bound to be a reward when I take them in."

But he wouldn't get that reward, not unless it covered the dead as well as the living.

"At least I'll pay for our traveling expenses," she said. Suddenly she was eager to get away from him, from her heightened sense of him, his scent and the lethal power of his body. "We still have a few hours to sleep before morning. Now that Frances and Judith are well enough to work, we should be able to cover the range more quickly than we expected."

Jacob seemed deeply preoccupied, though his final

glance as she left held a wealth of meaning she didn't know how to interpret. She slipped out and walked slowly back to the house.

She wasn't surprised to see Changying waiting for her on the porch.

"Revenge will not cure your unhappiness," the Chinese woman said as Serenity reached the door.

"I don't want revenge," Serenity said. "I want—"

"Justice, as you did with Leroy?"

The deep compassion in the other woman's eyes was more than Serenity could endure. She mumbled a vague response, went inside and returned to her room.

This time her mind and body were exhausted enough to let her sleep, but her dreams were laced with glittering yellow eyes, sharp white teeth and a voice that spoke the same words over and over again:

"Killing doesn't know any barriers between race or blood."

The barrier between her and Jacob was high indeed. But as long as she never forgot what he was, as long as she kept her distance, she would be safe until she didn't care about being safe anymore.

CHAPTER NINE

THEY RODE OUT on a warm June morning, an hour before sunrise. The season's most important work was done, the ranch was well stocked with supplies, and the other women were as prepared as they would ever be.

Jacob watched from the saddle as Serenity made her farewells. Most of the women seemed resigned to her departure, but a few of them—Changying and Caridad, in particular—didn't much trouble to hide their true feelings. Zora had been as stolid as usual. She and Jacob had hardly exchanged a word since their conversation in the stable, but Jacob had been sure that she'd resolved any problems between her and Serenity.

Unlike the women, Jacob had to conceal his thoughts and emotions. He couldn't let Serenity so much as guess what was going through his mind. Until he'd done what he had to do, the last thing he wanted was for Caridad or Victoria or one of the others to decide he couldn't be trusted to look after Serenity and her interests.

Can you? he asked himself as Victoria gave Serenity a hard embrace. He could still hear Caridad's challenge: *If you fail or betray her in any way, we will find you.*

The threat didn't bother him, though he didn't doubt that Caridad would try to kill him if anything happened to Serenity. He didn't plan to expose Serenity to any danger at all.

But he *would* betray her.

The voices of the women faded from Jacob's awareness. He stared blindly at his gloved hands resting on the saddle horn. If there'd been any other way, he would have taken it. But there wasn't. Serenity had done everything possible to make him believe she accepted what he was, that the Change hadn't affected her deeply. She'd spoken calmly and allowed him to take her hand. Few humans could do as much, let alone one whose family had been killed by werewolves.

It was her need to show him just how unafraid she was that had made her insist that they keep working as partners. She'd neither kept her distance nor given any indication that she so much as remembered their kiss, which should have made him glad. It would make things so much easier later.

But the constant ache of desire, the wanting that had come on him so hard and quick in the barn, made it impossible for him to ignore her as she pretended to ignore him. The smell of her, her constant nearness, the flex and bend of her body on her horse…all those things kept him aroused when that was the last thing he wanted to be.

So he'd worked himself to exhaustion every day in hopes he could get some relief in sleep. There hadn't been much. He'd ended up spending most nights running, though even that hadn't helped. He was weak, and finding out he was still subject to that kind of weakness had been a hard lesson to learn. Just as it had been hard to realize that the vengeful creature inside him hadn't been extinguished.

The men Serenity wanted were the men who had killed Ruth. And now that Serenity had set him on their trail, he couldn't turn back. He couldn't pretend it was better to leave them alone than add to the bloodshed that had kept the feud alive so long. Bonnie had brought that home to him. So had Serenity.

He would go after them, sure enough. But the Code, as much as it had been stretched these past few days, wasn't yet broken. He would do one thing he'd promised Serenity. He would bring them in and stick with them until they hanged or he was forced to finish the job himself.

But that would be the last resort. And it would be the end of the Code. Of himself.

A brief touch on his knee snapped him out of his thoughts.

Zora was standing at his stirrup, looking up at him with eyes as flat as the top of a mesa.

"Serenity has offered you money," she said. "I will give you more if you finish this hunt alone."

Werewolves couldn't read each other's minds, but Zora might as well have seen right into his.

"I don't need money from you," he said quietly. "But I've got the same plan in mind."

The Indian woman nodded. "You know these men she seeks," she said.

"I know *of* them."

"I think it is more than that. It is not only because of Serenity or the money she will give you that you hunt these men."

"My reasons don't matter. I'm doing what you asked me to do."

She rested her brown hand on his horse's croup. "Hatred is a powerful thing. It blinds Serenity. She has no sense where these men are concerned."

"That's why I plan to leave her somewhere safe before we get anywhere near them. I'll see her to some town where she can find her way back here with no trouble."

"How will you do this?"

He met her gaze. "I know what she hates and fears most," he said.

"You will not hurt her?"

"I'll do what I have to do, no more."

"You will do this soon?"

"Soon as I can."

"Then we will be watching for her." She paused. "She will hate you for this."

"She's halfway there already."

"Maybe not as much as you think."

Jacob kept all expression from his face, though his heart had contracted into a tight little ball. "Once this is finished, we likely won't lay eyes on each other again." He looked out across the desert grassland sloping away from the mountains behind them. "You take good care of her."

"We will."

She walked away just as Serenity rode up. Her eyes were sad, but her jaw was firm and her shoulders set.

"How do werewolves say goodbye?" she asked.

"Not so differently from anyone else."

Serenity cast one last look around the yard and the

women gathered to see her off. Caridad raised her hand, and she waved back.

"Let's ride," she said.

They set off at a trot, their spare mounts keeping pace at the ends of their leads. Serenity didn't look back again, but Jacob suspected he saw a wetness in her eyes.

She believed she might not come back from the hunt. She wasn't discounting the danger, at least the danger she imagined. It was just that she was willing to die if she could see her enemies destroyed. Any regret she felt about Leroy—and he'd become sure she did feel regret—wouldn't be enough to stop her from killing again.

Only he could do that. But not yet. He had to wait until he'd set things up just right. When he was done, she would be glad to get away from him, even at the cost of her revenge.

In the meantime, he would have to be close to Serenity every waking hour and every night, breathing in her scent, listening to her husky voice, struggling to remember that she was untouchable and always would be.

They rode south along the Rio Grande through the morning, stopped in the shade of the vast cottonwoods by the river during the hottest part of the day to rest and change horses, and continued on into evening. They made camp ten miles northwest of El Paso, taking advantage of the river's proximity to provide not only water but fuel for their fire. Jacob knew they wouldn't always have it so easy.

Not that it would be easy for Serenity much longer

after tonight. He had decided to wait until the next evening to begin putting his plan into effect. He gathered up an armful of fallen cottonwood branches, built a small fire and watched her boil the beans and coffee. They ate as they usually did, in silence, and then spread their bedrolls on either side of the fire. It didn't make much of a barrier, even a symbolic one, but then, that didn't really matter.

In the morning, they broke camp and continued on to El Paso under a brilliant blue sky. They reached the busy town in the early afternoon and stocked up on supplies, then kept riding south toward Fort Hancock. Though they still traveled along the river and parallel to the tracks of the Southern Pacific, the landscape away from the bosque had grown increasingly harsh, dominated by hardy desert plants and patches of grassland.

On the second night, when they camped at the edge of the bosque, Jacob slipped out of sight behind the trees, stripped out of his clothes and Changed.

Maybe Serenity sensed what was happening, for she was staring in his direction when he reemerged. She flinched a little when she saw him, struggling to get herself under control again.

"Are you going out to catch our dinner?" she asked casually.

He turned and burst into a standing run. He could feel her gaze locked on him as he loped away from camp. She would seem indifferent when he returned, but she wouldn't be. She would be thinking of the Reniers and everything he had in common with them. And he couldn't let her forget.

Jacob turned up a jackrabbit in less than five minutes, scented another one soon after and caught *it,* as well. The meat would be scanty and tough, but along with the beans it would be enough.

Just as he'd anticipated, when he returned, Serenity seemed relaxed as she boiled the beans over the fire. She hardly glanced up as he trotted into the firelight with the two rabbits dangling from his jaws.

"Good," she said. She patted a cloth she had spread on the ground beside her. "Please put them here."

Feeling like a cad, Jacob did as she asked and returned to his clothes. He Changed, dressed quickly and rejoined her. She had drawn the knife she wore at her waist and was reaching for one of the rabbits.

Jacob crouched on his haunches a few feet away. "Let me do that," he said, unsheathing his own knife. "I can skin a rabbit in my sleep."

She wouldn't look at him. "You did the hunting. I'll do the cooking."

Arguing would only make the situation seem normal again, so he lay back against his saddle, pulled his hat over his eyes and pretended to sleep. Two hours later Serenity "woke" him, and they ate beans and rabbit without so much as a word passing between them. Jacob moved a little more quickly than she did to clean up and dispose of the rabbits' remains. She left him to it and sat brooding over the dying fire, poking at the embers with a stick and studiously avoiding his gaze.

The next evening, when he Changed, Jacob upped the stakes. He turned his back and stripped in front of her, letting her witness the transformation as he had done the first time at Avalon. Before he left to hunt, he stalked around the camp, bristling up his fur and showing his teeth without ever turning his attention directly on Serenity.

Once again, they cooked and ate the brace of cottontails he brought in a silence fraught with tension and unspoken fears. Jacob reminded himself again and again that this ugly game was necessary, but he hated it all the same. For the first time in years, he despised what he was.

On the following day, they stopped in Fort Hancock, then turned west toward Sierra Blanca, riding into a country of vast, flat plains broken by high mountain ranges that seemed to spring straight out of the parched earth. That night, when they made camp in the open desert, Jacob behaved in as bestial a manner as he could, growling and snapping in the darkness just out of Serenity's sight, nearly tearing the night's prey apart before he brought it back to her, eating his bloody portion as wolf instead of man, and howling at the moon long after she had taken to her bedroll.

He didn't come back until dawn, when the fire had burned to ashes and Serenity's attention was focused on saddling her horse. Her shoulders twitched when she heard him trot into camp. Self-disgust curdled in Jacob's gut as he Changed, dressed and retrieved his own saddle and bedroll.

Acutely aware of Serenity's inner turmoil, he saddled his own mount and checked on his spare. The weak part of him wanted to apologize to Serenity for his behavior, but he knew one slip would undo any progress he had made. By tomorrow, or the next day, or the day after that, she would have seen enough of the beast that she would rejoice to be rid of him.

"Are you trying to frighten me?" she asked suddenly.

An unseen rock rolled under Jacob's boot, and he almost stumbled. "No," he said, half choking on the word. "What makes you think—?"

"Are you hoping I'll give up rather than travel with a werewolf?"

Hell. She'd seen through his ruse so easily. "Serenity…"

She stood very still with her palms flat on her horse's barrel. "You don't understand me at all, do you? If you think staring at me with those yellow eyes and howling all night will make me turn back…" She turned to glare at him just the way she'd done when he'd been lying in the barn after the rescue, completely at her mercy. "I saw Zora speaking to you before we left. I know she never wanted me to come with you. Was this your idea, or did the others put you up to it?"

"It was my idea," he said. He removed his hat and held it in both hands, forcing himself to meet her gaze. "I thought if you saw what you'd be up against—"

"You think I don't know?" She shook her head sharply. "When you changed the first time, in the barn, I thought I had passed your test. I thought we had an agreement. But you were lying all along. You never intended—" She caught her breath. "There is nothing—*nothing*—you can do to make me change my mind. If you try to leave me behind, I'll come after you. Even if you take the horses and all the supplies and leave me in the desert, I'll find a way."

Her blazing eyes did more than send his emotions spiraling into a black pit of confusion. Her stubborn courage didn't only arouse his admiration, but his body, as well. Her fresh and passionate face with its straight, sandy brows, high cheekbones and full lips had never been more beautiful. Her chest rose and fell rapidly, pulling her shirt taut across her breasts.

Jacob knew then that he hadn't wanted to get rid of her only for the sake of her own safety, or because putting her in danger would go against the Code. He hadn't wanted to feel again what he was feeling now, that powerful, pounding lust that was such a deadly trap for both of them.

If it hadn't been for the wild contradictions in the way she looked at him—angry and pleading, defiant and vulnerable, all at the same time—he might have done better at resisting her. He would have remembered the time she'd tried to buy him with her body. He would have remembered Ruth.

But he wasn't remembering when he dropped his hat, crossed the space between them and took her in his arms. He wasn't thinking as another part of the Code he'd lived by crumbled under his feet like the parched earth at the edge of a cliff. After his three nights of hunting and running as a wolf, his instincts were very close to the surface. He didn't have the will to fight them. And when she put her arms around his shoulders and raised her face to his, he knew nothing in the world could stop him from kissing her.

Serenity was as hungry as he was, as eager to feel his mouth on hers. Her lips were pliant and warm and demanding. He could feel all the wiry strength in her body as she laced her fingers in his hair and opened her mouth to accept the thrust of his tongue. Her heart was thumping so hard that he couldn't feel his own.

He kissed Serenity's cheeks, her chin, her forehead, as he moved his hands down her straight back and rested them on the gentle flare of her hips. No men's clothes could conceal her very feminine body from his eager fingers.

She leaned into him, her breasts flattening against his chest. A little prick of Jacob's conscience reminded him that they were moving much too fast. He had to stop before they went too far. He had to *remember.*

But the wolf and its primitive power would not be denied. He pulled her hips against his and slid his hands between them, cupping them over her breasts. She wasn't nearly as small as she appeared in a shirt meant to blur her shape. He'd known she didn't wear a corset, and there was only one other layer between the shirt and her skin, too thin to blunt the firm peaks of her nipples.

He kissed her again, swallowing her soft moans as he rubbed his thumbs across the heavy cotton covering her breasts. He tugged up on the shirt, freeing the tail from the waistband of her trousers. His fingers brushed heated silk, a woman's undergarment that served as a shallow nod toward propriety, a feminine indulgence he hadn't expected. He lifted that as well, exposing the soft skin of her waist, feeling the tremulous flutter of her breath. The undergarment lay too close to her body for Jacob to reach underneath it, but he slid his fingers up over the silk and found her nipples again.

She gasped, her body torn between resistance and surrender. Jacob didn't recognize her struggles for what they were until she pulled away, tearing the undergarment before he could get his hand free. She backed up, her shirttail flapping around her hips.

"I'm…I'm sorry," she whispered. "I can't."

It was the second time she'd encouraged him and then broken off, and Jacob reeled as if a bullet had just passed through his heart. His legs had gone weak as a newborn calf's, and his breath burned like a searing wind off the Jornada del Muerto. The wolf inside him snarled in frustration, slavering to finish what he'd started.

This time the man was stronger.

"Serenity," he said, holding his arms loose at his sides. "You've…got no call to apologize. I was the one—"

She pushed at the air between them, warding off his awkward attempt at an explanation. "I wish I could explain," she said, her voice catching.

She didn't have to. He'd been doing nothing but reminding her what he was almost since they'd left Avalon.

Better to leave her alone and give her a chance to recover her composure while he figured out how he was ever going to be able to look her in the face again. He turned to leave.

"No," she said. "No. Don't go."

"I reckoned you'd want to be alone."

"No. I…wasn't honest with you, either. I said I was willing to give you…whatever you wanted in exchange for helping me. Even though you refused, I never would have been able to go through with it."

"You don't have to say any more," he said roughly.

"I want to. Please. Look at me, Jacob."

He looked. She wasn't trembling now, though he could still smell the fear on her.

"We should be riding out," he said. "If you want to talk later…"

"With this standing between us?"

"You know I'd never hurt you."

"I know," she said, staring at the ground. "If it were only what you are…" She trailed off and sat on one of the nearby rocks. "I was engaged once," she said, "to a very good man. A gentle man who loved me."

Another bullet plowed through Jacob's body, piercing something more vulnerable than any flesh. When he had first met her, he had speculated that her skittishness around him, her disgust for the male sex, had to do with bad treatment by someone she'd known. He had put that speculation aside when he'd learned of her parents' deaths at the hands of his kind.

But he'd never thought she might have had a good man in her life. It didn't seem to fit. And it meant that someone else had…

"He died," Serenity said. "He died in the fire with my parents. He was visiting that day. We were planning our—"

She broke off, her throat working. "I loved him," she said, finding her voice again. "He was the only man I had ever cared for. When he died, I knew I could never feel the same way again."

Or give herself to any man, because it reminded her too much of him? Had her fiance touched her as Jacob had, or had their relationship remained pure, preserved in innocence until their wedding night?

Ruth had been innocent in every way but one until the day she died. And he had loved her.

"I'm sorry," he said.

She rubbed at her eyes. "Thank you. I hope you understand why—"

"I understand," he said. But he knew there must be a hell of a lot more he didn't know about her. That made everything harder, because his plan to leave her behind wasn't going to work, and he needed every advantage he could get. He would have to figure out another way to leave her. And of keeping his hands off her for the rest of the time they were together.

"We should go now," he said. "If you feel well enough."

Serenity got up, opened one of her saddlebags and took out a small fabric pouch. Inside were the pins she used to hold her hair close to her head. She began to gather up the long strands that had come loose during their embrace, the lines of her back subtly changing with every graceful motion.

"What is it like?" she asked suddenly.

Jacob didn't have to ask what she meant, though it astonished him that she would ask at all.

"Sometimes it feels like a miracle," he said, looking toward the sun rising over the mountains. "Having two ways to look at life. There's so much beauty out there most folks don't see because they don't take the time to look. But when you're a wolf…" He hesitated, as if searching for the right way to put his feelings into words a person like Serenity could understand. "You can't help but take the time, because right now is all there is. The future doesn't matter, and neither does the past."

"No future," she murmured. "No past."

"You're just alive, part of the night, with the blood of everything that lives pumping in your veins."

Serenity turned slowly, the little bag still clutched in her hands.

"Are you…born this way?" she asked.

He met her uncertain gaze. "We're born with the ability. But the Change doesn't start coming until a boy or girl starts changing in other ways."

"Oh." Serenity rubbed her flushed cheeks. "It must feel strange at first."

"When you grow up around it, you don't think much of it."

She lifted the bag, looking at it as if she'd never seen it before. "I've seen wolves teaching their young," she said. "Is it the same with your people? Do your parents show you how to hunt?"

"Something like that."

"What is your family like, Jacob? Do werewolves—the good ones, I mean—have regular occupations just like ordinary people?"

Jacob felt his muscles tighten. He wanted to put her at ease, but not like this.

"Ma took good care of us," he said. "Pa ran a livery stable."

"I would have thought that werewolves would frighten horses, but you never have any trouble," she said.

"Sometimes being what we are makes other animals easier to control."

She shivered once and looked up again. "Are your parents still living?"

"No."

"I'm sorry."

At once he regretted the coldness of his reply. "My brother, John, is alive. He studied law and went up to Oregon."

"A werewolf lawyer," she said wonderingly. "And you left to join the Texas Rangers."

He turned away from the sunrise, hiding his face in shadow. "That's right."

"But they didn't know what you were."

He shook his head.

"Was there…a woman you left behind?"

It was natural she should ask, after she'd told him about her fiance. But he couldn't talk about Ruth. Not with Serenity. Never with her.

"It's your past we're dealing with," he said. "Mine's of no consequence in what we've got to do."

"I'm sorry," she said. "I didn't intend to pry."

He steadied his voice again. "Sometimes we take things for granted. We think what we've got isn't good enough somehow. But that ranch you've got…it's something you don't want to lose. You can still change your mind."

She turned and tucked the little pouch back in her saddlebag. "I'm ready to go now."

They finished their preparations, mounted and headed west, away from the Rio Grande. It took them another two days to reach Sierra Blanca, a small and isolated town distinguished only by the fact that it had been founded at a railroad junction a few years before.

Jacob and Serenity replenished their supplies, the last time they would be able to do so for the next week or more. From there to Fort Stockton they would be riding straight across desert grassland and through barren mountains, most likely encountering nothing more than coyotes, rabbits and rattlesnakes. Even cattle were uncommon in this country.

It was the most difficult part of their journey, but Serenity never once complained, even when they had to ration their water and ride during the night to avoid the sun's searing heat. Mesquite and tarbush scraped at their horses' legs, and the weary animals began to droop. Each night or morning, when they made camp, Jacob and Serenity worked as partners with no relationship but that of fellow travelers.

As they approached Fort Stockton, the terrain became more hospitable, and they began to see small herds of cattle. Jacob put all his senses on alert, frequently smelling the air and scanning the horizon.

They spent a whole day camped near the fort and its bountiful springs, resting the horses, buying more provisions and sleeping. Then they moved westward again, moving ever closer to the Pecos River. Serenity became visibly more uneasy, shifting constantly in her saddle, looking anxiously in every direction as if she expected an attack. Her agitation became more obvious after they forded the Pecos at the old military road crossing near the ruins of Fort Lancaster.

Jacob knew why. They'd seen hardly a sign of anything human in the miles they'd traveled since leaving Fort Stockton, but by his reckoning they were within a day's ride of Bethel. Serenity was remembering what had brought her there the first time, and wondering if she would finally find what she'd been looking for.

They came on a dry, meandering wash at midafternoon and followed the barely visible wagon path alongside it until they came within sight of a tiny cattle town, blessed with a single live oak, and a dusty street bordered by a row of bleached and battered structures hardly distinguishable from the desert itself.

Serenity pulled up and stared at the ragged buildings.

"This is the place," she said.

CHAPTER TEN

IT HADN'T CHANGED. The town was no bigger than it had been six years ago, nor any less deserted in appearance. Serenity gripped the reins, hoping to conceal the trembling of her hands.

Coward, she thought. She had seen no other choice but to come here in spite of the risk that someone would recognize her and tell Jacob how she had arrived.

She and Jacob hadn't spoken of anything personal—especially their respective pasts—since the day of the second kiss, a day she hadn't been able to put from her mind for a moment over the weeks that had followed. What he had revealed that day…what she had revealed to him…had changed something between them.

Oh, not in any physical sense. Jacob had been a perfect gentleman, careful not to so much as brush her hand in passing. If he'd changed into a wolf during their long ride, he hadn't let her see it. He was clearly using his animal senses, but he did so subtly, and not once had he done anything to provoke her.

But that didn't change the fact that something was different. In all the time she'd known about the existence of werewolves, she'd never once considered that there could be anything admirable about the change from man to beast. All she had seen was the ugliness.

Jacob had opened his heart to her and shown her

things she couldn't have imagined in the midst of her captivity or the hatred that had consumed her after her escape. The poetry of his simple words had moved her deeply.

Yet as much as those words had stirred her, his reaction when she had explained about Levi had touched her even more. His acceptance had seemed a blessing, even though she'd been lying about the real reason she couldn't let him…

A gust of dust-laden wind made her blink, and she brushed her hand across her eyes. Even the idea that she could consider going beyond a kiss astonished her.

That was what Jacob had wanted.

But he would never, ever force her. He had understood and accepted her explanation, vague and untruthful as it was. And then, when she had asked about his family and he had told her of his parents and brother, she had felt the weight of her prejudice begin to dwindle from a crushing burden to a knot of uncertainty hardly bigger than her heart. There had been so little left of it that she could ask about the women in Jacob's life and feel the ache of loss when he refused to answer.

But she could expect no better when she was withholding so much from him.

She drew her horse closer to his. "There's something I need to tell you before we ride in," she said.

He met her gaze with an intensity that was all wolf, just like the way he smelled the air and cocked his head at sounds she couldn't hear. "You want me to go in ahead?" he asked.

"No. It's what I said about the last time I was in Bethel. I told you that I'd ridden in to look for the outlaws after they attacked my family." She let go of the reins and locked her fingers around the saddle horn, preparing herself to lie again. "It wasn't that way at all. This was the place I came to when I escaped the outlaws. I was inside the house when they set it on fire, but I was able to get out." Her vision blurred. "I couldn't help my family. It was too late."

A low sound like a groan of pain seemed to catch in Jacob's throat. "You were almost killed."

"Yes. I took one of the horses and rode east. I didn't know or care where I was going. I rode for days without stopping, until my horse died under me. I kept on going on foot, and this is where I stopped when I couldn't go any farther."

Jacob lowered his head as if he were facing an enemy. "You said your family's house wasn't far from Fredericksburg," he said. "That's over a hundred miles southeast of here."

"I wasn't in my right mind," she said. "I was weak and starving when I got here. If an old couple living here hadn't take me in…"

He gazed at her with a kind of quiet horror, and she wondered if she'd been too honest after all.

"I'm not weak and starving now," she said, meeting his gaze again. "I survived."

He shook his head. "Why did you think the outlaws would be here?"

"I remembered hearing the name 'Renier' in Bethel when I was recovering. The people I stayed with were very much afraid of the Reniers, and they had visited the town several times. The name didn't mean much to me then, but when all the evidence led me to believe the Reniers were the killers I was looking for…"

She thought from the way Jacob looked at her that he could well imagine her terror. "You didn't have to tell me," he said. "But I'm glad you did."

At that moment she wished she had the courage to lean into him and let him take her into his arms again. "Someone in town may remember me," she said. "They may talk about what happened. I didn't want them to tell you first."

"You all right to ride in?" he asked.

"Yes."

In spite of her reassurance, he insisted on taking the lead. She kicked her mare Cleo into a trot and rode after Jacob up to the hitching rail outside of the mercantile, which, except for the crooked sign, seemed much the same.

Almost immediately the proprietor appeared in the open doorway, squinting up at them with open curiosity.

"Howdy, gents," he said. He looked at Serenity more closely. "Ma'am."

He wasn't the same man. He was younger, though he couldn't have been much less than forty years old. His lean face held an eager expression, suggesting that business here was no better than it had been six years ago.

"What can I do for you folks?" he asked, glancing warily at Jacob.

Serenity dismounted. "My name is Sally Cumberland," she said, giving him the name she and Jacob had agreed she would use during their search. "This is Jack King."

The storekeeper arched grizzled brows. "You look like you been in the saddle some time. I got some tobacco straight from San Antonio, and some perfume for the lady, if you…"

Jacob swung out of the saddle and tossed his mount's reins over the rail. "Maybe later. You mind answering a few questions?"

"Reckon that depends," the storekeeper said. He took a few steps back until he stood within the shelter of the doorway. "Maybe you'd like to get yourself a drink first. Saloon's three doors down."

Serenity could hear raised voices from several buildings away. She remembered such laughter on another day, when even the sound of a male voice had frozen her with terror.

"Where is the old couple who used to work here?" Serenity asked, ignoring the man's suggestion.

"They left years ago," the storekeeper said.

So much for that, Serenity thought.

Jacob glanced at her, opened one of the saddlebags and pulled out Serenity's sketches, rolled up in another sheet of paper and tied with a string. He untied it and passed the loose roll to the storekeeper, who accepted it with visible reluctance.

"We want to know if you've seen these men around here anytime recently," Jacob said. "They may go by the name Renier," Jacob added.

Serenity noticed that the storekeeper didn't seem to want to look at the drawings too closely. "Might've seen 'em sometime," he said. "Months ago. I didn't see 'em too close."

"They didn't do business with you?"

"They look like rough customers," the man said. "There ain't much else here to interest men like these." He thrust the drawings back at Jacob. "Can't tell you no more."

All at once Jacob seemed to get bigger and more menacing, the wolf bristling under his skin. "You sure that's all you have to say?" he asked softly.

The shopkeeper wiped his hands on his apron. "Maybe Harrison can tell you. He runs the saloon."

With that, he hurried back into his store and closed the door.

"He was lying, wasn't he?" Serenity asked.

"He wasn't telling the whole truth, that's for damned sure," Jacob said. "Why don't you wait here while I go over to the saloon?"

She was just about to remind him that she could handle herself when the sound of hoofbeats coming from the west caught her attention.

Jacob swung around, hand on his gun. His nostrils flared.

"What in hell are *they* doing here?" he said.

Serenity squinted into the afternoon glare. Gradually three riders leading three barebacked horses resolved out of the haze of dust and heat, and she realized what Jacob had meant.

Caridad was in the lead, as always, her flashy black gelding kicking up a trail of dust that almost obscured the riders behind her. As she came nearer, the other two materialized: Zora on her tough chestnut pony, and Victoria atop Avalon's biggest and strongest horse.

Serenity realized how foolish it was to be surprised. Caridad hadn't wanted her to go in the first place. She'd wanted to come along. Serenity should have known better than to believe that Cari wouldn't follow her impulses.

Caridad reined in her mount, and leaped off with all the panache and skill of an acrobat in a circus. Victoria dismounted and joined her, while Zora remained with the remaining five horses.

"Praise God!" Caridad said, striding up to Serenity and embracing her forcefully. "Zora said she could track you, but—*Madre de Dios!* I thought we would never find you."

"What in hell did you think you were doing?" Jacob demanded, confronting Caridad. "This isn't a pleasure ride."

"We do not need to give our reasons to you," Caridad said with an arrogant toss of her head. "It is Serenity we came to see."

"You shouldn't have come," Serenity said, placing herself between the two angry warriors. "This is not your hunt."

"We came for another reason," Victoria said. She stepped forward with an unsealed envelope in her hand. "This arrived for you the day after you left. Cari thought it might be important, so she opened it. She decided you should see it."

The envelope in Victoria's hand was not nearly as battered as the one Serenity had opened a month before she and Jacob had left Avalon, and this time the address was clearly visible. It was postmarked two months after the first letter, but had reached Las Cruces in a third of the time.

Serenity took it from Victoria and stared at it with consternation. Another plea from Aunt Martha? Would Cari consider that important enough to send three women riding four hundred miles to deliver it?

"You'd better look at it," Jacob said, "so we can get on with our business." He looked over Victoria's shoulder at Zora, who was still waiting quietly with the horses. "We'll give you your privacy. Miss Zora, I'd like a word with you."

The Indian woman led the horses to the rail, exchanged quick glances with Caridad and Victoria, and followed Jacob across the rutted street. Victoria went into the store, and Caridad muttered something about finding a place to make camp. She swung up in the saddle and trotted away to the north.

Feeling abandoned and very much alone, Serenity noted the decidedly masculine writing on the envelope, which matched the script inside. The text of the letter was brief and straightforward.

When she was finished reading, Serenity carefully refolded the letter, tucked it back inside the envelope and placed it in one of her saddlebags.

She looked around for Jacob and Zora. They were engaged in an intense conversation across the street, where a fallen-down fence marked an abandoned corral. She realized that this was the first time she'd seen them so close since she'd learned that both were werewolves, and her heart contracted with an emotion she didn't recognize at first.

They were the same. Despite their different backgrounds, they must understand each other far better than she could understand either of them. What were they talking about? What did they see when their eyes met?

"Are you all right?" Victoria asked from the doorway of the mercantile.

Serenity shook her head to clear it and turned to the blacksmith. "You didn't read it?" she asked.

Victoria ducked her head. "I thought Caridad should have a second opinion."

Then she now knew far more about Serenity than she ever had before. She knew about Serenity's kin in Texas, who claimed to love her.

Once Serenity and Aunt Martha had been close, closer even than Serenity had been to her own mother. Aunt Martha had been a bit of a rebel, filled with fun, and far less somber than most in the settlement. She and Serenity had often gone out to pick wildflowers and watch the hawks soaring over the plains when the day's work was finished.

But now Aunt Martha was dying…or so Uncle Lester claimed. Serenity found it difficult to believe that so much could have changed in the mere two months that had passed between the letters. Her aunt and uncle had been anxious for her to return before, but that was all. Still, it would be strange for Quakers to lie for any reason, but if Aunt Martha was a little ill, they might justify exaggerating in hopes of luring Serenity back.

Why they should go to such trouble after so many years she didn't know, and no amount of speculation would give her the answers she sought. Now she had a painful decision to make. She could set aside her bitterness, go home and stay with Aunt Martha, just like the dutiful child she had been before the outlaws had come. She could stifle the grief and sickness that choked her when she thought of seeing the settlement, Tolerance, again.

Or she could finish what she had started.

"Serenity?" Victoria said.

"It's all right, Vicky," Serenity said. "I just need a little time to think."

"Are you going to your family?"

"Jacob and I still have business in town. We must see to that before anything else can be decided."

The blacksmith accepted Serenity's evasive answer, though her expression showed that she was far from satisfied. She gathered up the five remaining horses and led them to the water trough at the end of the street.

Serenity was left to wait for Jacob and Zora. They returned shortly, both tense and obviously at odds.

Strangely relieved, Serenity waited to speak to Jacob until Zora had walked off in the direction of the trough. "What's wrong?" she asked. "Why were you and Zora arguing?"

"She brought them here," he said, his face still taut with anger. "She tracked us. They never would have found us otherwise." He met Serenity's eyes, and his gaze softened. "What was in that letter?"

If she told him, she would give him every excuse to encourage her to leave for Tolerance immediately. He didn't know the place she would be going to was the same farm where her parents had died, restored by the Friends who had returned years later. He would only believe she had obligations greater than finding the Reniers.

"You don't have to tell me," he said. "But you look upset. If there's anything I can do…"

"It's nothing," she said quickly, hoping he would believe her. "I don't know why Caridad thought it was so urgent."

"Maybe it was just an excuse," he said. "But they aren't coming with us. They have to go back."

"I agree," she said, trying to imagine how ugly it would get with Jacob and Caridad riding together, even if she hadn't been concerned about the women's safety. "Let me tell them, but not until tomorrow morning. I—"

A raucous laugh sounded from the direction of the saloon. Jacob turned his head sharply toward it. Then, just as abruptly, he turned in the opposite direction.

Another rider was approaching from the west with a saddled horse in tow, sitting as easy on his mount as if he'd never walked a day in his life. He wore a broad-brimmed hat and a duster that flapped out behind him like a pair of low-set wings.

Jacob tilted his hat back and whistled softly. "Perry," he said. "I'll be damned."

Serenity took a closer look as the rider slowed his mount to a trot. "You know him?" she asked.

"An old colleague of mine. What's he doing out in the middle of nowhere?"

His voice was a peculiar mixture of curiosity, pleasure and wariness, and Serenity wondered just what kind of "colleague" this Perry had been.

But as the man came within hailing distance, Jacob strode to meet him.

"Jacob Constantine?" the rider said, leaning over his saddle horn. "That you?"

"Mordecai Perry!" Jacob said with a grin. "What in hell are you doing here?"

Perry swung down from his horse and gave the animal a fond pat on the neck. "I could ask the same of you," he said, thrusting out his hand.

Jacob took the other man's hand and shook it firmly.

Serenity had the feeling they were testing one another's strength, but both were still grinning like a couple of boys after a successful fishing expedition.

"You ain't still with the Rangers?" Perry asked.

"Left eight years ago," Jacob said, dropping his hand. "I've never gone back. You?"

"Thought I'd do better huntin' men for money."

"A bounty hunter?" Jacob's brows arched. "Never thought I'd see you give up the Rangers."

Perry shrugged. "We all change." He glanced in Serenity's direction. "Maybe you've changed more than I thought."

Jacob followed his gaze. "We all change," he said shortly.

"I'm right sorry to hear that, Jake. Why don't you come on over, and we'll get a drink?"

His tone seemed to dismiss Serenity in a casual way that hurt her more than she wanted to admit, but as he turned, Perry and his horse behind him, Jacob gave her a little nod of reassurance.

"Miss Sally Cumberland," he said, "this is Mordecai Perry. Mordecai, Miss Cumberland."

“Howdy, ma’am,” Perry said, tipping his hat.

“How do you do, Mr. Perry,” Serenity said. She studied Jacob’s friend covertly in the short silence that followed. Jacob hadn’t an ounce of fat on him, but Perry was leaner still, reminding her of a greyhound she’d seen once in San Antonio. His features were gaunt, and his hair and mustache were iron-gray, though Serenity was by no means sure that he was as old as his weather-beaten face made him seem.

Regardless of his benign appearance and friendliness with Jacob, she was no more inclined to trust him at first sight than she was any man. In fact, she realized, she had disliked him on sight.

“Miss Cumberland hired me to track some people she’s looking for,” Jacob said, seemingly aware of Serenity’s judgment of his friend.

“Oh?” Perry smiled at Serenity, then turned back to Jacob. “Didn’t know you was working for hire.”

“This is a special case,” Jacob said a little stiffly.

“Why you got a woman ridin’ with you?”

“Because I insisted on it,” Serenity said, not bothering to keep the ice out of her voice.

Perry gave Jacob a long look. “I see,” he drawled. “It *must* be a special case.”

“Miss Cumberland’s a damn good rider and a crack shot,” Jacob said, his good humor fading fast. “She’s the only one who can identify the men we’re looking for.”

Perry continued to smile knowingly, and Serenity began to lose her temper. She held it in check. “Perhaps you have heard something of these men, Mr. Perry?” she asked. “They go by the name Renier.”

"Renier, eh? Kin of yours?"

"Not kin, Mr. Perry. Enemies."

The lean man stroked his mustache. "If you don't mind my sayin' so, ma'am, you ought to be a little more careful pickin' your enemies." He looked at Jacob. "Dangerous game where a female's involved."

"You obviously don't know the right kind of females, Mr. Perry," Serenity said.

"Maybe you're right, ma'am. Still, you must be payin' Constantine a pretty penny—'less you have somethin' else worth his services."

She was preparing a scathing reply when Jacob cut in.

"You'd best watch your mouth, Perry," he said in his softest, most dangerous voice. "You don't talk that way to a lady, and I don't take kindly to the insult to myself and Miss Cumberland."

The other man seemed genuinely taken aback. "No harm meant, Jacob. Miss Cumberland." His gaze shifted to the end of the street. "I got business I should see to, myself. Maybe we'll have that drink later." He strode off in the direction of the saloon, then abruptly turned into an alley between a ramshackle boarding-house and an abandoned post office. Victoria was still watering the horses. Caridad hadn't yet returned, and Zora was nowhere in sight.

Jacob met Serenity's gaze for just a moment and then strode after Perry. Serenity was about to follow when she heard more raised voices from the saloon. She stopped.

Victoria left the horses and walked toward the bar,

pausing just outside the door. Quickly she turned toward Serenity and broke into a run.

She was breathless when she reached Serenity. "Where is Constantine?" she asked.

"Why? What is it, Vicky?"

The blacksmith cast an anxious glance over her shoulder. "Zora. She's in trouble. We'd better get Mr. Constantine."

Serenity wasn't interested in waiting. She checked her gun belt and ran straight to the open saloon door, where the laughing voices were more raucous than ever.

"Indian bitch!" someone was shouting. "Have a little more!"

Serenity burst through the door. Zora was slumped over a table, and a rough-looking man with a bottle was trying to pour whiskey down her throat while being cheered on by two others. Serenity didn't have time to wonder how Zora could have gotten herself in such a predicament or why she wasn't fighting back. She drew her gun and rushed toward the table.

The man with the bottle froze, and his dirty, stubbled friends looked up in surprise.

Almost immediately the men relaxed again, and one of them laughed.

"Another bitch!" he said.

"At least she's white," another said with a grotesque leer. "You want somethin' to drink, little lady?"

Serenity aimed and fired at the wall just over the second man's head. He jumped out of his seat so fast that the chair fell backward and banged into the table behind him. The third man lurched to his feet while the first was still clutching his bottle, and both men reached for their guns.

She was faster. She shot the bottle right out of the first man's hand, and he lost his balance and tumbled to the floor.

Zora flinched but made no move to get up.

The third man lunged, grabbed a handful of Zora's hair and put a knife to her throat.

"You care about this half-breed?" he snarled. "Then put the gun down."

Common sense told Serenity that she was outgunned and outmaneuvered, but she was too full of blind anger to listen. She aimed right at the third man's chest.

A bullet grazed his shoulder, but it wasn't hers. Jacob ran into the saloon, closely followed by Perry.

"Drop that knife," Jacob said, "or I'll put a bullet through your gizzard." He stared at the first man, who was pulling himself back into his chair with a moan of pain. "You, throw down your gun and stand against the wall."

If Serenity had forgotten sense, the three men had never had any to begin with. The third man, bleeding but determined, was about to slit Zora's throat when Jacob's bullet caught him in the chest. He slumped over the table. The first man, who had recovered from his fall, never had a chance to draw. He fell with a shattered kneecap. The second man got as far as shooting a single bullet, which went wide, before Perry took him down.

Serenity ran to the table and put her arms around Zora.

"Come with me," she said, pulling Zora to her feet.

Zora staggered and leaned heavily against Serenity, her face obscured by the dark fall of her hair.

Victoria joined them, supporting Zora on her other side.

Jacob and Perry remained behind to speak to the saloon keeper, who had just emerged from the back room, where he had taken refuge.

Caridad came running, guns drawn, her face suffused with emotion. “I heard gunshots!” she cried. She glanced at Zora, looked again and swore eloquently in Spanish.

“Is there no one left to kill?” she exclaimed.

“It’s been taken care of,” Serenity said wearily.

Caridad glared at the closed saloon door, blew out her breath and slammed her guns back into their holsters.

There were no benches or raised walkways along the street, so Serenity led Zora to the mercantile and eased her to the ground against the wall, while Caridad remained a little behind, still watching the saloon door. Serenity fetched a canteen and tried to make Zora drink. The woman’s head slumped before she had swallowed more than a few drops.

“How did it happen?” Serenity whispered to Victoria.

“I don’t know. I heard shouting about Indians and looked into the saloon.” Victoria shook her head. “I’ve never seen Zora like this.” She stroked her friend’s damp hair. “I can’t believe she didn’t stab them the moment they put their hands on her.”

“Maybe because she knows what happens to Indians who fight white men,” Jacob said, coming up from behind and crouching beside Serenity. His face was set and hard, and his eyes were like chips of gray-and-yellow stone.

"I still don't understand," Serenity said, keeping her voice low. "Zora may be an Indian, but she's also a—"

She closed her mouth and glanced at Victoria and Caridad, who were speaking quietly a little distance away.

"What people do doesn't always make sense," Jacob said.

That she knew only too well. She lifted Zora's head, wet her handkerchief from the canteen and bathed Zora's face. Zora showed no reaction.

"We should get her away from here," Serenity said.

Jacob showed his teeth. "Those men won't be making any more trouble, and neither will anyone else."

"But the men you and Perry shot…?"

"They didn't worry you much when *you* went to shoot them." Jacob's expression became even more grim. Victoria joined them, and he clearly thought better of what he was about to say. "Only one of them is dead. The other two are likely to recover." He rubbed at his stubbled chin "The saloon keeper saw how it started. He'll swear it was self-defense. No one's going to take the word of a couple of idle cowhands over two ex–Texas Rangers." He looked up at Victoria. "Will you look after Zora while I speak to Miss Campbell?"

Victoria knelt beside Zora and uncapped the canteen again. She looked as if she knew that Serenity was about to get a good tongue-lashing, and she obviously wasn't about to interfere.

And Serenity knew there wasn't any putting it off. Jacob got up, and she followed him across the street.

"What in hell were you thinking?" he demanded as soon as she was near enough to hear him. "Running in there with no backup? You should damned well have made sure I—"

"There wasn't time," she said. "Zora was in trouble."

"A few seconds longer wouldn't have made any difference," he said, all but snarling. "You could have gotten Zora killed. You could have gotten *yourself* killed."

He was right. All at once, without warning, Serenity began to shake. The physical reactions she'd held at bay consumed her, turning her legs boneless, and flooding her body with alternating currents of heat and cold.

It wasn't just the realization that things could have gone very wrong, that she and Zora might have died. She had run into a saloon occupied by men just like the Reniers, men who thought nothing of abusing a woman and breaking her spirit.

And she'd shot at a man, then watched him die, all because of her recklessness. At the time she'd felt glad, but now…

You were responsible for Leroy's death, she reminded herself. She'd come to regret the way she'd passed judgment on him without any thought of justice, but she still thought he had deserved to die, and so had the man in the saloon.

Yet she hadn't done the actual killing either time. Could she stand before Renier and his men and shoot them in cold blood?

Then again, they would be shooting back. It wouldn't be cold blood then.

"I did what I thought was best at the time," she said.

Jacob turned away, hooking his thumbs in his gun belt. "That isn't good enough, Serenity. You may think your life isn't worth a damn, but I..." He trailed off and kicked at the dirt with his boot. "You made me a promise to obey without question, Serenity Campbell. One more mistake like this..."

"Would you think it was a mistake if I was trying to save your life the way I did at Avalon?" she snapped.

"I don't plan on making any more mistakes like that," he said, swinging around to face her. "And I don't want to worry about you every damned minute."

"I didn't ask you to worry about me. I'm sorry you had to get involved in what happened in the saloon." She looked away. "I want only one thing from you, and that—"

He seized her by the shoulders and began to shake her. "You listen to me—"

Some sound, perhaps only the jangling of a horse's bridle or a footstep, interrupted his tirade. She and Jacob broke apart like two halves of a lightning-struck cottonwood. Serenity looked over her shoulder. Zora was still slumped against the wall, Victoria on one side of her, Caridad on the other. Neither one was looking toward her and Jacob.

She could only pray they hadn't seen.

"You'd better get Zora to camp," Jacob said, as if nothing had happened. "I've still got business here."

Her business. But he was right. Zora had to come first.

"Is there anyone left to ask about the Reniers?" she asked, echoing Jacob's pretense of composure.

"The saloon keeper will talk to me. There's an old miner in one of the cabins at the edge of town, and a..." He hesitated. "A lady in the other."

Serenity was fairly certain what he meant by "lady." Under other circumstances, Jacob's absurd and belated concern for her feminine sensibilities might have amused her.

"I'll take Zora, then," she said, "and send someone back to show you to the camp."

"I'll find you," he said. He took a step toward the saloon, then paused without looking back. "Did I hurt you?" he asked.

Her arms were still tingling, but his words made the discomfort go away as if it had never been. "No," she said. "You didn't."

He nodded and continued on his way.

Serenity walked back across the street.

"How is she?" she asked Victoria.

"A little better, I think," the blacksmith said.

"If only I had been there earlier," Caridad muttered. She sighed in resignation. "If you are ready, I can take you to the place I found to make camp." She bent close to Zora. "Can you ride, *amiga?*"

Zora lifted her head. Her eyes were dull. "I can ride," she said.

"I'll get the horses," Victoria said.

"I'm afraid you ain't goin' anywhere," Mordecai Perry said, appearing suddenly with a gun in his hand. "Victoria James, you're wanted for murder."

CHAPTER ELEVEN

JACOB MOVED WITH wolfish speed, sprinting across the street and planting himself between Perry and Victoria before even Caridad could reach for her guns.

"You put that down, Mordecai," he said. "I don't know what the hell you're talking about, but there won't be any more shooting here today."

The other man didn't relax his posture. "I don't make a habit of shootin' women," he said, "and I don't aim to shoot one now, 'less I'm forced to it."

Serenity had risen and was standing beside Victoria, a look of disbelief on her face. "You must be insane," she said. "Victoria never killed anyone."

Perry's eyes narrowed. "What exactly is she to you, missy?"

"She's my friend."

"That's too bad." Perry met Jacob's gaze. "I told you I had business in this town. I followed these three all the way from Doña Ana County, and I ain't givin' up now."

Caridad's fingers hovered above her guns, and Perry casually shifted his aim toward her. "If any of you have a mind to interfere, someone's likely to get hurt, and I don't think any of us want that."

No, Jacob didn't want that. He'd known Mordecai too long to doubt that he was after Victoria for a good reason. At the very beginning, Serenity had told him that nearly all the women who had come to Avalon had suffered at the hands of men, and they all had secrets.

Just how many such secrets was the blacksmith keeping? And did Serenity know about them?

"You have obviously mistaken Miss Curtis for someone else, Mr. Perry," Serenity said. "You are not taking her anywhere." She glanced at Jacob. "Mr. Constantine told you that I can shoot, and he wasn't lying. Caridad is even faster than I am. I don't think I need to tell you of Mr. Constantine's skill with a gun. You may disable one of us, but there will be two more to stop you."

Perry looked hard at Jacob. "That right, Jacob? You gonna stand in the way of the law?"

A few weeks ago Jacob would have had a ready answer. A few weeks ago, before he had lost his head, he'd still had a little sense left.

"Right now I don't know what the law is," he said. "I've known Miss Curtis a little while myself, and I've never seen anything to suggest she's capable of killing anyone." He looked at Victoria, who was trembling and seemed to be on the verge of tears. "You know what this is all about, Miss Curtis?"

"I don't want anyone to get hurt because of me," she whispered, gazing at the dirt between her boots. "I'll go with him."

"Chingados!" Caridad exploded. "What is this foolishness? You have done nothing!"

"Maybe you'd like to talk in private," Jacob suggested quietly to the women. "I'll hear what Perry has to say."

Serenity obviously saw the wisdom in such a course.

She caught Caridad's eye, and the Mexican woman helped Zora to her feet. Serenity took Victoria's arm, and together they walked away.

Perry looked as if he might protest, but he held his tongue. Once the women were out of hearing, he faced Jacob with a mixture of disbelief and hostility.

"What in hell's happened to you, Jacob?" he demanded, holstering his gun. "I never seen you try go against the law or cater to any woman."

"I don't cater to anyone," Jacob said coldly. "I just want a few more facts before you go carting Miss Curtis off to some jail."

Muttering under his breath, Perry returned to his horse, opened one saddlebag and withdrew a stained piece of paper. "This here's a warrant for Mrs. Walter James's arrest. You can see it's genuine."

Jacob took the warrant out of Perry's hand. It looked genuine, all right, and there was no reason Perry would be after Victoria if it wasn't. The charge was murder.

"What exactly did she do?" he asked.

Perry took the paper back. "Killed her husband. Knifed him in the belly. He died slow, they say."

If they'd sent a bounty hunter after her, it must have been pretty bad. "Who saw this supposed murder?" Jacob asked.

"She was seen running away from the house with blood all over her hands and clothes just before they found the body. She went on the run after that and managed to keep hidden until I went after her." Perry smoothed his mustache again. "I heard tell a woman of her description was seen at a ranch on the east side of the Organs. I was on my way there when I saw these females ride out. Pretty easy to recognize the murderess."

"You know why she killed her husband?" he asked.

"It ain't my business to know why. I only bring 'em back for trial. Maybe she found out he was gettin' a little on the side." Perry's lips thinned in an unpleasant smile. "I can understand why any man would want to get away from her. She's got shoulders like a buffalo bull."

Jacob smiled just as unpleasantly. "You ever seen her before that day in New Mexico?"

"Can't say as I have."

"She might have those shoulders because she's been working as a blacksmith."

A guffaw burst from Perry's chest. "A female blacksmith?"

"At the ranch you were looking for."

"I'll be damned."

Jacob had a feeling one of them would indeed be damned by the time this was over. "I think we should let her speak for herself before you take her into custody."

"I ain't no judge or jury. I'm here to do a job. Ain't nothin' personal in it."

"Then do it as a favor to an old friend."

A heavy silence fell between them. Perry clearly didn't like where this was going, not one bit. Jacob didn't, either. But he couldn't get Victoria's scared, hopeless expression out of his mind any more than Serenity's trusting look when she'd warned Perry that Jacob would be on their side.

He didn't want to see that look change to shock when she realized he wasn't.

"They're coming back now," Jacob said, keeping his hands well away from his gun. The women—including Zora, who seemed steadier on her feet—clustered protectively around Victoria. Serenity whispered something in Victoria's ear and embraced her, then marched directly up to Perry, Caridad on her heels.

"I've heard Victoria's story," she said. "She admits she killed her husband, but she says he was going to kill her. It was self-defense."

"That's for a judge and jury to decide," Perry said.

He wasn't smiling anymore, and Jacob knew the situation was getting trickier every second. "Go on, Miss Cumberland," he said.

Serenity glanced back at Victoria, then faced Jacob. "I'd like to speak to you alone."

Caridad folded her arms and took a wide stance in front of Victoria. Keeping one eye on Perry, Jacob let Serenity take him aside.

"Victoria told me everything," she said under her breath. "I always knew she'd had an unhappy marriage, but I never realized…" She looked up into Jacob's eyes. "Did you ever know a woman whose husband mistreated her, Jacob?"

The question hit him hard. He'd never mistreated Ruth. He'd only neglected her, too intent on his work to notice if she was unhappy, never loving her quite enough.

"Victoria was badly hurt," Serenity said, before he could find an answer. "She was beaten again and again by a man who took pleasure in hitting her with his fists until she couldn't stand or even crawl."

It never occurred to Jacob to doubt Victoria's story. He knew it played out a hundred times every day, all over the West. But that didn't mean anyone else would believe her. Victoria had admitted she'd done the crime, and eyewitness testimony about her bloody flight would stack the odds against her from the start. No justification in the world would seem good enough to the men who would sit in judgment over her.

"She had to defend herself," Serenity went on, grabbing Jacob's arm and holding on as if he might walk away before she was finished. "He had already beaten her nearly to death. She picked up the nearest weapon she could find. She wasn't even trying to kill him, just to stop him from killing her." She shook him. "It's true, Jacob. I swear it!"

He found it harder and harder to meet her gaze. "If it was up to me," he said, "I'd let her go. But Perry has the law on his side."

"The law!" She let go, took a step back and regarded him as if she'd never seen him before. "You've talked about justice. There's precious little of that for women in this country. They'll want her to be guilty, because men can't abide the thought that women might have their own minds and don't live just for their menfolk. They'll be afraid what happened to Walter James could happen to them someday." She wiped her palms on her trousers. "You've been a lawman for years. Can you deny what I'm saying is true?"

He couldn't very well deny it when he'd just been

thinking the same thing himself. "Serenity, you don't know—"

"Are you going to let Perry take her?" she demanded. "Just sit by, and let him tie her up and carry her off, even though they'll probably hang her?"

"Do you want her to be on the run for the rest of her life?"

"We can protect her."

"What you're suggesting is dangerous, Serenity," he said. "You'll make yourself a partner in Victoria's crime."

"But *you* don't have to be." She set her jaw and looked away. "We're not letting Perry take her. If you don't want to help us stop him, I understand. But don't try to get in our way."

"Serenity." He caught her chin with two fingers and turned her head toward him. She was flushed and angry and ashamed, her gaze accusing and pleading at the same time. She'd presumed on his loyalty to her and her women, and was beginning to realize how hazardous that assumption had been. If he turned his back on her and Victoria now, any friendship or trust between them would be gone. And he would be responsible for whatever happened to her and the other women.

The Code gave him a clear answer, but he couldn't accept its verdict.

Serenity jerked her chin out of his hand and spun to walk away.

He grabbed her arm.

"Can you trust me, Serenity?" he asked.

Her eyes widened with hope. "You'll help us?"

"If I can."

"What are you going to do?"

He had an idea, one he didn't like at all, and he didn't want her to know ahead of time, just in case she might get herself into worse trouble. "You'll have to trust me."

Serenity wet her lips, began to speak, then fell silent again.

Maybe he was asking more of her than he had any right to. They might have become friends, but any loyalty she felt for him couldn't stand against her commitment to her women.

"I can't," she said, her voice breaking. "Victoria is under my protection. No one will ever abuse her again."

She turned again and left him standing there like a man who had just lost his last nickel in a crooked card game. She rejoined the other women and stood silently beside Caridad, facing Perry with a look that could have stopped a speeding railroad train in its tracks.

Perry's fingers twitched. He was obviously ready to draw his gun the second anyone so much as fluttered an eyelash.

"Mrs. James," he said, "I plan on gettin' a little ridin' in before the sun sets. You got anything to pack up, you'd best do it now."

"I'm afraid we can't permit that, Mr. Perry," Serenity said. "You'll have to shoot all of us first."

Armoring himself against Serenity's contempt, Jacob walked up behind her.

"You can't stop the course of the law, Miss Cumberland," he said. "And I won't let you try."

Caridad spat a curse and went for her right-hand gun.

Jacob was faster. He drew, aimed and shot it out of

her hand, careful to hit the barrel instead of her fingers. She jumped backward, shaking her hand furiously.

Serenity stared at Jacob, stunned by his interference in spite of her decision not to trust him.

He couldn't bear to look at her.

"It's no use, Serenity," he said. "Mrs. James, you'd best step out if you want to keep your friends safe."

To her credit, the blacksmith didn't hesitate. She left the others, ignoring Serenity's muffled cry of protest, and walked straight to Perry.

Zora held Serenity back when she would have followed.

"You done the right thing, Mrs. James," Perry said, taking Victoria by the arm and wrapping a rope around her wrists. "I don't like to have to tie you, but if you try to make a run for it, I wouldn't want to shoot you."

Victoria hung her head. "I won't try to escape." She looked at Serenity, who was weeping silently, and then to Caridad and Zora, who showed no expression at all. No one interfered until Perry began to lead Victoria toward his horses.

That was when Serenity pulled her Peacemaker again and ran after them. Without conscious thought Jacob intercepted her. He wrapped his arms around her and let her struggle, kicking and swearing, while Perry threw Victoria up into the saddle of his spare mount and untied his own horse from the rail.

Jacob closed his eyes and rested his cheek against Serenity's hair. It was soft and smelled of sage. He tried to imagine he was holding her for very different reasons, feeling her melt in his arms and whisper that she trusted him. That she loved—

The unexpected blow to his stomach so surprised him that he almost released her before he realized what she'd done. She knew she couldn't hurt him, but she'd counted on catching him off guard so she could get free.

"Don't," Jacob said, pressing her face into his shoulder. "There's nothing you can do."

She wept with grief and rage, her arms trapped uselessly at her sides. Over her head, Jacob could see Caridad cradling her stunned right hand tightly against her chest. She wouldn't be using that hand any time soon. Zora had mounted her horse and was riding south out of town, slumped in her saddle like a woman already dead. Whatever had happened in the saloon had drained every last bit of spirit out of her.

Jacob had never hated himself as much as he did at that moment. He didn't let Serenity go until Perry and Victoria were well out of sight.

"You can't stop him now," he said, as she wrenched herself free. "He won't let you get close enough to shoot."

Serenity's eyes were cold, spearing him with ice instead of fire. She marched to the end of the street, where her horse still stood, rifled through her saddlebags and pulled out a sheaf of bills. She strode back to Jacob and threw the bundle at his feet.

"This is half of what I intended to pay you," she said. "I don't require your services any longer."

Jacob let the bundle lie there between them. "I can't take your money when I haven't done anything," he said quietly.

"You've done plenty." She gave the bundle a kick,

scrubbed at her cheeks and walked away again. "Cari, let's find Zora and get out of here."

With a savage glance in Jacob's direction, Caridad followed Serenity to gather the horses. Jacob knew he still had a little time; Serenity would be going after Perry as soon as she could, but she had sense enough not to go rushing off when she knew he might be expecting pursuit.

Knowing that he couldn't just leave Serenity's money lying in the dirt where anyone could take it, Jacob picked up the bundle, tucked it inside his vest, and waited until Caridad and Serenity were on their horses. Serenity cast him one final look full of anguish, contempt and profound loss. Then she kicked her horse into a trot, and she and the other women vanished behind the dry, rolling hills to the south.

His feet as heavy as his heart, Jacob went for his own horses. It wasn't until he was in the saddle that he began to think clearly again. Head cocked, he listened to make sure that Serenity, Caridad and Zora were still heading away from town, then reined his own mount east after Perry.

It wasn't difficult to find them, though Perry had taken the precaution of choosing the most broken ground and changing direction every quarter mile. Victoria was riding with her head hung over her saddle horn. It was pretty clear she had given up.

A swell of deep anger built under Jacob's ribs. He kept on riding until Perry, human though he was, couldn't help but hear him.

The bounty hunter reined in his horse and twisted in the saddle. Victoria lifted her head.

"Constantine!" Perry said as Jacob drew near, his hand falling to his waist. "What are you doin' here?"

So much for old friendship. Perry didn't trust him, and Jacob was about to justify his doubts.

"I wondered why you let us go so easy," Perry said when Jacob didn't answer. "You got somethin' to say, say it."

Jacob dismounted. "Victoria," he said, "you'd better get down."

Perry pulled his horse around to face Jacob. "I don't know if you've gone crazy," he said, "but you ain't interferin' with my prisoner."

Victoria glanced from her captor to Jacob and stayed right where she was.

Jacob couldn't blame her.

"I can't let you take her, Mordecai," he said. "I didn't want the women to get involved, but now it's just you and me."

"But it ain't." Perry drew his gun and aimed it at Victoria. "You make a move and she dies. I'll get the reward one way or another."

Jacob laughed. "You scared, Mordecai? So scared of me that you'd threaten a woman to get out of facing me in a fair fight?"

The mockery worked. Perry leaped from the saddle, all his attention for Jacob. Eyes wide, Victoria dismounted, as well, keeping her horse between herself and Mordecai.

"You her lover?" Perry asked with a sneer. "Is that why you want her free?"

Jacob refused to rise to the bait. "I'm helping these women find outlaws who've done far worse than Mrs.

James could imagine. Maybe they're the ones you should be going after."

Perry shook his head. "Never thought I'd see the day when you turned renegade, Constantine. You bring shame on the Rangers. They'll be glad when I report you dead."

"You want to see a renegade, Mordecai?" Jacob said. "I'll show you one." Slowly and calmly, he unbuckled his gun belt and tossed it on the ground. He removed his coat and vest, and began to unbutton his shirt, then sat on a convenient rock and pulled off his boots.

Perry stared with a complete lack of comprehension, his gun half-raised, as Jacob finished undressing.

"You *are* loco," Perry said, his voice dropping to a whisper. "Someone ought to put you out of your misery."

"You're welcome to try," Jacob said. And then he Changed.

With a shout of astonishment and horror, Perry aimed wildly, cracking off a single shot before Victoria flung herself on his back and threw him to the ground.

Snarling, Jacob attacked from the front, closing his jaws around Perry's wrist when he tried to take a fresh grip on his gun. Victoria jumped away, but she'd done enough. Jacob shook Perry's wrist until the bounty hunter was forced to drop the pistol, then planted his forepaws on Perry's chest. He lowered his head until his breath was puffing into Perry's face and his teeth were inches from the bounty hunter's nose.

He stayed there until Perry's eyes glazed over and

his body went limp. Perry didn't move when Jacob backed away.

Jacob Changed again, fetched his trousers and pulled them on. Victoria was standing beside her horse when he turned around, staring in wonder not at him but at Perry.

"You all right, Miss Curtis?" he asked.

Her head came up. "I think so," she said.

Few humans would have been as game as she was after what she'd seen. Jacob had an idea that she wasn't as calm as she seemed, but he would have to wait to talk to her. Right now Perry was his main concern.

He ambled over to where Perry still lay, and stood with his legs to either side of the bounty hunter's feet.

"Mordecai," he said. "You hear me?"

The other man groaned and lifted his injured arm, cradling it against his chest. "What…what *are* you?" he gasped.

"Most people would say I'm a monster. As far as you're concerned, they're right."

"But you…you…"

"I could have killed you, Mordecai. If I was after your life, that's what I'd have done. But there's only one thing I want from you. You need to ride back to wherever you came from and don't ever think of coming after Miss Curtis again." He leaned over, staring into Perry's eyes. "You understand me? If you ever try to take her, or come near any of those women, I'll kill you. No matter where you go, I'll find you."

Perry made a croaking sound.

Jacob nudged the bounty hunter's boot with his bare foot.

"Give me your word, Mordecai—your word as a Ranger—and I'll let you go."

"I…" Perry squeezed his eyes shut. "I give my word."

"Just one other thing. I wouldn't advise you tell anyone what you've seen here today. You'll be the one they call loco." Jacob stepped back. "Miss Curtis, can you ride?"

Shaken as she must be, Victoria nodded.

"Then mount up."

She did as he asked, while Jacob watched Perry struggle to his feet, still holding his arm against his chest.

"Ride out," Jacob said. "You can take your gun."

Crippled as he was, Perry was too good a horseman to need any help getting into the saddle. He stared at Jacob for another long moment, picked up his gun and clambered up onto his horse. Without a word or backward glance, he rode away.

CHAPTER TWELVE

THE SOUR TASTE of defeat flooded Jacob's mouth. Oh, he'd won, all right. But he'd lost, too. He had succeeded in humiliating a man he'd never seen show fear before. He'd gone against the law and the Code without knowing anything about the murder except what Perry had said…or what Serenity believed.

"Mr. Constantine?" Victoria said.

He shook himself. "Perry won't come back," he said. "Serenity and the others were riding out of town to look for Zora when I left. Let's go find them."

He spoke quietly as he finished putting on his clothes, explaining as briefly as possible what he was and why she didn't have to be afraid of him.

"Does anyone else at Avalon know?" she asked, twining her fingers in her horse's mane.

"Serenity does. And Zora. You're the third." He mounted, and drew his horse alongside hers. "I'd appreciate it if you'd keep it to yourself for now."

She laughed nervously. "I would never tell anyone," she said. "You said it yourself to Mr. Perry. They'd think I was crazy."

He inclined his head in appreciation of her courage and reined his horse back the way he had come, Victoria just behind him. They'd gone no more than a few dozen yards when Jacob caught a scent that raised the fine hairs on the back of his neck. He pulled up as a wolf with a pelt as dark as his own loped into view.

Zora was beautiful as a wolf, but when she Changed she was magnificent, all smooth muscle and shining dark hair. "Victoria!" she said, looking back and forth between Jacob and her friend. "Where is Perry?"

If she'd been dazed and barely conscious before, Zora was fully alert now and clearly ready to fight.

Jacob pointed his chin over his shoulder.

"Gone," he said. "He won't be troubling us anymore."

Zora's nostrils flared, and Jacob knew she would have liked nothing better than to give chase and teach Perry another lesson. She approached Victoria's horse on silent feet.

"I did not mean to make you afraid," she said. "I only wanted to stop Perry."

Victoria gave another hoarse laugh. "Are there any more werewolves I should know about?"

Zora met Jacob's gaze. "No," she said. She touched Victoria's leg. "I am glad you are well."

"I'm glad *you* are, too," Victoria said, holding out her hand.

Zora took it, and they shared a private moment of relief and happiness.

Somehow Jacob wasn't much surprised when he heard three sets of hoofbeats coming from the east. A little while later, Caridad and Serenity appeared, leading a third horse behind them.

Serenity's face was flushed with an emotion much less hostile than the one she'd shown Jacob when they'd parted. After she had spoken with Victoria and Zora, she left Caridad with the two other women and rode over to join Jacob.

"You stopped Perry," she said.

He nodded brusquely, not trusting himself to speak.

"I misjudged you without reason," she said hesitantly. "I should have known you would never have let him take Victoria."

Her apology released the knot in his belly. "You couldn't have known that," he said. "I've known Mordecai a long time. We rode together for years. I could have taken his side."

"And you believe in the law." She leaned over to touch his arm. "You had to compromise your principles for my friend. I owe you a debt."

The formality of her words erased his good feelings. He reached inside his vest and pulled out the wad of bills. "You're talking about paying me, aren't you?" he said.

She didn't flinch, but he saw the hurt in her eyes. "You have every right to be angry," she said. "I wish I could make it up to you."

The idea of just how she could make it up to him filled Jacob's mind and sent the blood rushing to other parts of his body, but he didn't let her see what he was thinking. He was half-ashamed he'd even let such thoughts enter his head after what she'd told him about her fiance.

"Did Zora lead you here?" he asked, quickly changing the subject.

Serenity seemed glad to follow his lead. "Yes. We followed her when she rode out of town. It was her plan all along to go after Perry herself." She glanced at Zora, who had taken a blanket from a bedroll and wrapped herself in it. "She seems all right now. We still don't know why she acted so unlike herself in the saloon."

But Jacob wondered if Zora's strange behavior had some connection to the same kind of suffering Victoria and Serenity had endured.

They rode back toward Bethel without any further words between them. Caridad had found a good spot for camp a quarter mile south of town, and Jacob suggested they settle in while he went on to question the saloon keeper. The women had called too much attention to themselves, and there might be more loose guns wandering around. He didn't want to risk getting into another fight.

To his surprise, Serenity agreed and sat down to speak to Victoria, while Caridad searched for sticks and kindling. Jacob thought that riding alone would help him get his thoughts in order, but it didn't. By the time he reached Bethel, he was ready to bite the head off anyone who crossed him.

Fortunately for the townsfolk, few as they were, no one tried to give him any trouble. On the other hand, none of them could answer any of his questions, either. While the barkeep wasn't able or willing to supply him with any more information about the Reniers, he was able to learn a fair bit more from the man he'd shot in the knee, who was lying on a cot in the saloon's back room. He was sufficiently scared to spill his guts when Jacob pressed him, refusing to admit any direct dealings with the Renier renegades but almost eager to tell Jacob the direction the outlaws had gone the last time they'd passed through. He went as far as to hint that their base of operations was within two days' ride of town.

Jacob knew the trail wouldn't be easy to follow after so long—not even for a werewolf—and two days' ride covered a hell of a lot of territory. But it was something to go on.

But when he rode out to join the women in camp, the one problem he still hadn't solved continued to hover over him like a hungry buzzard. However earnestly Serenity might promise not to take crazy risks again—and she hadn't actually made any such promise—he knew the time had come to find another way to leave her behind. He couldn't be responsible for her anymore. He'd gotten too close to her, enjoyed their kisses too much and let lust creep into his heart, risking not only the Code but the purpose to which he had devoted his life.

There was only one way to get rid of Serenity now. He would have to tell her that he'd learned nothing in Bethel, that the trail had gone as cold as a three-day-old corpse.

He laughed at himself. That wouldn't stop her. Neither would his riding after the outlaws by himself. She would simply convince Zora to track him again, and Zora would succeed.

But Zora had never wanted Serenity to go in the first place. When they'd argued after the women's arrival in town, she'd demanded to know why he hadn't managed to send Serenity back to Avalon. He hadn't had a good explanation, but he'd had plenty to say about her stupidity in leading Caridad and Victoria to him and Serenity. They'd parted with nothing resolved.

Now they might have reason to work together as allies—for Serenity's sake.

As if his thoughts had summoned her, Zora's scent came to him on the evening wind. She rode toward him slowly, looking as if someone had ripped the pride right out of her and left it lying in the dirt for the coyotes to finish off.

"Constantine," she said, raising her hand in a brief salute.

He reined in his horse. "Zora," he said. "Where are the others?"

"In camp. I told them I would make certain that Perry was really gone."

"But that isn't what you rode out for," he said.

She met his gaze. "I am ashamed."

Jacob didn't see any point in dancing around the subject. "What happened in the saloon?" he asked.

"I was a coward."

"You're no coward. What did those men do?"

Zora dropped her gaze. "They called me names. They tried to make me drink."

It didn't sound like much, but Jacob had an idea it had been worse than that. "It wasn't easy for you, growing up half Indian and half white."

She looked up again. "Life is not easy."

"I didn't know there were werewolves among the Apache."

"There are men and women who shift shapes, but they are not welcome in the tribes."

Jacob knew the Navajo beliefs about "skinwalkers" and their evil nature, but he'd never heard the Apache talk about wolf-men. It didn't surprise him that they felt the same way, just like most human beings of any color.

"Was it your mother or father?" he asked.

"My mother. She was cast out soon after she turned fifteen." Zora's mouth twisted. "She was lucky. She found a man to protect her before she starved or had to sell her body."

"Your father?"

"Yes. But he knew nothing of my mother's kind. He had come west three years before the war to settle in Texas. I was born a year after. When the war started, he went back to fight. My mother was not accepted by the other whites."

"And you were cast out again."

"Not cast out. But the time was hard on my mother. She knew no others of her own kind. She was alone. When my father returned, she died. He did not know what to do with me, but he had money to buy many things. He sent me to a white school."

About the worst hell someone like her could endure. He didn't have to ask what she'd had to put up with, the taunting she'd faced every day, the hatred. Having to hide her true nature without the companionship of her own kind.

"I escaped when I was fourteen," she said. "I went to my tribe. They would not have me." She looked away again. "I learned to find peace in a bottle of whiskey. It was a long time before I found myself again. I swore I would never go back."

But those men in the saloon had tried to make her drink. They'd humiliated her, driven her back to a time of grief and loneliness.

She hadn't been able to shed her past. But he had no more right to judge her than he did Serenity or Victoria. Not the way he judged himself.

"It is not an excuse," she said. "I will not forget that my weakness put Serenity in danger. I only tell you this so that you will not think I will weaken again."

"I didn't figure you would."

They were quiet for a time, sharing an understanding that went deeper than words. Finally Jacob spoke, seeing the chance to ask a few questions that had been on his mind.

"What was in that letter you brought Serenity?" he asked.

If she was surprised by the question, she didn't show it. "Caridad said it was from her family."

"Her family? I thought they were dead."

"Her parents were killed. I did not read the letter, but it was sent by the husband of her mother's sister."

Serenity had never mentioned kin other than her parents, and he'd never thought to ask her. "Where was it sent from?" he asked.

"I have not heard of it, but Caridad says it is near a place called Kerrville."

Kerrville was only a little closer to Bethel than Fredericksburg, and the two towns were only about twenty miles apart.

"Why did you come all the way out here to give her the letter?" he asked.

"Because her mother's sister is dying, and the woman's husband has asked her to come to their home."

So she had kin who cared enough about her to want her to be with her aunt when she passed. Serenity had said she'd ridden west after escaping the fire. If she had close relations living so close to her parents' farm, why not ride south to Kerrville? Why had she chosen to make her own life away from those who could have sheltered and comforted her after the loss of her parents?

He was sure of one thing. Serenity had been pretty upset after she'd read the letter. An idea came into his head, one that might solve his problem.

"What did she say about this letter?" he asked.

"She has not spoken of it. But I think…" Zora looked carefully at Jacob. "Why does this concern you?"

"I've learned a few things that may help me find the outlaws we're looking for," he said. "You asked me why I hadn't stopped Serenity from getting this far. I tried to—my plan didn't work, but I haven't changed my mind."

She studied him thoughtfully. "I do not argue with you," she said.

So far, so good. "Do you know anything more about these people of hers?" Jacob asked.

"I can only tell you that she comes from a place very different from most whites," she said. "Caridad says her people do not believe in fighting. They live away from other whites and worship their God in silence instead of with shouting and singing."

Jacob had seen plenty of "shouting and singing" in houses of worship where folks were more enthusiastic about showing off than following the Lord's Commandments. But silence…

That alone didn't really tell him anything. But the bit about not believing in fighting did.

"Quakers," he said, hardly believing it. "Is that what you mean?"

"I think this is the word Caridad spoke," Zora said. "You know these people?"

"A little." He knew that not all Quakers were alike, but from what Zora was describing, Serenity's people were traditionalists who'd stuck to the old ways instead of adopting the more open customs of most Protestant churches in America. Their communities tended to be close-knit, sharing resources equally, and valuing honesty and plain speaking. The few times Jacob had run across them, they'd made it plain they preferred to keep to themselves rather than be part of the corrupt society that surrounded them.

And they meant it when they said they didn't commit violence. They lived the Lord's admonition to turn the other cheek.

That made what Jacob knew about Serenity's past seem even worse than he'd thought, and at the same time all the more puzzling. If the outlaws had attacked a Quaker homestead, they would have found easy prey. There would have been almost no resistance. They might as well have been shooting infants in their cradles.

Serenity would have been raised to believe that things like hate and revenge were wrong. The murder of her family must have destroyed years of belief in pacifism and loving thy neighbor. She had become an entirely different person, willing to put a man to the noose. Willing to kill.

He'd always thought her name didn't match what he knew of her. Now he understood why. And he thought he could see why she might have set out on her own rather than go to her kinfolk, close as Quakers tended to be. If she hated so much, maybe she couldn't see her way clear to being around people who couldn't or wouldn't share her feelings—especially if she'd been planning revenge from the moment she found herself the only survivor of the outlaws' attack.

It must have been hell. Hell to be separated from her kin and community, hell to be alone with the feelings eating her up inside.

But maybe—impossible as the idea seemed right now—once she got back to her own people she would find some of the things she'd lost. Things that would take the place of her need for revenge. Things he could never give her.

His breath seized up in his chest. Zora's horse tossed its head and snorted, reminding him to breathe again.

"Quakers are good folk," he said. "If they're asking her to see her aunt, she should go."

"I do not think she wants to," Zora said.

"She just needs to be reminded of what's important. You can help me make that happen."

"How?"

"I'm going to tell Serenity that the trail's gone cold. I'll suggest that she go to her kinfolk while I keep looking, then come get her when I locate the outlaws."

"I do not think your idea will work."

"You don't think she'll believe me?"

"You will make it very hard for her. She will wish to believe you, but she will doubt."

Which wasn't any wonder after what had happened with Perry.

"You can help me make her believe," he said.

Zora held Jacob's gaze. "I wanted you to stop her from finding these men and going to her death. But there are worse hurts."

"If you mean her not getting her revenge..."

"You care for her very much. I know this is true. But is it not your intention to leave her and never return?"

That had always been his intention, hadn't it? If he'd managed to leave Serenity behind, he would have gone on to finish what they'd started. But after that...

He'd never thought about "after that." He hadn't needed to. He would go his way and she would go hers.

"She cares for you," Zora said. "You must know this."

He stared at her. That word, *care,* had been flung around pretty freely, and he still didn't know what in hell it meant. What it meant to *him*.

"I don't know what you mean," he said roughly.

"She has felt nothing but hate for any man since I met her," Zora said. "Since you came, she is different."

Different? Maybe she'd calmed down a little from the day she'd rescued him. She'd let him touch her—more than once. She'd trusted him, even if that trust had slipped a little today. But had he *changed* her?

His horse felt his agitation and tossed its head. He gentled it, struggling to gentle his own turbulent emotions, as well.

"What are you trying to say?" he asked Zora.

She touched her breast. "It is not enough to keep her from finding these men and killing them. She has lost much. You have begun to help her find those things again. She will need your help long after her enemies are dead."

He finally understood. She was asking him if he would stay with Serenity. Not just now, but for all time. And that was crazy.

His throat contracted painfully. "Why do you think I've helped her?" he asked. "You've barely seen her since we left Avalon." He swallowed. "Did she say—?"

"She has not spoken, but any fool could see it." She searched Jacob's eyes. "Do you deny such feelings?"

Her feelings? Or his own? He'd spent the past eight years living from day to day, like a wolf. If he saw the Reniers punished, that would mark the end of a phase of his life that had become so much a part of him that he didn't know what he would do when it was over. He had nothing and no one to go back to.

But Serenity did. She'd made a good place for herself, and once she finally let go of her past she could shape her life exactly the way she wanted it to be, with or without the companionship of a man. It was possible she might find some decent man who could make her forget she had ever hated the male sex. A man who would gentle her, caress her body, kiss her breasts, stroke her secret places until she opened to him like a blossom to the sun…

Pain that was far more than physical rose from Jacob's groin into his chest. Some man, but not Jacob Constantine. She might get over her dislike of men, but never of what he was. Not completely. And even if she accepted his nature—even if she wanted him to stay with her, which was a crazy idea by itself—she needed something he didn't know how to give.

She needed love. She needed devotion, someone worthy of her, who could teach her to trust and discover all the beauty she'd forgotten. Someone who could promise to settle down, respect her strength and accept her friends. Be the kind of mate he himself should have been for Ruth's sake.

"Maybe you don't see as clearly as you think," he said. "If she goes back to her kin, she'll have a hell of a lot better chance to find what she lost."

Zora looked out across the dry, rolling plain and watched a lone cow amble along the wash. "It is her happiness I wish for," she said.

"I can't give her what she needs. Maybe her family can."

Zora looked at him again. "She will not easily let you go. I do not think you will easily let *her* go, either."

"I promised Serenity I'd find these men, and I will."

It wasn't an answer, and Zora knew it. "I have wondered if you do not want to find these men for yourself," she said.

The sudden accusation startled him. "I'm a bounty hunter," he said. "As you once pointed out, I'm the best man to hunt other werewolves."

"But you said you would not do so when I asked you. What made you change your mind?"

"That's my business."

She held his gaze, wolf to wolf, half challenging and half apologetic. "Yes," she said. "I will help you to convince Serenity to go to her people. But it will be easier if you come with us to this Quaker place."

"You plan to go with her?"

"We will see her safely to her family. If you offer to do the same, she will not question."

The hell of it was, she was probably right. Jacob didn't believe for a minute that Serenity felt about him the way Zora had implied. But Serenity wouldn't think he was abandoning her if he accompanied her to Kerr County. She would believe he was waiting until she was done with her visit to resume their search. If he was lucky, by the time he left she would have a reason to stay behind, maybe even give up her hunger for revenge.

And he wouldn't see her again. That would be the best thing for her. For both of them.

"I'll come," he said. "But I won't stay long. Her folks aren't likely to want me there, anyway." He tried to smile. "I'm not the kind they'd approve of. You'll have to make sure she stays behind, even if she doesn't want to."

"We will find a way to keep her from going after you." Zora glanced past him toward Bethel. "Is your business finished here?"

"Yes. There's no need to go back there again."

"Then we should return to the camp. Serenity will be worried."

And he wouldn't be easing her feelings any when he told her he hadn't been able to learn any more about the Reniers. He would have to lie with complete conviction and keep on lying all the way to the Quaker settlement. He would still be lying when he rode off to find the Reniers, knowing he would forever be robbing her of her revenge.

But she would finally be safe, and so would the

Code. He would send word when the Reniers were locked up and facing the noose. He could do that much for her, even though they would never meet again.

Like a gut-shot man who doesn't know he's already dead, Jacob followed Zora back to camp.

CHAPTER THIRTEEN

TOLERANCE, TEXAS, LOOKED much the same as it had seven years ago. Once they had returned from San Antonio, the prodigal settlers had rebuilt the burned barn and house in the same simple style, and restored the other houses they had abandoned to the elements. There were new whitewashed fences and vegetable gardens, pigpens and chicken coops, and all the features of a prosperous farming community. Cattle and horses grazed in pastures among stately oaks and late-summer wildflowers. Across the road to the north, close to the Guadalupe River, where the most arable land was located, crops grew in fields protected by scarecrows and split-rail fences.

"It's very pretty," Victoria said.

Serenity came out of herself and tried to smile. "My…the Quakers are hardworking folk," she said.

It was all she was able to say at the moment. Her throat was too choked with emotion, her heart with memories that set it to aching like the phantom pain from a missing limb. She preferred anger; anger had kept her alive, kept her fighting, had given her the strength to rebuild her world when it had seemed shattered beyond recovery.

But in this place, so peaceful and serene, the anger was slow in coming. She was a child again. Papa was repairing a fence in the outer pasture. Mama, Elizabeth and Aunt Martha were baking pies. Levi and William were hitching the horses to the wagon, preparing to drive to Kerrville for supplies. Uncle Lester and all the other Friends contributed each in his or her own way, working not for themselves but for this small, hopeful community built in peace and love.

Maybe it would have stayed that way, if it hadn't been for the illness that had taken most of the cattle, the drought, the misfortunes that had befallen them one after the other. That last winter had been hard, and everyone but Papa and Levi had chosen to return to the community of Friends in San Antonio.

Closing her eyes, Serenity imagined she smelled the stench of burning wood. But it was all in her imagination. The blackened remains of the old house lay beneath the foundations of the new building. She wondered if they had gathered up the ashes and prayed over them before they buried them.

"This is not good," Caridad muttered to Zora. "We should go back."

Caridad had been against this visit from the moment Zora and Jacob had returned to their camp to tell Serenity that no one in Bethel had been able to reveal anything more about the outlaws or their present location. It didn't help that Jacob had pressed for the trip. Somehow Caridad sensed how difficult Serenity would find this homecoming. Or perhaps she had feared Serenity would never return to Avalon again.

There was no need to worry about that, Serenity thought. None whatsoever. True, she had been deeply discouraged when Jacob had told her that their journey to Bethel had been for nothing. But after the harm that had been done there—two men wounded, one man dead, Zora's abuse, the incident with Perry—even finding the outlaws' trail hardly seemed worth the price.

Then there had been her treatment of Jacob…her ugly assumption that he would side with Perry. She'd apologized more than once, but her conscience still wasn't clear. She'd seen the hurt in his eyes when she'd accused him of betraying them—hurt he, as a man, would never want anyone to see.

But that rare glimpse of vulnerability, so much like the sensitivity he had shown when they'd spoken of their families—that, and his selflessness in confronting Perry and revealing his true nature to Victoria for the sake of her safety—had brought to full clarity the realization she had tried for weeks to ignore. Which was just how much his companionship—his mere presence—meant to her.

It meant so much that she hadn't been able to refuse when he, along with Zora and Victoria, had urged her to see her family. Of course none of them, not even Zora, knew that Tolerance was the very place where her parents had died.

But Jacob's sacrifices for Victoria's sake had forced Serenity to admit just how selfish she'd been to even think of continuing the hunt before she'd seen Aunt Martha.

The decision had been made easier when Jacob had offered to escort her and the other women to Tolerance. In spite of her reckless behavior in Bethel and their falling-out over Perry, Jacob wasn't giving up, not on her or their search. Once she had seen Aunt Martha and assured herself the old woman wasn't as sick as Uncle Lester claimed, she would be off with Jacob again.

And then? What happens when it's all over, and you and Jacob go your separate ways?

Her mind stubbornly refused to settle on the question, but it had become less difficult to put it aside as they approached the settlement. There was no room now for anything but dread.

"*Muchacha?* Are you well?"

She blinked at the sound of Caridad's voice and looked around quickly. They were approaching the picket fence that ran between the wagon road and the cluster of houses and cottages that made up the heart of the settlement. A young man she didn't recognize was coming out of the barn across the yard from the largest house. He tipped back his hat, and stared at her and her companions in obvious surprise.

It was no wonder. Over the course of time more settlers would have come to the area—Serenity and her party had already ridden past several new homesteads and farms that hadn't been there seven years ago—and it would no longer be quite so uncommon a sight to see travelers on the wagon path that served as the only road west of Tolerance. Still, everyone in this part of the county would take note of all comings and goings, and strangers would be noticed.

There was no turning back now, no way to conceal that she was no longer the meek, obedient girl she had been the last time her aunt, uncle and cousins had seen her. Not even if she had wanted to. She didn't even own a dress, and if she had, she wouldn't have brought it on her journey from Avalon.

Yet it didn't really matter; she would appear out of place here no matter what she wore, and so would her friends. Jacob had indicated that he would make camp by the Guadalupe, but she had refused to consider it. The Friends were usually hospitable to outsiders. They would freely offer shelter, food…anything a traveler might require.

While no outsider would ever penetrate the soul of the community unless he or she chose to become one of the Society of Friends, Caridad, Zora, Victoria—even Jacob—would be welcome for a few days, a week, perhaps longer if it were necessary.

But it wouldn't be necessary. No matter how sincerely the Friends asked her to stay—*if* they did—she wouldn't do it. Even if she had to tell them the reasons she had never admitted in the two letters she'd sent to them after her escape.

The young man had walked quickly from the barn to the path that led toward the largest of the houses, casting glances toward the travelers with every other step. Serenity led the others to the gate in front of the main house, hearing the distant sounds of children's laughter. This was a happy place, where children could laugh so freely.

She didn't see the children themselves, but a few minutes after the young man entered the house a modestly dressed middle-aged woman appeared in the doorway, wiping her hands on her apron and raising her hand to shade her eyes.

Serenity didn't recognize her, either, but as she reined her horse to a stop another woman, perhaps ten years younger, joined the first. Her dress, like that of her companion, was almost absurdly plain, a nondescript brown of the most common cloth, with no decoration whatsoever. She wore an equally plain bonnet tied close under her chin. Her face was careworn and weary, as unremarkable as her clothing, but Serenity would have known it anywhere.

With Victoria, Caridad and Zora behind her, Serenity dismounted and tied her horse to the fence.

"Elizabeth Selden?" she called softly.

Elizabeth gasped. "Serenity Campbell?" she cried. "Is it thee?"

Serenity walked up the neat little path to the porch. "Yes, Elizabeth," she said. "It's me."

The woman Serenity didn't know addressed a whispered question to Elizabeth, who nodded vigorously. The other woman disappeared inside the house, and Elizabeth walked briskly out onto the path.

"Dear cousin!" she said, her faded blue eyes filling with tears. "I was afraid…" She held out her arms. "I thank God that thee has come to us."

Taking that one step to meet Elizabeth was like leaping over a chasm. Serenity returned her cousin's gentle embrace and awkwardly patted her back murmuring senseless little reassurances.

At last Elizabeth drew away, searching Serenity's eyes with pity and concern. If she were alarmed by Serenity's appearance, her worn and dusty men's clothing and hat, she was too polite to mention it. "I am so glad thee is well," she said.

"And I thee," Serenity said, the once-familiar cadences of the plain language coming back to her with surprising ease. "Aunt Martha. Is she…?"

"She has been waiting for thee," Elizabeth said, sobering quickly. "We prayed thee would receive the letter."

"She is not worse?"

"The same. But seeing thee will surely lift her spirits."

Perhaps, Serenity thought, Uncle Lester hadn't been exaggerating after all. She found it difficult to continue to meet her cousin's gaze.

"Elizabeth" she said, "these are my friends." She turned to give Victoria a nod of encouragement, and the three women stepped inside the gate. "Victoria Curtis, Caridad Garcia and Zora. They have been gracious enough to escort me, and I hope it will be possible for them to stay a few days before they return."

A spark of curiosity lit Elizabeth's eyes. "Thy friends are welcome here." She looked beyond the women to Jacob, who had dismounted a few yards behind them. "Will thee not introduce thy other companion?" she asked.

Serenity found herself blushing. "Jacob Constantine," she said, "will thee…will you come meet my cousin?"

Jacob removed his hat, holding it close to his chest as he walked through the gate.

"Elizabeth," Serenity said, "this is Jacob Constantine. Jacob, my cousin Elizabeth Selden."

"Ma'am," Jacob said, inclining his head. "A pleasure."

"As it is mine," Elizabeth said with a slight smile. She was obviously bursting with questions, but she had a true Quaker's patience. "You must be thirsty," she said, addressing all of them. "Please, come inside."

It was Victoria who seemed least reluctant to obey. Caridad and Zora exchanged glances and slowly followed her. Jacob came last. Elizabeth stood to the side until the four of them, followed by Serenity, had entered the house.

It was cool and dim inside, the late-afternoon sun no longer shining through the windows that served the common room and large kitchen. A dining table big enough to seat sixteen at one time dominated the room. In many ways it was very like the kitchen Serenity remembered, and she felt a pang of fresh grief.

The man Serenity had seen by the barn stood near a cupboard against one wall, hat in hand. Serenity judged him to be not much older than herself. He was quiet and reserved, but it was obvious that he was very interested in the visitors. The older woman waited by the large table, her hands folded in her apron.

"Cousin Serenity," Elizabeth said, indicating the woman, "this is Grace Hollander." She smiled at the young man. "And this is Virgil Thompson."

Surprise momentarily halted Serenity's reply. "Virgil Thompson?" she repeated.

The young man stepped forward, smiling warmly. "Thee remembers me, Serenity Campbell, though it is long since we were children together?"

A very long time. Yet they had been friends when she was ten and he twelve, before Virgil had left with his family to settle in Colorado. Serenity even remembered having admired him in the way of a girl on the cusp of womanhood.

"I remember," she said, offering her hand.

His fingers were calloused and warm and held hers with gentle pressure.

"I have heard thy name spoken often these past months, Serenity Campbell," he said. "It is a blessing that thee has come back to us."

Serenity slipped her hand free and smiled at all three Friends. "I thank thee for thy hospitality," she said, slipping easily back into the mode of speech she had grown up with. She beckoned Victoria, Zora, Caridad and Jacob forward to introduce them to Virgil and Grace.

Grace was obviously shy, and responded by bustling into the kitchen to fetch a pitcher of milk, some cheese and a loaf of bread. Virgil studied each of the women in turn, frowning a little as he tried to make sense of their appearance. Then he looked at Jacob, and his expression went flat.

It was no wonder. Though she had asked him and the others to leave their weapons with the horses, as she had done herself, everything about him, from the way he carried himself to the look in his eyes, marked him as a man who had known violence. The Quaker women were careful not to notice, but Virgil was evidently not so reticent.

"Will you sit?" Elizabeth said into the silence, gesturing toward the table.

Well aware that she was far too dirty to help the Quaker women in the kitchen, Serenity motioned the others to the sturdy chairs neatly tucked around the table. She felt as if she were moving in a dream, part of her acting within it and the other part observing from without. Every gentle word Elizabeth spoke drew her deeper into the past she had tried to forget. She could almost imagine that Virgil was Levi, gazing upon his future wife with affection as she worked beside the other women in the kitchen, preparing the evening meal.

Virgil, however, remained standing, and his gaze was fixed on Jacob. Feeling Jacob's eyes on her, Serenity nibbled at the bread and cheese the Quaker women offered. Her stomach rebelled, but she didn't want him or any of the others to know just how unbalanced and confused she was. It was up to her to make her friends feel as comfortable as possible…and never to let on to the Friends how little she wanted to be here.

"You will wish to rest after you eat," Elizabeth said to her guests with a firm authority that belied her humble manner. She looked at Serenity. "Thy uncle, Leah Burns and Rebecca Dale have gone to Kerrville, and should return by nightfall. William Burns, Adam Egan and Jonathan Dale are out with the cattle or working in the field, and Jane Goddard is with the children, but they also will be back soon. Grace and I will draw water for bathing, and find a place for thy friends to sleep."

"We don't want to be any trouble," Victoria offered shyly.

"I'll be happy sleeping in the barn, ma'am," Jacob said, perched on the edge of his chair as if he were in some dangerous situation that required his constant vigilance.

"I am certain we can find rooms for all of you," Elizabeth said, "if you do not mind sharing."

"We will be grateful for any shelter," Serenity said,

setting her plate aside. "But perhaps I should see Aunt Martha before I do anything else."

"Would thee not rest longer?"

"I am fine, cousin. If my friends might stable our horses…?"

"I'll see to it," Jacob said, almost jumping to his feet.

"I'll help," Caridad muttered.

Cari's sudden spirit of cooperation didn't surprise Serenity, since she looked just as ill at ease as Jacob.

"Of course," Elizabeth said. "Please let us know if there is anything you require. Virgil, will thee see if Martha is awake?"

The young man nodded, cast another cool glance at Jacob and walked out the door at the back of the kitchen. Jacob left by the front door with Caridad, the two of them for once in perfect accord. Grace was gathering up the almost untouched plates when Virgil returned.

"She is awake," he said, "and asks that Serenity Campbell come to her." He looked at Serenity. "Will thee come with me now?"

"Do not trouble thyself over thy friends," Elizabeth said. "I will see them to their rooms."

Serenity got up from the table. "I thank thee, Elizabeth Selden, for thy kindness," she said, and then turned to Victoria and Zora. "I will see you again tonight."

She went with Virgil out the back door and followed him along one of several intersecting paths that connected the main house, the cottages and the outlying farm buildings.

He turned toward one of the smaller cottages not

far from the main house and slowed his pace so that Serenity could catch up.

"May I ask a question, Serenity Campbell?" he asked.

"Only one?" she asked, attempting a smile.

He stopped. "I did not mean to offend thee."

"Thee didn't." She sighed. "We have ridden a long way today."

"I understand." He glanced down gravely at his folded hands. "I am sorry about thy parents and intended."

Serenity knew, of course, that everyone at Tolerance would be acquainted with the tragedy; word would have reached them in San Antonio long before the letter she had sent after her escape from the Reniers. She knew that they had believed her dead along with Levi and her parents until they had received the letter, but there had been nothing she could do to contact them before she reached Bethel. They would have looked after what remained of the farm and perhaps spoken over the ashes, but she had never come back to see.

"I thank thee for thy sympathy," she said.

"I was told thee had settled in New Mexico Territory, that thee has a ranch there."

He would know that, too, since it was unlikely Uncle Lester would hide such information from another in the community. The second and only other letter Serenity had sent to San Antonio, before the group's return to Tolerance, had been vague about her whereabouts but would not have made it impossible for them to locate her with a little effort.

"Yes," she said. "We call it Avalon."

"And thy companions…they live with thee there?"

"Yes, with several more women who are still there."

He peered at her keenly. "With their husbands?"

"None of us are married."

"Indeed?" He raised a fair eyebrow. "Thee surprises me."

"There are no men at Avalon."

"Saving this Jacob Constantine."

It seemed peculiar that Jacob's presence would be of more concern to Virgil than the fact that women could run a ranch alone. Even in the egalitarian Quaker society, few would find that either appropriate or sane.

"Jacob Constantine has been temporarily working at the ranch while we looked after the branding," she said. "When I received Uncle Lester's letter, he offered to accompany us."

"To watch over thee?"

"The land we passed through to get here has been known to harbor outlaws, as thee must know."

"He is good with a gun?"

The Friends so seldom spoke of such matters that Serenity was a little startled. "Thee need have no fear of trouble," she said, meeting Virgil's gaze. "He offered to camp by the river, but I assured him he would be as welcome here as I am."

Virgil had no ready answer for that, so they continued on to the cottage. "This is where Martha Owen rests," he said. "It is the house set aside for those who are ill or need special care."

Serenity hesitated at the door, gathered her courage and went inside.

Aunt Martha lay on the simple bed that took up

much of the single room. The walls were bare, the furniture exceedingly plain, but everything about it seemed to encourage healing and rest.

The woman on the bed was shockingly changed from the one Serenity had known seven years ago. Her skin was withered, her eyes sunken, her body thin and frail, as if her very bones had shrunk. Her eyes were closed, but when Serenity approached the bed she opened them and tried to focus.

"Serenity?" she croaked. "Is it thee?"

Any resentment Serenity still felt dissolved with her next, painful, breath. She rushed to the bedside and dropped to her knees.

"Aunt Martha," she said, laying her hand over the fragile fingers lying on the quilted bedcover.

The old woman sighed. "Serenity," she whispered. "It is good to see thee."

Serenity raised Aunt Martha's hand to her cheek. "Forgive me," she said. "Forgive me for not coming sooner."

"We were afraid the letters would not reach thee," Aunt Martha said. "It had been…so long since we had heard from thee." A tear rolled from the corner of her eye. "I did not want to trouble thee with this, but Lester…"

"Hush," Serenity murmured. "I am here now. I will stay by thy side as long as thee needs me."

Aunt Martha lifted her other trembling hand to touch Serenity's hair. "I have been so long troubled," she said. "I have prayed thee would forgive Lester and me. We have prayed that thee found peace in thy new home."

Serenity clasped her aunt's hand in both of hers and

gently laid it down again. “There is nothing to forgive. I will not have thee worry over me when thee needs rest.” She glanced at Virgil, who was standing in the doorway, then turned back to her aunt. “I will come see thee again tonight, after Uncle Lester returns.”

“Yes.” Aunt Martha closed her eyes again. “Yes.”

The effort of speaking seemed to have wrung all the strength from her, for within minutes she was asleep. Serenity rose and backed away from the bed as quietly as she could. Virgil stepped outside to allow her to pass, then closed the door behind her.

“The physician has been to see her?” she asked him, struggling with her own tears.

“Several times. He says it is a cancer and cannot be cured by mortal man. We pray for her daily.”

Of course they did. But Serenity had long since ceased to believe in the efficacy of prayer.

“Thee will stay?” Virgil asked.

“Until my aunt no longer needs me.”

“We had hoped…thee would stay longer.” He searched her eyes earnestly. “Every Friend here has prayed not only for thy safe journey but also that thee might consider returning to thy people for all time.”

Serenity had thought herself prepared for this. She hadn’t been sure how quickly they would recognize the changes in her, but her family would naturally encourage the return of their little lost lamb. It was her own fault for failing to make clear right away that she would never be one of them again.

The time to tell them must come soon, but not now. “Again, I thank thee, Virgil Thompson,” she said, “but perhaps we may speak of these things later.”

"Of course, Serenity Campbell. Thee must have time to recover from thy journey."

They walked back to the main house. As they approached the back door, Serenity heard the rattle of a wagon, and she and Virgil went around the side of the house to look.

The horses were gone, evidently taken to the barn by Jacob and Caridad. The wagon was a sturdy buckboard filled with sacks and boxes, driven by Uncle Lester and carrying two female passengers, one of whom seemed familiar to Serenity. Lester stopped in front of the gate to let the women get off, and then drove toward the barn without noticing the observers.

"Serenity," Elizabeth said, emerging from the front door. "I see that Lester Owen has returned. Virgil, will thee help him unload the supplies?"

With a long glance at Serenity, Virgil set off for the barn.

"I hope thee found Martha well?" Elizabeth asked.

"She was sleeping soundly when I left," Serenity said.

"Ah, that is good. The bathwater is prepared. Would thee care to make use of it?"

Unfailingly polite she might be, but Elizabeth's meaning could not be mistaken. The truth was that Serenity felt as if she had rolled in the mud with the pigs, and she couldn't resist the lure of a hot bath.

"The others—" she began.

"There will be more water when they need it," Elizabeth said, steering Serenity back along the path beside the main house. Just outside the kitchen door stood a small building that served as a bathhouse, where a large cast-iron tub had been filled to the brim with steaming water.

"Will thee need help?" Elizabeth asked.

"Thank you, but I can manage." Serenity looked down at her filthy clothing. "But if thee can lend me clothing until I can wash these..."

"Wash day is tomorrow. I have a dress that I think will fit thee."

A dress. It wasn't unexpected, but Serenity would have given much to be able to ask for trousers and a boy's shirt instead.

But Elizabeth wouldn't understand. And it wouldn't be appropriate to wear outsider clothes while she remained at Tolerance.

"I thank thee, cousin," she said.

Elizabeth left, and Serenity undressed. Even her tangled emotions couldn't erase the sheer pleasure of sinking into the hot water, and scrubbing the dirt from her skin and hair. She became acutely aware of her body, the firm muscles of her legs, developed from hard riding; the flatness of her stomach; the swell of hip and breast.

Oddly enough, in a place where physical matters were so much less important than the spiritual, such thoughts seemed almost safe. No one would know she was having them, or that her mind kept wandering back to Jacob...his burning eyes, his powerful arms, his demanding lips on hers.

Uncomfortable and increasingly all-too-familiar sensations began to trouble her peace, so she climbed out of the tub and used one of the flour sacks hung on a nail in the wall to dry herself. The water she left behind was tea-colored instead of clear. One more person might be able to use it, but the others would have to wait.

She was feeling a little guilty over that fact when Elizabeth returned with a plain gray gown, simple cotton undergarments, wool stockings, shoes and a bonnet. Serenity asked if more water might be heated, and Elizabeth returned to the main house to refill the reservoir on the stove.

Putting on the simple Quaker clothing felt to Serenity like donning medieval armor. But she was grateful; wearing one of the restrictive garments considered essential for outsider women would have been completely unbearable. There was, thank God, no real corset, only a starched garment just stiff enough to support her breasts. The bodice was loose enough to let her breathe almost as well as she did in her boys' shirts, though the high collar seemed to bind her neck like a noose. Nor was there a true bustle; the simple petticoats gave the skirts more fullness than was fashionable, designed for ease of work and movement. The sturdy shoes were too small and felt ridiculous on feet accustomed to working boots.

The bonnet came last, a relic from another era. Serenity pinned up her hair and settled the bonnet over it. Now she was the complete Quaker woman, modest and sensible.

And safe.

But safety was an illusion, even here. She had learned that hard lesson far too well.

Serenity shook her head and made the final adjustments to her dress. There were few mirrors in the settlement, of course. Not that it mattered; her appearance meant no more to her here than it had at Avalon.

Even though Jacob will be seeing you in a dress for the first time? Would he be shocked? Approving? Amused? She had no way of knowing. He had never once spoken of her choice of clothing, or indicated in any way that he would have preferred to see her dressed as an ordinary woman.

Much more nervous than she had expected to be, Serenity ventured outside. The air was releasing the heat of a long summer day, a pleasant temperature for the heavier weight of her clothes. She pretended her legs didn't feel confined under the skirts and walked back to the kitchen.

Elizabeth looked up from her pots, pushing aside the damp brown hair that escaped from her bonnet. "Thee is comfortable?" she asked.

"Yes," Serenity said, permitting herself the smallest of lies. "Thank thee for the dress."

"It fits thee well," Elizabeth said, as much of a compliment as one Friend was likely to give another on such a subject. "We were not certain what clothing to give to the others."

Now, Serenity thought, the questions would begin to come in earnest.

"Men's dress is best for traveling and the work we do at the ranch," she said.

"Ah, yes. Thy ranch. Thee and thy friends all own it together?"

She must have spoken to Victoria or Zora, Serenity thought. Most likely Victoria, who seemed to feel more at home here than she herself did.

"Yes," she said.

Elizabeth moved to the ancient stove, where the bathwater was heating, and poured tea from a kettle into a teapot. "It must have been difficult to begin this ranch with only women to help thee," she said.

"Quaker women are taught to be strong and work hard," Serenity said. "Does it surprise thee that others might be equally strong?"

"I do not doubt that thy friends are capable," Elizabeth said, returning to the table with the teapot and two cups. "But how did thee come to find such a place?"

How much to tell? Serenity thought. Explaining in too much detail might give Elizabeth ideas about Serenity's fate after the fire.

"I bought it," she said, "with money contributed by those who shared my hopes. Many of the women at our ranch have suffered at the hands of bad men. I wanted a place where such women could be safe."

Elizabeth, like most women among the Friends, was not as sheltered as she might appear. "It is a worthy goal," she said, taking a sip of her tea. "Did thee achieve what thee hoped?"

"Yes. Avalon has done well."

"Thee did not find Friends in New Mexico?"

Her tone made it clear that she meant other Quakers.

Serenity stared at her cup.

"No, Elizabeth. If there are any Friends in New Mexico Territory, I never saw them."

Because she had never looked for them.

Elizabeth wrapped her work-roughened hands around her cup. “There is one thing I do not understand,” she said. “Why did thee not come home to thy people after the fire?”

CHAPTER FOURTEEN

THERE WOULD BE LIES now, Serenity thought. Not of commission but of omission. "I could not come back to the place where I saw those I loved die," she said.

Elizabeth reached across the table toward Serenity, her eyes dark with sorrow. "Even though thee knew there were many who would help and succor thee?"

"I couldn't," Serenity said, keeping her hands folded in front of her. "I had hoped thee would understand."

"I am sorry," Elizabeth said, withdrawing her hand. "Thy suffering must have been very great."

Serenity bit down on her tongue to keep the confession from spilling out. "I had to find my own way," she said.

Elizabeth accepted the explanation, though Serenity suspected she wouldn't do so forever.

"What of this man, Jacob Constantine?" Elizabeth asked. "Thee has said he works for thee."

Everyone seemed interested in Jacob today. "Two of our women fell sick during one of the busiest times of the year," Serenity said. "We had no choice but to accept his help."

"He has proven worthy of your trust?"

"He has worked hard and treated us with respect."

Elizabeth nodded. "He seems a good man, though rough in his ways."

"No rougher than most, and more civilized than many."

She knew she'd spoken with too much heat when Elizabeth paused in midsip and peered curiously into Serenity's eyes. "Thee likes him," she said.

"As I said—"

Elizabeth raised her hand. "Yes." She put down her cup. "Thee chose not to marry," she said.

Virgil had asked virtually the same question, and given that they did not know about Avalon's purpose, it was not an unreasonable one. Though Elizabeth hadn't mentioned a husband or children, most men and women, Quaker or outsider, considered marriage essential to life and happiness. Once, Serenity had believed the same.

Still, it seemed strange that both should ask at the same time they spoke of Jacob. How could they have seen anything that would indicate more than simple companionship between her and Jacob, when she had been so very careful not to suggest that anything else—the "anything else" she still couldn't understand—existed between them?

"No, cousin," Serenity said, taking a deep breath. "I never met anyone I thought I could love."

"There is still time," Elizabeth said. And by that she no doubt meant that she, like Virgil, hoped Serenity would remain to marry one of their own, in spite of everything Serenity had told her. "Thee is content in thy life?"

"Very content."

"And thee—thy ranch—has not been troubled by those who covet what thee possesses?"

Serenity couldn't guess why Elizabeth had thought to ask such a question, but she recognized that she stood at a crossroads. She could lie and suggest that Avalon had escaped such problems, and that she had maintained the Quaker commitment to peace. Or she could make clear, as she should have done at the beginning, why she could never again be one of the Friends.

"There are always those who would see women alone as easy prey," she said. "The land we live in is a hard one, ruled by hard men. We learned how to defend ourselves from the beginning."

"Thee...defended thyself with weapons?"

"When it was necessary."

Abruptly Elizabeth got up, gathered the tea things and went back to the worktable. She revealed nothing of her emotions, but Serenity heard what she didn't say.

Did thee hurt these men? Has thee killed?

The questions hung between them, dimming the happiness Elizabeth had so clearly felt when Serenity had arrived.

But there was no help for that now. "I have done what I had to do to protect myself and my friends," Serenity said. "I saw this farm burned and my family killed. Should I let such a thing happen again?"

Elizabeth gazed at Serenity, her expression deeply troubled.

Before she could speak again, Jacob walked into the room. He came to a sudden stop when he saw Elizabeth.

"Sorry if I'm intruding, ma'am," he said, removing his hat, "but I was looking for Miss Campbell. You mind if I have a word with her?"

JACOB COULD SEE right away that he'd interrupted a difficult conversation between Serenity and her cousin. Their voices had been quiet as he'd approached the house, but he could smell the strain, and recognize it on their faces. He wondered what could have come between them so fast.

All the way to Tolerance, he'd been thinking about how it would be for Serenity when she arrived. It had been obvious to him from the moment she'd accepted his lies and decided to come here that she hadn't been looking forward to it.

He couldn't blame her. She'd chosen a very different kind of life for herself. And though he didn't know why she'd left her Quaker kin after the tragedy, he could understand why she would be reluctant to face people who would only remind her of what she'd lost.

He'd begun to feel pretty bad about urging her to come, even though it made things a lot easier on him. Yet, by the time they'd arrived, she'd seemed in control of her emotions, resigned if not happy. She'd greeted her cousin with obvious affection, and the other Quakers were clearly glad to see *her.* She'd started talking just like them, slipping back into the customs she'd been born to.

Once she'd belonged among these people. Maybe he wasn't too crazy thinking she still might do so again. Once she'd been here awhile...

"You have not interrupted, Jacob Constantine," Elizabeth said, sparing him thoughts he was glad enough to set aside. "Thee has no need to call me 'ma'am.' We use no such titles here." She smiled. "Would thee care for some tea?"

"No, thank you…Miss…Elizabeth." He glanced at Serenity, aware for the first time that she was no longer wearing her familiar shirt and trousers but a simple gray dress. In fact, she looked downright peculiar, as if she had draped herself in skins and furs. The bonnet she wore would have made any other woman look prim, but on her it only seemed ridiculous.

He put on his hat. "Miss Campbell?"

"Of course." Serenity rose, smoothing her skirts with nervous hands. "Elizabeth, I'll return soon to help thee with supper."

"There is no need," Elizabeth said. "Grace has only gone for a sack of flour. Please take as much time as thee wishes."

Serenity ducked her head, a flurry of emotions sweeping across her face, and strode toward the door, almost stumbling when her legs moved too fast for her dress.

Jacob caught her and held on until they were outside.

She eased her arm from his grip. "Is something wrong?" she asked.

"I just wanted to tell you that I hid the weapons in the barn, up in the hayloft. You think that's safe enough?"

"For the time being." She frowned. "But that isn't why you wanted to talk to me, is it? Have they given you a place to sleep? Are you—?"

"I came to see how you were doing." He gestured toward the gate, inviting her to precede him. "You and Miss Selden have an argument?"

"Nothing is wrong," she said a little too quickly.

"Elizabeth asked me a few questions about…where I had been since I was last here."

"How long ago was that?"

"I haven't seen them since before Levi and my family were killed."

That told him that his speculation about her actions after the tragedy were pretty close to the mark. She hadn't gone to her kin even after she'd recovered from her hard, wild ride west to Bethel.

He didn't think it would be a good idea to ask why right now.

"They knew where you were, didn't they?" he said softly. "They got a letter to you."

Serenity folded her arms across her bodice and lowered her head. "I wrote to them twice," she said. "Once soon after I'd left Bethel, and once from Las Cruces, when I was buying the ranch."

For a moment, all Jacob could imagine was just how bad she must have felt to choose the terrible odds of survival on her own over a safe place with her kin. If this was the first time they'd seen her since her parents had died, she was probably feeling a fair amount of guilt right about now. No doubt they wondered why she hadn't trusted them to help her, why she'd turned her back on them in her hour of need.

"This can't be easy for any of you," he said.

She shot him a look that might have been gratitude, or at least relief. He wasn't judging her, and that was something she cared about. It was little enough he could give her.

By unspoken agreement they walked toward the pasture on the east side of the house. "I guess they don't know too much about the ranch," he said.

"No."

"Your cousin must have been curious about an outfit run by women."

He was really wondering whether Elizabeth had disapproved, and Serenity had to know it.

"It is not something most Friends would do," she admitted.

"Friends, or just Quaker women?"

"If you know anything at all about the Friends, you must know that we…they believe in equality between men and women."

"That doesn't mean a bunch of Quaker females would set up their own place."

"No. They wouldn't."

"So that was why she was upset with you?"

She stopped, her skirts swinging around her, and stared at him with challenge in her eyes. "What do you want to know, Jacob?"

"Just that you're doing all right."

"Everyone has been very kind."

"Have you talked to your aunt?"

"Just for a few minutes. I will see her again tonight, when my uncle comes."

"How is she?"

Serenity began to walk again, brushing a persistent insect way from her face. "Very ill," she said.

"I'm sorry."

They reached the gate that opened into the field, its honey-colored grass painted orange by the sinking sun. A few cattle watched them with bovine curiosity, twitching their ears. Serenity ignored the gate, lifted her skirts and clambered over the fence with no thought to womanly modesty.

Jacob got a good look at her stockinged calf and caught his breath. He realized he'd never really seen her legs unless they were encased in baggy trousers. The sight aroused him, though there was nothing remotely seductive about her appearance or her behavior.

And this wasn't the time to think about what looking at her did to his body.

But when they were standing together in the long grass, he found out just how hard it was not to smell the clean, soapy scent of her skin or notice the way her bodice, modest as it was, outlined the swell of her breasts better than any shirt could have done.

Serenity closed her eyes and breathed in deeply.

Jacob could smell wildflowers somewhere on the other side of the fence, and stew simmering in the kitchen. Children's high voices shouted to each other among the houses behind them.

Serenity's expression softened as all the tightness and care were smoothed away.

"I can't believe..." she began, and trailed off.

"Can't believe what?" Jacob asked, wishing he dared do something as simple as taking her hand.

"I never thought it could be this way again."

Jacob's heart bucked. The wistfulness in her voice told him what she was trying to say. She felt at least some peace here, some sense of belonging, no matter what awkwardness there might be between her and her kin.

She had known happiness before the tragedy. She'd

been looking forward to marriage, a home, children of her own. Maybe some of the good memories—memories of a childhood and an innocence she had lost—were beginning to gain a little ground against the bad ones.

He had to give her time, even if that meant staying on longer than he'd wanted to. Staying among folk who would reject everything he was.

That didn't matter, as long as they accepted Serenity.

"It's good you came here," he said. "It was the right thing to do."

She looked up at him, and he saw that her eyes were filled with tears. He reached out and touched her hand, just a brush of his fingertips, but it must have helped, because she clasped her hand around his and held on tight.

"The last time I was here," she said, "this field was burning. The barn and the houses were turning to ash, and the cows were bawling...." She covered her face with her free hand.

A cold understanding gripped Jacob by the throat. "Here?" he asked.

She looked away. "I misled you," she said. "I made you believe my parents lived near Fredericksburg, but this was the settlement my parents, and my aunt and uncle and a dozen others, founded when they left San Antonio."

"There were others here besides your parents?"

"Life was difficult here," she murmured, seemingly unaware of his horror. "After a while, everyone but my parents and Levi decided to return to San Antonio.

But my parents believed it was worth staying on. So did Levi. With hard work, we made something of this place. Father was about to write to the others in San Antonio to tell them—"

Her voice cracked. Jacob let go of her hand and put his arm around her shoulders. She leaned into him, racked with dry, gasping sobs that tore at him like a panther's claws.

She didn't have to tell him the rest. Her family had been alone when the outlaws came. Not that it would have made any difference, since most Quakers wouldn't fight. But the outlaws might have had a little more trouble killing them if all the original settlers had been here.

Serenity hadn't wanted to come here, but not only because her last memory of this place was one of death and destruction. She remembered that the others hadn't been there when her family had needed them the most. To the terrified young girl she had been, it would have seemed like a kind of betrayal.

"I'm sorry, Serenity," he said, resting his chin on the crown of her head, where the bonnet cupped her bound-up hair. "We can leave. Now."

It was the old Jacob Constantine who spoke—not the bounty hunter and loner who couldn't settle down, but the man who had known how to love a woman. He wasn't thinking about leaving to go after the Reniers. In that miraculous moment, the old Jacob saw a real future: being with Serenity every day, sitting beside her at a roaring hearth, riding beside her, loving her, for the rest of his life.

He recognized his mistake as soon as the words

were out of his mouth. Carefully he eased his arm from around Serenity's shoulder.

She stared at him with parted lips and shining eyes. "Go back to the hunt?" she asked. "I thought you lost the trail in Bethel?"

A bubble of laughter swelled and died in his throat. *She* certainly wasn't thinking about going away with *him* to some snug little cabin and settling down as a wife and mother.

"I did," he said, trying not to let his bitter amusement show in his voice.

"I can't leave anyway," Serenity said. "Not as long as my aunt needs me." She gave him a forlorn little smile. "Don't worry about me. I'll be all right."

The danger was over. Jacob cleared his throat.

"I've set up my bedroll in the barn," he said. "It suits me just fine, but I plan to find a place by the river as soon as—"

"Why?" Serenity interrupted, her expression tightening up again. "You've come here for my sake. The least you deserve is a real bed."

"I'm not much used to real beds," he said. "I prefer a haystack or a nice blanket of leaves, myself."

Though he hadn't intended any double meaning, Serenity blushed as if she'd been put in mind of something else that might be done in a bed. But that, he told himself, was just his imagination. Two kisses, and they hadn't come anywhere near going that far, or even contemplating it.

At least *she* hadn't.

"It's better if I stay away," he said quickly. "Because of what I am."

Her gazed locked on his. "A werewolf? But no one would ever—"

"I use a gun to make my living," he said. "Your people might set themselves apart from other folk, but they aren't blind. They won't want me around."

"How can they know what you do? You aren't wearing a gun."

He shrugged, not quite sure how to explain. He'd known he wouldn't feel right here. He hadn't realized just how bad it would be until he'd met Serenity's kin, especially Elizabeth. In some ways she reminded him of Ruth, gentle as she was. She made him think about how many times he'd killed in the line of duty—seldom with anger, but killing just the same. Even being a werewolf didn't seem as bad a secret.

"Do you think they would consider Zora and Caridad any different from you?" she demanded when he didn't answer. "Or me? They've both killed in defense of our home. Victoria killed her husband to protect herself. I was responsible for Leroy's death. If they judge you, they'll have to judge me, too."

Passion flared in her eyes, challenge and that almost violent emotion he'd seen each time she responded to his kisses.

But there was something deeper there, too…something he didn't want to see and yet hoped for all the same.

"Your kin don't have to know what you've done," he said.

"But they *do* know. When I told Elizabeth about the ranch…" Her shoulders sagged, and all the defiance seemed to leak out of her at once. "She guessed that we might have been bothered by 'bad men.' I admitted it was true, and that we'd had to defend ourselves more than once."

And that was what their "argument" had been about. Serenity might feel some sense of ease here, in this quiet pasture with the cattle looking on, and the sound of children's laughter and the smell of wildflowers on the breeze, but she wasn't at peace.

"I don't want you to go," she said in a voice that would have been nearly inaudible to anyone but a werewolf. "I don't want to be alone here."

"You've got Caridad, and—"

"I don't want you to go."

Every time she was vulnerable like this, he felt as if someone had wrapped barbwire around his throat, and was pulling it tighter and tighter. She *needed* him, not just to take her to her enemies, but simply to be with her.

What had Zora said? *It is not enough to keep her from finding these men and killing them. She will need your help long after her enemies are dead.* Because in some strange way Serenity believed he understood her as no one else could.

And he *did.* As well as he could understand anybody, including himself. But he had to believe that what Zora had said was wrong, that what he saw in Serenity's eyes was just a passing weakness. She could easily turn that same gaze on some other man, someone like…

Virgil.

Jacob stiffened. What in hell had put that sneaking polecat into his mind?

His own vehemence startled him. Virgil hadn't

done a damned thing to him but stare at him with cold disapproval—*he'd* sure as hell sensed what Jacob did for a living—and welcome Serenity like a brother would.

But there hadn't been anything brotherly in the way the other man had looked at Serenity. He was hiding something.

You're imagining things, Jacob told himself. But the thought of Virgil's bland smile and flat eyes wouldn't leave his mind.

"I'll stay here," he said suddenly. "So long as they'll have me."

She gave him such a smile that the barbwire snapped in a million pieces. God, how he wanted to kiss her again. She took a step toward him, eyes half-closed, all sweet womanhood with the swell of her breasts and curve of her hips that even sackcloth couldn't hide. Jacob fought a savage inner battle between instinct and sense.

But there were still only three ways this could end: with Serenity staying here in the bosom of her family, returning to Avalon, or coming with him and giving herself up to violence and death.

"We'd better go back," he said. "Your cousin must be waiting for you."

Serenity's smile vanished. "Of course," she said. "Supper should be ready soon. I'd intended to…" She paused, a flicker of bewilderment in her eyes. "They'll expect you to come."

"I'll be there," he said, though he dreaded the prospect of sitting down with the Quakers—and Serenity—more than a bullet in the belly. But he didn't get much of a chance to think about how bad it might be. He smelled someone coming toward the pasture from the direction of the house, someone he definitely had no interest in talking to. He was about to make a break for it when Serenity heard the approaching footsteps and rushed toward the fence.

"Virgil Thompson," she said brightly. "Has thee spoken to my uncle?"

"I have," he said, shooting Jacob an unfriendly glance over the rail. "Jacob Constantine. I trust I am not disturbing you?"

"Not at all," Serenity said. "I was about to return to the house."

"Then perhaps your hired man will not object to my escorting you," Virgil said.

Considering how strongly most Quakers felt about equality for all people, pointing out that Jacob was a "hired man" was a pretty strange thing for Virgil to do. But Jacob knew why Virgil had spoken as he had. He wanted to be sure that Jacob knew his place.

"I don't mind if Serenity doesn't," Jacob said flatly.

Serenity barely looked at him as she climbed over the fence. Virgil was more than ready to help her. He took her hand and gripped it firmly until she was on the other side.

"Jacob Constantine," she called over her shoulder, "I will see thee at supper."

She didn't wait for his reply.

Jacob was left to watch her and Virgil walk away, the young man's arm brushing hers and her head tilted toward his. Instead of going directly to the house, Virgil led her along one of the little paths that curved away behind it.

As soon as the two of them had turned the corner, Jacob jumped the fence and went straight to the brushy wood across the road. When he was out of sight of the settlement, he tore off his shirt with enough force to pop two of the buttons and removed the rest of his clothes with equal indifference to their subsequent condition. The sun had left a streak of red across the sky, reminding him of blood, and the smell of deer and small animals seeking their dinners made his stomach growl and his mouth water.

But he had other prey in mind. He Changed, shook his fur briskly, and trotted back across the road.

CHAPTER FIFTEEN

"CAN I HELP, SERENITY Campbell?"

Virgil's voice was mild and pleasant, almost musical, with none of the harsh masculine tones that dominated whenever Jacob spoke.

But Serenity had been glad to hear Jacob's voice when he'd sympathized about the difficulty of her reunion with her family and her aunt's condition. She had basked in it when he'd put his arm around her to comfort her. She'd been grateful for his understanding, without her telling him, why seeing this place again had evoked so many painful memories and such violently mixed emotions. And when he'd offered to take her away, right now…

Oh, how she had wanted to go. And had realized, an instant later, how close she'd come to a terrible misstep. Jacob hadn't meant it the way her heart had heard…her foolish, overwrought heart. She'd been quick to make it seem as if she'd understood him correctly the first time, that they were both speaking of the hunt.

So he hadn't caught her slip. And she would have let it end there if he hadn't said he would move down to the river because he didn't belong in a place of such peace-loving folk.

She couldn't bear it. First she'd been angry on his behalf, that he would think himself somehow less than the

Friends just because he had not lived his life in a way they would approve. Then she had been angry on her own behalf for the same reason. Angry and ashamed, and trying not to let him know it.

But he'd seen through her, realized just how brittle her brief feeling of peace had been, how easily her sense of herself could be shattered. She had set aside all her pride and asked him, begged him, not to leave her. His answer had driven the darkness away and made her forget all over again that some things were impossible, and always would be.

Why couldn't she remember that simple truth?

"Something *is* wrong," Virgil said, halting her racing thoughts with a hand on her arm. "Is it the outsider?"

Serenity realized she'd done no better at hiding her emotions from Virgil than she had from Jacob. She was weary of others asking her what was wrong, and her first impulse was to tell her old friend to mind his own business.

But that would hardly be fair. Virgil's inquiry was meant in true Christian fellowship, just like Elizabeth's, and she couldn't find it in her heart to rebuff him.

"Jacob and I were only speaking of the journey," she said.

Virgil kept a firm grip on her arm. "I do not think that is why you are unhappy," he said. "It is difficult for you to be here again."

If he'd seemed to pity her, she would have broken away in spite of her decision to bear with his questions. But his gaze was straightforward, respecting her dignity, and so she told him the truth.

"Yes," she said. "It is difficult."

"Considering what thee has borne, thee has done well," he said. He smiled. "I remember thee as a brave child, Serenity. Young though thee was, I admired thee even then."

Admired her? She experienced a small unexpected flush of the pleasure that long-ago child would have felt if she had known of such admiration in happier times.

The pleasure quickly faded. "The child thee remembers is gone," she said.

"'When I was a child, I spake as a child, I understood as a child, I thought as a child,'" he quoted. "There is no shame in putting aside childish things."

He didn't know her. None of them did.

"Does thee think grief is childish?" she asked, unable to keep the bitterness from her voice.

"No, cousin," he said gently. "Not childish. But thy family is with God now, beyond pain and suffering. And thee has thy whole life ahead of thee." He let his hand fall from her arm. "Has thee thought of what I said about coming back to us?"

It had been only two hours since their last conversation, and already he expected an answer?

"Thee has been most welcoming," she said, "but I cannot think of such things yet. My aunt—"

"I do not believe it is thy aunt who makes this decision difficult for thee," he said, his tone hardening. "Or even thy memories. Serenity—" he sighed "—these outsiders with whom thee live are no good influence on thee. They are rough in their ways, and I fear—"

"That is enough," Serenity said, stepping away from him. "You don't know my friends, and you don't know me. I would ask you not to comment on such matters again."

Virgil blinked at the vehemence of her response. "I… Serenity, I did not mean…" His face fell. "I apologize. I spoke out of turn, and in ignorance. It is only that I remember our friendship, and how it was when we were children together. I ask thy forgiveness."

No apology could have seemed more heartfelt, and once again Serenity felt obliged to give him the benefit of the doubt.

"As you said, we are not children anymore."

"No. We are not." He gave her an uncertain smile. "Come. We will help lay the table."

Mollified, she accompanied him back to the house, where Grace, Elizabeth and a woman named Leah were placing bowls and plates of simple, wholesome food on the table. Elizabeth seemed glad to see Serenity after the awkwardness between them, apparently prepared to disregard their last conversation and what it had revealed of Serenity's life since the tragedy.

Relieved, and glad to pretend that nothing had happened, Serenity offered to help, and the work was done quickly. A short while later Elizabeth asked Virgil to ring the bell, and one by one the other Friends began to assemble in the kitchen. Elizabeth introduced Serenity to each of them in turn. They welcomed her with varying degrees of warmth or reserve.

Uncle Lester, however, was effusive in his greeting. He enfolded her in an embrace that all but shouted relief and joy.

"Serenity Campbell," Lester said, releasing her, "I thank God thee is here at last. To see thee again safe and well after so many years is a balm to my soul. I only wish thee had come to us sooner."

There was no rebuke in the words, no sign that he had been distressed by her failure to keep in closer communication with the Friends. He beamed at her as the other men and women took their accustomed places, turning away only long enough to ask those seated on either side of him if one would be willing to give up his seat for Serenity. When an older man by the name of William Burns quietly surrendered his chair, Lester waved Serenity to join him and continued to gaze at her with undisguised pleasure…and a less happy emotion he obviously intended to conceal.

Guilt.

Aunt Martha had said what he wouldn't. "I have prayed thee would forgive me and Lester."

Serenity laid her hand over his and smiled. "I am glad to see thee, too, Uncle," she said.

Tears welled in his eyes. He clasped her hands in his, then addressed the table at large. "We are indeed blessed this day," he said.

There were murmurs of agreement. Serenity flushed and glanced toward the front door. Virgil and one of the younger men had drawn up five additional chairs for their guests. The table was crowded, but no one thought to complain, and when Zora, Caridad and Victoria arrived—each one in a dress, though Zora looked a little uncomfortable and Cari much too vivid for the unadorned brown—they made room and saw to it that the women were comfortably situated.

Soon afterward a troupe of five children, ranging in age from what looked like three to ten, marched in through the back door, each one scrubbed and dressed like a little adult. They filed to the smaller table and chairs set out for them at one side of the main table and took their seats, glancing curiously at the strangers. They were too well-mannered to ask questions without permission, but a boy of about five made a remark that caused the oldest girl to giggle. The young woman caring for them cast Serenity an apologetic smile and shushed the child gently.

These were the good, honest people Serenity had known most of her life, and she felt the tightness begin to drain from her muscles as the comfort of familiarity pushed her conversations with Jacob and Virgil out of her mind. Virgil, engaged in a low-voiced discussion with his neighbor, sat two places away from her and didn't seem inclined to ask any more awkward questions. The only wrong note was the empty chair beside Zora's, waiting for its tardy occupant.

But Jacob didn't keep them waiting long. He came quietly through the kitchen door, wearing his spare set of clothes, boots carefully cleaned and face cleared of stubble. He paused just inside the room, removed his hat and nodded to Elizabeth.

"Ma'am," he said, then glanced around at the table's nearly two dozen occupants, waiting for someone to break the silence.

Uncle Lester rose. "Good evening to thee, Jacob Constantine," he said. "I am Lester Owen. Thee is welcome to our table."

He didn't offer to introduce anyone else, but Jacob had never been one to stand on formality himself.

"I'm honored to be here, Mr. Owen," he said. He

looked at Serenity as if she were a stranger, hung his hat on the rack near the door and went to the unoccupied chair.

Once Jacob was seated, there was a moment of silence as each of the Friends offered his or her private devotion. Victoria bowed her head, Caridad crossed herself, and Zora simply waited. Jacob gazed at some point in the center of the table.

Serenity attempted to pray with the others. The last time she had done so had been during her captivity, and she had never tried again after her escape. The words seemed empty, addressed to someone who had abandoned her long ago.

She was profoundly grateful when the others lifted their heads, and the plates and bowls of food began to make a stately circuit around the table. No one took more than he or she needed. The fare was as plain as it could be, but as substantial as hardworking people required. Conversation between neighbors was sporadic, but no one addressed the table at large, and Serenity knew why.

It was Jacob. He did nothing to call attention to himself, but he didn't need to. No matter how much she hadn't wanted to accept what he had told her in the pasture, he had been right. The Friends weren't blind. How could she blame him for wanting to stay away?

"Jacob Constantine," she said, her voice rising above the others at the table, "how are the horses?"

The quiet conversations stopped, and nearly everyone looked at Serenity. She smiled as if she hadn't noticed.

"The horses are fine," Jacob said, meeting her gaze. "Cleo's already lost that limp."

"That's wonderful news." Serenity gathered the other diners into the conversation with a sweeping glance. "We are fortunate to have such good horses."

"Your livestock are some of the best I've seen," Jacob said, addressing Uncle Lester.

"Thee are kind to say so, Jacob Constantine," Lester said. "We care for them as best we can."

"You keep beeves on your range?" Jacob asked.

"A modest number," Lester said. "Enough for our needs."

"Does thee have much experience with beef cattle, Jacob Constantine?" Virgil asked.

The question was perfectly civil, but there was no particular friendliness in Virgil's eyes or expression.

Jacob stared right back at him, and Virgil dropped his gaze.

"I wouldn't be much use to Miss Campbell if I didn't," Jacob said.

Virgil tried to conceal a grimace. "Thee must have encountered…they are called 'rustlers,' I believe?"

"That comes with the territory."

"How does thee defend thy property, Jacob Constantine?"

A heaviness settled over the room. Lester opened his mouth to speak, but Jacob was already answering.

"How do you defend yours, Virgil Thompson?" he asked.

CHAPTER SIXTEEN

UNCLE LESTER WENT very still.

Elizabeth closed her eyes.

Only a few words had been spoken, and yet to Serenity it felt as if two implacable foes were facing each other with guns drawn, each waiting for the other to shoot first.

"We recognize no enemies," Grace said, unexpectedly breaking the unbearable tension. "Only those who have been led astray."

Like me, Serenity thought. She set down her fork. "Uncle," she said, "if Martha has not yet been taken her meal, may I do so?"

He glanced at her with the expression of one abruptly awakened from an unpleasant dream. "Of course," he said.

"I will help thee prepare a plate," Elizabeth said, rising hastily.

A few Friends turned back to their meals. Others waited as if expecting yet another verbal duel. Caridad, Victoria and Zora exchanged surreptitious glances.

Abruptly Jacob slid back his chair and got up.

"It's a fine meal, ma'am," he said to Elizabeth, who had returned to the table with an empty plate. "But I reckon I'm not too hungry right now. Thank you for your hospitality."

He inclined his head to Lester and walked out the front door without taking his hat. Serenity couldn't decide if she wanted to shout at Virgil, apologize to the Friends, or follow Jacob and apologize to *him* instead.

But she did none of those things. Keeping her head down, she took the tray and newly filled plate Elizabeth offered, and went out the back. The night was cool and refreshing, its soothing silence, broken only by crickets in the long grass, easing a little of her agitation.

Aunt Martha was alert when she entered the cottage, propped up on her pillows and smiling as Serenity approached the bed.

"Niece," she said in her cracked voice. "I am glad to see thee again."

"And I thee," Serenity said, setting the plate down on the table beside the bed. "I have brought thy supper. I hope thee is hungry."

"I do not eat much these days," Martha said, "but I am a little hungry tonight."

Serenity pulled a chair up to the bed, picked up the tray and carefully laid it across her aunt's lap.

Martha refused to let Serenity help her eat, though her hands trembled as she lifted the fork to her lips. She permitted Serenity to cut the meat into smaller portions, but she ate less than half of the modest slice Elizabeth had provided for her, and almost none of the potato and squash.

"I thank thee," she said, setting down her fork. "I think I am finished."

Serenity took the tray away. She was more than a little worried about Aunt Martha's color and the way she sank back into the pillows.

"Will thee rest now, Aunt?" Serenity asked. "Is there something else thee needs?"

Martha smiled, white around the lips. "I need only to sleep a little. We will visit again tomorrow morning, if that is agreeable to thee."

"Of course." Serenity removed one pillow from beneath her aunt's head and helped her settle, drawing the sheets and blankets over her thin chest. She kissed Martha's forehead.

"Rest well," she said. "I will see thee tomorrow."

But Martha was already asleep.

Serenity picked up the tray and crept to the door.

Virgil was waiting outside.

"Let me help thee," he said, taking the tray from her hands.

Serenity glanced toward the main house. "Is the meal already finished?" she asked.

"I would speak with thee," he said.

Which was no answer at all, and Serenity didn't care. He was the last person she had any desire to speak with, but, judging by the look on his face, avoiding him would not be easy.

"I think it is better that we not speak now," Serenity said coolly.

Virgil flushed. "Thee are angry with me. Perhaps thee has good reason, but—"

"Please give me the tray."

Instead of doing so, Virgil walked back toward the main house and through the kitchen door. Before Serenity could escape, he was outside again.

She could see it wouldn't do any good to put him

off; she would let him say what he had to say, and then she could be done with him.

It soon became apparent that he wanted privacy for whatever he intended to say. He led Serenity away from the settlement, not into the fields surrounding it but toward the wagon road. Nothing moved on it now. It might as well have been the middle of the Llano Estacado, the barren "staked plain" that straddled the border between New Mexico and Texas.

When they were completely alone, Virgil stopped and turned toward Serenity with an expression of utmost gravity.

"I know thee would not have me speak of this again," he said, "but I cannot remain silent."

"If you intend to insult my friends—"

"It is Constantine who concerns me now," he interrupted. "You said that he is employed to work at thy farm, but he does not behave like a hired man."

"I am surprised at thee," Serenity said, meeting Virgil's challenging stare with one of her own. "Does thee not agree with the teachings that all men and women are equal in the sight of God?"

"He is arrogant," Virgil said stiffly. "He is the one who believes himself better than the rest of us."

"His ways are not yours. Thee cannot expect him to behave exactly as thee would wish."

"Does thee approve of the way he spoke tonight?"

She began to lose her temper. "Did thee not provoke him?" She folded her arms across her chest. "Tell me, why does thee dislike him so much?"

"Anyone can see what kind of man he is. The way he holds himself, the quickness of his movements…"

Virgil scowled. "The way he looks at thee…does thee not see that he lusts after thee?"

His frankness startled her. It was not generally the way of Friends to discuss such private matters with anyone, even close kin. And that Virgil could guess so much…

"He has never imposed upon me," she said, which was as close to the truth as made no difference. "He has behaved at all times with propriety."

"But that is not how he *wishes* to behave," Virgil said, his voice growing heated. "Thee has lived on a farm with only women. What can thee know of such men?"

Serenity choked back a laugh. She had nothing to lose now by letting him know what Elizabeth had already guessed.

"Does thee think I am an innocent?" she asked, as she had once asked Jacob. "I saw this place burned to the ground by evil men. Does thee truly believe that I have no experience of the world?" She closed her eyes. "Perhaps I am not so unlike the man you seem to despise."

"Thee is *nothing* like him. Thee is one of us, even if thee—"

"I have used weapons against men who would have hurt me and my friends," she said. "I have defended what I hold dear, with no regret. What does thee think of me now?"

He turned away from her, taking several jerky steps back toward the cluster of buildings. He clasped his hands tightly behind his back, pressing so hard that his knuckles whitened with the strain.

"It is that man who has influenced thee," he said.

"I have known him for only a few weeks. What I did, I did by my own choice."

She thought that would be the end of it, that he would march back to the house and never speak to her again. But it was not to be so simple.

"Thee..." Virgil began. He stopped, shook his head and began again. "Thee is not beyond redemption. Thee can repent, renounce the life that has led three astray and become one of us again."

Repentance. Renunciation. He had no idea what he was asking of her.

She bent her chin to her chest. "This is no longer my home," she said. "I have made my decision. I will not be staying after my aunt...after she no longer needs me."

"But this *is* thy home. Thy true home, where thee can find peace."

"You do not seem much at peace, Virgil Thompson," she snapped.

She regretted her words at once, but it was too late to call them back.

Virgil grew red in the face and pressed his lips together in a narrow white line.

"I have had concern for thee, Serenity Campbell," he said, "because I see how deeply thee are in error, and how much danger thee faces in pursuing thy present course. Someone must stop thee from destroying thyself. Or does thee think Constantine can save thee?"

"I need no one to save me."

"But thee will be going with him when thee leaves, will thee not?" He stepped toward her. "Will thee deny that there is more between thee and him than thee has admitted?"

Now she began to understand his anger. He was jealous. The idea was so startling that she could hardly keep from showing her amazement.

"We have been friends," she said. "That is all."

"It is a sin to lie."

"It is the truth."

"He is an evil man."

"That is ridiculous. He is—"

"Why does thee defend him so staunchly if he means nothing to thee?"

"I have no need to defend him to thee or anyone else." She began to move past him, but Virgil stepped into her path.

"Heed my warning, Serenity Campbell," he said hoarsely. "Thee must consider thy salvation and thy hope of eternal life. If thee will but surrender thyself to God, thee will regain everything thee has lost."

Oh, no. Not everything. And she couldn't surrender to anyone. Not now. Perhaps not ever.

But Virgil hadn't finished. "Thee will find someone who loves thee and will stand by thy side in thy struggles," he said, his eyes glowing with fervor. "Thee needs a husband to help thee find thy way."

She met his gaze in disbelief. It was clear he meant himself, but that seemed absurd. Aside from their childhood acquaintance so long ago, they had known each other all of one day.

"Serenity—" He looked as if he were about to fling himself to his knees in front of her. "Does thee know…" He flushed. "Thee are beautiful."

Serenity stared at him. Jacob had never called her beautiful. She had been glad, because she hadn't wanted to look beautiful to anyone…least of all Virgil. Now she became aware for the first time that he was no neutered male who would never look upon a female with anything but the purest intentions. She had been so young when she'd been taken, so naive. She hadn't had the chance to learn that Quaker men were men like any other.

And Virgil, for all his sober dress and gravity, would have been found attractive by many women. He was more than pleasant to look at, strong and straight in body.

She had no interest in him at all.

"I thank thee, Virgil," she said coolly. "It is a great compliment thee bestows upon me. But I will never marry."

"Thee doesn't know what thee is saying."

"But I do, I assure thee."

"If thee does not love Constantine…"

Serenity's mouth went dry. "I do not."

"Then if thee still grieves for Levi Carter, I have no doubt that he would wish thee to be happy. He would not wish thee to be alone."

"I am not alone. I have my friends—"

"Thee does not belong with them."

"She belongs wherever she wants to be," a deep and ominous voice said from behind her.

Jacob ambled onto the road from the stand of live oaks across the rolling meadow, loose-limbed and relaxed.

There was no hostility in his words, but Virgil went

rigid at once, his shoulders drawn up and his fists clenched at his sides.

"This does not concern thee, Constantine," he said.

Jacob ignored him. "Is he bothering you, Miss Campbell?"

It seemed the tension that had all but ruined everyone's supper had followed Serenity as relentlessly as a bad omen. "No," she said. "If you gentlemen have anything to say to one another, I suggest you say it and leave everyone else alone."

As she strode away toward the dim, flickering candlelight shining through the windows of the houses and cottages, she heard Virgil begin to speak. His tone was strident, but she couldn't make out the words.

It seemed incredible to her that they should quarrel over her, foolish and pointless. Virgil was jealous for no reason at all. And Jacob was very much mistaken in thinking she needed protection from Virgil. Unless *he,* too, was…

Jealous? Jacob? The very idea was ludicrous. Serenity stopped, laughed and shook her head. He'd never tried to hold her or put any kind of claim on her; if he had, she would never have let him come so close.

Too close.

She sighed and continued to walk, her feet pinching in their too-snug shoes. Hadn't she brooded over the very same thoughts before? Wasn't her lack of control at the very root of every difficulty that had come up since she and Jacob had left New Mexico? Hadn't she returned Jacob's embraces and his kisses with reckless abandon?

Because she had desired him. In spite of everything,

that part of her was far from dead. But that was all it was: a physical attraction.

"If thee does not love Constantine..." Virgil had used the word she had never so much as considered in connection with Jacob. Had she?

Of course not. Nor would Jacob. As little as she knew of his past, or what women he might have known and left behind, she couldn't imagine that his interest in any female would extend beyond the physical realm.

She increased her pace, eager for the familiar company of her friends in the guest cottage set aside for them. Victoria, Caridad and Zora would surely have many questions, some of which she wouldn't want to answer, but she would welcome even their interrogation rather than deal with Virgil or Jacob again tonight.

Serenity never knew what caught her attention, or why she froze like a doe scenting a panther. She turned her head toward the trees just in time to see a male figure darting among the oaks. He moved as if he didn't wish to be seen, and something metal in his hand briefly glinted in the light from the houses. Suddenly she was plunged back into the past, to the last time when strangers had come in stealth and silence.

The world around her disappeared. She was seventeen again, but this time she knew they were coming. This time she was ready to fight.

Ready to kill.

She picked up her skirts and ran for the barn. The horses snorted in alarm as she plunged through the door and climbed to the hayloft where she knew she would find the weapons she needed.

In the grip of blind instinct, Serenity buckled on

her gun belt and snatched up her rifle. She found the box of bullets and loaded both weapons, then rushed outside. She ran back the way she had come, turning toward the trees when she was well clear of the settlement.

If she had been thinking at all, she would have known that she was unlikely to find the intruder in the dark, moonlight or not. But as unlikely as it was, she saw him when she came within a dozen yards of the trees, crouched close to the ground and moving ever nearer to the houses.

A face turned toward her, blurred by shadow and distance. She had seen that face in hell, grinning like Satan himself, laughing at her pathetic attempts to protect herself. Jeering and taunting her, never letting her forget how her parents and Levi had been so mercilessly slaughtered. How she had been permitted to live for one reason only.

She lifted the rifle to her shoulder.

"Stop!" she shouted. "Stay where you are, or I'll kill you!"

The man straightened and lifted his hands. "Serenity," he said. "Go ba—"

She fired. She heard a grunt of pain, and the intruder dropped. Serenity's heart slammed in her chest, and a wash of dizziness nearly swept her to her knees. She fought to keep her balance and staggered toward the outlaw, eager to see that vile, ugly face as his blood ebbed and he realized who had taken it from him.

That was when the other man appeared, a gun in his hand, and stood over her victim. He looked at Serenity, and she glimpsed the flash of white teeth.

"I owe you a debt, ma'am," he said, touching the brim of his hat. "You saved me a heap of trouble."

"Perry," she whispered.

"Never thought you'd see me again, I reckon." He glanced down at the man at his feet. "Neither did Constantine. He didn't know me as well as he thought he did."

She followed Perry's gaze to the body. Horror, bitter as nightshade, robbed Serenity of her ability to speak.

She had shot Jacob.

"At least you didn't kill him," Perry said. "I plan to save that privilege for myself."

"No," Serenity whispered, finding her voice again. "It was a mistake."

"You must be crazy to defend a freak of nature like him," Perry said, contempt drenching every word. "What kind of female are you? Did you let this *thing* into your body?"

Serenity lifted the rifle again and aimed at Perry's chest. "Put down your gun."

"I don't think so. I've got other business here once this animal's dead. I think these people will see reason when I explain about the murderer sheltering with 'em."

"My people will never let you have Victoria," she said. "And you won't be killing anyone."

"I wouldn't like to hurt a woman, but if you don't drop that rifle—"

The body at Perry's feet erupted out of the grass, lunging for Perry's legs in a blur of motion. But Jacob was weak, and Perry stumbled away in time to escape his clawing hands. Perry braced himself on the trunk of the nearest tree and took careful aim at Jacob's head.

He never pulled the trigger. Serenity shot him, and he slumped against the tree. She dropped the rifle and fell to her knees.

"Serenity," Jacob croaked.

Still alive. She began to crawl toward him, dragging her skirts behind her.

Jacob was on his side, his right shoulder and chest smeared with terrifying quantities of blood that obscured most of his shirt and the wound itself. The deadly wound *she* had given him.

He lifted his head as she reached him, his eyes mere slits and his face taut with pain. "Serenity," he said. "I...need your help."

She crouched before him, lifting her hands helplessly, trying to think of what to do. The bullet would have to come out, and they would need rags to stop the bleeding and bind the wound. But if she left him even long enough to find help...

"I'm dying," he whispered. "Help me...undress."

Serenity knew he must be mad with pain. She ignored him and began to tear at her petticoats, struggling to rip the heavy cotton.

A bloodied hand settled on her arm. "I can...heal myself," he said. "I need...clothes off."

All at once she understood him. He meant to Change, and somehow that was going to heal him. But removing his clothing would only increase his bleeding, possibly enough to kill him.

"Trust me," Jacob said, his voice beginning to fade. He sank back, his breath rattling in his throat.

Serenity wasted no more time. She crawled closer and began to remove his boots, knowing she had to be fast as well as careful. Jacob groaned under his breath when she unbuttoned his shirt and tried to pull it over his shoulders. In the end she had to rip it to pieces with her bare hands, tearing her nails and hurting Jacob again. Grimly holding back her tears, she unbuttoned his trousers and tugged them off his legs.

The moment he was free of his clothes, Jacob shuddered and twisted as if he was caught in the grip of an agony Serenity couldn't begin to comprehend. Blood gushed from his wound, staining the ground beneath him crimson and emblazoning his skin like war paint. He shouted, a sound more howl than anything human, and the lines of his body grew blurred like a smudged charcoal drawing. Serenity glimpsed dark fur fused with pale human flesh.

Jacob scrabbled at the dirt with hands turned to paws. His face stretched, and his bared teeth glistened pointed and white. For agonizing moments he seemed to hover somewhere between man and beast, unable to complete the transition, dying a little more with every breath he took.

Serenity grabbed at him, holding on to any part of him her hands touched. It was like trying to capture mist, but she didn't let go.

"Don't give up," she whispered, praying silently as she spoke. "I won't lose you." She dug her fingertips into flesh and fur. "I love you."

It might not have been the words that gave him strength. He might not have heard them at all. But suddenly Jacob convulsed, arched his back and cried out.

The air around him shimmered, and then he was a wolf, big and black, scrambling to his feet.

The big head swung toward her. Jacob's eyes held hers, full of emotion even his animal nature couldn't conceal. He was whole, and alive, and the most beautiful creature she had ever seen.

She rose up on her knees and held out her arms, falling against his side and spearing her fingers through his thick coat. Her tears shimmered on his fur like tiny jewels.

"I'm sorry," she murmured. "I'm so sorry."

He nuzzled her hair and whined.

She drew back and took his broad head between her hands. "It will never happen again," she said. "I will never—"

A chill stole her breath. How could she have forgotten Perry? She had assumed he was incapable of attacking again, but if she were wrong…

She pulled herself to her feet, leaning heavily on Jacob's massive shoulder. He tried to block her way, but she stepped around him. Perry lay propped against the trunk of the oak, his vest and shirt as red as Jacob's, his eyes staring and empty.

Serenity reeled. *She* had done this. She had taken a life. All these years she had dreamed of shooting down the animals who had destroyed her world, but she had never imagined it like this…the waxy skin, the gaping mouth, the blood, the living spirit gone forever.

"Don't look at him," Jacob said behind her, human again.

It would have been so easy to obey him, but she wasn't going to run away from what she'd done. For her sake, Jacob had tried to take the burden of responsibility for Leroy's death. She wouldn't let him do it again.

"I almost killed you because I thought you were my enemy," she whispered, her body breaking into shivers of reaction.

"But you didn't." His hand settled on her shoulder, fingers squeezing gently. "I'm all right. Not a mark on me."

"If you hadn't been able to Change, you would have died. Wouldn't you?"

"The Change heals about every kind of wound, as long as you're strong enough to make the transformation."

Jacob had been strong enough. This time. How often had it happened before? When he'd healed so quickly at the ranch, before she'd even known he wasn't human? Did werewolves have nine lives, like cats?

If they had, she'd just taken one of Jacob's. And a man lay dead at her feet because she had made one too many mistakes.

"I warned him to stay clear," Jacob said, cupping his hand around her neck. "I misjudged him, and I'm sorry you had to be the one to stop him. I would have spared you that."

She closed her eyes. "If I hadn't been so blind with hate, this wouldn't have happened. After I left you and Virgil, I thought I saw one of the men who killed my parents, but it was Perry."

Jacob walked around her, coming to stand between her and the body. "Perry could have been one of them. He was willing to go pretty far to get his prey. It doesn't take much for a man to turn from what he was into a murderer."

She turned her back on Jacob, unable to meet his gaze. "It didn't take much for me to turn into a murderer. First Leroy, now—"

He grabbed her shoulders and spun her around. "You saved my life," he said harshly. "You protected your friend and God knows who else from a man who refused to back down. You had no choice."

Perhaps not tonight. But from now on—tomorrow and the next day and the next—there would be new choices. Hard ones. And she could not put them off much longer.

"Jacob," she began, but he wasn't listening.

A growl rumbled in his throat. Virgil was running from the direction of the road, his face a pale blur. As soon as he was close enough to see Serenity and Jacob, his feet stuttered to an awkward halt.

"Serenity? I thought I..." He stared at Jacob's nakedness, then at Serenity. "What has thee done?"

CHAPTER SEVENTEEN

SHE KNEW VIRGIL WASN'T referring to Perry's body, which he hadn't yet seen, but to Jacob's. Whatever he planned to say next was forestalled by the arrival of several people from the settlement. Zora was in the lead, running with all the grace and intensity of a wolf on the hunt. Caridad and Victoria were behind her, followed by Uncle Lester and William Burns.

Zora took in the situation immediately, her night-seeing eyes quick to pick out the body and the blood splashed across grass, earth and tree.

"Perry," she said.

Caridad skidded up beside her.

"Chingados," she spat. "I knew he would not give up!"

The Quakers followed her gaze, and Serenity saw them stiffen with horror.

"Who is this man?" Lester stammered, no longer the jovial, affectionate uncle he had been at supper. "Is he—?"

"He is dead," Serenity said, stepping forward. Jacob tried to hold her back, but she broke free and met Lester's gaze steadily.

"This man," she said, "was a bounty hunter who intended harm to one of my friends and would have stopped at nothing to take her captive, including killing anyone who stood in his way. He tried to kill Jacob, so I..." She swallowed and lifted her chin. "I shot him."

Lester and William exchanged shocked glances. "Where did thee get a weapon?" Lester asked.

"We had them when we came here," Jacob said. "We just kept them out of sight, in the barn. We figured you'd want it that way."

"Because thee wanted to hide what thee are," Virgil snarled. "But we know thee are no simple cowhand."

"I don't deny it," Jacob said. "I follow the same profession as the dead man, but I hold to the law."

"Killing is the law of Satan," Virgil said. He turned to Serenity. "Did thee recognize this man when thee shot him?"

"She saw someone with a gun sneaking toward your homestead," Jacob said. "I'd been stalking him myself just before she got here."

"Unclothed?" Lester asked in disbelief.

"Less noise that way," Jacob said. "But he saw me, and tried to kill me." He moved up so close to Serenity that she could feel his hot breath on her neck. "She saved my life."

Only after nearly killing him, Serenity thought. But telling the whole story would only make things worse.

Though as far as her fellow Quakers were concerned, it could hardly be any worse. "Thee knows our ways," Lester said to Serenity. "If thee had come to us instead of choosing violence—"

"What would you have done?" Jacob said. It was the same question he'd asked of Virgil at dinner, and it was no less stinging now. "This man would have killed you as soon as look at you."

"We cannot sanction violence here, even at the cost of our own lives."

"Jacob isn't bound by our…by the beliefs of the Friends," Serenity said. "He should not have to give up his own life for those beliefs. And I wouldn't let him."

The elder Quakers were obviously struggling for something to say, but Virgil was not so reticent. He stared at Jacob with undisguised hatred.

"It is you who have brought this evil here," he said.

"No," Victoria said. "He was after *me.* I was accused of—" She broke off, and then continued bravely. "I killed my husband."

"In self-defense," Caridad said. "Her husband beat her. Perry would have taken her back to be hanged by men who knew nothing of what she suffered."

Serenity knew what the Friends would say to that. They would deeply sympathize and mourn for Victoria's plight, but they would never condone what she had done under any circumstances.

"None of you should have come," Virgil said, his mouth twisted in a bitter sneer. "Serenity would have had some chance of salvation if you had not brought your outsider ways. Now she is as damned as all the rest of you."

"Virgil Thompson," Lester said. "Be silent." He looked at Serenity with deep sadness. "Has thee truly forgotten everything thee learned here, child? Has thee fallen so far?"

Heedless of his nakedness, Jacob imposed himself between them. "Serenity's family died because of your rules," he said. "They would have died even if you'd been here, along with the rest of you. I just hope nothing like that ever comes your way again."

"It would make no difference," Lester said, his face drawn with sadness. "We would stand by our principles and the teachings of our Lord."

"And do your principles allow for taking Serenity back after what she's done?"

"Jacob," Serenity began, "I don't—"

"There is always forgiveness with sincere repentance," Lester said, echoing the words Virgil had spoken so short a time earlier. "With prayer and guidance, there is always hope. But in light of what thee has told us, Jacob Constantine, I believe thy influence to be harmful. Thee is unlikely to renounce thy ways. Serenity cannot achieve peace in thy continued presence."

"But I'm not staying," Serenity said. "You expect me to choose between my friends and your world. But I left this world long ago and can never return."

In spite of all he had said, Lester seemed genuinely stricken by her words. "Does thee know what thee is saying, child? Would thee forever turn thy back on those who love thee?"

"I came for my aunt's sake. I would stay to tend her if you could accept my presence, but I would only be a blot on her peace. I am sorry, Uncle."

"Sorry?" Virgil spat. "I offered thee honorable and lawful marriage, a life of honest work and devotion, and thee chooses this man who will lead thee to damnation?"

"Yes," she said. "I choose Jacob."

Though she could see only a little of Jacob's face, she glimpsed his grim expression when he glanced at her over his shoulder. Had he heard her when she'd said "I love you," or had his nearness to death made him deaf to her pleas? Did he assume her declaration had only been that of a woman desperate to save a friend's life, and that her choice now was simply a means of defying her family?

If they had been alone, would he have reminded her just how deep was the chasm she was attempting to cross?

Spinning on his heel, Virgil strode away. Uncle Lester and William bowed their heads.

"We can do nothing more," Lester said. "Thy aunt will be deeply grieved."

Guilt and rending sadness thickened Serenity's voice. "If you…if you will permit it, I would see her one more time."

Lester considered for a dozen painful seconds and then lifted his head. "Come to the house in the morning. Elizabeth will return thy clothing, and thee may see Martha to make thy farewells. We will think of some reason to explain the necessity of thy going." He glanced at William. "We must see to the burial of this man. Will thee wait here while I gather the other men?"

"That won't be necessary," Jacob said. "I'll bury him here. You can say your words over him once I'm done."

Serenity expected Lester to argue, but he only looked one last time at Serenity, his eyes brimming with tears, and then, with William beside him, started back for the settlement.

Jacob was already speaking to Caridad when Serenity rejoined him. "I don't think we'll be wanted in

Tolerance tonight," he said with heavy irony. "Can you get our gear and horses? We'll make camp where the river makes that big bend about a quarter mile west of here." He paused. "I think Serenity needs a little more time to herself."

Obviously relieved at having something to do, Caridad headed for Tolerance. Zora lingered, glancing between Serenity and Jacob.

Serenity wondered how long the other woman had known just how she felt about him. Longer, Serenity guessed, than she had herself. Even Frances had sensed it, back at Avalon.

After a moment Zora left, and only Victoria remained.

"I'm so sorry," she said. She covered her face with her hands. "This is all my fault."

"Don't be foolish," Serenity said, pulling Victoria into her arms. "We would never have let him take you. Jacob would have stopped him if I hadn't…if I hadn't shot him first."

"But you wouldn't have had to if I'd gone with Perry."

"That's enough." Serenity released Victoria and pushed up her friend's chin. "It's over now. Go help Caridad and Zora."

Victoria scrubbed at her face and turned away, her big frame bent with grief.

Serenity's heart ached for her, but she knew there was nothing she could do. Jacob's words of comfort had done nothing to ease her own sickness at what had happened.

What must never happen again.

"Serenity."

Jacob's voice was gentle, but she dreaded what he might be about to say. "I'm all right," she said quickly.

"That pasty-faced, mealymouthed son of a bitch," Jacob growled. "For two bits I'd have laid him out right where he stood. Hell, it was hard just to keep from telling that uncle of yours what I thought of his pious hogwash."

"Thank God you didn't."

"I don't see what God has to do with any of this. Your kin turned their back on you for trying to protect them from what happened to your ma and pa."

"But I wasn't really protecting them. The man I imagined I saw…the one I thought I shot…that wasn't Perry, much less you."

"One of the Reniers," he muttered.

"Yes." She closed her eyes. "I was a little crazy, Jacob. But that doesn't excuse—"

"I would have done exactly what you did."

"You said you wouldn't kill them when we found them," she said. "You were going to see they faced justice under the law."

"I'm not so sure anymore."

Not sure, when she had become so sure herself?

She turned to face him. "Your devotion to the law is what sets you apart," she said quietly. "It makes you better. Don't ever think of giving it up."

He touched her cheek with a fingertip. "It's good I have you around to remind me. Maybe I'm going to need more reminding from now on."

Serenity forgot to breathe. Were his words careless

rhetoric, or was he acknowledging what she'd said to Jacob, making a declaration of his own?

Was he saying *I choose you?*

Don't, she told herself. *Don't think.*

"Perry," she said, forcing herself to remember the body still lying under the tree. "We should look after him. At least he deserves a decent burial."

Jacob blinked, caught off guard by her abrupt change of subject. "Are you sure you want to help?" he asked softly.

"Yes."

"Then this is as good a place as any. I'll dig the hole."

It didn't surprise her when he Changed into a wolf. He made short work of digging a man-size hole in the soil under the oak's gnarled branches, shoveling with his broad, sharp-nailed paws and pushing the dirt behind him with thrusts of his powerful hind legs. The grave wouldn't be deep; the soil was too shallow and rocky. But it would do its job.

As Jacob dug, Serenity prepared herself to touch the man she had killed. She crouched beside Perry's body, reached out slowly and brushed his eyelids closed, then straightened his arms and legs. He looked almost at peace now, the harshness gone out of his face, his heart no longer driven by the need to kill.

In that one way, though she was still alive, Serenity was like him. She had learned her lesson just in time.

Now she only had to explain to Jacob that his job was over.

As if he'd sensed her thoughts, Jacob gave her a long, wolfish look and Changed again.

"You ready?" he asked.

She nodded and moved to Perry's feet. She knew Jacob could easily handle the body himself, but even if her assistance was only symbolic, it was important.

Together they lifted Perry and carried him to the grave. Jacob took most of the weight as they lowered the other man into the ground. When the body was settled, Serenity straightened it again, folding Perry's arms over his chest.

"I'm not one for ceremony," Jacob said, hovering with unusual awkwardness over the grave. "Anything you want to say?"

Serenity bowed her head and stumbled through a silent plea for forgiveness, with a wish that Perry might truly find peace in whatever place his soul found itself.

Then she nodded to Jacob, who used his human hands to push the dirt over the body. It took some time, but neither he nor Serenity was in any hurry to leave. When the hole was filled, Serenity helped Jacob tamp down the earth, and they collected rocks to cover the grave and give the body a little more protection.

After that they stood in silence for a while, absorbing the night-sounds that gradually resumed around them.

"You've got to get cleaned up," Jacob said at last. He gathered the remaining shreds of his clothing. "Let's go down to the river."

With a last glance at the grave, Serenity left the shelter of the trees, pausing to let Jacob take the lead. Five minutes' walk brought them to the bank of the Guadalupe River at the place where Jacob had suggested setting up camp. The water was quiet there, with a low, grassy bank that ended in gravel next to the water.

The other women still hadn't arrived, and Serenity was glad. She sat down on the bank, too exhausted to move another inch. Her skirts were liberally spattered with blood, but she couldn't imagine finding the strength to remove them, let alone the petticoats and bodice and underthings to which she was so unaccustomed. Jacob continued to the river's edge and waded in, carrying his ruined trousers.

Serenity had seen Jacob naked on several occasions before tonight, each time when he had been about to Change. She had noticed his beauty before and tried to pretend she hadn't.

But now she was keenly aware of his body, of the way the rising moon's light slid over the contours of his back and shoulders and flowed down to his waist and below. He kept his back to her, a small concession to modesty, but there was nothing self-conscious in his movements.

Why should there be? He and Serenity had shared every intimacy possible between a man and woman. All except one. She watched him as he emerged from the river, water glistening on his chest and dripping from the trousers he had carried in with him. He laid the trousers out on the rocks and came toward Serenity, crouching on the bank a few yards away with his hands dangling between his knees.

"You ought to wash up," he said. "I can go a little ways off while you do it. I'll know if anyone comes."

She sighed. "I don't want you to go away."

"Then I won't look. You've got to take care of yourself, Serenity."

Others had said that to her before. She wasn't sure what it meant anymore, if she ever had been sure. For a year after the tragedy, "taking care of herself" had meant personal survival, and then it had been making sure the ranch survived. When Jacob had arrived, the only thing she'd wanted for herself was revenge.

Now that purpose was gone. What could possibly replace something that had driven her for seven years? If she removed her dress and bathed the blood from her flesh, would she wash away her sins, as well?

It was too good to be true. All the things she had imagined in the most secret corners of her heart were too good to be true.

"Jacob," she said wearily, "I have something to say to you."

He met her gaze, his gold-flecked eyes intent and worried. Was it fear that she would declare her love for him again? Ask him to return the sentiment? Beg him to marry her?

"I—" She drew in a hard breath and let it out again. "I won't be going on after the Reniers."

Whatever he had expected her to say, it obviously hadn't been that. "Why?" he asked.

She laced her fingers together and clenched her joined hands. "I always intended to kill them, Jacob."

"I know."

Of course he had. That was why he'd tried so hard to discourage her from the beginning. He hadn't wanted her to become a murderer.

"I've changed my mind," she said, forging ahead.

"Even after Leroy, I still didn't understand what it would be like to kill someone with my own—" She opened her red-stained hands and stared at them blankly. "Never again. I'm finished."

THERE HAD BEEN more than a few times in Jacob's life when he'd had to hide his feelings. There had been times when it hadn't been easy, but this was one of the hardest.

This was what he'd been hoping for. He'd just about given up when he'd realized that Serenity could never return to her Quaker ways or find acceptance among kin who had no comprehension of what she'd been and what she'd done to survive.

But he hadn't counted on Perry. He hadn't counted on what Serenity had had to do to save his life again, or how much that would change her.

He should have been relieved, but his feelings were as tangled up as petticoats on a barbwire fence, and he couldn't seem to sort them out. Just like he couldn't forget the words Serenity had spoken when he'd been fighting for his life.

I love you.

Jacob stared at the soft earth between his feet, wishing he could dig a hole deep enough to bury himself way down where no one could ever find him. When she'd blurted out her feelings, he'd been too busy trying to survive to really understand the words. And afterward, he'd had plenty more to think about, especially where it came to Serenity's well-being and the clucking of the Quakers with all their high-minded rules.

Now he felt her avowal all through his body, tightening every muscle and shortening his breath. In all the time they'd spent together, even when he'd had her in his arms, those words were the last ones he'd ever expected to hear her say.

Not because she couldn't learn to love a man. She'd done it once. Hell, he'd thought that someday if she could only let go of her hate, she could find someone who would treat her decent and soothe her hurts and make her happy. He'd just known it wouldn't be him.

The only thing that made sense was that she hadn't meant what she'd said. Maybe she'd only intended to help him when he was losing his fight to live.

And she *had* helped him. He'd felt her words, even if he hadn't fully understood them. They'd given him strength. She'd done what she'd set out to do, if that had been her purpose. But that knowledge didn't help him, either. Not when she'd gone and made it so clear that she'd chosen him over her own kind.

Chosen him for what? Virgil had wanted to marry her. Jacob had heard the proposal himself when he'd been listening to their conversation after supper.

Serenity had rejected him firmly, but had she been tempted by Virgil's offer, even for a moment? Had that put some idea in her head that Jacob wanted the same thing? Could her brief time at Tolerance have changed her in ways he hadn't recognized?

A hollow pit opened up in Jacob's chest, a cage where his heart rattled around like seeds in a dried-up yucca pod. He had to be wrong about that, too. She'd only wanted to show her kin that she was serious in her intention to go her own way, and get rid of Virgil at the same time.

If she *had* meant the other thing, she would tell him. She was too honest not to. And now that she'd decided to give up her revenge…

It didn't mean he had to give up the hunt, too. *Your devotion to the law is what sets you apart,* Serenity had told him. He'd come dangerously close to forgetting that when he'd realized that Perry had ignored his warnings. He would have killed his old friend without hesitation.

But Serenity had brought him back to himself again. He could entrust her to her friends, knowing they would do everything in their power to heal her sadness, that she would become all the stronger for what she'd suffered. He would go after the Reniers using the information he'd picked up in Bethel. He would bring the outlaws in under the Code, as he'd always intended.

Everything would be the way it was before he'd met her.

A fish plopped in the river, and Jacob came back to himself.

Serenity was still gazing at him steadily, her eyes filled with profound sadness.

"I understand," he said slowly. "You're no killer, whatever you think. Letting go is the right thing to do."

Serenity tugged her bonnet off, pulled the pins out of her hair and shook it loose around her shoulders. "I have a chance to start over now," she said. "And that's what I plan to do."

Jacob's mouth was crowded with words he couldn't speak. "You're strong," he said. "You'll find your way."

Serenity glanced away, and Jacob realized how what he'd meant as encouragement must have sounded to her.

Your way. Not *our way.* If she looked at him again with hurt in her eyes…

"I don't know if I'm strong," she said. "I only know I can't go back to the way I was before I came here."

He wondered if *he* could.

"You're going back to Avalon?" he asked.

"I was always going to go back," she said. "I just didn't know it would be so soon. Or so difficult."

"It won't seem that way when you're home."

Serenity drew up her knees, tucking her skirts around her legs. "I guess we won't be seeing each other again after I leave."

There it was. No more circling around, each waiting for the other to make the first move, speak the words out loud. Serenity had just answered the questions that had been haunting Jacob since they'd left Perry's grave.

So why in hell did he want to tear the whole world apart with his bare hands?

"My work takes me to New Mexico Territory pretty often," he said thickly. "There's no telling…"

But he knew, as she did, that once they parted it would be for good.

There was nothing left to say. Jacob became suddenly aware that he was still naked. A few minutes ago it hadn't mattered; now it did, and his trousers were still sopping wet. Until the other women got back with the horses and his other clothes, he would find somewhere in the brush to wait, maybe even go for a run and work this sickness out of his head.

Serenity moved before he did. She got to her feet, reaching behind her to the fastenings of her skirt. She let it fall in a puddle at her feet, kicked it aside and began to unbutton her bodice. Underneath she wore some kind of a modified corset, fastened with hooks and worn over an unbleached muslin chemise. She removed her petticoats, made for an old-fashioned kind of dress, one without a bustle. Her drawers were unadorned, without even a hint of ribbon or lace.

Jacob clenched his teeth and forced himself to look away. He'd urged her to bathe, sure enough. But she had to know better than this. He jumped up and started for the trees.

"Jacob."

He stopped in his tracks. The sound of his name on her lips filled that empty place in his chest with air too hot and heavy to breathe.

Move on, he told himself. But her voice had bound his legs, his whole body, with silk and thorns. He turned his head. As Serenity unbuttoned the placket of her chemise and pulled it over her head, baring her small, firm breasts, he knew the situation was already out of his control. And when she stepped out of her drawers and cast them aside like the skirts and petticoats, he didn't figure it was much good trying to hide the part of him that gave him away.

He'd imagined her body naked plenty of times, just as she was now, slender and curvy all at the same time, innocent and seductive as a siren. He'd felt a little of that sweet body—the firmness of her belly, the plumpness of her breasts. But he hadn't seen her bare legs, sleek with muscle earned from days in the saddle, soft and feminine all the same. Or the gracefulness of her bare arms. Or the little fluff of hair over her—

"Do you think I'm beautiful?" she asked, her voice husky.

Virgil had called her that. Jacob never had, even though he'd thought it more times than he could count.

"Yes," he said. "And you'd better get on with your washing up. I'll just go over to the—"

"No." She came toward him, moonlight caressing her skin with eager fingers. "I want you to stay with me."

Jacob's heart seemed to swell up as big as his cock. "The others will be here anytime now. It's time you—"

He lost his train of thought as Serenity turned toward the river, hips swaying as she glided down to the water's edge and slipped in. It wasn't very deep, but she crouched until she was floating on the surface, then swam out to the middle. She stood upright again and began to splash water over her face, her shoulders, her back, dunked her head and came up with her hair sliding over her neck and shoulders like drifts of seaweed.

It was a struggle, but Jacob managed to consider the idea that she still might not completely understand what she was doing. Maybe she thought since he'd been so easy being naked that she should be, too. But he couldn't quite convince himself that she could be that naive after what they'd already done.

Serenity glanced back at him over her shoulder, her hands moving where he couldn't see. He imagined them stroking her own breasts, the nipples hardening to stiff peaks, and the ache in his cock became almost unendurable. He'd been ready for this for a long time. So ready that he would have to watch himself once he got inside her.

If that was what she really wanted, and if he didn't have the sense and discipline to refuse. He was about to walk away again when Serenity waded out of the water, bold as you please, and all he could think about was licking the glistening drops from her breasts and belly, and hearing her little cries of surrender.

She held out her hand. "Jacob," she said, a little crack in her voice, "I want to be with you. In every way."

"Serenity," he said. "Listen to me. I—"

"I want you."

Oh, she knew what she was doing. Maybe too well. There was a chance—he despised himself for thinking it—that she saw sex as a way to bind them. That this was a trick, and all the quiet acceptance of their separation a lie.

He wouldn't believe it of her.

"I know it's only this one night," she said, oblivious to his ugly speculation. "I won't ever ask anything of you again. But I want something to remember you by. Something I can never forget."

Jacob was ashamed, but he wasn't done worrying. In giving herself to him, Serenity might get far more than she bargained for. He had to think for both of them, as long as he could still think.

"Have you thought..." He started again. "You know there's a chance...a danger that..."

"I don't think it's possible, Jacob." She looked down, her hair swaying over her face.

Jacob couldn't ask her how she knew. For most women, it would be a tragedy. There was nothing he could do to take that pain away. But he could show her she didn't have to be alone.

He took her hand and pulled her into his arms.

CHAPTER EIGHTEEN

SERENITY WASN'T AFRAID. She didn't fear Jacob's touch, or the arousal that made itself so plainly known as he embraced her.

And she wasn't afraid of what the others would think if they returned too soon. None of that was important now. What had Jacob said about the way wolves saw the world? *No future, no past.*

Tonight she was a wolf.

Like a wolf, guided only by instinct, she searched for his mouth and found it, opened her lips to welcome the gentle push of his tongue.

There had been two other kisses, only two, and yet it felt as if they'd done this a thousand times. A thousand times, and every one as arousing and exciting as the last. Jacob was incredibly gentle as he explored her mouth, probing the subtle dips and hollows with flicks of his tongue.

She had never been kissed like this. It was an act of love in itself, demanding nothing more than what she had already offered. If she had asked to stop here, Jacob would have let her go, even though she had seen the extent of his arousal and felt it pressing against her thigh as he leaned above her.

Once that would have terrified her. Later, she had trained her body not to feel anything at all. But with

Jacob she was a virgin again, clean, untouched, eager to know the mysteries into which every young bride was initiated.

But there was no bride here. Only a lover, in every sense of the word. And that would have to be enough.

She suddenly became aware that Jacob's mouth was no longer on hers. His face was a few inches away; he hadn't left her. But he was searching her eyes, looking for…what? Fear? Uncertainty? Second thoughts about continuing what she had always stopped short of before?

No words could reassure him. She reached down to feel for his hand, twined her fingers through his and lifted it to her breast.

The last time he'd touched her there, she had been caught in a kind of desperate pleasure, as if she were snatching joy from the mouth of an abyss. But when Jacob cupped his palm around her now and began to tease her nipple with his thumb, the abyss was nowhere to be found. Only the exquisite sensation of his big hand on her soft flesh, gentle and firm at the same time.

Her nipple hardened under his caresses, aching so badly that it seemed nothing Jacob could do could take away the pleasure-pain.

But he found a way. He kissed her lips again, then her chin, then the hollow of her neck and the upper slopes of her breasts. When his mouth closed over her nipple, she cried out in surprise. Heat flowed like an invisible current up to her head and down to the warm, wet place where her thighs met her belly.

Jacob's tongue stroked over her nipple, curled around it, drew it into his mouth. Serenity arched her back, pushing herself deeper as he began to suckle. The obvious satisfaction he took aroused her even more.

He *did* think she was beautiful. He worshipped her body as he sucked, running his hands over her hips, along her thighs, around her belly. And he made her realize, with the part of her mind that could still hold a thought, that her body was something wonderful. Not a thing to be used, not a vessel to serve a man's lust, but a source of joy.

That was why, when Jacob cupped his hand over the mound of soft curls below her stomach and slid his finger into the tender cleft below, she didn't try to push him away, or struggle or resist. It was the most natural thing in the world to feel the flood of moisture nourish what had been dry for so many years, feel the petals plump and swell like flowers bursting from the desert earth after a summer rain.

"Serenity?" he murmured into her ear. "Am I going too fast?"

If she had been able to laugh, she would have given him his answer. There was nothing quick or impatient about anything he was doing to her.

But since she couldn't speak, she slipped her hand between them and followed the length of his arm until she found his slick fingers and pressed them into her again. He dipped in, rubbing gently, and all of a sudden brushed against something that set off an electric current, shocking her whole body at once.

Her thighs opened of their own accord, inviting him to continue. He didn't hesitate to accept the invitation. He returned to that remarkable nub of pleasure, gradually applying more pressure as he circled it with his thumb. Serenity could feel something building inside her, a strange and almost frightening sensation that could not be compared to any other, not even the things Jacob had already done. It was as if she was poised on a high pinnacle above a deep valley, wings pressed tight against her back, and was only awaiting the moment to unfurl them and fly.

But something held her back, and it seemed as if she stepped back from the edge when he slid his fingers deeper into her cleft and downward. Then they found her entrance, and she began to fall. There were no wings to save her; the abyss was there again, bottomless and black.

"Serenity." Jacob's rough cheek pressed against hers, a simple, affectionate touch that brought her back to herself again. "What's wrong?"

She opened her eyes. The sky was full of stars, splashed across the darkness like spatters of paint. There was no cavern here, no chains or ropes to bind, no mocking voices.

Only Jacob, who simply held her in his arms, lying beside her so that she could no longer feel the weight of his shaft on her thigh.

She turned toward him, resting her forehead against his. "I…I only need a little time," she whispered.

"Am I hurting you?"

"No. No." She smiled and kissed him, the barest touch of her lips on his. "I'm just not used…" She swallowed. "It's been a long time."

It occurred to her then that he might think—correctly, even if for the wrong reason—that she was not a virgin. A woman alone, without a man, and still young… He might think she had been with Levi before their marriage, but if he did, he had never shown in any way that it bothered him.

They had come to this without obligations or promises on either side. He knew he was getting her out of wedlock, with no real knowledge of what her life had been like since her family's deaths. He would have no right to judge.

But that was the wonderful thing. He wasn't judging her at all. He was cupping her face in his big palm and stroking the tears away with his thumb, so very, very tenderly.

"We can stop now," he said. "It's all right."

She covered his hand, trapping it against her cheek. "I don't want to stop," she said. "I want to give you—"

"You don't need to give me anything," he interrupted huskily. "If this is all we ever do, it won't make any difference."

But it would. To her. She wanted Jacob, wanted to be one with him completely. She turned on her side, rolling her body against his, and hooked her right leg over his left thigh.

"I want you inside me," she whispered. "Please."

"You sure?" he asked, stroking her hair away from her forehead.

She let her body speak for her, snuggling even closer, making it impossible not to feel his very hard erection and the quickness of his breath on her face.

But he didn't take her then, as he could so easily have done with a little adjustment and a single deep thrust. Instead he gently pushed her onto her back again, then began to work his way down her body with his lips and tongue, beginning with her lips and ending at the mound of curls he had so intimately touched before. He didn't stop there but dipped his tongue where his fingers had gone, sliding it between the swollen folds of those other lips. He stroked downward, almost teasing her entrance, and then licked up again, flicking the nub, his mouth hot and wet.

The wings of ecstasy began to unfurl from Serenity's shoulders. Jacob drew the fleshy nub into his mouth just as he had her nipples, and suckled. Her heart nearly burst with indescribable pleasure. Liquid gushed from between her legs, and she was almost embarrassed. Nothing like that had ever happened to her before. But Jacob lapped the wetness up as if it were honey and stroked lower once more, his tongue circling around and around the place that now felt so empty, so desperately in need of filling.

Jacob filled it with his tongue. He pushed inside her. Serenity cried out and arched her back, stretching her legs farther apart. He withdrew his tongue and pushed it in again, mimicking what would inevitably come later.

Still, it was not what she wanted. Once again she reached between them, tugging on his thick, dark hair, forcing him to slide back up along her body.

His mouth was wet with her juices, and he slowly licked his lips.

"I love the taste of you," he murmured.

Serenity shuddered. Even the few words he spoke drove her near to madness. But she kept enough presence of mind to reach down between them again, feeling for the shaft trapped between his stomach and hers. She brushed the silky head with her fingertips.

Jacob stiffened. Serenity closed her hand around him, and moved it up and down, very gently.

He closed his eyes and moved against her palm.

"Serenity," he rumbled, "you can't keep this up if you want me to…to…"

Nothing would have pleased Serenity more than to continue, seeing all the control slip from Jacob's body. But she spread her thighs again and firmly guided him down until he was poised at her entrance, just one easy move away from filling her up completely.

He hesitated only a moment, then thrust inside her. There was nothing hard or brutal about it; he seemed to glide in, moving easily over the slick surface her body had made for him. There was no pain, no discomfort of any kind, only a profound sense of rightness. This was how it was supposed to be, the way she had never imagined it *could* be.

Love made all the difference.

Jacob rested once he was fully within her, bending his face to hers. His unspoken question hung between them. He had seen how skittish she was at every touch—until tonight. How many times, she thought, had he wondered why?

After tonight, he wouldn't have to wonder any longer. For now, she could only reassure him with her fingers in his hair, her smile, her eyes. And her lips claiming his.

Slowly he began to move again. He withdrew almost all the way, teasing her, then moved in again. He set up a rhythm that seemed to stroke Serenity inside the way his hands had stroked her skin, creating a delightful friction that made her catch her breath. His thickness stretched her, but again there was no discomfort. She lifted her hips to take him even deeper, and he obliged, cradling her bottom with one hand and driving all the way to the hilt.

Serenity gasped, and once again Jacob hesitated. She locked her thighs around his waist.

"Don't stop," she moaned.

He began to move faster, no longer measuring his strokes the way he'd done before. She moved with him, eagerly, breathlessly. She spread her enormous wings and looked down into the chasm.

Light exploded up from the depths, enfolding her, carrying her out into the currents that swirled with a million colors. Then she was flying as the light pulsed and throbbed around her, sending velvety shivers over the surface of her skin and deep inside.

Jacob sighed and relaxed, holding himself up on his elbows above her. He kissed the side of her jaw and her ear, and nuzzled her hair. Serenity closed her eyes and settled back onto the precipice. The abyss no longer held any terror for her. She knew she could always find her way out again simply by spreading her wings.

Rolling onto his side, Jacob murmured something she couldn't quite hear, pulled her against him and hooked his arm around her shoulders. She tucked her head under his chin. A little while later Jacob's breathing slowed, and she knew he was asleep.

Her heart was overflowing, spilling joy throughout her body and keeping her wide-awake. She listened to Jacob for a while, then watched the stars and wondered how there could be so many miracles in the world that she had never noticed.

That was part of the wolf, too, Jacob had told her. Now she was beginning to understand. And though Jacob's goodness could never erase the evil of the Reniers and others like them, it had showed her that she had learned to hate a phantom that didn't exist. Just as she had learned that there could be deep, abiding pleasure in the joining of woman and man. It was the greatest of gifts except one.

And if she never received the other, she would be forever grateful to Jacob for giving her wings.

SERENITY'S QUIET WEEPING woke Jacob from a sleep crowded with dreams of brilliant color and soaring wings. He was up at once, on the verge of panic before he saw her kneeling in the grass a dozen yards away, her head in her hands, her shoulders shaking with her sobs.

He ran to her, moving as loudly as he could to warn her of his approach.

She looked up, composed her expression and surreptitiously wiped the tears from her face.

"I'm sorry," she said, attempting a smile. "I didn't mean to wake you, but I should have realized you would hear me."

He sat beside her, began to put his arm around her shoulders and then thought better of it. She'd never liked looking weak, especially when she was at her most vulnerable.

"I don't usually sleep past dawn," he said, resting

his elbows over his updrawn knees. "Did you get any rest?"

"As much as you'd let me." She grinned, but he knew it was only for his sake.

"Did I make you cry?" he asked softly.

"No! Don't think… It wasn't you. At least not in the way—" She broke off, her breath shuddering out in a rush.

He touched her shoulder with the tips of his fingers. "You sure I didn't hurt you?"

"No. No. Please believe me." She smiled at him again, warm enough to make him wish they had the night to share all over again. "I was only happy."

"You were crying because you were happy?"

She lowered her head, her hair falling around her face so that he could no longer see it. "Women do that sometimes," she said. "Maybe you wouldn't understand."

"Try me."

A bird sang tentatively in the bushes nearby. Jacob smelled rain, maybe only a few minutes away. Down near the river, metal jingled. Jacob had heard the women coming with the horses and stop a discreet distance farther down the bank, but he hadn't wanted to wake Serenity.

Right now she was struggling with something—a secret, maybe—she wasn't sure she should tell him. If she chose to keep it from him, he wouldn't press her; he didn't have a right to ask anything more of her when they would be parting so soon.

Parting. Never to see her again. Never to kiss her,

hold her in his arms, feel her thighs gripping his waist as he took her again and again to joyous completion.

"I didn't know it was possible to feel this way," she said. "To feel so good, so safe. It was like a miracle."

Jacob felt humbled, but he sensed it would be better not to interrupt her with clumsy words of thanks he didn't know how to give.

After a moment she continued, speaking as hesitantly as if she were feeling her way through some vast darkness.

"You must have realized that I wasn't a virgin," she said.

He'd known as soon as he entered her, but after that he hadn't been doing much thinking about anything. It hadn't shocked him then and it didn't now, but it meant something that she was telling him this. Something important.

"Before tonight," she whispered, "the only thing I knew about lying with a man was ugliness. Pain and humiliation."

Every muscle in Jacob's body tightened. He'd wondered more than once if a man had hurt her, but she'd absolved her late fiance with her loving words and never hinted at anyone else in her life.

"Who was it?" he demanded.

She turned her head swiftly, her hair swinging away in a silken arc, and looked into Jacob's eyes. "Does it matter to you that I wasn't…wasn't pure?"

In answer, he put both arms around her and pulled her against his side, pressing his face into her hair. "I wasn't exactly pure, either," he said.

Her laugh was more of a hiccup than anything else.

"It's different for men. Didn't you know that? Not many men would think—"

"I don't give a damn about what other men think."

Tucking her head under his chin, she curled against him as if she wished she could fold herself into his body and disappear. "I'm glad," she whispered.

Jacob wasn't sure he could ever be happy about anything again. "Who was it, Serenity?"

She twisted in his arms to touch his cheek. "Is it so important, Jacob? I'm not who I was before you came to Avalon. The past is dead for me now. Last night took away all the rest of the pain."

Serenity took his clenched fist and kissed his knuckles. "Can you be content with knowing that you have changed everything for me?"

Could he? Could he stop himself from imagining what she'd gone through, what pain she must have suffered to have completely cut herself off from male companionship?

Zora's words in Bethel came back to him then. *She has felt nothing but hate for any man since I met her. Since you came, she is different.*

He'd been more than willing to accept her renunciation of her revenge against the Reniers, just as he'd renounced his own. Letting his anger keep the past alive would do nothing to change it. The Code had taught him that.

How much do you care for her? How much?

Enough to want to make her tormentor suffer. But not at any price.

"Jacob?"

Her voice was very soft now, hardly a breath of air

grazing his chin. "I said I'd never ask anything of you again, but…"

He knew then that nothing she asked him would be too much. "What is it, Serenity?" he asked, pulling her close again.

"Will you…will you at least consider coming back to Avalon?"

Only a few hours ago he would have flinched at the question. It didn't seem so terrible now. Not after last night. Not after what she'd told him. She'd said he'd changed her life.

But he'd changed Ruth's life, too. He'd cut it short with his stupidity and neglect. Serenity had to know that, even if he never told her who had shot Ruth eight times and left her lying on the kitchen floor.

"There's something you have to know," he said. "I was married once. Her name was Ruth, and I loved her." He had to swallow twice before he could continue. "She was killed. Murdered, like your parents."

He told her the rest, about how he'd spent so much of his time away with the Rangers, coming home for only a few weeks out of the year, taking her for granted in spite of her devotion and selfless love for him, or maybe because of it.

He didn't tell Serenity who had murdered Ruth. He couldn't ask her to share that burden now.

"I should have been there," he said, staring into a darkness that no wolf's eyes could penetrate. "Ruth's dead because of me."

"Oh, no." Serenity dragged his head down to hers and wrapped her arms around his neck, rocking him like a motherless child. "No, it wasn't your fault."

No one in the world could have told him that and made him believe it. No one but Serenity. Something happened to his eyes, something that spilled into his chest and dissolved the shame he'd carried with him ever since he'd found Ruth's broken body.

"It's all right," Serenity whispered, stroking his hair. "It's all right to cry."

The rain began to fall then, small, cool drops that blossomed into warmth as they touched Jacob's head and shoulders. He covered Serenity with his own body, lifted her into his arms and carried her into the shelter of the nest he had made for her the night before, easing her to the ground and lying down beside her.

They listened to the summer rain, accepting the gentle gift of moisture that nourished cattle and crops, bad and good men alike. Jacob closed his eyes and breathed in the new life coming. The new life he could have if he would only reach out and take it.

If he let the Reniers go and gave up the Code forever. Let them continue their depredations on behalf of powerful men who didn't want to get their own hands dirty, even after he'd finally decided he couldn't let that happen any longer.

You don't have to take them yourself. But who else would? Other humans? The very reason men like the outlaw Reniers were still running loose was because they *weren't* human.

Serenity's warm, slender hand came to rest over his. "About what I said before..." she said softly. "You don't have to decide now. We can stay here for a few days. Do whatever you must to be sure of what you want."

Did he finally know what he wanted? Was peace—

a final, lasting peace for him and Serenity—within his grasp?

The damp grass rustled as Serenity got to her feet. "The rain has stopped," she said. "Caridad and the others must have set up camp by now. I'm going to dress and walk a little before I go down to see them. I won't stray far."

Jacob was slow to rise himself. He waited until he heard Serenity finish dressing and walk away, then examined his ruined trousers. They were stiff and stained, almost unwearable, but his spares were in his saddlebags down by the river, so he put on what clothes he had and went to find the other women. He knew they would have plenty of questions for him, but it was up to Serenity to decide what to tell them.

Zora, Caridad and Victoria were down on the bank, Victoria examining one of the horse's hooves, Caridad wading in the river with a sharpened stick in hand, and Zora sitting on a bedroll mending a shirt. She heard Jacob before he left the tangle of bushes that screened the bank from the woods nearer the road and came to join him.

"How is she?" Zora asked.

Jacob didn't have to ask if she knew what had happened. Her wolf senses would tell her even if she hadn't already guessed.

"She's all right," he said. "She went through hell last night, but it's over now." He glanced over Zora's head toward the river and the women still intent on their work. "She wants to go back to Avalon."

"She has chosen not to pursue the outlaws."

"That's right."

Zora didn't ask the obvious question: why Serenity had changed her mind so abruptly, abandoning the very thing that had driven her for as long as Zora had known her.

And Jacob didn't see the need to tell her. She knew Serenity as well as anyone; she could probably figure it out for herself. But there was something he very badly wanted to ask *her.*

"Serenity told me something this morning," he said, watching Zora's face. "She said the only time she'd been with a man had been bad for her. Do you know what she was talking about?"

Zora bowed her head and began to walk away. Jacob caught up with her.

"I need to know," he said.

She stopped and swung to face him again. "Why?"

"Because she's asked me to return to Avalon with her."

"What did you say to her?"

"I didn't. There are things I have to know about her past before—"

"Do you love her?" Zora demanded.

"I—"

"If you love her, then what happened long ago should not matter."

"You were so damned worried about my hurting her. I don't want to risk hurting her again."

"Whether you leave her now or later, you will hurt her."

And that was the one bitter fact he couldn't escape. "I'm not judging her," he said. "But I can't live with ghosts I don't know and can't fight."

She weighed his words with a hard stare, and the wariness of one who knows all too well what it is to be scorned and abandoned. "If I tell you," she said, "you must swear never to let her know what you have learned."

"I swear," he said.

Zora glanced toward the river. The other women might notice and wonder about her absence at any time, just as they must be wondering about Serenity's. Obviously the explanation would have to be brief.

"The Reniers," she said. "You know them."

It wasn't a question. She'd asked him something like that before. She'd guessed he had personal reasons for wanting to find them.

Zora had more than earned the right to the truth, or as much as she needed to know. "I know them," he said heavily. "Their family and mine have been enemies for generations."

Zora must have been surprised, and she was plenty justified in being angry, but she clearly realized that this wasn't the time to demand explanations. "You were not hunting them before Serenity hired you?"

"I couldn't. Not for a long time." How could he explain the Code to anyone, let alone a woman who had been abused like Zora? "These men are vicious killers, used by more powerful men in the Renier clan to do their dirty work for them. I didn't want to continue a war that's brought nothing but misery as long as I can remember. I didn't want to become like them." He looked away from Zora's quiet face. "Serenity's family never would have had a chance against them, even if they weren't Quakers. If she hadn't escaped..."

"But she did not escape."

Jacob's heart turned as brittle as the skin of ice on a lake after an early-winter freeze. "What do you mean?"

"The men took her."

Still he refused to understand. "As a hostage?"

"They had no need of a hostage. They had no reason for burning the farm or killing Serenity's family. They kept her alive because they had another use for her."

It took all Jacob's effort to keep his howl of rage in his throat. "She told you?"

"Yes. She did not have to say much. Even when I first knew her, I could see how much she had suffered."

"How long?" he said hoarsely.

"Nearly a year. She survived, and when the time came she escaped. She took some of their stolen money with her."

Joseph remembered what Serenity had told him about buying the ranch in part with money "contributed by those who shared my hopes." Had it also been bought with her suffering and ruination?

God help him, no wonder she'd wanted to conceal her femininity and distrusted, even hated, men. She'd been an innocent when they'd taken her. Even an experienced woman might not have come through such an ordeal with her sanity and will intact, but Serenity had done it. She'd more than survived. She'd made a place for women who needed a sanctuary, a place where women who'd suffered at the hands of men could be safe.

He swallowed. "Do the others know?"

Zora shook her head. "They might have guessed, but they would ask nothing. We—" She laughed under her breath. "We were supposed to forget the past at Avalon."

But that wasn't easy. Hell, in Serenity's case it would be impossible. She had tremendous courage to be willing to go after her tormentors at all, let alone face them directly enough to kill them. He realized just how much faith and trust she'd put in him, working at his side, asking help of a man of violence to find other men of violence.

How much faith and trust—and love—would it take for her to offer her body to a man when all she had known was pain?

Pain from the same men who had killed Ruth, who might have done the same thing to Serenity.

Jacob's vision went dark. He shoved past Zora and strode toward the riverbank.

"Jacob!"

He stopped, but only because Zora's voice was filled with such uncharacteristic emotion.

"What are you going to do?" she asked, grabbing him by the arm.

"What I should have done a long time ago," he said, shaking her off.

"You will kill these men."

Yes, he would kill them. Slowly, if he could. All the hatred he'd kept in check for so many years, the vicious rage the Code had channeled into the search for justice, had broken loose from its chains. The wolf was in ascendance, the primitive half of him that didn't care about Man's law. Or what humans called love.

He bared his teeth. "I remember a time when you would have been happy to see them dead."

"You said Serenity has given up her revenge. Will you go against her wishes?"

"I'm not asking her to do anything but return to Avalon."

"She will try to stop you if she finds out what you are planning."

"Then it's up to you to make sure she doesn't know."

Zora didn't anger easily, but now her eyes were as sharp as chips of obsidian. "What would you have me say to her? That you have abandoned her when she needs you most? When you have marked her as surely as those other men?"

The wolf would have gone for her throat. Jacob had a little more discipline.

"Say that again," he said, "and I won't much care if you're female."

She held her ground. "Do I not speak the truth?"

That was the hell of it. She did. He would be abandoning Serenity just as he would be abandoning the Code that had been the very framework of his life.

"Tell her whatever you want," he said. "Tell her I don't think I'm any good for her. Tell her I can't settle down. Tell her I could never love her." He stepped closer to Zora, so that their faces were only inches apart. "If *you* care about her, you'll make her believe it. You'll stick to your part of the plan we made in Bethel and get her back to Avalon."

The anger went out of Zora's eyes. "Yes," she said. "I will take her back to Avalon. And I will never tell her what you have done."

It was what he'd wanted, but he had no gratitude left in his heart to give her. He jerked his head in acknowledgment and continued toward the river. Whatever the other women thought of what had gone on between him and Serenity, he wouldn't give them any chance to ask him about it. He would come up with some excuse for a "temporary" ride away from Tolerance, and be packed and ready to ride within the hour.

Ignoring the organ that still pumped beneath his ribs, he let the wolf claim him.

CHAPTER NINETEEN

SERENITY MET VIRGIL as she was wandering near the road, her mind and heart still torn between joy for herself and sorrow for Jacob, faith in his courage and fear of the answer he had yet to give her. The confession she had made to him and his trust in telling her about his murdered wife had lifted a burden she'd thought she would have to bear for the rest of her life, even once the Reniers were dead.

But they were safe from her now, and she had no regrets. Only a profound sense of peace and a new hope that not even yesterday's horrors could diminish. She was hardly aware of her surroundings when Virgil appeared in her path.

Nothing, not even her newfound happiness, could have compelled her to speak to him. Immediately she turned to go.

"Serenity," he said. "Wait, I beg thee."

She refused to look at him. "What do you want?" she asked.

"I… Serenity, I know thee has reason to despise me," he stammered. "I well know I have earned thy contempt. But if thee will hear me one last time, I will never trouble thee again."

Serenity had heard that note of contrition in his voice

before, and it had meant nothing in the end. Surely it meant nothing now.

"As we are not likely to see each other after today," she said, "I have no need of your promise."

"If it were only for myself..." He sighed. "I bring word from thy family, if thee will listen."

Word from her family? Serenity's heart lifted again. In spite of her realization that she might finally begin to forgive herself for her many mistakes, she was still haunted by the way she and her uncle had parted. If Virgil carried some message of reconciliation, she had to hear him out.

She faced him and waited for him to speak. He shifted from foot to foot, glanced at the ground, opened his mouth and closed it again.

"I owe thee an apology, Serenity Campbell," he said in a low voice. "I had no right to judge thee or thy... thy friend. It was the sins of pride and covetousness in me, and I have prayed to purge them from my soul." He bowed his head. "I ask that thee accept my good wishes for thy future happiness."

His words and manner were so deeply humble that Serenity had difficulty doubting them. Everything was possible now, even Virgil's sincere regret.

"We were all deeply distressed last night," she said. "What was done and said..." She hesitated as the shadow of her guilt for shooting Perry fell over her happiness. "We cannot undo it. But we can try to live with greater care and reverence for life."

Virgil's sorrowful expression was transformed into one of heartfelt relief. "I could not agree with thee more. If we cannot be friends, I hope that now we may not be enemies." He sobered again. "Thy uncle has also regretted what passed last night. He has no wish to part with thee under such a cloud of recrimination."

"If this is true," Serenity said, "nothing could bring me more joy."

"There is more. Your aunt has grown very weak. It is thought she has little time left, perhaps only hours. Your uncle urges that you return immediately."

Serenity had hoped to go to the camp on the river and change her clothes before seeing Aunt Martha, not least because she didn't want to bring any taint of blood into the old woman's sight. But there was no time for that now.

Nor was there time to consult Jacob or the other women. "I'll come," she said.

Immediately Virgil set off for the settlement, and Serenity fell in beside him. The sky had cleared, and the sun was a little above the horizon now, painting golden halos around the oaks and casting shadows like questing fingers stretched across the grass. The settlement seemed suspended in silence, like a common stone in precious amber. There was no sign at all of men and women about their morning chores, or children stealing a few minutes of play before they were called to their books.

"Quickly," Virgil urged, taking her hand. She found it difficult to abide his touch, but she knew she wouldn't have to endure it long. They were through the gate and on the gravel path leading to Aunt Martha's cottage when Elizabeth came hurrying out of the main house.

"Virgil!" she cried. "Thee mustn't do this!"

Still keeping a firm grip on Serenity's hand, Virgil

stopped to face the older woman. "Thee should go back inside, Elizabeth," he said. "Others need thee now."

Elizabeth cast a wild glance at Serenity, who knew that something must be very wrong. She tried to pull her hand free.

"Let me go, Virgil," she said.

He released her hand but continued to stand very close.

Serenity met Elizabeth's frightened gaze.

"What is it?" she asked. "Do they not want me here after all?"

Elizabeth's eyes welled with tears. "Go away," she said. "Please. Take Jacob Constantine and never return."

"Thee don't know what thee are doing," Virgil snapped.

"The price is too high," Elizabeth said.

"If no one else will protect our home, I will." He seized Serenity's wrist again, but this time his grip was like a blacksmith's tongs, relentless and unbreakable.

"Release me at once, Virgil," Serenity demanded.

"I cannot do that, Serenity." He cast a final hard stare at Elizabeth and dragged Serenity not toward her aunt's cottage, but behind it and beyond the rearmost house to a small, sturdy shed standing against the rear pasture fence. There was a padlock hanging from the door latch.

Serenity planted her feet and refused to move another step. Virgil dug his fingers into her skin and tugged. Even without benefit of Jacob's extraordinary power, he was too strong for her. He slung her toward the shed, opened the door and pushed her inside.

"This is best for thee, Serenity," he said without expression. "Thee will thank me later."

"Thank you! What are you—" She flung herself toward the door, but Virgil was already closing it. She heard the padlock click into place.

Without a moment's hesitation she began to pound on the wood, hoping that someone else would hear her and let her out. Whatever Virgil was doing, it couldn't be what the other Friends intended. There was only one reason Serenity could think of for him to confine her here: he wanted her out of the way so that he could go after Jacob. There was no doubt in her mind that he hated Jacob enough to do him great harm if he could, his Quaker beliefs be damned.

But all her banging and shouting did no good. No one came for her. The silence was absolute. She backed away from the door and began to search the black interior of the shed for something to use to break it down.

"I NEED THY HELP," Virgil said.

Jacob stared at the Quaker's face in disbelief. It bore no resemblance to the way he'd looked last night; the man was clearly not happy to be here, but there was no animosity in his voice.

Only fear. And that was exactly the emotion he *should* be feeling, particularly since Jacob was barely able to keep himself from breaking Virgil's neck.

"You'd better get out of here quick," Jacob growled, "or I might forget you were Serenity's friend once."

The Quaker had kept a healthy distance between himself and Jacob, but Jacob's threat hardly made him flinch.

"I would not have come here if not for Serenity's sake," he said, glancing nervously at the women who had gathered behind Jacob. "But thee are the only one who can save us."

"What is it?" Victoria asked. "What is he talking about?"

"Is Serenity in trouble?" Caridad demanded.

How could she be in trouble? Jacob thought. She'd left him less than two hours ago.

Jacob lunged at Virgil, grabbed the collar of his coat and yanked him close. "You'd better explain yourself—and fast."

Virgil's face blanched. "It is…these men, these outlaws thee are following…they—"

"How the hell do you know that?" Jacob snarled.

"Serenity told me, before…"

"You're lying. Serenity would never have told *you* anything about it."

"She was troubled, and I—" Virgil coughed weakly. "I offered to listen to her worries. She told me about the men who killed her parents and fiance. She described them to me, and I remembered seeing—" he gulped for air "—seeing one such man in Kerrville when I was there a week ago. Of course I…didn't tell her, but…"

He kept on talking, but Jacob didn't hear him. It was too damned convenient. The Reniers in Kerr County, right when he most wanted to find them?

But Virgil couldn't have known about the hunt unless Serenity had told him, or told one of the other Quakers and Virgil had found out. Virgil didn't know that Serenity had given up on her quest for revenge last night.

And the Renier gang had been here at least once before. Maybe they had a reason for coming again.

"What was the man's name?" Jacob said, tightening his grip on Virgil's collar.

Virgil wheezed. "Lafe Renier. He…fit the description of one of the men Serenity described to me."

"And just why did you happen to notice him?"

"He and a few other men were causing trouble in town. It was impossible not to notice him."

That sounded convincing, all right. But it still wasn't enough.

"Why are you here now?" Jacob asked, giving Virgil a hard shake. "You think you'll make Serenity grateful if you lead us to the Reniers? They're long gone by now."

"No." Virgil flailed his arms as if he could break free with a few random movements. "I…I think they have made camp by the river to the east of Tolerance. I fear for the Friends. If these men are planning to… do what they did before…"

A red film like a splash of blood fell over Jacob's eyes. If there was even a chance Virgil was telling the truth…

Jacob let him drop, stepping back as the other man sprawled to his knees. "You're going to take me to this camp," he said. "If I find out you're lying about anything, I'll skin you alive."

Virgil's mouth gaped and closed and gaped again, like one of the fish Caridad had caught earlier that morning. "I know," he whispered.

"Do not trust him," Caridad warned. "His sheep's skin hides a scorpion's tail."

"I will come with you," Zora said.

And interfere with what he planned to do...*if* the Reniers were there at all.

"No," he said. "You three wait here for Serenity."

"She was going to return to Tolerance to see her aunt," Victoria said, worry in her voice. "Maybe she's already there."

"She wouldn't have gone without changing her clothes," Jacob said. "But if she isn't here in an hour, find her and bring her back. Then ride west and don't look back."

His horse was already saddled and ready. He secured his spare horse, mounted and met Zora's gaze.

"Get Serenity home safe," he said. He rode to where Virgil had come awkwardly to his feet and flung the second horse's reins at the Quaker's chest.

"Get on," he said.

Virgil stared up at the animal as if he had never been on a horse before, then made a clumsy attempt to mount. Zora walked up behind him and boosted him onto the horse's bare back.

"Start riding," Jacob said. He circled around Virgil's horse and slapped it on the rump. It broke into a trot, Virgil clinging to its mane for dear life. After a few moments, he grabbed the reins, got control of the animal and turned it east along a deer path roughly paralleling the river.

They were halfway to Tolerance when Jacob became certain that something was wrong. There was a taint in the air, a scent he couldn't place. If it was the Reniers, they were still too far away to identify. Jacob pulled up his mount and listened, taking in deep lungfuls of air. Virgil kept on going.

Jacob kicked his horse into a canter, rode alongside Virgil and grabbed him by one arm, not caring if he pulled the limb out of its socket.

Virgil cried out and jerked his horse to a stop.

"Where are they?" Jacob growled.

"Please," Virgil whimpered. "Don't hurt me."

Jacob released Virgil's arm and pulled his gun from his holster. "You trying to get away from me?"

"No. No. It's only a little farther, I swear."

Jacob had heard once that Quakers never took oaths, but since Virgil smelled about ready to empty his bladder, he was probably too scared to lie. Jacob prodded Virgil's wrenched shoulder with the revolver.

"You find them," he said. "Now."

That was when the wind shifted, a sudden gust blowing out of the northeast, and Jacob smelled a stench he couldn't mistake. He knew that scent. Someone had set wood on fire, and there was too damned much stink in Jacob's nose to suggest anything less than a burning building.

Jacob bore down with his heels, and his horse leaped into a gallop, running away from the river and into the acrid wind. Black smoke billowed above the trees that marked the western boundary of the settlement. Jacob was almost within sight of the settlement when he caught a whiff of another scent that had been masked by the burning. He had barely pinned down its source when the first wolf raced out of the underbrush alongside the road and leaped straight at him.

Jacob got off one shot. He didn't get a chance for

another, because the wolf was on him and carrying him out of the saddle before he could pull the trigger. Jacob twisted in midair, trying to grab the wolf around the throat and keep its jaws from connecting with his own neck. He and the beast landed together, locked in a struggle that gave Jacob no time to Change. Razor-sharp fangs pierced his forearm as he and the wolf rolled across the rocky ground, and he heard his horse squeal in fear.

That was when he knew he'd failed. Others were coming, both men and wolves, every one an enemy. The arm the wolf had bitten had gone numb, and his fingers could no longer grip his pistol. For a few seconds he managed to get on top of the wolf and pin its head to the ground with his good hand, but then one of the others came, and something hard, cold and heavy struck the back of his head.

Someone laughed, and then he knew nothing more.

THE ROARING IN Jacob's head slowly began to subside, and he became aware that everything around him had changed.

Even before he opened his eyes, he knew he was in the main house of the Quaker settlement. The smell of scorched wood was overwhelming, drowning all other scents, but he felt the presence of at least seven people in the room, most of them strangers, and heard the sounds of rapid breathing. Frightened Quakers and dangerous enemies.

But he couldn't move. He had been bound to a chair, his arms wrenched and tied behind the back of it and his ankles tied to its front legs.

He opened his eyes, already braced for what he would see. A man was perched on a backward chair directly in front of him, his legs astride the seat and his arms folded casually over the back.

Jacob knew him. His sense of smell might be compromised by all the smoke in the air, but he could never forget the face he'd glimpsed eight months before. Lafe Renier had helped kill Ruth. Her death had been only the end result of a petty war between a handful of Constantines and Reniers, but Jacob had never dreamed she'd be in any danger. He hadn't wanted to get involved.

In the end, he hadn't had any choice.

"Renier," he croaked.

The man grinned lazily. "Constantine," he said. "You've been a busy boy."

Jacob tested the ropes. He could snap them easily enough, but Lafe Renier wasn't the only one of his clan in the room. There were five others, and behind Renier and against the wall stood Lester and Virgil, both pale and wan with fear. Jacob had no doubt that they would suffer if he struggled, though he had a pretty good idea that Virgil would deserve whatever he got.

The only good thing about any of this was that Serenity and the other women weren't there. He prayed that Serenity had gone to the river when she hadn't found him waiting where she'd left him.

"What are you doing here, Renier?" he asked calmly.

Lafe Renier leaned back, hooking his thumbs in his gun belt. "I'm surprised you thought we'd never find out you was after us," he said. "Fact is, we expected it a long time ago. For a while there, we wondered if you'd turned yellow." His grin broadened. "Thought maybe you didn't put much value on your pretty human wife."

Jacob lunged in his chair and fell back, sucking air through his teeth.

"Now don't get so riled up, Constantine," Renier said. "We got a few things to talk about before you die."

Slowly releasing his breath, Jacob relaxed his body again.

Renier nodded.

"Good boy," he said. "You just stay that way, and we'll get along just fine."

Renier's expression darkened. "Nice and safe, so long as you cooperate."

Something told Jacob that Renier wasn't completely happy with the situation. Maybe he didn't have *all* the Quakers under his thumb. If any of them had escaped…

"I guess you want to know how we found you," Renier said, interrupting Jacob's thoughts.

Jacob did want to know how the Reniers had followed him without his smelling or sensing them, even if it was too late to make any difference. He could blame himself for that along with everything else.

"We got a message from Bethel the day after you left," Renier said, returning to his original position. "See, we have a nice little camp out there and do a lot of business in town, especially with the old storekeeper. Seems he met a man and a woman who were askin' questions about us and where we were. The man called himself 'Jack King,' but it seems the old man heard his real name during some trouble with a bounty hunter." Renier chuckled. "When we heard the name Jacob Constantine…well, we figured it weren't no coincidence. So we started makin' a few inquiries, and found out a man and three women were seen ridin' east toward San Antonio. I sent one of my men ahead and rode after you…keepin' well out of smellin' range, o' course. Harl spotted you a day ahead of us, and we just kept on your trail." He smirked. "And I heard you was pretty good at man-huntin'. Guess you was too busy with all them females to notice us."

Jacob kept his expression blank. He'd been too busy to know that the enemy was right behind them. Too busy even to sense Perry, who was only human. Too busy to use the instincts God had given him.

"Well," Renier went on, "you can imagine how surprised we was when we figured out where you was goin'. Gave me some pleasure to recall the fun we had here a few years back."

One of Renier's men laughed. Lester's jaw trembled, and Virgil twitched like a corpse full of maggots.

"Now, what we *couldn't* figure was why you'd come to a place like this," Renier went on. "You ain't no Quaker. Maybe you heard tell of our last visit?" He eyed Jacob as if waiting for an answer, then shrugged when none was forthcoming. "We moved in a little before dawn this mornin'. A lot of blood on the air. You can imagine how sad we was to hear you wasn't here." He glanced over his shoulder at the two Quakers. "The old man denied you'd ever been here, but we knew he was lyin'. Your scent was all over. Didn't figure it would take much to make these sheep talk, but then *Vir*-gil—" he pronounced the name with contempt "—told us you'd come and gone. We was goin' to look for you, but he said he could bring you right to us. Save us some trouble."

Jacob stared at Virgil. "You son of a bitch," he said.

Renier shook his head. "Just a little lamb, like all of 'em," he said. "Ba-a-a-ah. Feeble and scared." He snapped his fingers, and one of his men brought him a freshly rolled cigarette. "*Vir*-gil said he'd tell you he'd seen us in Kerrville. Now, we figured watchin' you walk into a trap would be a sight more satisfyin' than huntin' you down. So we agreed we wouldn't hurt anyone here if he did like he said." Renier plucked a match from his vest pocket, bent down and struck it against the floor. "We set the fire to keep you from smellin' us and just bided our time."

A trap and an ambush. And Jacob had fallen for it, all because he'd been weak. Weak with too much caring. And with hate.

"Now, this is all fine 'n' dandy," Renier said, lighting his cigarette, "but we knew you had some females with you, four of 'em all told, includin' the one the storekeeper said was interested in us. *Vir*-gil said you had a fight with 'em, and they rode out alone. I figure we can run 'em down easy enough once we're done with you. But I do wonder why you'd be ridin' with a bunch of human females in the first place. Tryin' to start your own hay-ram?"

He guffawed, and his men joined in.

Jacob held his rage in check. Virgil had lied in telling the Reniers that Jacob and the women had fought. That must mean something.

"I was escorting the women to San Antonio," Jacob said.

"Do tell." Renier took a pull on his cigarette. "The old storekeeper said you was pretty cozy with the lady who called herself Sally Cumberland. He said she was pretty handy with a gun. Shot up a saloon." The outlaw's gaze sharpened. "This particular female means somethin' to you. I smell it."

"You killed the only woman who ever mattered to me."

"Maybe you just wanted a pretty piece to give you a little relief on lonely nights."

Jacob couldn't help himself. He snarled a curse and lunged against the ropes.

Renier watched with great interest.

"Make it easy on yourself, Constantine," he said. "All I want to know is who she is, and why she was after us."

Jacob was determined to live long enough to visit that storekeeper again. "Guess you'll have to keep wondering," he said.

"You should cooperate, Constantine. We might go easy on those females when we find 'em."

"The way you went easy on my wife?"

"That was business. Orders from the top. Needed to teach your kinfolk a lesson about messin' with the Reniers."

"You must have felt mighty big, killing a lone human woman."

Renier didn't even blink. "All in a day's work. But you ain't answerin' my questions. Who's that female, and why did you come here?"

"One of the women with him was a Quaker," Virgil said. "She paid Constantine to bring her here."

Renier scooted around to face Virgil. "Which one?" He chortled. "The Mexican or the half-breed? Or the white woman with shoulders like a bull buffalo?" He chortled. "Couldn't have been this Sally Cumberland. Never heard of a Quaker shootin' up saloons."

"Victoria has been away a long time," Virgil said. "She couldn't fit in among us. That is why she left so soon."

Renier cocked his head. "Funny thing about that," he said. "Storekeeper said that bounty hunter Constantine had trouble with was lookin' for that big woman. Wanted her for murder."

"I know nothing about that."

"You seem to like the company of hard women, Constantine," Renier said, swinging around to face Jacob again. "I'm gettin' impatient to meet 'em. Where are they?"

"I don't know," Virgil said.

Lafe Renier got out of the chair. "Guess we'll have to find 'em ourselves. Then we'll all have a little fun." He signaled to the men behind Jacob. "Harl, Rayburn, you go find 'em."

The two men walked out the front door. *Three left,* Jacob thought. The odds were getting better—if he could figure out how to keep the Quakers safe when he went for the Reniers.

But whether or not Serenity and the other women had ridden out, they would soon be facing a pair of depraved, inhuman killers. Jacob hadn't gotten a good enough look at Harl and Rayburn to know if they matched the two other men in the sketches. What would Serenity do if they did? She and the others wouldn't have any choice but to try to kill the outlaws, and Zora would give them a decent chance to succeed. But what would it do to Serenity if she forgot her vow to give up her revenge and went after them as she'd gone after Perry?

Jacob closed his eyes and prayed as he'd never prayed in his life.

CHAPTER TWENTY

SERENITY RAN. SHE ran because all she could think of was getting to Jacob, no matter what might be happening in Tolerance.

All the time she'd been looking for a way out of the shed, she'd remembered Elizabeth's fearful protest: *Virgil, do not do this. The price is too high.* And Virgil's answer: *If no one else will protect our home, I will.*

Serenity had assumed he'd meant protecting it from Jacob, and that he intended to go after the man he hated. But now that seemed too simple an explanation. It didn't explain the silence in the settlement, the absence of children and workers. There was something else going on, and whatever it was, she knew she couldn't deal with it alone and weaponless.

So after she had escaped the shed through the slats she had broken with the ax she had found inside, she had headed for the road at as fast a pace as her feet would carry her, continuing west through the woods and across brushy meadows to the place where she'd left Jacob. The dress slowed her, but when she stumbled, she simply picked up her skirts again and stubbornly kept on.

She had gone only a few dozen yards away from the road when someone rushed out of the trees to the south.

"Serenity!" Victoria said, skidding to a stop in front of her. "Where have you been?"

"Tolerance," Serenity said. "Victoria, something is wrong."

"I know. Come with me."

Victoria turned and led Serenity south at a fast walk. Hidden behind a thick stand of oaks were Caridad, Zora…and Elizabeth, with the five children Serenity had briefly met in the settlement. Elizabeth had the three-year-old in her arms; the other children pressed close around her, frightened and silent.

"Serenity!" Caridad exclaimed. "When we could not find you, we were afraid—"

"I'm all right," Serenity interrupted. "Virgil met me on the road while I was out walking. He asked me to return to Tolerance immediately to see my aunt. He was lying." She looked at Elizabeth. "What has happened? Why are you here?"

Zora took Serenity aside, out of Elizabeth's hearing. Her expression was grim. "There are strangers in Tolerance," she said. "Werewolves."

Werewolves. Serenity registered the word with disbelief.

"Who are they?" she asked with sudden, choking dread.

Zora ignored her question. "Elizabeth says they are holding hostages in the settlement, and—"

"Hostages?" Serenity glanced toward Elizabeth. "But why? Who would want…?"

But she already knew, and so must Zora. There might be other werewolf gangs in this part of Texas, but Serenity could think of only one that would have a particular interest in Tolerance…and who might be staying there.

Panic would help no one now. "Go on," she said to Zora.

"Elizabeth was barely able to escape with the children when the strangers were distracted by—" She hesitated, her eyes full of sadness. "When they took Jacob."

Serenity reached for the trunk of the nearest tree and leaned against it heavily. "Took him?"

"Captured him. I saw signs of a fight near the road. Blood was shed, but there were no bodies."

That was all Serenity needed to confirm her worst fears. She strode back to Elizabeth. "Did you see Jacob?" She demanded. "Was he all right?"

"I saw little of what happened," the Quaker woman said, bending her head to the child in her arms. "I, Grace, my father and Virgil were in the kitchen when they came. Six men with guns walked into the house, and said they were looking for a man and several women who might have come recently to Tolerance. We knew at once that they were dangerous men, so we said nothing."

"Did you see Jacob?" Serenity repeated.

"I saw these men drag someone into the house as I was leaving to gather the children."

Surely the outlaws wouldn't have bothered to hide Jacob's body if he were dead.

Serenity forced herself to remain calm. "How did you get away?"

"These men pay little attention to women or children," Elizabeth said. "It was soon after I saw Virgil return with thee, and I tried to reason with him. While the intruders were arguing, I gathered those I could, and we ran."

She looked up, tears in her eyes. "What do these men want with thee and Jacob?"

The situation was too precarious now not to share some part of the truth. "Jacob is a hunter of those who break the law," Serenity said. "These bad men may carry some grudge against him because of that, but I don't know how anyone could have found us here."

"Thee knew about this grudge when thee came?" Elizabeth asked in disbelief. "Did thee know these men were searching for thee?"

Serenity looked away. "We would never have come here if we believed we would bring trouble with us."

"Yet a man of violence attracts violence," Elizabeth said, anger behind the quiet cadence of her voice.

"It is more than that," Zora said. She faced Serenity, speaking to her as if Elizabeth were not even there. "Jacob knows these Reniers. His family and theirs are ancient enemies. They have reason to hate him as he hates them."

After so many other shocks, Serenity found this one remarkably easy to accept. It all made sense. Jacob had admitted at the beginning that he knew *of* the Reniers. But there had been an odd note in his voice then, a heaviness that had suggested he was hiding something important. And he'd said werewolves sometimes killed each other.

But there was more to this than a feud between families. The Reniers could have come after her and Jacob because they'd found out Jacob was hunting them, and this feud Zora spoke of would give them even more reason to want to hurt him. But what if it was personal? What if Jacob had harbored his own reasons for wanting the Reniers, and her own quest had only made it easier for him to go after them?

What if the same men who had attacked Tolerance seven years ago had also killed Jacob's wife? What if they'd always intended to kill *him,* too?

She brushed the painful question aside. Jacob's motives, and his decision to keep them hidden from her, didn't matter now. She couldn't say anything to make the situation better. But she could act to save the people she loved.

"What did they do when you didn't answer their questions?" Serenity asked, deathly afraid of the answer.

"They threatened us. Then my father and Virgil asked if Grace and I could leave if they remained. Their leader was going to refuse, but Virgil said he could lure Jacob Constantine to Tolerance without trouble." Elizabeth bit her lip. "We tried to reason with Virgil, but the leader had already agreed. He said he would keep us in the house until Virgil brought Jacob to a place where his men could catch him. Before he left, Virgil was able to tell me and my father that he would see that you were safe."

So Virgil had betrayed both her and Jacob, seeing that betrayal as a chance to protect his own people.

And if he could hurt Jacob at the same time…

"That's why he locked me up in the shed to keep me safe?" Serenity asked. "Did he know if I'd realized what was happening, I would have tried to stop it?"

"Thee could not have saved us even had thee tried, nor can Jacob. It is not right that he should have been asked to try. We do not sacrifice others for our own safety."

But Virgil had been willing to sacrifice Jacob. And now, if Jacob was still alive—and Serenity refused to believe otherwise—it was still one man against six, unless one or more of the outlaws had been killed or injured in the fight.

Jacob might be badly injured himself.

"What about the fire?" Serenity asked, trying to think.

"The outlaws told Virgil to set it after he brought you back. I do not know why."

Serenity did. The smell of smoke would have made it impossible for Jacob to detect strangers in the settlement. God knew what Virgil had said to lure him in. She had an idea it might have had something to do with her.

"Did these men know my name, or who else rode with us?" she asked.

"They did not mention it." Elizabeth frowned. "Why would *thee* be of interest to them if their grudge was with Jacob?"

Serenity ignored the question and wondered how the outlaws had known where to go in the first place. Had someone in Bethel told them of "Jack" and "Sally's" pursuit?

If they saw her again, would they remember the girl they'd once held captive, that pathetic creature broken in body and spirit?

Serenity laughed grimly. She'd stolen a substantial

portion of their loot when she'd escaped. That alone would give them cause to remember.

Would they want her back to punish her for that theft? Want her badly enough to give her an advantage in doing whatever she had to do to help Jacob and the Friends?

Zora, Caridad and Victoria wouldn't hesitate to help her, but Serenity wasn't about to underestimate her enemies. She knew them too well. This wasn't like the incident with Leroy's gang. A direct attack by four humans against God knew how many werewolves would be doomed to failure. The outlaws would know they were coming as soon as they approached the house.

Unless they were sufficiently distracted.

Serenity gulped in several shallow breaths. Her legs felt hollow, and her ribs seemed to be squeezing her heart so tightly that it could hardly beat at all. If she followed the plan that had just come into her head, she wouldn't be facing the Reniers with gun in hand and Jacob at her side. She would be surrendering herself as surely as if she were willingly locking their collar around her neck.

She glanced at Zora and the other two women who stood with her. "The men Elizabeth speaks of are the ones we've been hunting," she said. "I can't ask you to put yourselves in more danger because of Jacob and me. It would be better if you left now."

Victoria shook her head, and Caridad laughed.

"Do you think we wish to miss the fun?" Cari asked.

"We will not leave," Zora said. "But Elizabeth and the children should be taken to a safe place."

Once again Serenity was reminded why she loved

these women. "Elizabeth, is there somewhere you can go where no one will look for you?"

"There is an abandoned cabin a mile west of here, away from the road," Elizabeth said.

"Victoria, will you take them there?" Serenity asked.

Victoria nodded and ran into the trees, returning with three of their horses. "Two children can ride on each of these horses," she said, indicating two of the geldings, "and I'll ride with you and the littlest one, Elizabeth."

Victoria, Caridad and Zora helped the children up, reminding them to hold on tight, while Serenity took the toddler from Elizabeth. She held the child while Victoria mounted her own horse, sliding back on the animal's croup and then, with Zora's help, pulling Elizabeth into the saddle in front of her. Serenity handed the child up to Elizabeth and stood back.

"I'll return as soon as I can," Victoria said, taking the reins of the children's horses from Caridad. She urged her mount into a fast walk, picking a path heading west through the woods, well away from the road.

"What now?" Caridad asked, lovingly stroking the polished black handles of her guns.

Serenity turned to face her. "Will you follow Victoria a little way, just to be sure no one sees them?"

Caridad nodded and trotted off the way Victoria and her charges had gone.

Once she was out of sight, Zora said, "We should also leave this place before those men smell us."

"But that's exactly what I want them to do," Serenity said. "I want them to smell you and hear you, Zora. But not until we're ready."

Serenity explained her plan. It wasn't really a plan at all, just a desperate ploy that was more likely to fail than succeed. So much depended on the behavior of the Reniers and their greed, and her own ability to convince them that they would soon be facing enemies of their own.

And she had to pray that Jacob was not too badly hurt to take advantage of any opportunity she could give him. He would fight if he could. She just had to do whatever she could to make that possible.

Even though that meant delivering herself into the hands of her enemies all over again.

JACOB THOUGHT he was dreaming.

He opened his eyes, the lids swollen from repeated blows to his face, and struggled to clear his vision. He thought he smelled Serenity, felt her footsteps in the soles of his boots, heard her voice.

But that couldn't be. She wasn't anywhere near Tolerance. Once Serenity had returned to the river, Zora would have given her some excuse for Jacob's absence and led the others away immediately.

Still the voice persisted, joined by others: Virgil's and Lester's raised in protest; laughter, crude and disbelieving. Jacob tried to smell the air, but his nose was too clogged with blood and mucus to detect any scent at all. Blurred human shapes began to appear in his line of sight: the Quakers, Renier's men, Renier himself, his back to Jacob as he stared at someone on the other side of the room. Jacob blinked several times, praying that his eyes were playing tricks on him after the repeated beatings.

But he couldn't deny it. Serenity was standing there between Harl and Rayburn, chin raised, legs braced as if for battle. She was unarmed. There was almost no color in her face.

Jacob tried again to rise, ready to spend the last of his strength to snap his bonds and go to her. But then Serenity met his eyes across the room and gave an almost imperceptible shake of her head.

Had she refused to believe Zora's necessary lies? Had she escaped and come looking for him after he hadn't returned? She would never have come to Tolerance if she'd known the Renier gang was here. She had suffered too much at these men's hands. And Zora would never have let her.

Still, she *was* here, and she must know now whom she faced. Maybe the Reniers hadn't recognized her. She couldn't look anything like the sheltered Quaker girl they had tormented seven years ago.

That was probably too much to hope for, but Serenity's brief acknowledgment had been deliberate. She'd managed to keep her head and was clearly determined to stand up to her fear. She must have some kind of plan, though God knew what it was.

Jacob knew that she was going to need his help, though—and soon. He had let Renier hit him because he'd figured any resistance on his part might endanger the Quakers, but he couldn't sit by any longer. He focused on gathering his strength, pushing aside the pain of his cut and bruised flesh. If he could weaken the ropes, he could move that much faster when the time came.

"...don't remember me?" Serenity was asking as he

focused on her again. "Do all your kind have such poor memories?"

"Remember you?" Lafe Renier drawled, ambling toward her. "I think I'd remember a body like yours." He licked his lips and grinned. "I don't remember sending for any whores, but we'll be happy to give you what you want. We might even pay you for it."

There were appreciative murmurs of agreement and several crude jokes.

Jacob jerked on the ropes and reminded himself to work slowly. All attention was on Serenity now, but that might change at any time.

"She is no whore!" Virgil said, moving closer to Serenity. "She is one of us."

Renier's expression cleared. "So she's the one," he said. "A Quaker who shoots up saloons. Where's your gun now, little lady?"

"We have a bargain, Renier," Virgil said, drawing on some hidden reserve of courage. "You have the man you were looking for."

"Bargain?" Renier said. "I don't remember no bargain about this bitch. She was ridin' with Constantine."

Virgil clenched his fists. "You would rather torment a woman than face a man in a fair fight?"

For the first time Renier showed some emotion other than smug satisfaction. "You?" he asked incredulously. "You challengin' me, Quaker?"

"*I'm* the one challenging you," Serenity said.

Renier's gaze snapped back to her. He looked her up and down, and the mocking smile returned. Jacob knew the exact moment when Renier recognized her.

"As I remember," the outlaw said, "you was never

much of a challenge. But I can see you've changed." He walked around Serenity, examining her from every angle. "You Constantine's whore now, bitch?"

Jacob's wrists were already bloody, but the rough fibers of the ropes were beginning to give one by one. He knew he didn't dare let Renier think his relationship with Serenity was more than one of convenience, even if the truth came out about her purpose in riding with him. Somehow he kept his mouth shut and his head slumped against the chair back, reminding himself again how he would make Renier suffer once he got free.

"Mr. Constantine was escorting me home," Serenity said.

"Then why was you askin' about us in Bethel?" Renier demanded. "Don't deny it, 'cause we know all about it."

Serenity didn't so much as twitch a muscle. "I hired Constantine to find you so I could kill you."

The outlaw widened his eyes in a mocking imitation of terror. "Kill me?" He glanced around the room, expecting derisive laughter.

One man guffawed, and another snickered. The others said nothing.

"How do you think you're going to kill me? All of us?" Renier asked. He jerked his head toward Jacob. "Did you think he'd do it for you? Did he tell you he wants us dead, too?"

"No," she said.

"Well, let me let you in on a little secret. We killed his wife, same as we did your kinfolk. His family and mine go way back, and it ain't been a friendly relationship. I reckon he hates us just about as much as you do. But he ain't much use to you now, and he'll be even less when he's dead. Or do you want to beg for his life?"

"I don't care what you do to him," Serenity said coldly. "He is only a hired man. He lost your trail in Bethel, and I learned I was needed here, so I stopped looking."

Renier stared at Serenity through narrowed eyes. "That almost sounds like truth." He gestured toward Virgil. "But *he* said you didn't 'fit in' no more. Guess you was damaged goods and these pure folk couldn't have you around to remind them what could happen if we came by again someday."

Serenity held his stare. "It doesn't matter what they think. I have a deal to make with you. I'll give you something you want in exchange for leaving these people alone."

Dropping back into his chair, Renier stroked his stubbled chin. "Now what could you bargain with, I wonder? I can take you anytime I want. Hell, you're still the best-lookin' woman in this town." He snickered and crooked his finger. "Maybe, if you're good enough, I'll think about letting some of these sheep go."

Serenity stayed where she was. "I have something better to offer," she said. "You think you took everything from me. But I stole something from you, too. Didn't you ever wonder what happened to those bags of money? *Your* money."

Abruptly Renier's demeanor changed, and he was all wolf, predatory and bristling with rage. He jumped out of the chair again.

"Where is it?" he snarled.

"I'll tell you—if you agree to my terms."

His hand shot out, ready to lock around her throat, but Serenity deftly moved out of his way just as Virgil lunged forward to stop him.

"Get your hands off her!" Virgil shouted.

With a casual gesture Renier struck Virgil across the face, sending him reeling across the room.

Jacob clenched his teeth with such force that he nearly bit through his tongue.

If he moved too soon…

Renier swung to face Serenity again. "You must think you're pretty smart, comin' in here like you have some chance of gettin' out again." He grabbed for her shoulder, and this time Serenity wasn't fast enough to move out of his reach. Renier twisted a lock of her hair around his finger, pulling hard enough to hurt her. "You say you still got our money?"

Serenity stared him in the face without the slightest trace of fear or pain. "I hid it after I escaped. Most of it is still where I left it."

Renier yanked her toward him. "You're lyin'."

Jacob tasted blood in his mouth. God help him, in a few seconds he would lose what control he still had. But Serenity glanced at him again—a glance of complete indifference—and he forced himself to stay still. He moved his wrists carefully and felt the ropes begin to separate. There were only a few strands left holding them in place.

Just one sign from Serenity. Just one.

"What would I gain by lying?" Serenity asked. "I

can prove it to you. I can lead you right to it…if you leave these people alone."

"You think we can't kill everyone here and still make you take us?"

"If you hurt anyone," she said, "if you so much as touch a hair on a single Quaker head, you'll never see that money. I'll kill myself first, and you won't be able to stop me."

Renier started to laugh again, then stopped and abruptly let go of Serenity's hair. "Maybe I should take a couple of these sheep along with us, just to make sure you keep to your 'bargain.'"

"I said you'll get nothing if you touch anyone in Tolerance."

"There were three other females with you. We'll find them, and then you won't be singing so pretty."

"You might as well slit my throat now, Renier, because I promise I won't ever sing again."

That was when Jacob witnessed a miracle.

Renier backed down. He opened his mouth to threaten again, but the words never came out. He stalked away, glaring at everyone in the room, and spat on the once-spotless floor.

"You'll pay for this, bitch," he said. "Once you've taken us to our money, you'll suffer. You think the last time was bad…" He found his grin again. "You'll never be off your back."

"I don't care what happens to me," she said in a voice bare of emotion. "I'm already dead."

"Then maybe you won't mind watching us kill Constantine before we go."

"Do whatever you want with him, but don't take too long."

"Why not?"

"Because I think pretty soon you're going to lose your chance to come with me."

CHAPTER TWENTY-ONE

AS IF AT SOME UNSEEN signal, a howl rose outside the house. It came from the direction of the road, and no werewolf could mistake its meaning.

For it wasn't a common wolf crying out to its pack mates, but another werewolf, and not one of the Reniers. They all turned to stare at the front window.

Jacob forgot to breathe. It had to be Zora. But what did she think she could gain by attracting the Reniers' attention? A distraction? They would slaughter her once they caught her, though they might pause to abuse her first.

The howl broke off, and there was a long silence. Renier signaled to his men, drew his gun and ran to the door, where he dropped into a crouch.

"I saw them when I was coming to the house," Serenity said. "There were about ten of them." Her mouth twisted in a bitter smile. "One of them found me watching the house and asked me if I was the woman who had been traveling with Jacob Constantine. He said his family was at war with the Reniers, and Jacob had sent his kinfolk in the North a message from Bethel saying that he'd found where Lafe Renier and his gang were hiding." She shrugged. "I guess they must have followed us when I asked Constantine to bring me here."

"How could he have sent a message?" Renier demanded, still crouched by the door. "There ain't no telegraph in Bethel."

"By rider," Jacob croaked. "More than one man in need of work in that hellhole."

Renier straightened. "It's a lie. Louis was standing guard. He would have warned us. Whoever's out there, it ain't no—"

A second howl came, higher-pitched than the first, from the rear of the house. Renier's men turned as one toward the sound.

"I don't know what happened to this Louis, but you haven't got much time left," Serenity said. "I don't want my people caught in the middle of a fight between animals."

Renier hardly seemed to notice her insult. Sweat had broken out on his forehead, and Jacob realized Serenity—and Zora—had all but convinced him that the house was surrounded.

"Harlan," Lafe snapped. "You and Ned go out and take a look. Harl, you take the front door. Ned, check the back."

The men in question glanced at each other. "Maybe it would be better if we all went out," Ned ventured.

"Get out there," Renier said, showing his teeth.

Werewolves weren't wolves in every way, but in any group of them there was usually a pretty solid pecking order, and neither Ned nor Harlan was willing to stand up to Lafe. Harlan approached the front door at a near crawl, while Ned slunk toward the back. They stripped and went outside wearing only their gun belts. Renier paced the floor, glaring first at Jacob and then at Serenity. Jacob knew the man was on the edge of an explosion that could consume the entire settlement.

Serenity must have known it, too, but no doubt crossed her face. She watched Renier as if he were an insect in a jar, scurrying and scrabbling for purchase against the glass. The hair-trigger tension in the room increased a little more with each minute that passed without word from Ned or Harlan.

Jacob prepared himself. He wouldn't have time to take off his clothes once he freed himself from the ropes and went for Lafe Renier. He would have to tear them apart with the Change itself, and that would take an enormous toll on his strength. But there were only three of the gang in the room now, including Lafe, and he would never get a better chance.

He looked straight at Serenity, willing her to look back. She was turning her head toward him when there was a howl of pain from outside, followed by the report of a gun. Another gunshot, a third, and then the unmistakable sounds of a struggle.

Jacob surged upward, snapping the weak fibers that stretched between his wrists, kicking out to crack the legs of the chair and free his feet from their bindings. He felt the resistance of his boots and clothing as the Change began, confining his body as he struggled to complete the transformation. Leather and cloth gave way with a violent hiss.

Renier shouted at his men. Serenity seemed to move as if through water, her limbs dragging as she tried to dodge the man coming after her. Jacob shook off the tattered scraps of his clothes and charged Lafe, jaws wide to sever the pulsing veins in the outlaw's throat.

Everyone around him, werewolves and humans alike, seemed to slow to a crawl.

The man going for Serenity caught her, and Renier swung his pistol to aim at the center of her forehead.

"Stop!" his thick, muffled voice shouted from somewhere far away. "I'll kill her!"

Part of Jacob heard the words. Part of him wanted to stop. But the hatred was stronger.

It was too late. Too late to go back, too late to remember that he had once chosen not to be like his enemies. All he could see was Ruth, horror distorting her pretty face as she tried to run from the monsters who had come to steal her life and destroy Jacob's with it. All he could feel was the wolf's lust for blood. Revenge was a heartbeat away.

The world groaned, shuddered, came to a grinding halt. The powerful muscles in Jacob's hind legs bunched. His forepaws left the ground. All his massive weight hurtled toward Lafe Renier, roaring, flying.

Then Ruth looked at him with Serenity's eyes, and the last of Jacob's humanity recognized their message.

Forgiveness. No fear, no reproach, no hate. Only complete and utter acceptance.

The man remembered. The wolf twisted in midair before his body struck his enemy, twisted and flung himself sideways, one paw striking the floor before he leaped up again. He plowed into the woman, knocking her aside as the bullet whizzed past and buried itself in the wall behind the place where Serenity had stood a moment before.

Lafe Renier laughed. He aimed at Serenity again. Jacob's nails raked the floor as he scrambled to his feet and flung himself over the one who held his soul in her hands.

The second bullet flew past Jacob's ear, taking a tiny crescent of flesh with it. Jacob didn't move. He had but one purpose now and for the rest of his life, even if that life was to be counted in seconds.

The third bullet never came. Renier was falling, a look of amazement on his face, and Virgil was standing over him with a gun in his hand. Then he, too, was falling, and a flurry of struggling bodies spun past Jacob like a dust devil made of limbs and fur and flashing white teeth. A female voice swore in voluble Spanish. More shots, and then…

Nothing. No movement, no sound. Jacob lifted his head. Serenity's breath puffed against the fur of his neck, and she opened her eyes.

It was over. As the crimson haze cleared from Jacob's eyes, he smelled the stench of gunfire and blood and sweat.

And something more. Something that couldn't be defined by man or wolf. He rose, taking Serenity's weight as she dug her fingers in his fur and pulled herself to her feet.

There were bodies—Renier's men and Renier himself—but only two were bereft of life: Renier and Virgil, who lay on his back almost as if he were sleeping. Of the gun there was no sign. Lester crouched beside the younger man, tears running down his weathered cheeks.

Lafe Renier was on his stomach, his face hidden from sight, but from the look of him he'd taken Virgil's bullet straight through the heart. The other two outlaws who had been in the room were down as well, but both were at least partly conscious and moving, if feebly.

Caridad, Victoria and a naked Zora stood over their prisoners—Caridad, as always, prepared to shoot at the slightest sign of opposition. Victoria was nursing a wounded shoulder, hastily bound with strips of torn cloth.

Serenity bent her head to kiss Jacob's forehead, smiled into his eyes and then ran to her friends, embracing each of them in turn. She took special care with Victoria, who gave her a shaky grin.

What they said after that was only so much noise to Jacob. He crept to the open back door and slipped out.

There were bodies there as well, but Harl was still alive, bound hand and foot, and clearly too weak to attempt escape. The second man—Louis, Jacob figured—was moaning over a shattered knee. Ned lay on his side in wolf shape, but no breath lifted his ribs.

Three dead. There was only one for whom Jacob mourned. Virgil had set aside his deepest beliefs to defend one he considered a rival and an enemy. His sacrifice had been more than honorable, whatever his motives. And Lafe Renier's death had expunged the fell purpose Jacob had always carried in his heart, masked, but never erased, by the Code.

The Code was dead now, too. Jacob had shattered it beyond repair. He had forgotten all the principles of justice. He had deceived Serenity about his relationship with the Reniers, and put both her and the entire Quaker community in danger because of his deception. He had given himself over to bloody vengeance. And he had put that vengeance ahead of the safety of those he was sworn to protect.

Ahead of Serenity.

The pall of smoke that had hung in the air had begun to disperse on the late-morning breeze, leaving a faint stain of brown and gray that smelled of sorrow. Jacob trotted to the skeleton of the cottage Virgil had set afire, dipping his paws in the ashes. He circled it twice, then followed his nose to another cottage, where a dying woman lay.

There were five women inside, two weeping. All were still breathing. Jacob set off again, sniffing out the Quakers in hiding without letting them see him. No one else had suffered more than an ugly scare. Elizabeth and the children were gone, but Jacob was certain they had escaped before threat had erupted into violence.

He could do no more for any of them. If he showed himself, they would see only a monster.

Because that was what he had become.

Breaking into a run, Jacob raced away from the settlement and across the road, forcing his way through the brush and trees. He burst out onto the riverbank and plunged into the water, drenching his fur to the skin.

It made no difference. He couldn't wash his shame away. The only thing he could do now was keep on running—away from the end of the Code, from the shreds of his honor, and from Serenity most of all. He would take nothing with him. There would be no farewells. He would go naked into the wilderness, and perhaps—one day, before he died—he would find himself. And forgive.

He dragged himself to the opposite bank, flung back his head and howled.

"Jacob!"

Serenity ran out onto the bank across the river, her loose hair flying.

"Jacob!" she cried again, sliding down to the water's edge. "Where are you going?"

He backed away. A few short steps would carry him into the thicket behind him.

"No!" Serenity waded into the river, soaking her skirts, stumbling and righting herself again. "Whatever it is, Jacob, you can't give in! Not now!"

Her struggles were more than Jacob could bear. He plunged back into the water, seized her skirts and pulled her the rest of the way to the bank. She sat down hard, breathing fast. When he tried to move away, she wound her fingers in his waterlogged coat and refused to let go.

"Why are you running?" she asked, her eyes bright with tears. "Because you wanted to kill Renier?" She tugged his fur, forcing him to move closer to her. "That wasn't you. That was your hatred. I know how it becomes your world, consumes every good thing inside you. For so long you resisted it, but none of us can reject our darkest selves without paying a price." She buried her face in his mane. "Letting go means losing yourself. It's like being born again and having to learn life from the beginning, like a child."

Little by little, relentless as drops of water wearing down a mountain, her words reached through the darkness. *Being born again.* Wasn't that what he had wanted?

"Come back, Jacob," Serenity whispered. "Come back to me."

With a groan of surrender he Changed.

Her fingers slipped on his bare chest, gripped again at his shoulders.

"Jacob?" She searched his face, his eyes.

Still, he didn't hold her, though it was the only thing he wanted to do for the rest of his life. She was his anchor. She had been the strong one from the very beginning. She had become his life.

But he couldn't ask her to feel the same about him, not when he had nearly gotten her killed.

"I can't stay with you," he said hoarsely.

Her gaze was as steadfast as her hold on his flesh. "Because you can't love me?"

He laughed, and moisture ran from his eyes. "How could you love me after my failures? I let you believe I hardly knew the Reniers. I didn't tell you about the feud. I didn't tell you they were the ones who killed my wife."

"I know you had your reasons."

"They weren't good enough. I would have killed Renier and let you…let you—"

"Did you hear anything I said?" She took his face between her hands. "You didn't let me die. You would have given your life for mine. Not only today, but a hundred times since the day we met. You are the best man I have ever known."

"Lester, William, all the others…they're the good ones."

"It's not so hard to be good when you live by rules

you have known all your life," she said. "The hard part is making your own and staying true to them."

Jacob closed his eyes. "Virgil broke his rules saving my life."

"It was his choice. I will always grieve for him, and I will always be grateful for his sacrifice." She pulled his face down to hers. "You can't punish yourself forever. Ruth wouldn't want that if she loved you the way I think she did. I know you loved her very much, and maybe you can't feel that way about anyone else ever again. But I…I will take anything you can give, even if it's only your friendship for the rest of our lives."

New lives. New hope. A rebirth into a new world of their own making, a new Code of joy. Of love.

He cupped her cheek in his hand. "You'll take me… as I am?"

"Forever."

"Then I'll come with you. But only if you let me love you."

He kissed her then, and she laughed and wept and murmured endearments as he laid her down on the bank and loved her until they were both reborn in a blaze of light.

VIRGIL WAS LAID TO rest in a little grove where Lester and the other Friends had interred the ashes of Levi Carter and Serenity's parents seven years before. It was a quiet farewell, without ceremony, each prayer spoken in the silence of the mourner's own heart. Serenity knelt beside the simple grave when the others were gone and laid a bunch of black-eyed Susans across the freshly turned earth. Even Caridad and Zora, who along with

Victoria had been essential in deceiving and defeating the Reniers, gave sober thanks for his selfless courage.

There was no more talk of Serenity and the others leaving Tolerance, though it took Lester some hours to recover from the shock of witnessing Jacob's Change. He listened soberly to Jacob's explanation, then quickly agreed that it would be best to keep the matter of werewolves a secret from the other Friends.

Aunt Martha passed a week after Jacob took the Reniers to the Kerr County Jail. Serenity shared her sadness with the Friends, but not with Jacob; he had determined to stay with the surviving Reniers until they were tried and sentenced. Before he left, he had warned Serenity and the Friends that they might be called as witnesses in any trial, but his letters from Kerrville contained no news of any such need.

Serenity missed him terribly, but the time came when she knew she and the other women had to return to Avalon. After they were packed and ready, she said her farewells to the Friends, embraced Uncle Lester—who was bravely doing his best not to show his own grief—and exchanged another tearful hug with Elizabeth.

"Thee will be happy," Elizabeth said. "Perhaps thee will never be a Friend again, but thee will do much good in the world. It is in thy nature." She kissed Serenity on both cheeks, smiled and walked away.

THE JOURNEY BACK TO New Mexico seemed interminable, not only because Jacob wasn't with them, but because Serenity was eager to get home.

When they finally rode in sight of the ranch house,

Caridad whooped, spurred her weary mount into a gallop and blew into the yard like a storm. Victoria rode in after her, just as Helene, Changying and the others ran out to meet the home comers.

Zora and Serenity rode on together. Serenity found that her joy was mingled with a sorrow she was only now beginning to understand.

"It looks the same," Zora said. "Yet so much has changed."

Serenity nodded, unable to speak.

Zora reached over to touch Serenity's arm.

"He will come home soon," she said. "The time will pass quickly. You will see."

And it did. Once Serenity had convinced her astonished audience that Jacob Constantine was coming back to Avalon to stay, they all quickly settled back into a daily routine.

But Zora had been right. So much *had* changed.

Serenity rode more lightly, as if her hate had been like shackles that had grown heavier with every year she had let it fester. The bright New Mexico sun warmed instead of burned, and the sky stretched all the way to Heaven. Helene's baby boy was born on the last day of August. Peace settled over Avalon like a benediction.

BABY JOEL WAS two months old when Jacob rode in. He was bathed in dust and weariness, his lips cracked and his gray eyes webbed with new lines. But when Serenity straightened up from the cow she'd been tending and he saw her, he transformed before her eyes. He leaped from his horse's back, bounded across the grass like something with wings and gathered her up, lifting her and spinning her around until she was too dizzy even to laugh.

And when he kissed her, the sky burst open and wept with joy.

They walked back to the house together, leading their horses, wet to the skin, and so lost in each other that they didn't see Michaela and Judith waving as they passed, and hardly realized when they had reached the outer corral.

Caridad was gentling a new horse, and she was the first to see them.

"It is about time you returned," she said gruffly.

Helene came out of the house a moment later, beaming and holding her little boy in her arms. Victoria emerged from her workshop, sooty as usual, and Frances followed Changying out of the bunkhouse, slowing when she saw Jacob.

Changying bowed. "It is good to see you again, Mr. Constantine," she said.

"And you," Jacob said. He looked at the other women with a warm, slow smile. "It's good to be home."

Greetings were exchanged all around, and quiet congratulations extended to the lucky husband-to-be. Frances hung back, shy and a little sad, but then Jacob whispered something in her ear and she was all smiles again. Serenity loved him for making the girl feel better in her loss of the man she adored, but she never asked him what he had told her.

Near sunset the other women rode in, but Zora had still not returned from her work on the range. After supper, when Jacob had bathed—watched over and thoroughly scrubbed by his soon-to-be wife—he and Serenity strolled up to the yucca-spiked hill overlooking the house. They sat on a tumble of rocks and held hands as they surveyed the valley below.

"What happened in Kerrville?" Serenity asked.

"The Reniers went to trial," he said. "Faster than I had any right to hope. Seems they were wanted for a dozen different crimes, but no one had ever been able to find them, let alone bring them in."

"And they were found guilty?" Serenity asked softly.

Jacob nodded. "Funny thing is, not a single respectable Renier showed his face during the trial or after. None of their kin came to their defense." He sighed. "I stayed to see them punished, but I didn't take any satisfaction in it." He cradled Serenity's hands between his own. "My days as a hunter are finished."

"As well they should be. Do you think I'd let you wander around the country without me?"

"I'll never leave you." He bent to kiss her. The benevolent stars continued their stately dance across the sky.

"I made a visit on my way home," Jacob said a little while later. "To the place where Ruth is buried." He pulled Serenity into the crook of his arm. "I know she's at peace now. She always was. I was the one who didn't know it." He nuzzled Serenity's hair. "I told her about you. Maybe it's loco, but I felt her give her blessing."

"I don't think that's loco at all," Serenity murmured. "I'm glad. She was a good woman. I know that because she loved you." She sighed and snuggled closer. "What about the feud? If no Reniers showed up to defend the gang or try to interfere, maybe it's finally over."

"Maybe it is."

"If werewolves can learn to live in peace with each other, maybe werewolves and regular people can, too."

"I guess it has to start somewhere."

"I think right here is a very good place. I figure we could get married next week, if that isn't too soon for you."

"Tomorrow wouldn't be too soon."

She hesitated. "You know, we might not ever have any children," she said softly.

He tipped up her chin. "You tend to collect people the way other folks collect stamps. I figure someday a kid is likely to show up needing a home."

They kissed again, long and slow. A shooting star flashed its tail like a salmon returning to the place of its birth.

"I wonder where Zora is," Serenity said, lifting her head from Jacob's shoulder. "It isn't like her to be gone so long, and I know she wanted to see you as soon as you returned."

"She did, Serenity." He drew back and pulled a folded piece of paper from his vest. "She left this for you. I was waiting for the right time...."

Serenity took the letter out of his hand. The writing was almost childishly precise, each letter carefully formed as if for a school assignment. She read the message, then folded the paper up again.

"You know what it said?" she asked Jacob.

"She told me." He touched Serenity's cheek. "You can see why she has to go?"

"Yes." She wiped her tears away with the back of her hand. "She has to find her own way. There is a path for her, too. She has to shed her skin before she can live in the sun again. But…I wish she'd said goodbye."

"She couldn't. As long as she doesn't say it, she can believe she's coming back."

"She'll come back," Serenity said. "This is her home."

"That's what she has to find out. Like I did." He gazed into her face, the golden flecks in his eyes like tiny constellations in a deep gray sky.

"There's one more thing I haven't told you," he said.

She braced herself. "What is it?"

"I love you."

* * * * *

You've just finished your book.
So what did you think?

We'd love to hear your thoughts on our 'Have your say' online panel
www.millsandboon.co.uk/haveyoursay

- Easy to use
- Short questionnaire
- Chance to win Mills & Boon® goodies

Visit us Online

Tell us what you thought of this book now at
www.millsandboon.co.uk/haveyoursay

YOUR_SAY